LIFE IMITATES ART.

The scene that followed was surreal, mostly because I had written it so many times. In some ways, it felt as though I were still writing it. We were herded into the restaurant so it could be closed off; an Oceanside officer stood guard in the parking lot, carrying out the first rule at the scene of a suspicious death: nobody in, nobody out. Every vehicle in the lot, including Parisi's new Escalade and my old Schwinn, had to be accounted for. All our statements had to be taken. And, of course, the press had to be kept at bay.

In the dining room, my family and I, Lori, Cal, and Tim were all crowded around one table. "Why? Why," Nonna asked, wringing her hands, "did he have to pick *here* to die?"

"Tuesdays are slow anyway, Ma," my dad said, in a masterpiece of understatement. "Thank God nobody was in the dining room."

Murder and Marinara

◇◇◇◇◇◇◇◇◇◇◇◇◇◇◇◇◇◇◇◇◇◇◇◇◇◇◇◇◇◇◇◇

An Italian Kitchen Mystery

◇◇◇◇◇◇◇◇◇◇◇◇◇◇◇◇◇◇◇◇◇◇◇◇◇◇◇◇◇◇◇◇

Rosie Genova

AN OBSIDIAN MYSTERY

OBSIDIAN
Published by the Penguin Group
Penguin Group (USA) LLC, 375 Hudson Street,
New York, New York 10014

USA | Canada | UK | Ireland | Australia | New Zealand | India | South Africa | China
penguin.com
A Penguin Random House Company

First published by Obsidian, an imprint of New American Library,
a division of Penguin Group (USA) LLC

First Printing, October 2013

ISBN 978-0-451-41514-1

Printed in the United States of America
10 9 8 7 6 5 4 3 2 1

For Anthony Paul,
the hero of his own life, with love and pride

Acknowledgments

Like a good meal, this book had many helping hands behind it. It wouldn't have happened at all without a suggestion (and a nudge followed by a push) from my agent, Kim Lionetti, aka K-Lion. Her guidance and advice always serve me well. Ditto to Sandra Harding at New American Library, who took a chance on Victoria and the gang and who has been the best of editors— honest, supportive, and kind. I'd be remiss if I didn't send shout-outs to Jackie Cantor of Berkley Books and to Michael Neff of the New York Pitch and Shop, who both have my undying gratitude for jump-starting my writing career. And Assistant Art Director Maryellen O'Boyle and cover artist Ben Perini gifted me with a fun, beautiful cover that tells a story all its own.

My critique partners and bosom buddies Loretta Marion and Sarah Pinneo provided thoughtful feedback, comic relief, and shoulders when I needed them. My neighbor, retired Fanwood police Sergeant Brian L. Bantz, and e-mail pal, retired detective Mike Marsillo, answered my often obtuse questions about police procedure with patience, humor, and more gory detail than I really needed. I am grateful to them both and must add the disclaimer that any errors are all my own. Former student and valued friend Nick Pisa read early drafts and gave me the benefits of his mystery expertise. My brother, Joseph Genova, and his buddy Donato Basso, Italian cooks extraordinaire, helped me with details of harvesting and canning tomatoes. My colleague Bailey

Verdone read pages and shared her experiences of waitressing in an Italian restaurant. Fellow New Jersey author and sensei K. M. Fawcett explained how to bring someone to the ground with an elbow jab. The town of Ocean Grove, the Asbury Park boardwalk, and the wonderful library in Spring Lake gave me exactly the Jersey Shore inspiration I needed to write. And former student Benji Schwartz provided a great idea in the nick of time.

On the home front, I am indebted to my fabulous sister, Terri Harms, and my special SIL, Teresa Genova, who both provided the inspiration for Vic and Sofia's special bond. They've cheered me on throughout the journey, as have my beloved parents, Sam and Maryann Genova. (Mom also serves as my first-draft reader, as she can spot a plot hole from a mile away.) My sons, Anthony, Adam, and John, have been staunch supporters of my writing, even when it meant a fast-food dinner or an empty sock drawer. Special thanks to Adam for providing tech support, as well as listening to my plot ideas and supplying a few of his own. Finally, to Anthony, who once told me he liked my poetry and who has been with me from the beginning—*grazie mille, caro*.

Chapter One

"Vic," Josh said, "I don't think you have any choice. You have to get rid of him."

I stared at the phone in disbelief. "Absolutely not," I said. "It's too drastic. I won't even consider it."

"Why not? You complain about him enough. And think about what you could do with him out of the way. You could start over—a new name, a new guy. Maybe even a younger guy."

"Look, I know what you're suggesting. You're asking me to"—I dropped my voice to a whisper—"to *kill* Bernardo."

"Don't you get it, Vic? It's the easiest way out. The only question is how." He paused. "I mean, a bullet's kind of mundane, don't you think? And a knife's out of the question. I do hate a messy crime scene," he said, more to himself than to me.

"Do you hear yourself?" I gasped. "What's wrong with you?"

"Ooh, I know." His volume got louder with each word. "You could do a *Rear Window* kind of thing and really send him out with a bang. It has a nice retro appeal, too."

"Why don't I just shove him over a waterfall and be done with it?"

"Too obvious." Apparently my sarcasm was lost on him.

"Listen, Josh," I said. "You can just forget this, okay? Because I don't intend to harm one slicked-down hair on Bernardo's head."

"But Vic, aren't you tired of him? His annoying little gestures and that stupid accent—"

"Hang on a minute," I interrupted. "This is Bernardo you're talking about. He and I—" *Have been together for almost eight years. We have a routine, a formula for our relationship. And truth be told, wasn't I getting a little tired of him? Of his constant pronouncements? His shiny shoes and perfectly pressed pants? And, yes, the accent was kind of silly.*

"And he's right *all* the time," Josh continued. "He's never been tripped up, not once."

"He's not supposed to be tripped up," I said. "That's the way I made him. And I'm not killing him off; that's final. Anyway, what would Sylvie say? She loves Bernardo." Sylvie Banks was my editor, my hero, and she had come to be a dear friend. She'd fished me out of the slush pile, and I owed my career to her.

"Vic," Josh said quietly, "it was Sylvie's idea that you consider a new series."

"It was?" My heart tightened in my chest. "But my sales have been steady."

"Steady, yes, but nothing special. And the last one didn't hit any of the lists."

"So the new one will." But even as I said it, I could feel the uncertainty creeping over me like a chill.

"We hope." I could imagine him shaking his head, rubbing his eyes behind his glasses. "Listen, maybe we don't have to kill him," he said. "Maybe he can go on a long trip. Like the time you sent him to Venice, remember?" I could hear the sound of Josh's agent wheels grinding away.

"I guess I could do that. But what about that guy you were talking to at HBO? We can't end the series now."

"Okay, yes, if HBO picks it up, Bernardo can have a nice long life. But that's a big if. At the very least, I think you should take a break, maybe try something else."

Try something else. As Josh talked, a memory stirred. Fresh out of college with a business degree, I'd dreamed of writing a novel. Not a mystery, but a historical work based on my family. I'd jotted down a few notes and even had a name for my main character—Isabella—but that was as far as I'd gotten. Maybe the time had come to tell her story.

I looked out the window to the park below, watching the kids jump from monkey bars to swings while their parents chatted on benches. Across the street, the wine bar was getting ready to open as the café next to it was closing its doors. As I took in the bustle of the East Village, I thought about how much I loved this neighborhood. Yet a part of me knew it would never be home. "You know what, Josh?" I said slowly. "You might be right. Maybe a hiatus for the series is not such a bad idea."

"That's my girl! So listen, maybe you go with a woman detective this time. I've got an idea—"

"So do I. I know the story I want to tell." And suddenly, it all came back to me. The young Italian couple arriving on these shores with nothing but their few possessions and a dream. The first wooden stand on a nineteenth-century boardwalk. An old-fashioned Ferris wheel. It was all there—the smell of the food, the sounds of the ocean: a perfect backdrop for the book I'd dreamed about all those years ago. "Josh," I said, "I want to write a historical based on my family."

The silence that followed was so complete that I couldn't even hear breathing. "Hel-lo!" I called. "Paging Josh Silverman."

"I'm here, Vic. I just can't believe what I'm hearing."

"You just told me you wanted me to try something new."

"But not this! This is crazy. You're a great mystery writer—why mess with that?"

"I've been Vick Reed for seven years. We've released one Vitali mystery every year, and number eight's ready to go. But maybe the series is losing steam. You said it yourself."

He groaned. "I should have kept my big mouth shut. So instead of playing to your strengths and coming up with a new series—for which you have a built-in audience, I might add—you're gonna write the Great Immigration Novel."

"I know how it sounds. But why not?"

"I'll tell you why not: Vick Reed is a known quantity."

"Yes, but Victoria Rienzi has a different story to tell. This project has always been in the back of my mind— the setting, the characters, all of it." As I spoke, I could feel the excitement that comes with a new story. And every instinct was telling me this was a good one. "Don't you see, Josh?" I said. "This could be such a cool book. And it will give me a chance to learn about my roots."

"You hate your roots! You yanked them out of the ground when you left Jersey."

"Maybe that was a mistake." I hesitated, taking a deep breath. "Listen, to do this right, I need to go back to Oceanside Park. Back to the Casa Lido."

"Back to the restaurant?" He spoke in a whisper, as though I had shared some terrible secret with him. "To get bossed around by the granny in the black dress?"

I couldn't help smiling. "Shows how much you know. Nonna wears print blouses and polyester pants." But he had a point. My grandmother was bossy, and our relationship was as rocky as an Italian hillside. And I would need her for this project. I braced myself for his reaction to my next statement. "Maybe I'll ask her to teach me to cook. You know, real Italian cooking."

Josh's loud bray of laughter assaulted my ear. "Oh, that's rich."

"No, what's rich is Nonna's red sauce. And I'm determined to learn how to make it."

He sighed loudly. "How much time are we talking about?"

"Give me a year," I said. "To immerse myself in the family business, learn the family history."

"You'll be back in Manhattan in a week."

I looked back out the window at the familiar city streets. "Maybe. But I need to do this, and not just for the book." I wasn't ready to think about the other reason. Not yet.

Josh sighed again; he was starting to sound like my mother. "Look," he said, "if you really want to do this, I'll work to get it out there, but I'm not making any promises."

Thank you, I mouthed silently to the Fates, and added one to the Holy Mother for good measure. "You're the best little agent a girl could have—you know that? And if you can't sell it, I promise I'll work on a new mystery for you. In the meantime, have a little faith, okay?"

"I have faith in *you*. It's that crazy family of yours I'm not so sure of," he said as we hung up.

And with that, Josh voiced my first dark doubt. Going back to Oceanside meant going back to being a daughter and granddaughter, a kid sister and a hometown girl. Falling back into a role I'd shrugged off like an old coat and with nearly as little thought. Was I ready for that? And what of that second dark doubt, the one that loomed over me like a shadow? Wasn't it time to dispel it, once and for all?

I stood at my desk and picked up my latest mystery from the Agatha Press and smiled at the cartoon image of my moderately famous detective. "I'm gonna miss you, Bernardo. But I'm certain this is the right thing to do."

His eyes seemed to mock me from under his trademark Panama hat, as though any moment he would stroke his neatly trimmed beard and make one of his Vitali-esque predictions: *Fate has plans for those who are sure....*

A couple of months later, I headed south on the Garden State Parkway, the backseat of my newly purchased used Honda stuffed to its windows with boxes, clothes, and books. I had sublet my New York apartment for a year, and as I approached the Driscoll Bridge, I imagined myself as an epic hero on a quest. Because once I crossed this mighty river, there was no going back. But below me wasn't the Rubicon, only the Raritan, and beyond that, the bay, and finally the ocean. I opened my window and inhaled the mingled perfumes of seawater and industrial pollution. From the car's fuzzy speakers, Springsteen's voice was a plaintive wail on "Meeting Across the River," and I couldn't help but see it as a sign.

It won't be long now, I thought. A tiny frisson of apprehension traveled up my spine, and despite the warm May morning, I hit my window button to close it. Out of habit, or maybe for luck, I touched my necklace, a silver choker with a pendant made of green sea glass. *Please don't let this be a mistake.* As the words formed in my brain, I flashed on his changeable eyes and the swift bright grin that reduced me to the consistency of mascarpone cheese. My other dark doubt. *You are a big girl, Victoria,* I told myself. *Do not let this—do not let* him—*get in the way of your plans.*

From Route 35 I turned onto the jug handle that would take me into town, down Ocean Avenue toward the boardwalk and the Casa Lido. It was still early in the season, and the same street that would be crawling with cars on a Saturday in July was nearly empty now. But here were the old landmarks of my childhood: the Carvel stand with its giant aluminum ice-cream cone, Mrs. Parker's Fudge Shoppe (note to self: stop in for a pound this week), and Harrison's Department Store, which sold everything from sunscreen to hardware to hermit crabs. I let out a small sigh, startled at the thought that I had actually missed this—the boardwalk, the ocean, sand between my toes. Even the restaurant. All the things I had left behind eight years before.

We'll see how sentimental you feel as you face down Nonna, I told myself. *We'll see how warm and fuzzy this homecoming will be when you're trying to write your magnum opus during the day after waiting on hungry tourists all night.* As I passed each of the alphabetized beach blocks—Absecon, Barnegat, Cape May, Deal— the flutters in my stomach grew to an insistent thudding. The restaurant was on the corner of Ocean Avenue and Seaside Street, and I was already past the Ms.

Without thinking, I pulled over, got out of the car, and crossed the wide, quiet street. As I made my way up the ramp, I relished the echo of the wooden boards under my feet. Most of the stands were still closed, but the smell of popcorn drifted in the wind, and behind that, the unmistakable smell of the sea. I stood at the railing looking out over the ocean, feeling my shoulders slacken and the tension in my body ease. I was home. And starting tomorrow, I would write the story that was already forming in my heart and brain. But that meant facing all the things I had run from, starting now. I got back in the car.

As soon as I pulled up to the familiar redbrick building, I saw him. He was leaning against his squad car, arms crossed and a knowing grin on his face. His light brown hair was cropped close in a style that announced he was either a cop or a fireman. As I got closer, I could see some gold highlights, but there was also more silver. His face was tan, as always; he still spent his days off fishing or surfing. The lines around his eyes had deepened—and why did that always look so good on guys?—but his hazel eyes, the same color as mine, were warmly welcoming. He was still my Danny.

"C'mere, you." He held out his arms to me and pulled me into a tight hug that lifted me off the ground. Then he grabbed my face and gave me a loud kiss on the forehead. "You're too skinny."

"I won't be for long. I stopped for a pork roll and cheese on the way down." I smiled up at my big brother, and the world righted on its axis.

"Well, get ready," he said. "They've been cooking for three days."

"That's what I'm counting on." I looked up at the sign over the green-and-white-striped awning: THE CASA LIDO. FINE ITALIAN FOOD SINCE 1943.

"But I gotta say, I was surprised when you told me you were coming back," Danny said. "I know you want to research the new book, but it's not like you loved working in the restaurant."

"Neither did you," I said, poking him in the chest. "But because you were a guy, you got out of it easier than I did."

"But I never wanted to leave Oceanside. You couldn't wait to get out."

I looked up at his face, saw the affection and concern, and rested my palm against his cheek. "Danny, you know why. I had to get out of here to get started as a writer. And I had to put some distance between him and me."

"You know, he hasn't seen her in a couple of years, Vic. And I don't think he's been serious with anyone since."

"Right. Knowing him, I find that a little hard to believe." I ducked my head to search for my car keys, hiding my burning face and burning curiosity. So, he was still single. And probably still living in town. I gripped my keys with sweaty fingers, my hand shaking as I locked the car.

Danny caught my free hand. "He's grown up a lot, hon. And I'm not just saying that 'cause he's my friend."

"I don't want to talk about this, okay?" I glanced up at him and risked a question of my own. "How's it going with you and Sofia?" Instantly, my loving brother morphed into Bad Cop, all hooded eyes and tight jaw.

"It's not. And I don't want to talk about it."

"Fair enough," I said, and nudged him with my elbow. "At this rate, Mommy's never gonna get that grandchild she wants so bad."

"She never shuts up about it. Then her and Nonna double-team me." He grinned. "Now you're here, so some of the pressure's off."

"I don't know, Dan. I think they've given up on me. At the ripe old age of thirty-three, I'm pretty much on the shelf. At least you've *been* married."

"I'm still married. And if it was up to me, it'd stay that way." He refused to meet my eyes, and I knew better than to pursue it.

"Well," I said, looking back up at the Casa Lido sign, "I guess it's now or never."

Danny rested his hand against one of the wooden doors and winked at me. "You ready?"

I sighed. "As I'll ever be, brother."

Chapter Two

I ducked under his arm through the open door and took a step back into the past. Not just my past, but the past of this place, originating with World War II. As my eyes adjusted to the cool darkness, I saw the dark-paneled walls, the ornately carved bar, the tables with their classic red-checked tablecloths. My great-grandparents had started with a wooden boardwalk stand that sold sandwiches and ended up building a business that's been flourishing for nearly seventy years.

I inhaled the mingled smells of simmering sauce and fresh basil and the licorice scent of anise flavoring in Nonna's ricotta cookies. It was a Monday, the only day of the week we were closed, so I knew that sauce was meant for me. From the time I was old enough to set a table, the Casa Lido had been my second home. I spent every summer of my life here, and I'd done everything except cook. I'd waited and bused tables, served as hostess and greeter, and worked behind the register. Before we used a laundry service, I'd washed and ironed linens. I'd helped my grandmother plant and harvest the tomatoes from the plot out back; I'd picked basil and parsley and mint. At twenty-five, I was driven to break the grip of the Casa Lido, and now, nearly a decade later, I was running back to its tight embrace.

But that metaphor shriveled and died the minute I caught the glint of her eyeglasses in the shadows. Behind those thick bifocals was a glare so hard, I flinched. Her arms, hardly outstretched in welcome, were crossed tightly over her chest like protective armor.

I swallowed, my mouth instantly dry, and tilted my head to peer closer. "Nonna?" I said weakly.

She didn't answer, but only took a step toward us. At eighty, my grandmother still had the ramrod posture of a soldier and was just as fearless. Tall and angular, she was handsome rather than pretty, but she still indulged in two small vanities: hair dye and red lipstick. As her face creased into a smile, I smiled back in a rush of affection—not to mention relief. And then she walked past me.

"*Daniele!* Did you come for lunch?" She caught my brother's two hands in her own and led him to the back table, where the family always sat.

"I can't stay long, Nonna." Dan kissed her cheek and motioned toward me. "But look who I brought with me. Victoria. She's back, and she's gonna stay for a while."

"She knows perfectly well who I am." I stalked over to the table, pulled out a wooden chair, and plopped down. "I doubt she's forgotten me since Christmas."

Nonna made a small hissing sound, like a snake about to strike. "But you missed Easter," my brother said by way of interpretation.

"Again with that," I groaned. "For God's sake."

My grandmother's eyes widened, the nostrils of her enviable Roman nose flaring.

Danny looked at me in warning. "You shouldn't take the Lord's name in vain."

"I don't need a translator, Danny. I am well-versed in Nonna-ese." I smiled straight into her basilisk stare, surprised I hadn't yet turned to stone. "And I am happy to see her, even if the feeling isn't mutual."

This time Nonna went deaf as well as dumb and disappeared into the kitchen. I pointed toward the large silver doors. "I can't believe she's still pissed off about Easter."

"*I* can't believe you're surprised. You know her. She thinks you should be here every weekend."

The we-don't-see-you-enough refrain was one I knew well. New York, a mere fifty miles away, was "too far." *Oh, honey*, my mom would say, *you know Daddy hates all that traffic.* My brother barely left the confines of our little shore town, and to my grandmother, Manhattan was a place of sin and corruption. And everyone knew it was the girl's duty to visit her parents, right? I know I should have been here more, but for a long time, twice a year was all I could muster. Besides cooking, researching, and writing, I would now have to add fence-mending to my list. I sighed. "Where are Mom and Dad, anyway? I need reinforcements."

"They'll be here." He drummed his fingers on the table, and I caught a quick flash of gold on his left hand. Still wearing his wedding ring. *That's hopeful*, I thought. He glanced at the giant timepiece on his wrist. "It better be soon, though. I gotta get back."

"Hey, Dan, I've been meaning to ask—is Daddy behaving?"

"Do you mean is he staying out of AC?" My brother wiggled his palm. "*Mezzo, mezzo.*"

Our father had an unfortunate predilection for the blackjack tables in Atlantic City, among other forms of speculation that involved numbers, horses, and the occasional bookie. "As long as he doesn't bet the restaurant away," I said.

We were silenced as the kitchen doors burst open and Nonna set a plate down in front of each of us. Apparently, her punishment of me did not extend to starvation. Thank God. In front of me was a thing of beauty. A plate filled to its edges with homemade hand-cut cavatelli, blanketed in my grandmother's fresh marinara sauce. The secret to Nonna's sauce was the fresh tomatoes she put up every August; our pantry shelves were lined with Mason jars full of bright red-orange *pomodori*, accented with basil leaves from the garden. I sniffed deeply at the rising steam from my plate, and my salivary glands wept with joy. *Nonna, bring me your worst*, I thought. *I'll put up with anything as long as you feed me like this.*

But before I could have a bite, I was startled by a series of thuds. *Bang!* Water glass. *Bang, bang!* Cheese plate followed by a salad plate filled with fresh arugula. I looked up and smiled sweetly into my grandmother's scowling face. "Thank you, Nonna. And you made me my favorite, so you can't be that mad at me." I forked several cavatelli and a nice chunk of tomato into my mouth, closed my eyes, and let out a low moan that under other circumstances might be taken for an altogether different sort of pleasure. "Mmmm," I said. "This is sooooo good." I opened one eye a crack. Did I spy a twitch at the corner of Nonna's mouth? She was a tough cookie, but she'd have to crumble eventually. She took a seat next to Danny and looked on approvingly as he inhaled his lunch.

I was about halfway through my own plate before the door to the restaurant swung wide. "See, I told you she was here!" Nicolina Maria Spinelli Rienzi tap-tap-tapped her away across the floor in a pair of heels that were far too impractical for restaurant work. "Where's my girl?" she shrieked, holding her arms open as she tottered toward me.

I wiped my mouth and jumped to my feet, hoping I wouldn't have to catch her if she fell off those shoes. "Hi,

Mom." I gave her a kiss and was enveloped by a cloud of floral scent as I was pressed to my mother's generous bosom. She reached over and squeezed my face. "We don't *see* you enough!" *Oy*, I thought. *Here we go.*

"Well, that's about to change. I'll be here for a whole year." *If my sanity holds out.* I looked down at my mother's pretty, suspiciously unlined face. *May I look so good at her age*, I thought. Though I had inherited her light olive complexion, her eyes were a deep brown. At almost sixty, my mother still sported lots of hair and even more cleavage—another area in which we differed.

My mom pushed my bangs aside and scrutinized my hastily assembled "style"—my shoulder-length hair twisted into a clip on the back of my head. "You could use a few highlights, honey."

I lifted a strand of her stiffly sprayed locks. "I think you have enough for both of us." My mother and I had both started out with the same dark blond hair, but over the years hers had ranged from platinum to auburn to everything in between. This month's choice was a more natural color, but there was nothing natural about her wild mass of waves, half of which were extensions. Under all that hair, though, was a brain as sharp as her acrylic nails. A trained accountant, my mom managed the finances of the restaurant and those of the family. I glanced down at her red tunic top, worn over black tights. "You're rocking those leggings, Mom."

"Thanks, hon." She held out a still shapely leg. "They're the latest thing."

"Doesn't she look great?" My dad reached over and pulled my mom into a sideways hug. Whereas my mom jumped on each new fashion trend, my dad remained frozen in 1965—a choice that put him right in style these days. He wore a short-sleeved knit shirt, sharply creased sharkskin trousers, and brown Italian loafers. The en-

semble was topped off by a straw fedora, set at a rakish
angle on his head. "Hi, Daddy." I smiled into Danny's
face twenty-five years on.

"Hey, baby. Great to have you back." He folded me
into a quick hug, but lost no time in dutifully kissing his
mother as well. "Hey, Ma," he said. "Smells great."

Though they declined something to eat, setting off a
prolonged exchange with my grandmother, my parents
joined us at the table. In seconds, my brother was on his
feet. "Hate to interrupt the reunion, but I gotta get back
to the station." He sent me a wink, and I shook my head
at him. The traitor.

My dad pushed my plate toward me. "Finish eating.
Now that you're home, we can put some meat on those
bones." Nonna made a rumbling sound of assent. Her
own silence was killing her, and I wondered how long
she could keep it up.

My dad patted my free hand. "Honey, we are so
pleased that you've decided to take your rightful place
here at the restaurant." I wondered why no one bugged
Danny to take *his* rightful place at the restaurant. I
guess being a police detective, as opposed to a writer,
was considered a real job.

"Daddy, working here is just temporary. You understand that, right? I'm here for research." I was conscious
of my grandmother's eyes burning holes into me; I felt
like a dry leaf under a magnifying glass in the sun.

"Frank, darling, we can talk about all that later," my
mom said. She linked her arm through mine, seriously
compromising my ability to finish the rest of those cavatelli. "It is so wonderful to have you back with us. I
can't wait to catch up on all our girl talk. We'll be Nikki
and Vicki again!"

I winced, hoping it didn't show. "Listen, Mom, before
you go out and get us matching outfits—"

"Oh, and I told Gale down at the library that you'd do a reading or a signing, or something. And the book group has *Molto Murder* slated for its June pick, so I think they'd like you to lead the discussion. And we're so excited about the new release!" She stopped to take a breath, her heavily lashed eyes fluttering under the weight of her mascara. "Now, what else did I want to tell you?" She tapped a fuchsia-painted fingernail against her cheek. "Oh well, I'll think of it later. But in the meantime," Mom went on, "you're just in time for the rally."

Somewhere in the dark recesses of my mind, a tiny red flag was waving. "What rally?"

"I left a message on your Facebook, hon. Don't you remember?" She produced a newspaper clipping from her purse and shook it at me. "You're the one who inspired it."

I looked from my mom to my dad to my grandmother. "I'm lost here."

My grandmother cleared her throat loudly. "It's about that show."

"What do you know?" I said. "She speaks." I narrowed my eyes at her. She wasn't going to scare me. Much. "You want to explain, Nonna?"

"That show with the *puttanas*," she said, using the Italian word for, shall we say, loose women.

"That awful reality show." My mom held up the clipping. "You know, honey, the one you wrote to the *Times* about."

As a professional milestone, having a letter published in the *Times* was second only to signing my first book contract. Glints of light were beginning to shine through the darkness. Last year RealTV premiered a reality show about the escapades of a group of twentysomethings at a Jersey Shore rental a few miles from Oceanside. Their antics gave the rest of the nation a somewhat skewed view of our beloved coastline, so I felt called upon to correct that impression. Not that it mattered, since the show was a runaway hit. "You mean the letter I wrote about *The Jersey Side*?"

"We were so proud of you, honey," my dad said, beaming at me. "How you talked about our heritage and what the shore meant to you and—"

But I was allowed about a nanosecond to bask in my father's praise before my grandmother interrupted, pounding her fist down on the table. "They think we'll put up with their filth and their shenanigans. This is a family town. Let them take their dirt up north, where it belongs."

"Wow, Nonna, that's the most you've said since I walked in." I grinned at her. "Actually, *Filth and Shenanigans* would make a great title for a reality show."

In answer, she crossed her arms and grunted, lowering her thick brows at me disapprovingly. At this rate, I wouldn't be in her good graces long enough to learn how to boil water for pasta.

"Anyway, honey," my mom said, "the producer, Gio Parisi, has taken a rental here for the summer. They're scouting locations for filming, and we're worried the town might actually let them."

"God, I hope not," I said. "I came here to work. This place gets crazy enough in the summer." I shuddered at the thought of tourist caravans streaming into our little town to gawk at the kids from *The Jersey Side*. I shook my head. "I can't imagine that Oceanside will let them film here."

"We hope not," my dad said. "But we need to get our message out there." He leaned forward eagerly. "Tomorrow, Parisi and a couple of the stars are making an appearance on the boardwalk, so we're holding a rally out here in response."

"When you say 'here,'" I said slowly, "do you mean *here*?" I pointed down at the floor.

"No, darling," my mom said with her *oh honey, don't be silly* laugh. It was one I heard often. "Not in the restaurant. Out in the parking lot."

I closed my eyes, wishing I'd never crossed that damn river. "Let me get this straight." I looked around at their expectant faces. "Tomorrow, the town is holding a rally here in *our* parking lot to protest this show?"

"At eleven sharp." My mom patted my hand. "And you'll speak, of course."

"What?" I said, choking on my last bite of pasta. "I will not. I'm not getting involved in this." I looked around in a panic. "You'll need somebody in here, anyway."

"No, we won't," my dad said helpfully. "We're closed for lunch tomorrow because of the rally. We're only serving pizza outside. Our contribution to the cause."

"But what about the dinner prep?" That straw I was grasping at was moving farther and farther from my fingers.

"Oh . . . the new sous chef will get things started in here," Mom said, looking down at the table.

"But I'm rusty, Mom. Maybe I can just watch them. I know, I'll do the silverware setups and fill the salt and peppers," I said, naming the two jobs I most loathed.

"Yes," Nonna said, looking directly at me. "That will be good for Victoria. I will have a list made up for her."

I'll just bet you will, Nonna, I thought. I'd be scrubbing the table linens against a rock if she had her way. But it was still better than making an impassioned speech in front of strangers. "Anyway, guys, I'll be here bright and early tomorrow. I really need to unload my stuff." I stood up, gave my dad and my mom a quick kiss, and glanced at my grandmother. "And I hope the rally goes well tomorrow."

"Don't you worry," my dad said. "We'll show these people that Oceanside Park doesn't want them here. Parisi can just take his offensive show to another town. He'll get the message, all right."

"*Sì.*" My grandmother stood up and raised her right hand like some Neapolitan oracle. "By tomorrow," she pronounced, "we'll be rid of him for good."

Chapter Three

I jumped out of bed at six, fully expecting to knock off a thousand words before I headed down to the restaurant. I had such plans for my main character, Isabella Rossi, and I thought I'd at least get her on that boat to America. But those doubts wouldn't stop whispering questions into my ears. *Will I run into Tim? Will Nonna break her vow of silence? Will I remember what to do after all this time?* Poor Isabella never even left her house, let alone her village.

My rental bungalow was at the tail end of a beach block, a tiny four-room cottage that had about the same number of square feet as my apartment in Greenwich Village. The house had little to offer except for the solitude and the ocean view. But it came with a seasonal beach badge and an ancient Schwinn, and by nine o'clock I was swerving, wobbling, and swaying my way down Ocean Avenue to the Casa Lido.

I leaned the bike against the old shed that bordered one side of the parking lot with the back garden. There were pots of summer perennials next to the large plot that was already turned and ready for planting. Along its edge were also boxes of tomato flats, lined up like leafy little soldiers ready to do battle with the sandy soil. There would also be cucumbers, peppers, and herbs out here; my grandmother had been a locavore long before it became fashionable.

It was a little early for the lunch setup, but I was psyched to get started. Probably the best I could hope for today was vegetable and salad prep. Sketchy culinary skills notwithstanding, I was pretty good with a knife. But the minute I pushed my way through the silver doors of the kitchen, I came face-to-face with my past.

"I heard you were here, Vic," he said, "and, man, you look great."

Great didn't begin to describe how Tim Trouvare looked, but *luscious*, *delectable*, and *mouthwatering* might top the list. The dark curls that fell oh so invitingly over his forehead. Lashes so long they cast shadows over the blue-gray eyes, changeable as the tides. A face that looked as though it had been chiseled from Roman stone and a lean, rangy body that was equally at home on a surfboard as behind a stove. And in other places as well. This guy's Irish mother and Italian father had produced a varietal blend so potent that even one taste caused sensory impairment. And I had spent way too much of my life intoxicated. (Once, when I asked him which half was Italian, he looked deep into my eyes and whispered, "Whichever half you want it to be.") I might have ignored the danger signals then, but I was much smarter now. And I would not let this black-hearted Black Irishman complicate my life again.

I assumed a tone of cool professionalism that was at odds with my sweating palms and pounding heart. "Thanks, Tim. May I ask what you're doing in the kitchen?"

"Didn't they tell you?" That little note of amusement in his voice was enough to send a ripple of panic down my spine. "The Casa Lido just took me on as sous chef."

Ah, so that's why my mother couldn't look me in the eye

when she mentioned the new chef. "How interesting that no one thought to inform me of that fact." Was my voice shaking? *Stop that,* I told myself. *Stop that right now!*

"So now you know." He lifted one finely formed shoulder. "And what does it matter, anyway?"

"Because I happen to be working here myself."

"Are you, now?" A year in Ireland had inflected—or infected—Tim's speech. I half expected him to call me "lass" and spout Yeats. "Well," he said softly. "My job just got a whole lot more stimulating."

I took a deep breath. "I don't think so, Tim. I plan to stay far out of your way, and I'd ask you to do the same for me. I'm here for one reason only—research for a new book."

He grinned, and I steeled myself. "Don't tell me Bernardo's gonna find a corpse in a restaurant?"

"It's not a mystery." How many times would I have to explain this? "I'm doing a different kind of book, a historical based on my family history." I hesitated. "And I'm also going to learn how to cook. Finally." I waited for the inevitable crack about my lack of culinary skill, but none came.

"Good for you." He rested his hand on my shoulder, only briefly, but it was enough to feel the warmth of his palm against my skin and to soften my resolve like a piece of boardwalk fudge. "I like your mysteries, though," he said. "I've read 'em all."

"You have?" That resolve was softer and stickier by the minute.

He nodded. "I've been following your career ever since you broke my heart."

"Oh no, you don't. I am not going there, Tim. If I remember correctly—and my memory is very good—there was plenty of heartbreaking to go around." I lifted my chin and looked directly into his eyes; they were an interesting slate color in this light. "We have to work together, and there's no reason we can't be friends—"

"No reason at all," he interrupted, reaching for my hand.

I pulled it away quickly. "Let me finish. There are some ground rules. One: no touching."

He grinned. "What if the kitchen's on fire and you're overcome with smoke? Am I allowed to drag you out?"

"Are you ever serious? Rule Two: no nostalgia. No talking about the old days, no references to our past. We. Are. Done."

"You sound very sure of that, Vic." His grin faded. "People can change, you know. *I've* changed."

"You just broke the second rule."

"Okay. Am I allowed to say I'm glad to see you again?"

"Yes," I said with a smile, "just as I am allowed to tell you not to get any ideas."

Tim dropped his voice. "You know me, Vic. I'm full of ideas."

He certainly was. And the memory of those ideas had me regretting my first rule. "Right," I said, avoiding his eyes. "Where are Nando and Massimo?"

"They're not coming in until later. I'm doing the pies and starting dinner prep on my own." He grinned. "I think your grandmother's testing me."

"That reminds me. Did she leave a list around here for me?"

He crooked a finger at me to follow, and I hated how quickly I complied. He handed me an index card from the counter, his mouth twitching. On the card were two words:

Napkins
Tomatoes

I frowned. "Napkins?" Conveniently ignoring Rule Number One, Tim took my elbow and steered me toward the pantry, outside of which stood an ironing board, spray starch, and a giant silver iron that would have been right at home in Lucy Ricardo's kitchen. Under the ironing board was a clear trash bag stuffed full of red-checked napkins. Based on the condensation inside the bag, they were still damp.

"No," I whispered. "She does *not* expect me to iron these. Maybe there's a roomful of straw I can spin into gold when I'm done."

"Uh, no," Tim said. "She had something else in mind." He pointed to the back door. "Tomatoes."

"Tomat— Ohhhhh no. No! Does she actually think I'm going to get out there on my hands and knees and plant tomatoes?" I shook my head. "She's crazier than I thought."

No longer able to control his amusement, Tim pointed to me, his voice breaking with laughter. "You should see your face, Vic."

I glared at him. "I am *so* not in the mood."

His raised one dark brow. "That's new."

"Rule Number Two, Tim," I said through my teeth.

"You're absolutely right," he said, and made a little bow. "From now on I will honor both rules."

"Good." I looked into his eyes, hoping my disappointment didn't show too much. This was going to be much harder than I thought.

He smiled politely, as though we were new acquaintances and not two people who'd known and loved each other for years. "And now if you'll excuse me, Vic, there's some pizza dough that needs mixing."

After he left, I tried to focus my attention to the jobs at hand. I could start with the ironing, the lesser of the two Nonna-inspired evils. I squinted down at the bag, which seemed to have ballooned in size while my back was turned. There were easily a hundred napkins in there. At least it was cool here by the pantry; the sun was already warming up that garden plot. And with such an automatic task, I could let my mind range and jot down ideas for the book. I felt for the pad and pencil in my jeans pocket and put it out on the ironing board. What Nonna didn't know couldn't hurt her. Or me.

But as I sprayed, ironed, and folded, I wasn't thinking about my characters or my story line. I was seeing the long-haired, fifteen-year-old Tim the day he had walked into the Casa Lido and asked for a job as a busboy. I was remembering a thirteen-year-old Victoria, instantly smitten, trailing around behind him to clear tables. I set down the iron and sighed. Here I was breaking my own rule.

I jerked my head up at the sound of a muffled thud coming from the bar area and then the sound of footsteps. I crept out past the pantry and peeked into the dining room. A man stood behind the bar, running his hands over the carved wood. He wore a faded gray tank top and a black ball cap jammed on backward over longish sun-streaked brown hair. I probably should have been nervous about an intruder in the restaurant, but I was a little distracted by his tanned, well-muscled arms.

"Excuse me? May I help you?"

"Nope. I'm good," he said, without turning around.

His voice was husky, with a bit of a drawl. *Not from Jersey,* I thought. That's for sure. I squinted at the embroidered fleur-de-lis on his cap. "Uh, can I ask what you're doing behind the bar?"

Taking a pencil from behind his ear, he leaned on the back counter to write something in a notebook. "Doin' my work, ma'am." There was a pause. "If you don't mind."

I strode over to the bar, indignant and out of patience. "Look, I don't know who you are, and I don't appreciate talking to your back, okay . . ." My voice trailed off as I got a closer view of said back, as well as his tight faded jeans.

He shot me a grin over his shoulder, and I glimpsed a small gold hoop in his ear. "And here I thought that was my best side." He turned around, setting both hands down on the bar. His eyes widened, and his brows did a slow rise. As did my own. I looked into a pair of sleepy green eyes rimmed in brown, took note of the lines on his face that suggested a man a bit older than his boyish look. Not to mention a charmingly crooked smile that suggested a whole lot more. He stuck his hand out across the bar. "I'm Cal."

"Nice to meet you." I pulled my hand from his warm grasp. "But what are you doing here?"

He stuck his hand into his back pocket and then slid a business card across the counter. CALVIN LOCKHART, RENOVATIONS AND RESTORATIONS.

"So they finally got around to fixing the bar."

"Yes, they did, *cher*." He winked, stuck his pencil back behind his ear, and heaved a battered toolbox up onto the counter.

"I'm Victoria, by the way. The owner's daughter." My voice rose in irritation. "In case you were wondering."

"I wasn't, but nice meetin' you anyway," Cal said, turning again to his study of the woodwork.

Lucky me, I thought, as I walked back to the pantry. To have *two* disconcerting encounters with men on my first day back in town. Those napkins and tomatoes were starting to look better and better.

In another hour I had ten perfect stacks of pressed and folded napkins to show for my labors, while Tim bustled around the kitchen readying pizzas for the outdoor grills. Soon the protesters would start arriving; the fact that she was feeding them for free was testament to my nonna's displeasure with Gio Parisi and the RealTV channel.

"Hellooooo!" My mother's not so dulcet tones rang out from the open doorway. "How's it going here, everyone?"

I walked out to greet my parents and grandmother, this time risking an air kiss in the vicinity of Nonna's cheek. She only grunted, but in a nice way. I was making progress.

"So, Mother," I said. "I've met the new sous chef."

My mother's glossy lips froze in a tight smile, and her eyes looked pained. "About that, honey. I know I should have told you, but I wasn't sure how you'd respond and—"

I held up my hand. "It's fine, Mom. I'm a big girl, and it was all a long time ago."

My dad put an arm around my shoulders and gave me a classic Frank squeeze. "I'm glad you see it that way, hon. Tim's bounced around a lotta places over the years, but I think he's settled in now. He's a good chef and basically a good boy."

You got that right, Dad. He's a thirty-five-year-old boy.

I patted my father's arm before sliding out of his grip. "Shouldn't you be checking on things outside, Daddy?"

"I already did, baby. And they're here."

"Who, the protesters?" I looked out our front window at an empty parking lot. "I don't see anybody yet."

"No, honey," Mom said. "The people from *The Jersey Side.* They're already out on the boardwalk."

I stepped outside to get a better look. Memorial Day was still two weeks away, but Ocean Avenue looked as though the season were in full swing. Most of the parking spots were filled, and a number of stands were open.

A crowd was gathered around a platform occupied by a middle-aged man, probably Parisi, a dark-haired guy in his twenties, and a tiny, buxom young woman. Even from across the street, I could make out their dark tans. The kids were signing autographs, and the older man was chatting with the onlookers. In that moment I understood what it would mean to my quiet little shore town—and to my own plans—if these people were allowed to film here.

"We can't let this happen," I said as I came back inside.

"We won't." Nonna stared out the front windows, no doubt putting a curse on Parisi. "We will stop him." She turned back and smiled at a point over my head. "*Ciao*, Calvino." *Calvino?* I must have heard wrong, because a sure sign of my grandmother's approval was getting christened with an Italian name.

"'Mornin', Giulietta," he said pleasantly, and nodded to my parents.

I hung on to the nearest table, for surely the floor would now open beneath my feet. At the very least, a thunderbolt would come flying through the front door and strike Cal where he stood. How was this Southern saw-wrangler on a first-name basis with my prickly grandmother?

While I struggled with this new knowledge, Nonna looked back at me, still smiling. *Uh-oh*. "Victoria," she said, "have you made any progress on your list this morning?"

"The napkins are done." My voice sounded unnaturally chirpy.

"And the tomatoes?"

"Right, well, it's a little sunny out there now, and I thought you guys might need some help serving the protesters and—"

She nodded her head and spoke calmly. "So you'll do it later."

It wasn't a request; it was an edict. I sighed. At some point today, I'd be digging in that garden. I wouldn't put it past Nonna to set up a spotlight so I could work all night. "You bet, Nonna," I said brightly. "But right now, shouldn't we get ready to feed the starving hordes?"

But the "hordes" turned out to be a dozen people, two of whom had made signs, one reading "Not in Our Town" with a big thumb pointing downward; the other said "Pasta-tute," an epithet suggesting an Italian who was willing to sell out, presumably aimed at Gio Parisi. In the group, I recognized Gale the librarian, our produce man, Mr. Biaggio, and Mr. and Mrs. Pak, who owned the dry cleaners. They marched vigorously in a little circle chanting the slogans on the signs, with my mom pulling up the rear. (It's a little hard to protest in heels.) My father alternated between making short speeches and serving pizza, while Nonna perched on a lawn chair in the shade.

"That display outside," I said as I walked back into the kitchen, "is at once the bravest and most pathetic thing I have ever seen in my life."

"God bless 'em," Tim said. "Want a pizza to take home? We got plenty left." Since he was cooking, he had a blue bandanna tied around his head. Only Tim could make health code compliance sexy.

"Sure. Who are those for?" I pointed to a stack of foil-wrapped pies.

"I'm gonna bring them over to Father Tom at St. Rose's. A couple families in his parish are having tough times."

"Oh," I said. I couldn't imagine the Tim I knew driving out of his way to donate leftover food. "That's really nice."

He shrugged. "There's a lot of waste in restaurants. But there are health regs regarding perishable food for donation." He grinned at me. "Father Tom and I get around them. He doesn't ask and I won't tell."

"Neither will I." We stood smiling at each other, and a tiny ache tugged at my chest. "Well, I'm off to bring some cold drinks to the righteous," I told him, determined to stay out of that kitchen for the rest of the day.

Outside, it appeared our little rally was still going strong. A reporter had left the throng on the boardwalk to get some comments from our group. At the moment, my mother was speaking animatedly into a large mike, while behind her rose chants of "Pasta-tute! Pasta-tute!" *Please*, I prayed, *don't let this turn up on the cable news.* Across the street, the boardwalk was packed, the crowds were laughing, and the food stands looked to be doing a brisk business. I walked down to the sidewalk for a better view, only to see our mayor, Anne McCrae, up on the makeshift stage. The crowd cheered as she pumped her fist in unison with the show's stars.

"Oh no," I said aloud. "This is not good." There was no doubt that *The Jersey Side* could bring major profits to the businesses in Oceanside, but it might do some real damage as well. And apart from our ragtag little band of protesters, did anyone even care? Would any of us be able to stem the RealTV tide that was threatening to engulf our hometown?

After all the excitement died down and the crowd dispersed, our protesters, including Nonna and my parents, took their signs and went home. I was left alone with Tim, Cal, and the tomatoes, wondering which I should most avoid, when a customer appeared at the door and I got my first real look at the villain of the piece.

Gio Parisi was a good-looking man, if your taste ran

to dissolute Roman emperors. His heavy-lidded eyes were dark and hard, the kind of eyes that missed nothing. But everything about him suggested the words "well kept." His thick silver-streaked black hair was artfully cut, and his firm tan face owed more to artistry than nature. His clothes were expensive, from his hand-tailored shirt to his Italian silk tie and designer suit, not to mention his pricey two-toned black–and-cordovan oxfords, polished to a mirrorlike shine.

"Table for one," he said, crossing his arms in a clear signal.

"Uh, Mr. Parisi, we're not doing a regular luncheon service today, and we don't serve dinner for an hour and a half—"

"'Luncheon service,' is it?" He looked pointedly around at the Casa Lido's interior. "Please. As if you can't find me something to eat in this glorified pizza joint."

I gripped a luncheon menu tightly. "We offer grilled pizza as a summer dish. We are *not* a—"

He held up a large palm. "Spare me the details." He stalked past me and took a seat at a table for six. "I'd like a house salad with grilled chicken. And not some soggy piece of meat you pull out of the fridge. Cooked to order." He smiled and crossed his arms again. "I'll wait."

A sound from the bar caught my attention, and Cal jerked his head in Parisi's direction. I frowned and shook my head, hoping he wouldn't feel the need to leap over the counter and protect me. I'd handled worse customers than Gio Parisi. Frankly, I was more afraid of what my grandmother might do if she came back and found him eating in her restaurant.

"Oh, and, miss?" Parisi said. "You can also bring me a bottle of San Pellegrino and hot water for tea. And that I *don't* want to wait for," he said softly.

"I'll bring that right out. *Sir*."

"And I want that chicken well-done," he called after me. "And the dressing on the side!"

In the kitchen, Tim had dinner prep well under way. I watched his skilled hands slicing and trimming veal for the special, and I hated to break his concentration. "Hey, Tim, can you throw some chicken on the grill?"

He wiped his forehead with the back of his hand and scowled at me. It was a look I remembered well. "What for? I just cleaned it."

"Listen, Gio Parisi's out there. He's insisting we serve him. Just make the chicken. He wants it well-done. I'll throw the salad together."

"Forget it." He slammed his knife down on the counter. "I'm not feeding him. No way."

"*Chi*?" Mr. Biaggio came through the door with a large cardboard box filled to the top with lettuce and other assorted greens. He set the box down with a grunt and grinned broadly. "Who are you refusing to feed, Timoteo?"

I couldn't help smiling at his accent and at his efforts to make Tim's Irish name Italian. "Hi, Mr. Biaggio," I said. "Gio Parisi is out in the dining room."

"No!" He lowered his thick brows, and his face reddened. "That *cafone*, the nerve he has to come here." He shook his fist high in the air. "Victoria, I will be happy to throw him out for you, just like the garbage that he is!"

"I appreciate that—I really do, Mr. B—but I don't want any trouble. That's the last thing the Casa Lido needs." I filled a kettle and set it on the stove to boil, sliced some bread, and pulled a San Pellegrino from the drinks cooler. "Tim, please. Let's just give him lunch and get him the hell out of here before Nonna comes back."

"Oh, I'll give him lunch, all right." He struggled to

jerk open the door of the heavy refrigerator, then threw a pack of chicken on the counter and scrubbed his hands with a fury. "I'll make the damn salad."

"Okay, but don't dress it."

"Got it. And by the way, tell Lockhart to stay the hell out of my kitchen."

Oh, it's your *kitchen now, is it?* I thought, and backed out of the doors, holding the water bottle and bread basket, stopping at the coffee station to ready a plate and a tea bag. It was a little frightening how easily I'd fallen back into my old routine.

I set the water and bread down in front of my customer. "Here you go. Hot water's coming up."

Parisi waved his hand. "No bread." Then he looked up at me with a sly grin. "How does it feel to be serving a 'pasta-tute'? Bet they don't come in here every day."

Do not engage, Vic. "We take good care of all our customers, Mr. Parisi." I picked up the basket and turned to go.

"Then maybe you can bring me my hot water, Ms. Reed," he said from behind me.

I fought the temptation to answer him and headed back to the kitchen, where I filled a metal tea carafe with shaking hands.

When I brought the tea things back to his table, he emptied a packet of sweetener into his cup and pointed. "Water, please." As I poured his hot water, he winked at me. "Surprised you there, didn't I, *Vick Reed*? Though I don't know why you should be—your mug's on the back of all your books." He dunked his tea bag vigorously. "I do read, you know."

"I'm sure you do." I held up the carafe. "Would you like me to leave this?"

"Nah, you can take it. Where's that salad?"

"It'll be right up," I said through my teeth.

"Hey, it's a shame about that HBO deal!" he yelled to my retreating back.

Back in the kitchen, I took a deep breath and washed my hands. Neither Mr. Biaggio nor my temperamental chef was anywhere to be found. But there was a telltale smell of burning chicken and smoke drifting inside the open door. Apparently, Tim defined well done as "charred." But the salad was ready on the counter, so I took a small gravy boat and filled it with house dressing. While I waited for the chicken, I peeked through the kitchen doors at our guest, who was occupied with his phone. I pulled my head back inside before he could see me. *C'mon, Tim. Bring me the chicken already. This guy's not the patient type.* A few minutes later, Tim walked in; without a word, he dumped the blackened chicken pieces on top of the salad.

"Thanks, chef!" I called as he slammed out the back door.

I looked down at the unappetizing sight, but when I brought it out to Parisi, he dug right in.

"Is there anything else?" I asked.

"Not at the moment." He shoveled a load of salad into his mouth, his thick lips glistening with dressing, then followed that up with a loud slurp of tea. If I stood there any longer, I'd be in danger of losing those two pieces of pizza I'd had for lunch. "By the way," he said, shaking his fork at me and talking through a mouthful of food, "I don't know what you people are so damn upset about. Your mayor's on board, and I think your town council will be, too. You might as well get used to the idea that we'll be filming here." He opened his water bottle and poured a full glass. "You know the amount of business my show would bring you?" When I didn't answer, he tried another tack. "Or . . . the amount of business it could *cost* you?"

"I don't know what you mean." But I was pretty sure I did.

"Well, all it would take is for one of the kids to say—on camera, of course—how bad the food is here." He took another sip of tea and grimaced. After another sip, he folded his hands on the table and looked up at me. "How busy do you think you'd be after that?"

"That would depend on the season, Mr. Parisi. Now, if you'll excuse me." I wheeled around blindly, my fists clenched at my sides. The guy was scum, threatening us like some two-bit mobster. At the coffee station, I set up the two machines, one for American coffee and one for espresso, keeping Parisi in the edge of my vision and willing him to finish that darn salad.

My concentration was interrupted by a female shriek. "Vic!" Lori Jamison yelled. Then she threw her arms around me and stepped back. "Look at you, you skinny thing."

I looked down at her round, freckled face, and suddenly I was back in high school, when the two of us waited tables during the lunch shift every summer. But after I left, Lori stayed on.

Now married with a young son, she was our primary waitress and as much a part of the family as Danny or I was.

"It's so good to see you again, Lori. I could use some moral support around here."

"Why? Is Nonna around?" She grinned broadly, and I couldn't help smiling back.

"Not yet. But we've got kind of a tricky customer out there. Maybe you passed him on your way in?"

"I came in the back, hon. The only person I saw was Dreamboat in the kitchen."

"Right." Strangely, my cheeks grew warm, and I couldn't meet my old friend's eye.

"You gonna be able to work with him?"

I shrugged. "I have to, don't I?"

"So your mom tells me you're here to work on a new book. That's exciting, huh?"

"Neat change of subject there, LJ." I gave her a thumbs-up. "Well played."

She tucked a fresh order pad into the pocket of her apron. "Listen, don't let your nonna or Dreamboat back there get to you." She shook her pen at me. "Or get in the way of that new book. We're all so proud of you, Vic."

"Thanks, kiddo. Listen, would you mind checking on that customer at Table Five? See if he's ready for his bill."

She peeked out into the dining room. "Hey, isn't that the guy who was just up at the boards? From RealTV?"

"Gio Parisi." I shook my head. "And he is really unpleasant."

"I was wondering whose big ol' pimped-out Escalade was in my spot. And how lovely of him to mess up that whole table for me." She turned to me and grinned. "Maybe we can arrange a nice case of food poisoning."

"I think Tim already tried it with his chicken."

She winked at me. "I'll take care of him. Then I'm gonna go say hi to Cutie-Pie Cal."

"'Cutie-Pie Cal'? 'Dreamboat'? Does Billy know about you and the men of the Casa Lido?"

"I'm married, babe," she called as she walked away. "Not dead."

Lori came back with Parisi's plate and nodded toward the dining room. "He's just finishing his tea, but he's ready for the bill. I'll clear up when he's done."

"Thanks, Lori." When I brought Parisi the check, he handed me his credit card without a word. I pointed to his nearly empty teacup. "Are you through?"

"Leave that," he barked. He downed the rest of his water and wiped his sweaty forehead with the back of his hand. "You can take the water glass."

I tucked his card and a pen into the black billfold and set it down next to him. His face was pale. "Would you like more water?" I asked.

He shook his head. "No. Where's the men's room?"

"Around that wall and to the right." Holding his glass with two fingers as far away from me as possible, I brought it into the kitchen and then dumped the San Pellegrino bottle in the recycling bin. Then I scrubbed my hands again. Twice. Relieved that Tim was still missing from the kitchen, I backed out through the doors quickly, shaking my still-wet hands. But when I got back to his table, Gio Parisi was gone.

The Casa Lido started to come to life as dinner prep got under way. Cal was wrapping up his work at the bar, and Lori was in the back getting the specials from Tim. As promised, I filled and wiped all the salt and peppers, my nose twitching furiously. As I was finishing, Massimo Fabri, our executive chef, swept through the front doors and paused dramatically.

"*Cara!* You return!" He held his arms out to me, and I gave him a European double kiss, one for each cheek. "You look wonderful."

"So do you, Massi." Our chef, with his swept-back hair and luxurious mustache, looked as though he would be more at home in the Metropolitan Opera House than in the Casa Lido. And he did occasionally break into arias in the kitchen. When readers asked me if any real person had inspired my fictional detective, I always lied and said no. But there was more than a little Massimo Fabri in Bernardo Vitali. "Listen, Massi." I looked around to make sure my grandmother was nowhere in sight, but lowered my voice anyway. She had ears like a bat's. "I'm trying to get Nonna to teach me to cook."

"Ha!" he said. "Good luck with that, little one." He set his toque on his head and rubbed his hands together. "And ... Tim, he is in the kitchen?" He looked away from me as he asked the question; he, like the rest of the staff, as well as most of Oceanside Park, knew our history.

"Yes, he is." I dropped my voice. "And you can say his name. It's okay."

"Good." He patted my shoulder. "Look. Here is another of your old friends."

"*Hola*, Nando!" I said. "It's so nice to see you." His bright gap-toothed grin and round face reminded me of a cheerful jack-o'-lantern. He stuck out a plump hand and gave me his usual greeting. "Hello, Miss Victor." Despite years of trying, I could never get Nando to drop the "miss" or add the feminine ending to my name.

Nando Perez hailed from Ecuador and had worked here for nearly half his life, starting as a busboy and moving up to line cook. He spoke to my grandmother in Spanish and she responded in Italian, a communication style that confused the rest of us but worked for them. As always, Nando's glistening black hair was ponytailed and braided, the top of his head covered by a hairnet. I don't know whether he wore the net for reasons of health or beauty, but in fifteen years, I'd never seen him without it.

My parents and grandmother came in right behind Nando. My dad headed to the bar to set up, and my mom took her place behind the reservation desk.

"So, honey," Mom said. "How was your first day back?"

"Uh, good. Got all the napkins ironed and the setups

made." I risked a look at my grandmother's impassive face. "Now all I have to do is plant a dozen tomato flats."

"That's nice," my mom said vaguely, her nose in the black reservations book.

"I have something for you, Victoria," my grandmother said, handing me a rusted garden spade that was probably older than she was. "You still have a couple hours of light."

"Thanks, Nonna." I held up the dirty tool. "I'll get right on it."

Feeling very much like a child sent off to bed while the grown-ups partied, I headed out the back door toward the garden. My mood wasn't improved by the sight of the gold Escalade still occupying Lori's space in the employee lot. What was Parisi's car doing here? He'd left well over an hour ago. "You'd better come back and get this car, buddy," I grumbled. "Or I'm calling my brother to come and put a big fat ticket on it."

As I stood and surveyed the garden plot, I caught a foul smell on the breeze. *Ugh*, I thought. *Nonna's got a heavy hand with the fertilizer.* Knowing I couldn't put it off one minute more, I sighed and dropped to my knees, dug into the soft soil, and settled the first plant into its bed. Only 143 to go.

I had nearly a whole row planted when I spotted something in the grass near the shed. I stood up, my knees stiff, and took a few steps toward the object. When I bent my head for a better look, goose bumps prickled up and down my bare arms. It was a shoe—a two-toned black-and-cordovan oxford that had no business being in my grandmother's garden. My feet, of their own accord and certainly without my permission, carried me around the corner of the shed. I pressed my hand against the wall to steady myself and looked down at a sight that I had only ever seen in my fevered imagination.

But this was real. And that smell wasn't fertilizer. There on the ground, his arms and legs splayed out and his face in a puddle of vomit, lay Gio Parisi.

Chapter Four

Why couldn't I move? Why couldn't I speak? A voice, calm and rational, was saying, "Call nine-one-one. You *need* to call nine-one-one." My mouth dry, I opened it to answer, only to realize the voice was in my head. Holding my breath against the odor, I dropped to my wobbly knees. Careful not to disturb anything (I had learned at least that much in eight years), I reached out to touch Parisi's wrist, but my hand froze in midair. *He might need help*, the calm voice said. *You have to check and see*. I swallowed, breathing hard through my nose, and closed my fingers around the cold skin. But Gio Parisi was beyond any help I could give him. Still shaky, I fell backward in the grass, but pushed myself to my feet. I dug my hand into the pocket of my jeans for a phone that wasn't there.

I jerked my head up at a sudden rustling in the grass, expecting—no, willing—my fictional detective to show up. I desperately wanted Bernardo Vitali, jauntily arrayed in a summer linen suit and straw hat, his notepad and fountain pen in hand, to take over the case so I could run the hell back to Manhattan. But it was only Tim, rounding the corner from the other side of the lot, the empty compost bucket in his hand. When he saw my face, he dropped the bucket and ran toward me.

"What's the matter, Vic? What's wrong?"

I pointed, still unable to utter a word. Tim looked down at the spectacle behind the shed, his face swiftly draining of color. He gripped my arm with a clammy hand. And then he did something I'd been waiting half my life to see: He dropped into a dead swoon at my feet.

The scene that followed was surreal, mostly because I had written it so many times. In some ways, it felt as though I were still writing it. We were herded into the restaurant so it could be closed off; an Oceanside officer stood guard in the parking lot, carrying out the first rule at the scene of a suspicious death: nobody in, nobody out. Every vehicle in the lot, including Parisi's new Escalade and my old Schwinn, had to be accounted for. All our statements had to be taken. And, of course, the press had to be kept at bay.

In the dining room, my family and I, Lori, Cal, and Tim were all crowded around one table. "Why? Why," Nonna asked, wringing her hands, "did he have to pick *here* to die?"

"Tuesdays are slow anyway, Ma," my dad said, in a masterpiece of understatement. "Thank God nobody was in the dining room."

My mom frowned. "No matter how we may have felt about him, or how this affects our business, a man is dead out there."

He certainly was. I took a huge gulp of the wine in front of me, catching Cal's eye over the top of my glass. When I was outside with Tim in a crumpled heap next to me, I finally found my voice. Cal was the one who came running. He got Tim back on his feet and put a strong arm around each of us to get us back inside. He called 911 and then Danny, who materialized in what seemed like seconds.

Cal's expression now was warm and concerned; he slid his whiskey glass toward me. "Try a sip of this, *cher.* Good for what ails ya."

I held up my hand. "That's okay, but thanks. For everything, by the way." I smiled, and caught Tim scowling at us. "Are you feeling any better?" I asked him.

"I'm fine." Tim looked down at his glass; he was the only one drinking water. "It was just the shock of seeing him out there like that." He ran his hands through his thick curls, unwilling to meet our eyes.

Lori reached over and patted his arm. "Don't you worry, hon. We understand."

"Yeah, man. No worries," Cal said in a hearty just-us-buddies tone. "Coulda happened to anybody." *Except me, of course,* said the look on his face.

We all jumped at the sound of the door opening, and I was relieved to see my brother. He sat down, covering my hand with his. "You okay?"

I nodded. "Don't they need you out there?"

"I can't be part of this investigation—conflict of interest. Strictly speaking, I shouldn't even be here." He smiled faintly, but I knew my brother. He wasn't happy. "Anyway, I think this might be one for the county prosecutor."

I didn't like the sound of that. "What's going on out there?"

"The county coroner's office just picked him up."

My grandmother was the only one honest enough—or cold-blooded enough—to voice what all of us were thinking. "Good," she said. "The sooner he's off this property, the better."

"Listen, guys." Dan looked around the table. "We need to be prepared for the possibility this wasn't a simple heart attack."

"Danny, lots of people having heart attacks vomit, if

that's what you're thinking," I said. "I've researched it. And he was definitely sweaty and clammy looking before he left."

"But, Vic," Lori said, "he didn't look like he had chest pain or anything. I mean, he didn't mention it."

I shrugged. "Why would he? He probably just thought it was indigestion or something."

My mother's eyes widened. "You don't think it was a food allergy?"

"I don't think so, Mom." I shook my head. "He was so particular about what he ordered. If he had a food allergy, I think he would have made that loud and clear."

"Was the chicken fresh?" Cal asked, looking straight at Tim.

"What the hell?" Tim said. "Of course it was fresh. And that produce was clean." He glared at Cal. "Anyway, people don't drop dead of salmonella in minutes, Lockhart."

"Easy there, guys," Danny said. "I'm only saying that we don't know what killed him. And if it wasn't a heart attack, this could have some real repercussions for the restaurant."

My mother closed her eyes and rubbed her temples, as though her head hurt. "The season's about to start. If people think he died because of something he ate here—"

"Don't think that way, babe." My father picked up her hand and kissed it. "We'll be fine."

I glanced over at Danny, and I knew we were thinking the same thing: Our gambler father was a big believer in long shots. "Hey, Dan? Is the press out there yet?"

He shook his head. "But it's only a matter of time. The guy's high profile."

"Oh God." My mother held her head and moaned. "I didn't even think about reporters."

But I had. Including all that lovely footage they already had of the rally, in which both my parents and several townsfolk had publicly excoriated the dead man. My mother wasn't the only one with a headache. This could become a circus, with the Rienzi family in the center ring.

Nonna rapped on the table. "Nicolina! Get hold of yourself. *Daniele* will keep the reporters away. We will ride this out like a storm. In the meantime, we do what we always do—prepare for the season ahead."

I wondered, absurdly, if that included planting the rest of the tomatoes. I wasn't sure I could face that back garden again.

My head jerked up at the sound of a chair scraping across the floor. My brother stood with his hands on the back of the chair, his face serious. "I'm gonna head out there and see how long it will be before you can all go home. It shouldn't be much longer."

When we were finally allowed to leave, I declined all offers of rides. Instead, I biked along the empty boardwalk, breathing in the cool sea air and listening to the sound of the waves. The same words played over and over in my head: *It had to be a heart attack. It had to be a heart attack.*

By the time I reached the cottage, I had myself convinced. Gio Parisi had died of natural causes. Of that, I was certain. But as my own detective might have reminded me, fate usually had plans for those who were sure.

Chapter Five

Isabella clutched ~~pulled~~ *her tattered shawl closely around—*

No.

Isabella clutched ~~at the corners of~~ *her shabby wool shawl—*

God, no.

Isabella pulled the frayed wool shawl closely around herself. Chilled by the November wind, she—

She . . . she what? I took another slug of my coffee—like most of my old boyfriends, it was strong, dark, Italian, and slightly bitter—and stared at the blinking cursor on my screen. Who was I kidding? After yesterday's drama, did I really think I'd get any work done today? I put my head down on the desk, trying to ignore the slide show in my head that kept showing the same nightmarish image, Parisi facedown in my grandmother's tomato garden. When my cell phone vibrated, I grabbed it like a lifeline.

"Vic, what the hell's going on down there?" Behind the concern in Josh's voice, a different emotion was hiding, one that sounded suspiciously like excitement.

"Listen, it's not that big a deal, really," I lied. "Some guy had a heart attack out behind the restaurant."

"'Some guy'? You're kidding me, right? Gio Parisi is

one of the biggest producers in reality show television. Mindy's been glued to the TV since last night."

Josh's wife was a big fan of RealTV. "Wait—it hit the networks?"

"Where've *you* been?"

Right in the middle of this nightmare. Thank you. "There's no TV in the cottage."

"But it's all over the net."

"I'm trying to stay *off* the Internet. I'm here to work, remember?" I didn't mention that the last thing I wanted to do was see my family all over the news. I sighed. "Not that I'm getting anything done."

Ignoring my last remark, Josh went on. "They're calling it foul play, you know." His voice dropped. "And they're saying you found him."

I stared at the phone in my hand, then at my coffee cup, then at my screen, then out my window at the ocean. *Remember this moment, Vic*, I told myself, *because this is when it all goes south.* "Yes, Josh, I found him. But there hasn't even been an autopsy yet."

"There's a lotta chatter on the Net about it."

"I'm sure there is, but . . ."

"So I guess you haven't seen your sales numbers." Josh's jump to this particular topic left me confused. In a mental scurry to keep up, I took another swig of coffee.

"What are you talking about?" I glanced out the side window of the cottage, where a large white shape caught the corner of my eye. Plastering the phone to my ear, I hurried down the narrow stairs to the first floor, the coffee in my empty stomach rolling like a wave.

"Don't you get it, Vic? You're a mystery author, in the middle of a real-life mystery. Check out Amazon. *Molto Murder*'s on a steep climb, with *Ciao, My Darling* not far behind it. And the preorders for *Murder Della Casa* are through the roof. Bernardo just got a new lease on life!"

"Wow. I mean, that's great and all, but . . ." Now at the front window, I peeked through the old-fashioned metal blinds. The white shape had strange equipment attached to the top of it, and a big blue number 10 painted on its side. I turned quickly, flattening my back against my door.

"Listen," I said in a whisper, "much as I'd like to discuss my book sales with you right now, I have a little issue that needs my attention. The Channel Ten news van is parked in front of my house."

"That's awesome!" His voice was so loud, I was convinced he could be heard outside.

"Josh, you're a ghoul. You know that?" Still whispering, I made a dash for the staircase at the moment the first knock sounded. "I need to go. And please—if anyone calls you for a comment, you have none. Okay?"

"Okay," he said. "But you'd better keep me in the loop."

"I will, but I've gotta go."

The knocking was growing louder and more persistent, accompanied by calls of "Ms. Reed! Ms. Reed!"

I stood in the middle of my small bedroom, still clutching the phone, wondering if I had enough food in the house to last me through the media onslaught. I was suddenly in the middle of a horror movie, the last human alive, with bloodthirsty zombies circling my door.

Just then a shrill voice cut through the muffled tones of the gathering hordes. "Ya got nothin' better to do than hang around here? Ms. Reed has no comment, and neither do I. So why don't you just take your nosy butts off this property before I call my highly placed contact in the police department?"

I couldn't help grinning as my hero arrived—Sofia Delmonico, who also happened to be my landlord and erstwhile sister-in-law. I pulled my bedroom door closed and sat on the bed, waiting until I heard the front door slam.

"You can come out, Vic," she called. "It's only me."

I stuck my head out the bedroom door, and a welcome sight met my eyes—Sofia at the bottom of the stairs holding two coffees and a white bakery bag marked in familiar red letters. "Oh my God," I said. "Are they doughnuts from the Snack Shack?"

"Yes, but you don't get any until you tell me what happened in that restaurant." She shook the bag. "Are you coming down or am I coming up?"

"I'll come down." It was no surprise that Sofia was here for every detail, gory or otherwise, of yesterday's incident. And any information I didn't offer willingly, she'd worm out of me anyway. She beckoned again from the bottom of the stairs, this time using the coffee as bait. No match for her or the cinnamon doughnuts, I crept down the stairs.

"It is *so* good to see you." I threw my arms around her skinny-but-curvy five-foot-two frame. "And you look awesome, as usual." Sofia was a classic Italian girl, olive-skinned and dark-eyed with a shiny waterfall of black hair. "I can't believe you got through that mess out there," I said.

"Please," she said. "How long have you known me?"

"Since you used to climb trees to sneak peeks at my brother. Sit." In the kitchen, I grabbed napkins and two mismatching plates from the cabinet. Once I took a bite of warm cinnamon-sugar doughnut, I nearly forgot about the media zombies lying in wait outside. "I'm gonna be two hundred pounds before I leave here."

"Quit moaning and talk to me, SIL," Sofia said, using our shorthand for "sister-in-law." She cut her doughnut into quarters, of which she would allow herself exactly one, having already eaten her high-protein, high-fiber breakfast. As a dance teacher, she took great care of herself, and it showed. She took a sip of her unsweetened black coffee and raised her eyes expectantly. "Tell me."

"I assume you're talking about the dead guy in the tomato garden?" I tried to sound flip but didn't quite carry it off.

"He's not just any dead guy—he's Gio Parisi." She paused. "Well, he *was*, anyway." She pointed to the front door of the cottage. "He's the reason that van's out there."

I dropped my head in my hand. "Don't remind me."

Sofia leaned forward in her chair. "Is it true you found him?"

"Unfortunately." I described the scene as though it came from a book, and not my recent memory, but I couldn't help a little shudder as I remembered wrapping my fingers around his cold wrist.

"That sounds awful," Sofia said. "So what's next?"

"They're doing an autopsy and probably a tox screen. They took a whole bunch of food and trash from the kitchen. It looks like a heart attack. And that's the result we're all praying for."

"You don't think—" Sofia began.

"I don't know what to think. All I know is that he had lunch at the restaurant and died about an hour later."

She shook her head. "Not good."

"That's putting it mildly. Especially since there's a well-documented protest that happened outside the Casa Lido this afternoon."

"I forgot about that." Her face brightened. "Guess that solves the problem of them filming here."

"Don't even say it!" I gestured toward the windows. "They'd have a field day with that. And at some point, I'm gonna have to deal with them." I looked around the cozy cottage, with its musty seashore smell and mismatching furniture, and sighed. "This was such a perfect place for me to work, too."

"What do you mean 'was'? You're here for a year. I've got your name on a lease." She squeezed my hand. "Don't worry. This will all blow over and you'll write your book. What's it about, anyway?"

As I told her, I watched her bright eyes grow dim. "That sounds really . . . interesting."

"Ah, the adjective every writer wants to hear. Thanks, Sofe."

"I'm sorry, but I think you should write a romance. A really hot one, like Nora Roberts."

I couldn't help laughing. "I'm no Nora Roberts."

"At least give Bernardo a girlfriend." She paused. "Or a boyfriend, I don't care. Give him somethin', will ya?"

"It's hard for me to imagine Bernardo with a sex life." I wrinkled my nose. "Come to think of it, I don't *want* to imagine Bernardo with a sex life."

She looked at me sideways and lifted one eyebrow. "Speaking of romance—how's Not So Tiny Tim?"

"Funny. Did you think that one up yourself?" I wiped the sugar from my fingers and contemplated another doughnut.

"Actually, you came up with it."

"I guess I did. It all feels like a million years ago now. And yesterday." I pushed the plate of doughnuts away and concentrated on the coffee instead. I would need lots of caffeine to get through today.

"I know what you mean. Was it hard to see him again?"

"I'm over Tim, Sofia."

She pointed to my neck. "Right. And that's why you're still wearing the necklace he had made for you."

"I like it, okay?" I looked into her dark eyes. "Yes, it's hard to be around him. But I don't have to tell you. When *is* the last time you talked to your 'highly placed contact in the police department'?"

"Please." She waved her hand. "Your brother's a pain in my ass."

"But you love him, right?"

"Somethin' awful." she said with a sigh. "Hey, does he know I'm renting you the cottage?"

"I haven't mentioned it, but I know he wouldn't care. He knows we're close."

At this, Sofia broke into a passable imitation of my brother and jabbed her finger at me for emphasis. "'You two, you're thick as thieves.'" She broke off abruptly, her grin fading. "God, I miss him."

"He misses you."

She pressed her hand against her chest. "It feels like my heart is bruised."

"Because it is. And it's the same for him," I said quietly. "Don't you want to work things out?"

"You know I do!" She shook her head. "He's so stubborn. He won't give an inch."

"Is it so important to you to enter the police academy? To give up the dance studio and everything you've worked for? To put this kind of a strain on your marriage?"

Her lips tightened. "I guess it's natural that you'd be on his side."

"C'mon, Sofia, be fair. Yes, he's my brother, but I love both of you. And I want the best for both of you." I shook my head. "It's hard for me to understand."

"What's so hard? I want a career in law enforcement, and your brother won't accept my choice."

"You know why. It's not just Danny being macho—"

"Of course it is."

"He's worried about you. He knows the risks that

cops take, even in small towns. He doesn't want anything to happen to you."

"Don't you think I worry about *him* on the job? But I've been training on my own, going to karate class every week. And I'm smart; I can take care of myself."

"I'm not diminishing that. But there's more to it. You've got a nice little business in town. Do you really want to risk that for this dream of being a cop?"

Sophia's eyes narrowed. "You've got a nice little mystery series going that sells lots of books. But you're taking a risk for a dream. Why shouldn't I?"

"Got me there, SIL," I said. "We're probably both crazy." I drained the rest of my coffee and strained to listen. Above the chatter outside, I could hear a lone female voice speaking into a microphone. "Crap, I think they started filming."

Sofia frowned. "What is there to film? Your empty front yard?"

"I don't know. Background stuff, maybe?" I craned my neck to peer into the living room. "I wish I knew what was going on out there."

She stood up. "Let's find out."

"Are you crazy? I'm not going out there now."

"Who said anything about going out?" Sofia crept out to the living room, and dropping to her hands and knees as quietly as a cat, she slinked her way along the floor. If she had a tail, it would be twitching. She looked back at me over her shoulder. "Well, what are you waiting for? C'mon."

Knees creaking, I bent down to join her on the floor, my canine posture a sharp contrast to her feline grace. I wrinkled my nose. "Eww. This rug needs shampooing."

"Tell it to the landlord." Sofia had reached one of the two front windows; she poked her nose through the slats, her chin resting on the sill.

"Wanna tell me again why I'm crawling on a stinky rug with my butt up in the air?"

"Quit complaining. It's probably the most fun you've had in weeks."

While I pondered the truth of this statement, I reached for the sill to pull myself up. From my vantage point, I could make out only the van and a couple of guys moving some big cords. "What do you see?" I whispered.

"Oh my God!" Sofia's voice rose to a squeal. "It's Nina LaGuardia!"

"Will you keep your voice down?" I shoved my face further into the blinds, the metal edges digging sharply into my nose. "Who's Nina LaGuardia?"

"God, Vic, you live under a rock. She's the new Channel Ten anchor." Sofia lifted the blind a fraction. "Oooh, I love her dress."

"Will you forget the dress?" I hissed. "What is she saying?"

She shook her head. "I can't make it out. But it looks like she's practicing. She's really pretty in person."

My knees were getting numb and my face was marked with dirt from the window. I turned around to sit with my back against the wall and rubbed my sore nose. "There's got to be some way to make them leave."

She shot me a sly, sideways glance. "We could call Danny."

"We could. But then he'd have to meet the lovely Nina. And for all you know, she might have a weakness for men in uniform."

"Never mind." She scrambled to her feet. "Let's just sneak out the back door."

I stood up and groaned, my calves tight from the unaccustomed biking. "Well, I'm gonna jump in the shower."

"Why? What are you doing?" She looked at me as I trudged up the stairs.

I stopped with my hand on the rail and turned back to look at her. "What do you think? I'm getting ready for my close-up."

Chapter Six

*A*fter managing to escape the zombies in one piece, I jumped into my car and headed into town. It was a gray day, and the low clouds threatened rain. The streets were quiet after yesterday's crowds. I pulled into the restaurant with trepidation. My hands shook a little as I got out of the car, and I hesitated in front of the big wooden doors. *I can turn around now. I can be back on the Parkway in fifteen minutes.* But could I really leave my family at the mercy of Nina LaGuardia and the rest of the media? That van would likely end up here sooner or later, and how would that affect our business? Besides that, my curiosity was getting the better of me—what *had* happened to Gio Parisi?

When I stepped inside the restaurant, something felt off. It was just too quiet. Instead of the usual bustle of lunch prep—the clank of pots, the whoosh of the swinging kitchen doors, the calls of the deliverymen, there was only silence.

"Tim? Massimo? Anybody here?"

"Just me." Tim came through the kitchen doors, wiping his hands on a towel tucked into his apron. One dark curl had escaped from his bandanna; his jacket sleeves were rolled up to reveal his forearms—as Tim's body parts go, two of my all-time faves—and I took a nice cleansing breath. Luckily, the sight of his orange kitchen clogs brought me to my senses.

"Where is everybody? Are you doing lunch all by yourself?"

"Looks like it." He gestured toward my mother's precious black book. "We had a bunch of cancellations, so I'm just doing the minimum."

"Oh God. Is it happening already?"

"I guess so. I had Mr. B bring me about half the regular produce, and the butcher's been here. I mean, we needed stuff because the cops cleaned us out." He shrugged. "I just don't know how much of it we'll use."

I glanced toward the bar. "Is Cal in today?"

"I don't keep tabs on Lockhart. Anyway, the guy keeps whatever hours he wants. He's been and gone already this morning."

"Well, he can't work when we have customers, right? So that leaves Mondays, early mornings, and the gap between lunch and dinner service." As I spoke, I flashed back to the day before; Cal was in the restaurant while Parisi ate, and I remembered Tim's words: *Keep Lockhart out of my kitchen.* Why would Cal have been in the kitchen at all? And was he anywhere near the dead producer's plate? *Cut it out, Vic,* I told myself. *Yesterday you were convinced it was a heart attack, and today you're lining up the suspects.*

Tim's expression hardened as I talked about Cal, so I thought it prudent to change the subject. "Listen, can I do anything? Silver setups? Coffee station?"

"Done and done," he said as he headed back to the kitchen, "unless you want to give Lori a call and tell her not to come in until later." He grinned at me over his shoulder. "I think even you can handle today's lunch rush."

And he was right. The "lunch rush" consisted of one

elderly couple who ate Tim's pasta special (rigatoni with sausage, spinach, and fresh ricotta) with relish, apparently unaware of the previous day's happenings at the Casa Lido. They had probably never had such service in their lives; I kept their water glasses full, brought their food promptly, and even gave them a cannoli and two coffees on the house.

After they left, I sank into one of the dining room chairs, one eye on the front window in case that News Ten van should roll up to the door. But the only vehicle that arrived was my dad's Lexus, and I steeled myself for Nonna's reaction to an empty dining room at the height of lunch hour.

She stood inside the door, hands on her hips, her face stern. "Victoria, where are all the customers?"

"Oh, I don't know, Nonna. Maybe they've been kidnapped. Or they're hiding from us." I lifted the corner of one of the tablecloths. "Nope, no customers under there." I spread my palms out. "Where do you think they are? They're too afraid to eat here."

"We don't need your sarcasm, young lady," my mom said, and then opened the reservation book. Her eyes widened, and she slammed it shut. At that, my father looked around at the women in his life and, without a word, beat a hasty retreat to the bar. My grandmother held out one iron hand. "Nicolina, the book please."

My mother and I looked at each other guiltily. "We did have one table of two," I said, trying not to sound sulky.

Nonna didn't answer. She closed the book slowly and adjusted her glasses. "I notice we have some cancellations."

"A few." As my bravado evaporated, I squeaked like a seventh grader.

"More than a few." She handed the book back to my mom.

"Now, Mama," my mom said, "we'll weather this. Once they know how Mr. Parisi"—she paused—"um, expired, people will realize that it had nothing to do with the restaurant."

We hope, I thought, looking at my mother's worried face and my grandmother's stern one.

"But the season starts in less than two weeks!" Nonna's voice echoed across the empty dining room.

"We know, Nonna. We know." I patted her arm. "Listen, Danny said the autopsy results are coming soon."

She made a grunting sound either of skepticism or dismissal, or both, and I took the hint. I had also neglected to mention that toxicology results could take weeks. I sneaked into the kitchen and helped myself to a small portion of Tim's pasta special while I mulled over our predicament.

Any chef, waitress, hostess, or busboy will tell you that there is nothing slower than a slow night in a restaurant. Massimo, Tim, and Nando ended up cleaning the refrigerator and freezer, while Lori and I wiped every surface in sight. When I heard the rumble of thunder in the distance, I knew our fate was sealed; if not the corpse, the rain would keep people away. We ended up with only two customers, and when one of them turned out to be a reporter for the *Oceanside Chronicle*, our town's weekly rag, Nonna's response wasn't pretty.

As the evening wore on with nothing to do, the men drifted from the kitchen to the bar. I was about to join them when I saw my dad, Tim, Massimo, and Cal crowded around a laptop screen. The Casa Lido bar did not have a television, so I assumed they were watching a baseball game. Until I heard a female voice coming from the screen.

"We're here today outside the cottage where mystery writer Vick Reed, aka Victoria Rienzi, is on an apparent writer's retreat . . ."

Oh God. Nina's voice chirped on. "Ms. Reed, what can you tell us about the real-life mystery that's unfolding right here in your hometown? Can you confirm that producer Gio Parisi was found dead behind your family's restaurant?"

"Pause it right there," Massimo said. "Ho, look at her. Like a frightened horse!"

I stood behind them, straining to see the small screen. And there I was, looking just as Massimo had described me, rearing back from the microphone with my eyes rolled back until the whites showed, whinnying my "no comment" at the camera. I stared at my pale face, frozen by the pause button. My quick dabs of blush and lip gloss were no match for Nina's artfully made-up face, and the contrast was so painful I winced.

"Play 'er again," Cal said, and Tim and my dad chuckled.

"I'm glad you're finding this funny," I said.

Cal swung around on the barstool. "Lord, girl, you give a man a heart attack, sneakin' up on him like that." He patted his chest, and my eyes strayed to his broad hand, work worn and a bit beat-up. I hadn't seen many hands like that in Manhattan.

"You might want to watch your choice of words there, ace," I said. "What are you still doing here, anyway?"

He lifted his beer in a toast. "Just having a friendly drink, ma'am."

My dad pointed to a spot of bare wood among the scrollwork on the bar. "Look at the work he's done here, hon. He already stripped this whole section."

"That 'whole' section, huh?" I shook my head. "At this rate, we will no longer be able to afford you, Mr.

Lockhart." I gestured toward the empty dining room. "And unless business picks up, we won't even be able to pay the electric bill."

"C'mon, baby, things aren't that bad," my dad said.

"Yes, they are, Daddy." I swept my hand across the empty dining room. "Do you see any full tables? In fact, do you see anyone at all?"

"The night is young, hon." So said my father, player of long shots.

When the door finally opened again around nine, I turned hopefully, but it was only Danny, wearing street clothes damp from the rain. But even off duty, Danny was never off the job. He flashed me a look as he came in; I sent him a silent question back, and he shook his head slightly. Did the headshake mean, *No, the autopsy results aren't in yet*, or, *They're in, but don't ask me about them*?

"Somethin' smells good," he said, giving me a quick kiss. "And I haven't eaten."

I was about to tell him there was nothing cooking when the scent of sautéed onions wafted my way. Massimo emerged with a large black skillet, Nando behind him with a basket of bread.

"Massimo, is that a frittata?" I looked at the Italian version of comfort food, a glorious golden omelet made with greens, cheese, herbs, and bread crumbs.

"*Sì, cara*. I make it with the arugula and fontina cheese. And we need to eat, do we not?" He shrugged. "And as we have no customers at the moment . . ."

"And I don't think we're likely to have any."

Tim brought over plates and silverware while Massimo cut the frittata into wedges. We all squeezed around one table, passing the bread basket, suddenly aware of how late it was. As I was about to take my first bite, I had a discomfiting thought.

"This arugula is from the stuff Mr. Biaggio delivered, right?" I asked. All around me, forks were frozen in midair, poised inches from open lips.

"I'm not sure, *cara*," Massimo said, "but this was from a bag in the 'frigerator."

"From when?" Danny asked, still holding his fork aloft.

"By all the saints!" Nonna said. "It's a new bunch. The police took the rest last night." She gestured with closed fingers in the familiar Italian manner. "I ate a salad from this today. What's wrong with all of you?"

"We're just a little jumpy, Nonna." Danny took a healthy bite of his frittata; fueled by both hunger and relief, the rest of us did the same.

As we ate in silence, I looked around the table at the people I'd be working so closely with over the next year—my family, the Casa Lido staffers, Tim, and finally Cal. Except for Cal, I knew them as well as I knew myself. My brother's suggestion that there might be more to Parisi's death had unsettled us to the point where we were afraid to eat. But if it wasn't a heart attack, what was it? I knew that a reaction to the food was a remote possibility, but what if someone had tampered with his meal?

My eyes rested on each of the faces around me. The only people in the Casa Lido yesterday while Parisi ate were Tim, Cal, and Lori. I would vouch for Tim and Lori any day, but what about Cal? I watched him fold his egg into a slice of bread, taking careful, slow bites, eating just like he talked and worked. What did we really know about this guy? I shook my head and forked the last piece of egg from my plate, savoring the bitter taste of the greens. I stopped in midswallow. *The greens.* Mr. Biaggio had come into the kitchen with a delivery. He was a protester. He made no bones about his antipathy to

Parisi and his show. His face red and angry, he had compared Parisi to garbage to be thrown away.... *Stop it, Vic.* Do you really think the chubby little produce man is a murderer? My writer's imagination was clearly getting the best of me. And then Danny, who was sitting to my right, slid a piece of paper under my plate. On it was one word. I crushed the paper in my hand and jumped to my feet.

"Hey, Dan? Could you help me with something out back?"

"Sure thing, sis."

I hurried down the narrow hallway, my brother close behind me. As we stepped out the back doors, the sensor light illuminated the dark outline of the shed. The rain had stopped, leaving us in a chilly mist, and I shivered, both from cold and the memory of my last trip out here. I held up the crumpled paper. "Your handwriting sucks, but this says 'petechiae,' right?"

He nodded, his face grim. "So you know what that means."

"It means there were broken blood vessels in his eyes. And that maybe he didn't die of natural causes."

"There's more, sis. Tomorrow morning the county prosecutor's going on record with the press that it's a suspicious death."

"Oh no—"

"What are you two whispering about?" The voice that sliced through the darkness was as sharp as aged cheese.

I jumped, slapping my hand against my chest. "Geez, Nonna. You scared me to death. Danny's just looking at my car."

"Nonsense. Your car is on the other side of the lot. And I know exactly what you two are talking about."

"She don't miss a thing," Danny muttered.

Nonna pretended not to hear him and instead reached out and patted my arm. "Victoria, dear, you no longer have to worry about the tomatoes."

Touched by her concern, I smiled. "Thanks, Nonna." But that stone face never cracked. She tilted her head, her eyes calculating and just a bit scary behind her bifocals. "No, you need not worry about the garden. In fact, you don't have to worry about the restaurant at all for a while."

I narrowed my eyes at her. "Why?"

Her lips curled in what might have been a smile or a snarl. "Because I have another job for you. One you are well suited for." She jerked her chin toward the shadowy building behind us and pointed. "You're gonna to find out who killed that rich *cafone* and dumped him behind my shed."

Chapter Seven

"**O**kay, you are not gonna believe this one," I said as I walked into Sofia's office at the dance studio the next morning.

Sofia's voice came from behind her computer screen. "Your grandmother wants you to figure out who killed Parisi."

I plopped down in a nearby chair and shook my head. "Are there no secrets in this godforsaken town? Have you been in touch with my brother? And who said anyone killed him?"

"No, yes, and everyone." She peeked her head around her laptop. "By the way, I've already started doing our research." As she spoke, the printer began to whir.

"Did you say 'our' research, SIL?"

"You don't think you're gonna solve this without me, do you?" She handed me a sheet from the printer.

"Sofie, there's nothing to figure out. And even if there were, that's for the cops to decide, not me." I held up the paper. "What is this, anyway?"

"That's our list of suspects." She grinned. "I called Lori first thing this morning."

"I can't believe you did that." I looked down at the sheet, and my eyes widened. "What the— *My* name is on this!"

She shrugged. "You were there. You had access to his food." She pointed at the sheet. "So did Tim, Lori, and Cal."

"Oh my God, Sofie. You can't really believe one of us murdered him."

"Aha!" She shook her finger at me. "You just said it. He *was* murdered; I knew it."

I sat forward in my chair. "This is crazy and you know it."

"I'm already on it." She had turned back to her screen and hit the print key again. "I've begun compiling a dossier on Parisi. Business contacts, investments, people in his life. And everything I can dig up about those idiot kids on the show." The sound of the printer was accompanied by her nails tapping on the keyboard.

"I don't care what my grandmother says; I'm not doing this." I pointed to the growing stack of pages emerging from the printer. "I don't need a 'dossier,' and I don't need a list of suspects."

"Oh, yes, we do."

"And what is with this 'we'? You're not getting involved, so you can just forget it, Watson."

She waved her hand, and I caught a glimpse of her new French manicure. "Please. As if I would ever be a Watson." She frowned at the screen. "Ya know, I can't seem to find a thing on Parisi's wife."

"Get away from that screen." I grabbed Sofia's rolling desk chair and pulled her around to face me. "You can just stop Google stalking or researching or whatever it is you're doing. We are not investigating this death. Just because Nonna has the crazy idea that I should solve this so-called mystery doesn't mean we need to buy into it."

She crossed her arms and pouted in a manner my

brother could never resist, but it had little effect on me. "Why not, Vic? It's not like you have anything better to do."

"Are you kidding me? I have a book to write."

"Oh, right," she said, rolling her eyes. "Your great work about Isabella on the boat to America." She made a show of yawning behind her hand.

"Hey, this book means a lot to me. And I don't have time to snoop around Parisi's business. That's for the cops to do, not me." I had no choice but to play my ace card. "Danny would kill you if he found out you were involved in this."

"I can handle your brother." She smiled slightly, her cheeks pink under her already tan face. "We've kind of been talking again."

"That's great. But it's all the more reason to stay out of this."

She wheeled her chair close to mine so that our knees were touching and gripped both my hands. "Tell me you haven't wondered," she said. "Look me in the eye and tell me you don't already have a list of people in your head that matches the one I just gave you."

I sighed, letting out a great breath and my last bit of resistance. "Actually," I said, "you're missing somebody."

Sofia looked around the empty office and lowered her voice. "Who?"

"Mr. Biaggio."

"The fat little produce guy?"

I nodded. "He delivered the greens that day." *The greens that were in the salad that Tim made.* "But the police confiscated them, with all the other food. They even took the trash."

Sofia's eyes were gleaming as she scribbled Mr. B's name on the printed sheet. "What about Parisi's plate? Did they take that, too?"

"Uh, no." I hesitated. "Tim had already run the dishwasher."

She raised one eyebrow. "Did he, now? That was clever of him."

"Oh, c'mon. What motive would Tim have for putting something in Parisi's food?" It was a question I'd already asked myself several times, along with why Tim had fainted at the sight of Parisi's corpse.

Sofia shrugged. "What motive do any of you have? That's what we need to find out. Danny told me they already did the autopsy, so it should be easy to figure out what killed him."

"Not necessarily." I knew there was no way Danny had told her about the broken blood vessels in Parisi's eyes, but she was already off and running. I tried desperately to slow her down. "Look, the autopsy tells us some things, but not everything. They take fluid samples from the scene and—"

Sofia held up her hand. "Spare me the ick, please, and cut to the chase. When will we know what really killed him?"

"When the results of the tox screen come in. And that's the problem. Those results take a while, and until we know the cause of his death, people are going to assume he died because of something he ate at the Casa Lido."

"That's all the more reason to get started, Vic." She took the papers from the printer and placed them neatly in a bloodred folder marked "Parisi" in black uppercase letters. I was surprised there wasn't a skull and crossbones drawn on it. My sister-in-law is not known for her subtlety.

I shook my head. "I don't think so. We need the cause of death. To paraphrase Lord Peter Wimsey, until we know *how*, we won't know who."

"The hell with Lord What's-His-Name." In one wave of her manicured hand, Sofia dismissed Dorothy Sayers, along with all logic and reason. "There's a lot we can do in the meantime. We can find out if he owed anybody money, who he had fights with, particularly his wife. I hear she's a lot younger than he is."

I grinned. "That makes her guilty for sure."

"Too bad she wasn't there. Not that I'm counting anybody out at this stage of the investigation."

"Hey, don't you have classes to teach or something?"

Sofia glanced at the corner of her computer screen. "Not for another hour." She looked up at me and smiled. "You'd be amazed at what I can find out in sixty minutes. And don't try to act like you're not interested—because you are."

She was right; I *was* interested, but more than that, I was worried about protecting the Casa Lido. I stood up and pushed in the chair. "Okay, I give. We can do some research. But that's all."

She jumped from her seat and high-fived me, nearly knocking me off my feet. (For a little girl, she packs a punch.) "You go, SIL," she sang out. "And keep me posted." She settled back in her chair, her eyes glued to the screen. "In the meantime, I'm gonna dig up all I can on the widow."

I had just pulled into the restaurant parking lot when my phone buzzed, but I didn't recognize the number. "Good morning, Victoria," purred a female voice in my ear. "This is Nina LaGuardia from News Ten."

I muttered a forbidden word and sighed. "How did you get my number, Ms. LaGuardia?"

The lovely Nina chose not to answer and instead fired a few questions of her own. "How are you and your family holding up? Is it true that your brother used his position on the police force to keep them from closing the Casa Lido? And could you tell me a bit about the protest that was held the morning of Gio Parisi's death?"

"Hey, what do you think you're doing?" I bolted upright in the seat. "I did not agree to an interview, Nina. And I'm not answering any of these questions."

"That's a shame, Victoria. It's such a fascinating story. And what a great hook: mystery writer finds herself in the middle of real-life murder." She sighed. "Well, I understand if you'd prefer not to answer any questions at the moment. We can just keep replaying your 'no comment' video."

"That's big of you."

"However," she continued, "other journalists might not be as sympathetic as I am. In fact, I imagine that cute little cottage of yours might just be surrounded again today. Now, if you were to promise me an exclusive—"

"I'm listening."

"I might be able to call them off, at least temporarily."

What sort of Mephistophelian deal was this? "Are you telling me you have the juice to keep other journalists away from me?"

"What a quaint way of putting it. And, of course, I couldn't promise that no one would bother you, but I *could* put it out there that you were giving me an exclusive."

"Assuming I say yes." I leaned back against the seat in resignation. Did I really have a choice?

"Assuming you say yes. Do we have a deal?"

"Maybe." My mind whirled with possibilities. If the press were kept away, I'd be left in peace to get some work done. But an interview with Nina might bring more attention to the restaurant and not the kind likely to bring in customers. If only I knew how Parisi really died, but that information wasn't coming anytime soon. It always came back to time, didn't it?

"Victoria?"

"I'm here. Listen, how soon would you want to do this interview? Would you be willing to wait awhile? Say a week or ten days?"

She laughed. "My dear, this will be old news in a week."

"Not if I solve the . . . mystery of how he died." I had nearly said *murder*.

"Tell me more." Nina was clearly interested in the bait, and it was time to reel her in.

"What if I'm able to figure out exactly what happened to him? Wouldn't that make a better story?" I offered up a small prayer to St. Jude, patron of lost causes.

"Hmm," she said. "That could work. Mystery author *solves* real-life murder."

"Who said anything about murder?"

She laughed again. "Only everybody, darling. All right, Victoria. We have a deal. But one week—no more. And you'll be hearing from me," she said before hanging up.

"I just bet I will," I said into the dead phone. And now I had an even more compelling reason to unravel the mystery behind Parisi's death, and the clock was ticking. It was time to plunge in; I would start with a search of the kitchen and pantry, in case the cops had overlooked something. I could always act as though I was cleaning—an act my grandmother would heartily approve and one that nobody else would question.

I didn't see Cal's truck in the employee lot when I arrived, and once again I wondered about his hours, not to mention his background. Who was this guy, anyway? How much had my dad known about him when he hired him for the restoration? Had he gotten references? I fished in my purse for a pad; it was time to start keeping track of things. I scribbled a note to talk to my dad and to do a little Google stalking of my own.

Tim was alone in the kitchen when I walked in. He turned to look at me, and I felt the familiar catch in my chest. I truly believed I was over Tim Trouvare; I certainly wanted to be. But my feelings for Tim had deep roots, a childhood crush that had grown into something much more. And in the years we'd been apart, I'd had only one serious relationship. That had ended a year ago, and more with a whimper than a bang. I had to face it: There was a part of me that would always love Tim.

"Hey, Vic." He held my eyes a bit longer than necessary, and the catch in my chest turned into a flutter.

I tried to keep my voice neutral. "You on your own this morning?"

He nodded. "They figured I could handle things alone, at least for lunch. Lori's coming in, though; your mom wanted to give her the tables, if that's okay."

It was more than okay, as it freed me up for some snooping. "Of course. I know she needs the money, and I'll get enough practice later in the season."

"We hope." He looked tired. There were shadows under his eyes, and I wondered if he'd had trouble sleeping. "I keep getting phone calls from reporters."

I nodded. "I think my parents have, too. And, of course, you've seen my fifteen seconds of fame."

He smiled briefly, but seemed distracted. "I just want us to stay open. I grew up in this place. And now that you're back—"

I jumped in before he could go any further. "Listen," I said, "the Casa Lido has weathered wars, economic downturns, hurricanes, and the odd mobster or two." I pointed outside. "That boardwalk gives Seaside and

Wildwood a run for their money and still manages to stay family friendly. It's gonna take more than one dead body to change that."

Tim's eyes strayed to the back door of the restaurant, and I knew we were both remembering the sight of Parisi's corpse out there. He shook his head. "I don't see them filming that show here now, do you?"

"I doubt it." I started to ask Tim about the salad, but then closed my mouth abruptly. As much as I hated to admit it, he could be a suspect. I couldn't tip my hand.

He frowned. "What?"

"Nothing." I turned to hang my purse on a hook behind me, but not before I slipped my pad and pen into my pants pocket. "Hey, Tim," I said over my shoulder. "Does Massimo still keep that box of gloves in here?"

"Hang on." Tim reached under the sink and tossed me a balled-up pair of latex gloves. "What do you want them for?"

"I'm planning to do some cleanup in the pantry." I slipped the gloves on and wiggled my fingers. "Gotta protect the manicure."

I left the kitchen hurriedly, realizing my mistake too late. Tim was no fool. Aside from prepping messy food, there were few uses for gloves around here—unless someone didn't want to contaminate evidence, for example. *Gotta brazen it out, now, Vic. Get moving.* I took the key to the pantry from its usual place on the row of hooks along the kitchen wall.

Opening the pantry door was like entering a portal into my childhood. The shelves of Mason jars holding bright orange tomatoes from the last harvest. The herbs hanging to dry from the open rafter beams, and the dusty bottles of my father's homemade wine. As my eyes got accustomed to the dimness, I took in the shelves of staples and canned goods and an old dresser that held our linens. It was all as I'd remembered it; more important, nothing looked disturbed. I made a note on my pad to ask Danny if the cops had been in here at all.

I started with the dresser, but the drawers yielded only my carefully pressed napkins and an old flashlight. The shelves held nothing more than restaurant supplies, with no bottles marked "poison" hidden behind the bags of semolina flour. Feeling ridiculous in my latex gloves, I turned to go but stopped at the sight of the dried herbs. There were some I recognized easily by sight or scent: rosemary, basil, and parsley. But there were others whose green leaves were blackened and, to my suspicious eyes, noxious looking. Nonna was big on herbal tisanes, and some of the stuff she used might have toxic properties. We used our herbs in the house dressing, and one dried-up leaf looks just like another.

I closed my eyes briefly and tried to summon my memories of Parisi's lunch order. He had asked for dressing on the side, and he had used some, because I remembered it dripping from his mouth. I was about to pinch off some leaves when I realized I had nothing to put them in. *Some detective, Vic. You don't even bring an evidence bag with you. Bernardo would not approve.* I grabbed a roll of plastic wrap from the shelves and tore off several pieces, then made three small packages of herb samples and tucked them into my pockets. I wasn't sure who I could get to identify them, but I would worry about that later.

I locked the pantry behind me, as my grandmother was convinced that strangers would come in and steal her tomatoes, and my father was certain that all of Oceanside coveted his spurious Chianti. I stuck the keys in my pocket and headed down the hallway for the most distasteful task ahead of me—searching the bathroom.

The last time I saw Parisi, he was heading to this

room. But did he ever reach it? He had vomited outside before he died. If those broken blood vessels were indicators of poisoning, he would have been feeling really sick—likely nausea and stomach cramps. I felt a flicker of pity for the guy. Even jerks don't deserve to die like that. I looked around our cozy little unisex restroom, complete with Italian tile and prints of the Amalfi Coast. It was as spotless and sanitary as usual, smelling of the lavender my grandmother grew outside. The police had been over this room, and I wondered if Danny knew what they might have found. In the meantime, the cleaning service had been in here, followed by Nonna, who always cleaned again after they left. But even my eagle-eyed grandmother might have missed something against these patterned floor tiles. I stood staring at the toilet, my gloved hands on my hips, knowing there was only one thing to do: I dropped to my knees in front of that bowl. *Like Bernardo would ever do this.* I had to smile as I thought of my elegant detective with his face inches from a toilet, scrabbling around a bathroom floor, looking for God knows what.

I turned my head sideways and squinted at a tiny white triangle sticking out from the back of the porcelain base. Reaching around, I tugged it out and scrambled to my feet. The paper curled in my hand, and I held the edges open carefully. A register receipt from the Tiffany store in Red Bank, it showed a $250 purchase for a silver necklace, paid by a credit card, the number x-ed out but for the last four digits. It also had Monday's date on it. Now, *this* was interesting, particularly if those last four numbers matched Parisi's credit card receipt from his lunch.

I slipped the paper into my pocket and washed my hands, gloves and all, and wiped up the sink with paper towels. I crumpled up a few more to take outside with me for the sake of appearances and sailed out of the bathroom exhilarated by my little search.

But what have you really got, Vic? my rational mind asked. *A pocketful of herbs that are probably harmless and proof that someone—not necessarily Parisi—bought a necklace the day before he died.*

"You done in there?" Tim popped his head around the kitchen door, and I jumped.

"Yeah," I squeaked out. Sleuthing was a distinctly unnerving experience. How did Bernardo stand it?

Tim frowned. "What's the matter?"

"Nothing." I heard a muffled buzz from the kitchen and pointed. "Isn't that your phone?"

Without answering, he pulled his head back inside the doors, and some instinct told me not to follow. I stood on tiptoe to peek at him through the thick glass window. His phone was on the counter, still vibrating, but he only stared at it. I pushed through the door, and he turned to me, his cheeks pink. He swept the phone off the counter. "Gotta take this. Sorry." His head down, he put the phone to his ear and hurried out the back door.

I replaced the pantry key and positioned myself at a window with a full view of the back lot and garden. Tim walked to a spot a few feet from the shed, realized where he stood, and suddenly wheeled around so that his back was to it. He spoke closely into the phone, his free hand cupped around it as though he were whispering. But there was no one to hear him. At this hour of the morning, the restaurant was—you should pardon the expression—*dead*. And much as I wanted to trail him out there, I couldn't risk it. Now he was agitated, stalking back and forth and shaking his head. *What's going on, Tim?* I thought. *Why are you acting so guilty? More to the point, who the heck are you talking to?*

*   *   *

I took advantage of Tim's absence to search the kitchen, but I knew it was a fruitless effort. The police had been through every cabinet and drawer and over every inch of countertop. If there'd been anything to find, it was sitting in an evidence room at the county prosecutor's office. I tucked the herbs into my purse, but kept the jewelry receipt handy. I had to get into the office and check my mother's files before any of the other staff came in. It was 10:40, which meant that Lori would be arriving in less than twenty minutes. More than enough time to go through Tuesday's receipts.

But the minute I opened my mother's brown accordion file, I realized my mistake—there were no receipts for Tuesday, because the police had taken them. I shoved the file back into the desk drawer and slammed it shut. Unless . . .

Tapping my fingers while waiting for her computer to come to life and counting on my mother's mania for duplicates of everything, I clicked open the Casa Lido folder and sighed. There were dozens of subfolders with abbreviated names, in a code only my mother could understand. (It was her way of keeping my dad out of the accounts.) I could be here all day looking through this stuff, and Lori was probably on her way. I glanced at the clock and back at the screen, clicking on folders as fast as the computer could respond. After getting a virtual tour of all things Casa Lido, I finally found a folder of scanned receipts, and there it was—his credit card receipt for lunch.

Same bank. Same credit card. Same four digits. "Bingo," I said. Parisi *had* been in Red Bank on Monday afternoon, and he *had* bought that Tiffany necklace. It wasn't much, but it was a start.

I stepped out of the office and caught the sound of voices in the dining room. When I rounded the corner, I saw Tim and a woman, their backs against the bar, their heads close together as they spoke.

She was striking, with side-swept black hair that was stark against her fair skin. In her four-inch heels, she was nearly shoulder to shoulder with Tim; her shoulder, in fact, was brushing his, a detail I registered but quickly suppressed. Standing across from me in my flats, she dwarfed my measly sixty-five inches, and I had the sense that she and Tim belonged to some superior race of tall, beautiful beings to which I could never aspire.

Straightening my spine and lifting my chin, I did my best to sound confident, in control, and not vertically challenged. "Were you looking for me?"

She reached out with a pale long-fingered hand. "I'm Anjelica." She paused, and I watched in fascination as one tear gathered in the corner of each eye. What were the odds that those tears would spill over and ruin that perfectly made-up face? Only the kind my dad would bet on. Her voice was a whisper when she spoke again. "Anjelica Parisi."

Uh-oh. Parisi's widow? I raised my hand slowly to take hers, all the while staring at her creamy skin, arched brows, and dark blue eyes. Her nose was small and straight. *Either she's not Italian,* I thought, *or she's had some work done.* And while I was sure I'd never met her, there was a vague familiarity about her features. I watched her closely, taking rapid mental notes to share with Sofia later on. The silk blouse she was wearing revealed a willowy neck but a bare throat—no silver necklace.

"You must be Victoria." She blinked, and her full raspberry-colored lips trembled. "I understand you served my husband right before he died." She gave a shuddery breath. "Would you mind telling me about his last moments?"

I glanced instinctively at Tim, who swiped his forehead with the back of his hand. He looked as though he would rather be hanging upside down from the scariest ride on the boardwalk than standing between the two of us. What the hell was making him—quite literally—sweat?

"I'm sorry for your loss," I said, and she nodded. "But I don't think there's much I can tell you." *Or much I should tell you.* "He came in on Tuesday around four. He ordered a salad and some tea." I did not add that his table manners were disgusting, as my mother has taught me not to speak ill of the dead. "At the end of his lunch, he looked pale and asked for the bathroom. That was the last time I saw him until—"

She gasped, and her hand flew to her mouth. "Oh my God," she said. "You were the one who found him!" Her dark blue eyes widened and again filled with tears.

Given my debut on the local news, I found it hard to believe Anjelica Parisi didn't know that I was the one who discovered her husband's body. *Give her a break*, I told myself. *She's grieving.* Or was she? Despite the tears, her eyes held a canny expression, and I would swear the lip tremble was the result of years of practice. As Danny had recently remarked about our grandmother, this one didn't miss a trick. She was probably capable of a few of her own as well; she inched closer to Tim, her arm resting along the length of his. He, on the other hand, held himself stiffly, as though she had some communicable disease. As I watched them, my stomach gave a little thump of warning. Whatever my five senses wouldn't or couldn't tell me, my gut was screaming. Something was definitely off here.

"Yes," I said. "I'm sorry. But I probably don't know any more than you do."

Anjelica took a tissue from her purse and dabbed at her now-dry eyes. "The police won't tell me anything."

"They don't know anything yet." Tim's voice came out in a croak, a sound so unexpected, I jumped. When I looked over at him, he refused to meet my eye. My stomach thumped two more times, like an impatient person knocking at a locked door. It was a summons I'd have to answer sooner or later. I turned my attention back to the widow.

"I understand he had a heart problem?" That much had been on the news, so I figured I was on safe ground.

"Yes," she said, sniffling and wrinkling her tiny nose in a gesture that was both pathetic and flirtatious. "But he was doing well." As she spoke, she gazed up at Tim, who shrank against the bar, wide-eyed. I watched in sick fascination as her hand crept to his forearm, my eyes glued to the five pink ovals of her nails against his skin. Her hand still clutching his arm, she turned her attention back to me. "I can't help wondering," she said quietly, "if it was something he ate."

Well, there it was. The lovely young widow had just voiced the suspicion that hung over the Casa Lido like a dark cloud in hurricane season. I had a sudden image of Anjelica holding a press conference, and from there it was all too easy to picture the storm breaking right over all our heads. "No, Mrs. Parisi," I said automatically. "There's no question of that." *Except for the one looming in my mind, of course.*

Anjelica took a deep breath, as though preparing herself for the answer to her next question. "Can you tell me who prepared his lunch, please?"

I was about to say I didn't know when my treacherous little eyeballs swiveled in their sockets, stopping only at Tim's face, now the color of ricotta cheese. Anjelica dropped her hand from Tim's arm.

"Oh, Tim," she cried. "What have you done?"

"I didn't do anything! I made him a salad. I swear to

God, that's all." He turned and gripped her two shoulders tightly. "Angie, you have to believe me."

Angie. Angie. Angie. The blood pounded rhythmically in my head, those two syllables sounding over and over like a death knell. There was only one Angie. She was the woman who'd taken a wrecking ball to my life. The woman who'd sent me running off to New York without once looking back.

The woman Tim had left me for.

Chapter Eight

"**W**ell, if it isn't Angie 'Even One Is Too Many' Martini. I don't know why you bothered with introductions," I said to the woman now calling herself Anjelica. I stared her down in my best imitation of Nonna. "You know very well who I am."

She nodded, trying hard to appear apologetic, but there was no mistaking the flash of triumph in her eyes. "I do," she said. "But I wasn't sure you knew who I was."

I leaned my head sideways and studied her more closely. "Your hair's longer—and darker. You're wearing blue contacts, and you've got some nice veneers in your mouth now." I smiled, baring a few teeth of my own. "And your lips are a bit fuller than I remember." I shrugged. "Then again, I'd seen you only in passing, and it's been a number of years. Right, Tim?"

Tim, who had dropped his hands from Angie's shoulders, flinched at the sound of his name. The misery on his face was evident, but it was nothing compared to what he'd caused me all those years ago. Standing in front of me was a pale, frightened-looking stranger with shaking hands. "Vic, please," he said, his voice nearly a whisper. "You have to believe me."

"It doesn't matter what I believe. It's the police you have to worry about." I marched past them into the kitchen, my head, back, and neck so erect I should have been in uniform. Lori stood behind the door, her eyes wide. She pointed past the kitchen doors toward the bar.

"Isn't she—?"

"Yes," I interrupted. "She sure as hell is."

"Holy cannoli," Lori said. "Tim's ex-girlfriend Angie went and married Gio Parisi."

I plopped down on a nearby stool. "Yup." *And she all but accused Tim of murdering him*, I thought. "Only now she's his widow."

Lori nodded. "His very rich widow."

I didn't say anything, but my mind was reeling with possibilities. And questions. If money was an issue, Anjelica certainly had a motive for wanting her husband dead. But she hadn't had access to his food. Could she have given him something at home? But he'd spent several hours on the boardwalk looking the picture of health, and he was fine when he came into the restaurant. The most logical explanation was that he ingested something that had killed him while sitting right there at Table Five.

I thought back to Lord Peter's dictum: If you know how, you know who. Well, we still didn't know how. But I was beginning to have a pretty good idea of who. And I wasn't sure it was a solution I could live with.

I spent the rest of the day and most of the evening helping Lori and avoiding Tim—not hard to do since there was no reason I needed to visit the kitchen. The Casa Lido was so quiet that Massimo and Nando didn't come in, and neither did my parents, much to my relief. It was too hard to look into my mom's worried face or listen to my dad's false cheer. All I knew was that another day without customers brought us closer to closing our doors for good.

By nine I sent Lori home, her apron pocket not exactly bulging with cash. While cleaning up behind our one table of the dinner service, I noticed that Cal was back and appeared to be packing up his tools. *He's finishing now?* This was a man who kept his own hours—that was for sure. And it was time I learned more about this stranger whose name was on the short list of those in the restaurant on Tuesday.

I stepped behind the bar and held up a bottle of our best single-malt Scotch. "You interested?"

"I wouldn't say no." He dropped his toolbox at his feet and sat at the bar.

I poured him a generous splash and then filled a wineglass with pinot grigio for myself. I came out and took a seat next to him.

"So it's been a day around here," he said. "I heard the widow"—or "widduh" as Cal pronounced it—"made an appearance."

"It sure has, and, yes, she showed up." I waited for a comment of some kind, but none was forthcoming.

I glanced sideways at him, keenly aware of his forearm resting close to my own, his large, work-worn hand resting on the table. He had taken off his hat, and his shaggy hair was tucked behind his ears; there were deep lines around his eyes that attested to days in the sun. He raised the tumbler, and I clinked my wineglass against his.

"*A votre santé*, Victoria." He drew out all four syllables of my name in a low drawl, Vic-TOW-ree-uh, lingering over the second and softening on the last. It was an accent one didn't hear much in Jersey, and I couldn't help smiling.

"You're a long way from home, Calvin Lockhart."

He nodded, still staring at the bar. "That I am, *cher*."

"Yup, between that Saints cap you wear and that

faux French you just dropped—which, by the way, we Northern girls don't find so endearing—"

"I'll remember that." He flashed me a grin that *was* pretty endearing, though.

"So are you from New Orleans originally?"

He winced. "Girl, don't ever say 'Or-LEENS.' You sound like a straight-up tourist. I grew up in Baton Rouge, but went to the city when I was eighteen. You ever been?"

"Are you kidding? I love that place. The food, the music, just the feel of it." I leaned my chin on my hand, dreamy-eyed as I remembered my trip there. "I went once after college and fell head over heels for that place." I grinned at him. "That city is like a bad boy you can't resist—you know he's all wrong for you, and you'll hate yourself in the morning, but you just can't help yourself." My eyes met his, and I was surprised by the little jolt of electricity that jumped between us. *Uh-oh*, I thought. He caught it, too; his eyes widened. They were a smoky, woodsy green in the bar's dim light.

"I know exactly what you mean," he said, amusement coloring his every word.

I looked down at my drink. "So how long have you been up here?"

"A while now." He ran his hands over his chin. "Goin' on eight years, I think."

Eight years was long enough to establish connections up here. Might he have one to Parisi? But suddenly the import of leaving New Orleans when he did became clear. "So you must have left right after Katrina."

He nodded. "I had a custom furniture business downtown." He lifted his whiskey glass and swirled the dark liquid. "The workshop was a little old place, but everything at hand, if you know what I mean."

I thought of my small office at home in New York

and my room in the beach cottage where I did my writing. *Everything at hand.* "I do, yeah."

He shrugged. "Well, then she hit. She did her worst, all right. I lost everything—the shop, the stock, all my tools. And after that, my wife." He gave a small, twisted smile. "She didn't cotton to waitin' around for me to get back on my feet."

I fought the impulse to touch his hand. *Don't pity him, Vic. Do not feel sorry for him. He's on the list.* "Sorry. I'm really not trying to pry." But of course I was.

"It's okay, Victoria. It was a long time ago." He looked up from glass. "So, what's the story with you and the Iron Chef in there?"

"Oh. Well, he was my first kiss. My first love. My first everything." I sighed. "Tim Trouvare and I have been dancing this dance since I was fifteen years old." And then, despite my determination to treat Cal like a suspect, I spilled it all. My girlhood crush on Tim. Our first real date the summer after I graduated high school, after which Tim left for Ireland and I didn't see him for a year. His decision to go to culinary school and the on-again, off-again nature of our relationship, which finally cemented itself when Tim showed up at my college graduation with a bouquet of flowers and a declaration of love. "Then things got serious," I continued. I shook my head. "I hadn't planned to come back home, but Tim was here."

"In town, you mean?" Cal asked.

I grinned and pointed to the floor. "No, here, in the restaurant. He was a line cook at the time."

"What about you?"

"I had a shiny new business degree that my parents assumed I'd put to use for their business. But I got a job with a local marketing firm."

"Did ya like it?"

I nodded. "I did. I had a job, an apartment, and Tim. I thought my future was planned."

I drained the last of my wine. "And then Tim"—*left me for the slut who showed up this afternoon*—"met someone else. And I ended up in New York writing mysteries."

He gave a quick nod and then took another sip of his drink. If I thought my confession might move Cal to spill some secrets of his own—like whether he knew Parisi or "the widduh"—I was barking up the wrong magnolia tree. I studied his unreadable face. "You sure don't say much."

"Actually, I got two things to say. First, you let that guy get to you. And second"—he knocked back the rest of his drink, then gestured to me with his empty glass—"you're much too good for him." He set the glass on the bar, shot me a crooked grin, and tipped his cap. "G'night, ma'am," he said. "And thanks for the drink."

I couldn't help smiling as I watched Cal saunter away.

"What the hell was that about?" Tim's voice cleared the pleasant fog in my brain. Speaking of suspects.

"We were having a nice chat. And anyway, it's none of your business."

Tim pointed toward the doors of the restaurant. "We don't know anything about that guy. And you've known him, what, two days?"

"I've known you for more than half my life, and God knows you're still full of surprises."

"I wish you'd let me explain." He reached out a hand, and I fought the urge to slap it away.

"No, thanks, Tim."

"Okay." He sighed. He turned toward the kitchen. "You might as well head out. I'll go finish cleanup."

As I watched him go, the front doors burst open, spilling my sister-in-law, Sofia, inside. She looked as though she had run all the way from the studio. "Vic," she said, still huffing from her sprint and waving her red folder. "I finally found Parisi's wife, and you're not gonna believe who she is."

I held my finger up to my lips and pointed toward the kitchen. "He's here," I mouthed, leading her to a table in the far corner.

Sofia's butt had not even touched the chair before she spoke. "Do you have any idea who she is? She's—"

"You mean Tim's ex?" I asked. "Angie?" *Wow*, I thought. *I said her name without choking on the syllables.*

"So you know." She shook her head. "Angie Martini. Sure didn't see that one coming."

"SIL, you have a gift for understatement. But there's more you don't know." I took a breath. "She was in the restaurant earlier today, clinging to Tim like poison ivy. I met her."

Sofia's large eyes were now two dark moons. "You're kidding me. What was she doing here?"

"Fishing, either for information or her old boyfriend. Maybe both." I stopped, remembering her question to Tim: *What have you done?* "Then again, she all but accused Tim of killing her husband."

Sofia dropped slowly into a nearby chair. "Oh my God." She looked up at me, her eyes serious. "This gives him a motive, Vic. I don't care how long ago they broke up."

A sharp little pang struck in the vicinity of my heart. Did he still care enough about this woman to kill for her? Was he jealous of Parisi? Did he want her back? Somehow that thought was almost worse than Tim as a murderer.

I took a chair across from her and sat down. "I know it does. He was here. He had an opportunity—maybe

the best opportunity—to put something in Parisi's food."
Saying it aloud felt like a betrayal. And what if I had to
say it again to Nina LaGuardia, perhaps on national
TV? My stomach clenched at the thought.

Sofia opened the red folder and fished a pen from her
oversized designer purse. She scribbled something on a
legal pad and then reached over to pat my arm. "I know
it wasn't easy seeing her."

"It wasn't at first, but I'm handling it." I shook my
head. "Honestly, between her and this thing with Tim
and Cal today—"

My sister-in-law eyed me sharply. "Cal? You mean
the Southern dude working on the bar? Kind of cute
but needs a haircut and a scrub?"

"He's clean, Sofie!" In fact, I had a clear memory of
his spicy soap smell. "He's just a working guy, you know?
A little rough around the edges."

She frowned. "That's not usually the way you like
'em."

"Who said I like him?"

"Your red face, for one thing." She waggled her index
finger in my face. "And you're shifty-eyed, all of a sudden." She narrowed her eyes at me. "There's more to
this, SIL. I can always tell, so you might as well give."

"There's nothing to give. We had a drink is all."

"And?"

"And nothing." My cheeks *were* warm, come to think
of it.

She narrowed her eyes at me. "You think he's cute."

"Yes, okay, I think he's cute. Is that a crime?"

"Interesting choice of words, there, Detective. He's
on the *list*, Vic. For all you know, he's trying to keep you
off guard. And from that goofy look on your face, it
looks like he was successful."

"I get it, Sofe." I rested my chin on my hand and re-

played Cal's words in my head: *You're too good for him.*
"But can I just enjoy a little attention from a man,
please?"

She patted my hand. "God knows, you need a little
fun." But then her voice grew stern and she raised her
eyebrows in a manner reminiscent of Sister Theresa, my
sixth-grade CCD teacher. "But you can't go around flirt-
ing with suspects."

"I didn't flirt with him. He flirted with *me*."

"I don't care. We need to be objective." She pointed
the folder at me. "You'd better get it together, or I will
take you off this case so fast your head will spin."

"I don't want to *be* on this case! I want to write my
book and learn how to make sauce." I let out a loud
breath. "But now I'm stuck."

"What do you mean?"

"I mean that Nina LaGuardia called me this morning." While Sofia listened with shining eyes, I explained
the terms of my deal with the journalist.

"Wait," Sofia said. "You told her you'd solve this in a
week?"

"I didn't really have a choice."

"Okay, then." She slapped her palms down on the
table. "We gotta get moving, girlfriend. Did you look
around here today, by the way?"

"I did." I glanced at the kitchen to make sure Tim
wouldn't be coming out of it anytime soon and then dug
into my pocket. "I found these." I spread out the packets
of dried herbs.

Sofia pointed to the plastic-wrapped leaves. "What is
that crap?"

"That's what I need to find out. Herbs of some kind, I
think. They were in the pantry, but I don't recognize them.
My grandmother grows a lot of this stuff."

She grinned. "Think Nonna's been smoking it?"

"No, but she makes tisanes—special drinks with herbs." I wrinkled my nose at the memory of the stuff she used to try to foist on me when I was sick. "There's dried bunches of stuff all over the pantry."

Sofia's eyes widened as the light dawned. "And some of it might be poisonous."

"C'mon, Sofe. That's kind of a leap, don't you think?" But even as I said it, I thought of our famous house dressing, flavored with dried herbs right from the Casa Lido garden.

"Right now, SIL, nothing's a leap. And nothing's off the table." She pointed. "Including your grandmother as a suspect."

"She wasn't even here!" As far as I knew. Couldn't she have slipped in and out of the kitchen? To what lengths would my grandmother go to keep "filth and shenanigans" out of her beloved shore town? It was ludicrous to imagine my grandmother as a murderer. And she had specifically asked me to find out who killed Parisi. Yet I could still hear her words: *By tomorrow, we will be rid of him.* I shook my head as if to rid myself of the thought. "Oh, hang on—I almost forgot." I flattened the receipt out on the tabletop. "Check this out. I found it in the bathroom."

"Good work." She picked it up and peered closely. "Ah, my favorite store. So it's a silver necklace, but I'm not sure which one." She pressed her palms together in prayer to the God of Little Blue Boxes. "But it doesn't matter, because I love them all."

"Hang on there, princess. Before you get carried away—don't you even want to know who bought this jewelry?"

She rolled her eyes. "It was Parisi, of course. Why else would you be showing it to me? And you found it in the bathroom, where he probably went when he felt pukey."

She shook her head. "Do I have to do all the deducing around here?" She stood up and stretched. "It's getting late, SIL. Keep snooping." She winked at me. "I'm gonna go work on your brother to see if he knows anything."

"He won't tell you a thing!" I called after her.

She stopped in the doorway and shrugged her sweater off her shoulders to reveal a pink leotard with a deep V-neck and lots of golden brown cleavage. "Wanna bet?"

As I watched my sister-in-law sashay out the door, I was inclined to agree with her. But I was torn between hoping Danny would tell her something and worrying whether he'd compromise his position on the force.

I looked around the empty restaurant and sighed. We couldn't have many more nights like this one. I wandered over to the bar, resisting the urge to have another small taste of whiskey. Had Cal corrupted me already?

"Did Sofie leave?" Tim's voice came from behind me. I shifted on the stool to look up at him.

"Yes. If you knew she was here, why didn't you come out and say hello?" I shot him a tight smile. "Maybe you're feeling guilty."

He ran his hands through his hair, a sure sign he was nervous. "Vic, how many times do I have to say it? It's not how it looks."

"It's not how it looks? Please. Even in books that's a cliché." I swung around on the barstool, unable to look at him.

He rested his hand on my shoulder. "You have to let me explain."

Just as I turned around, the alarm system blared once and stopped. The next second, the room was completely dark. Tim's hand tightened on my shoulder.

"Please tell me we don't have a fire." My voice sounded unnaturally loud in the darkness.

"No," Tim said. "That's the sound it makes when the

system loses power. I think a breaker's been tripped. There's not a light on in the place."

"Great." I shivered, my anger with Tim all but forgotten in my panic. Tim patted my shoulder.

"Don't worry," he said. "I know this place like the back of my hand. I'll go check out the panel."

Steadying myself on the edge of the bar, I slid down from the stool and grabbed his arm. "You're not leaving me out here by myself. I'm going with you."

I could almost hear his grin. "C'mon, scaredy-cat. There's probably a flashlight in the kitchen."

Still holding on to Tim's arm, I strained to see any source of light. There was a faint glow near the front doors, probably from lights on the boardwalk. But inside was pitch-blackness. As I shuffled behind Tim, I was startled by a metallic creak coming from the back of the restaurant.

"Tim!" I whispered. "Did you hear that?" My heart thudding in my chest, I squeezed his arm tightly.

"It sounded like the back door. I had it propped open and it probably just swung shut. Hey, ease up on the grip, okay?"

"Sorry." I loosened my hold as we made our slow way down the narrow hallway. As my eyes got accustomed to the darkness, I could just make out a rectangular shape a few feet ahead of us, and I halted. "Tim, wait! The pantry door is open, and I know I locked it."

"Are you sure?"

"Yes." In my mind, I saw myself replacing the key. "Absolutely."

"I'm going to check it out. You wait here."

"No." I gasped. "You can't leave me in this dark hallway."

"Then follow the light from the front door and wait outside."

I considered my rather limited choices. Wait here alone while Tim walked into the pantry where someone could be waiting. Stumble out toward the dining area alone where someone could be waiting. Go with Tim and hope—no, pray—that we could get the lights back on quickly. My fingers tightened on his arm again. "I'm going with you."

"Okay, but stay behind me."

As if I would consider any other course of action. Wishing I'd poured myself that whiskey, I slid one heavy foot in front of the other while the pantry door loomed closer. Tim shook off my arm and strode into the dark room. "Is someone here?" he called, his voice like the crack of a gun shot in the silence. I jumped and moved quickly into the pantry myself. "Hello?" he said again, turning to look at me. "Vic, there's nobody here. C'mon. We gotta get downstairs to that electrical panel."

"I think there's a flashlight in the dresser over there," I whispered. But just as the words left my mouth, I heard the creak of the floorboards in the hallway. And then the pantry door slammed shut behind us.

Chapter Nine

"**H**ey!" I shouted, frantically turning the knob. I opened my mouth to yell again, but Tim clapped his hand over it.

"Stop, Vic! We need to hear what's going on out there." As he spoke, soft footsteps sounded in the hall, then died away. "There's definitely somebody in the restaurant."

I turned and leaned my back against the door, my heart still pounding. "Your powers of deduction are amazing there, Sherlock."

"Shhh. Listen, will you? I think that's the kitchen door."

"I said that before, Tim," I hissed. "Somebody's in that kitchen."

"But why, Vic? They gonna steal my Cuisinart? The money's out in the dining room." He shook his head. "It doesn't make sense."

It does if you're not looking for money, I thought, *but something incriminating you might have left behind. My God, we could be trapped in here with a murderer running around the restaurant.* I took a deep breath to steady myself and slow my frantic heartbeat. "We are such idiots," I said. "We did everything wrong."

"What do you mean?"

"That open pantry door was a trap. We should have either slammed it shut or turned around and left the restaurant." In the dark, windowless pantry, the herbs hung like black bats over our heads. I shivered, due to the room's chill and a healthy dose of fear. "I've been writing some version of this scene for years. What we did was the equivalent of walking up the dark attic steps in the haunted house." I slid down against the door and landed on the floor in a helpless heap.

Tim sat down next to me and put his hand on my arm. "Don't worry. We'll—" He paused, dropping his voice to a whisper. "Do you hear that?"

I pressed my ear against the solid oak door. There were definite sounds coming from the kitchen: muffled thumps and crashes as drawers and cabinets were opened and closed. "Yeah, I do." I shivered again, and unconsciously moved closer to Tim. What could they be looking for that the police (and I) had overlooked? And if they found it, would they leave—or come and find us?

"When the hell did they get in?" Tim asked.

"They could have gotten in anytime. Don't forget, you propped the back door open. At some point they slipped in and threw that breaker, knowing we'd head straight for the panel box and right past that open pantry door."

"How'd they know which key locks this door?"

"I don't know." But I had some ideas I wasn't yet willing to share. It could be someone connected to the restaurant who knew the layout and our routine, like Mr. Biaggio. But Mr. B was thickset, with a lumbering walk. The tread I'd heard in the hallway belonged to someone sure on his feet, even graceful. *Like Cal*, a voice in the back of my mind said. I shook my head. Anybody on staff could have shared information about that key, even innocently, to the wrong person. I turned to look at Tim, and the dawning suspicion forced me to my feet. "Maybe someone told them," I whispered.

"What are you saying, Vic?"

"I'm saying that maybe you sent your ex-girlfriend here on a mission tonight."

Then Tim did something I've never heard a person do: He laughed in a whisper. "Vic," he said, "I was in the kitchen all day. I'm in the kitchen *every* day. If there was something to get rid of, don't you think I would have done it by now?"

"You washed his plate." The words flew from my mouth and echoed in the dark room.

"Right. To get rid of all that poison I put in his salad." Tim reached his hand out to me and smiled. "Come back and sit down, will ya, please?"

I sighed and sat back down, allowing several inches between us. "Tim, admit it. You've been acting guilty as hell."

"Because I knew how it would look. I served the guy. I had complete access to him, and I used to be involved with his wife."

I shifted a few more inches away from him on the floor. "Why'd she come here today? To case the joint?"

He shook his head. "You really have been writing mysteries too long. That imagination's working overtime. I mean, we still don't know for sure that it's murder."

Not officially, I thought. But it was clear somebody did away with Parisi, and I had to make sure it wasn't Tim. "You haven't answered my question."

"I think she came for the reason she said. She wanted to know about his last moments and try to get a sense of what killed him."

" 'Cause she's so grief-stricken, right?"

But the sound of the back door closing heavily jolted

us before he could answer. "You think they're gone?" Tim asked.

"Wait." I put my hand on his arm just as the sound of a car engine reached our ears. "They weren't parked in the lot; that sound is too far away." I strained to listen as the sound of the car died away. "Well, let's hope they're not coming back."

"They won't risk it." Tim got to his feet. "Did you say there's a flashlight somewhere in here?"

"In one of the dresser drawers." Blinking in the darkness, I could just make out its square shape in the corner of the room. "And watch out for the shelves."

"Please," he said. "I told you. I know this place like the back of my hand."

Before I could answer, the crash of canned goods started my heart thudding again. "Will you please be careful? I jumped a mile, and I don't need any more scares tonight."

"Sorry." His voice softened. "Do you remember the first time we were in this pantry together?"

My face grew warm, and I smiled in spite of myself. "A girl doesn't forget her first kiss. You were sixteen and had just had a growth spurt. Your hands hung out of your shirtsleeves."

Tim held the flashlight out between us, and I had the strange sensation that we were telling stories around a campfire. Not scary ones, though. "You followed me in here," he said.

"No way. You followed me."

"Whatever." Tim grinned, and in the soft light he became that sixteen-year-old I had so crushed on. "It ended up the same way. We were right there." He pointed with the flashlight to the corner where my father's wine was stored. He shook his head. "I remember it so clearly. Your nose was peeling from sunburn."

"Your lips were chapped. They felt rough." I touched my lips at the memory.

Tim grinned at me. "I was too cool for lip balm. You didn't seem to mind, though."

"I didn't. But then when school started, you ignored me. And continued to ignore me for four years."

"C'mon, you were only a freshman. I was waiting for you to grow up."

"Right." I stood up to stretch. "But we're breaking Rule Number Two. And, anyway, we don't have time to reminisce. We need to figure out a way out of here."

He shook his head. "Not gonna happen. Even if I could find a screwdriver in here, we couldn't budge that oak door, assuming I could get it off its hinges. Nope, we got only one choice. We have to spend the night here."

The thought of spending the night in the same room with Tim was only marginally less frightening than fighting off the mysterious intruder. "You're kidding me."

Instead of answering, Tim used the flashlight to find his way to the very spot we'd kissed nearly twenty years before. I heard the crash of breaking glass, and the unmistakable odor of grapes hit my nose.

"Did you just break the top of one of my father's wine bottles?"

"How else could I get it open?" He held out the broken bottle and a small flowerpot, which he handed to me. "I think I got most of the dirt out of it."

I used my shirt to wipe it out for good measure, then held it out toward the flashlight. "No drainage hole. Good work."

Tim poured me a full pot of Chianti and lifted the bottle. *"Salute."*

"Wait—you can't drink from that bottle."

"Damn right." He pointed to my flowerpot. "We're gonna share."

"That's kind of intimate, don't you think?"

"Well, we're in kind of intimate circumstances, aren't we?"

"You could say that." I took a deep swig of my father's swill, and it rushed to my head like a freight train. The next swallow went down a bit easier, though my legs were shaky. I sat back down and Tim joined me on the floor. I took another quick sip for courage and wiped the rim of the pot before passing it to Tim.

"I don't mind your germs, Vic." He filled the little pot again and swirled the wine as though it were the finest Montepulciano instead of Frank's Thursday Chianti. "Not a bad nose." Then he took a sip and choked. "Geez, that's got a kick."

"It tastes better as it goes down," I said, feeling warm and cozy as the Chianti coursed through my veins. "With each successive sip."

Tim laughed. "You said 'suh-cess-ive.'" He took a deeper swallow this time and pounded his chest as it went down.

I reached for the flowerpot. "Lessee how good you talk after another ounce of this crap." I sipped again and then sniffed; the air was filled with the smell of old wine. "Nonna's gonna kill you for making a mess in here." I handed him back the pot. "She scrubs the cement."

He drained what was left in the pot and grinned at me over the rim. "She '*shrubs* the cement,' huh?"

"Oh, ha-ha." I flapped my hand at him and he grabbed it, pulling me closer to him on the floor. I got to my feet as quickly as my rubbery legs and foggy head would allow. "Wait a minute, there, buddy. Whoa. Don't get any crazy ideas." I swayed a little. "That's Rule Number One." I frowned, trying to remember. "Or maybe it's Rule Number Two. Anyway, it's one of them."

"You're right, Vic, and I'm sorry." But his expression

was anything but sorry. He jumped to his feet pretty quickly, considering how much wine he'd put away. "But if we have to stay in here tonight, we might as well be comfortable." He shined the flashlight onto the dresser and began opening the lower drawers; he threw us each a couple of tablecloths.

"Those are clean, Tim! And I just ironed all those!" I wailed, as several napkins sailed toward me.

"We need pillows, don't we?"

I sighed. Even the image of all those crumpled linens that would need laundering wasn't enough to keep me from creating a makeshift bed. Fear was exhausting. Tim's "bed," set suspiciously close to my own, resembled a pile of soon-to-be-dirty laundry.

As we struggled to get comfortable, I turned my back to Tim. Much safer. But the wine had loosened my untrustworthy tongue.

"Are you involved with her?" I asked over my shoulder. Despite my stupor, the words rang out clearly, as did the meaning of "involved."

He didn't have to ask whom I meant. We knew each other far too well for that. Instead, he just sighed. "No, Vic, I'm not. She got in touch with me about a week ago, out of the blue. She wanted to know how I was doing. I told her I was here, and she stopped in to see me." He paused. "She thought Parisi was cheating on her."

I had to stop myself from bolting upright in my pile of tablecloths. Another woman equaled another suspect and another motive for Miss Angie. I tried to keep my voice casual. "Is that so? What made her think that?"

"She didn't really get into details. It's not like she made a habit of confiding in me. Angie and I were over a long time ago."

I shifted on my pile of damask cloth, feeling every bump in the cement. "Then why did she show up today?"

He lifted himself up on one elbow, treating me to the shadowy outline of his muscled arm. "I told you. I don't know. She was hysterical. Maybe she had nowhere to turn."

Men, I thought. She was hysterical, all right. Hysterical enough to come snooping around here and throw suspicion on her old boyfriend. "I wonder what he did die of," I said.

Tim spoke through a long, loud yawn. "It was probably just a heart attack, Vic. And as soon as the police release those results, this will be old news."

"I hope so," I said. "The Casa Lido's future depends on it." *And maybe yours as well. But if it was just a heart attack, why were there broken blood vessels in his eyes? Why was somebody ransacking the kitchen? And more to the point, why are we locked in this pantry?*

"Hey, Vic?" Tim's voice interrupted my thoughts.

"Yeah?"

"I'm glad you're back. I missed you."

The sound of his voice—deep, warm, and familiar—coursed through me as thoroughly as my father's homemade wine and with the same potency. A little light-headed, I tried to control my response, but my answer came out as a sigh. "I missed you, too," I said, and tried to settle myself into my bed.

Whether it was the wine or utter exhaustion, I slept pretty well, considering we'd probably had a brush with a murderer and that my bed was a tablecloth and my pillow a pile of slippery napkins. When the dim light of morning broke through my consciousness, I groaned and put my hand over my gritty, foul-tasting mouth. Ugh. A toothbrush followed by about seven Tylenol was the first order of the day.

"Hey," I croaked.

Tim turned to face me, rumpled in that morning sexy

way that is usually only true on television. "'Morning, sunshine," he said brightly.

I held my head and groaned. "Turn it down, will you? Frankie's Chianti is having its terrible revenge."

Just then came the scrape of the key in the pantry lock, and the door swung open to reveal my grandmother, fists on hips and thunder in her face. I listened in dazed, hungover horror as Italian invective rained down over us. The words dropped with painful thuds onto my aching head, and I could only imagine the scene as she saw it: spilled wine, broken glass, crumpled linens, and the two of us lying side by side on the pantry floor. I winced as she went on, ever louder, ever more virulent. Finally, after shaking her fist at the two of us, she turned with a jerk and stalked down the hallway into the kitchen. I took a breath and looked at Tim.

"You speak Italian—what'd she say?"

Tim stood up with a groan, stretching his stiff arms and legs. He rubbed his hand over his stubbly chin and grinned. "I didn't get it all," he said. "But I'm pretty sure we're engaged."

Chapter Ten

"**F**lirting with one suspect and sleeping with another. *Tsk-tsk*, Vic. Bernardo should have such an exciting life."

"Cut it out, Sofie." I rubbed the temples of my still-aching head, but I was glad to be in my cottage and far away from my irate grandmother. "And I didn't sleep *with* him. I slept next to him. There's a world of difference." I got up from my kitchen table to pour myself another cup of coffee.

"If you say so," she said.

I sat back down and sipped my coffee, willing the caffeine to do its work on the pulsing blood vessels in my brain. "Look, it's not like I had a choice. Somebody was in that restaurant last night. Tim and I both heard him, and then he locked us in that pantry."

"You think it was the murderer, don't you?"

"Who else? Nothing was stolen. The kitchen was pretty messed up, but that was it. Clearly, somebody was looking for something." I held the sides of my head and moaned. "I just went over all of this with the police."

"What'd they say? Did they take you seriously?"

"I guess. I called Danny right away, and he sent me down there to file a report. As his sister, I have some cred." I sighed. "They're probably sending everything over to the county prosecutor anyway."

"If it was the murderer," Sofie pointed out, "this lets Tim off the hook." She paused. "Unless he's in cahoots with the Widow Angie."

"If he is, he's a pretty damn good actor." I shook my head. "I don't buy it, SIL."

"You're not exactly unbiased where Tim is concerned."

"I'll give you that one." I said.

"By the way," Sofie said, "why are your teeth blue?"

"Ugh. I know." I automatically put my hand to my mouth. "I brushed twice. Apparently, my father's home-made swill pierces tooth enamel. The desk sergeant kept staring at my mouth."

She pushed my plate of cold toast across the table. "Eat. You'll feel better."

I groaned. "If I had a dollar for every time somebody in my family said that to me."

"We say it because it's true. Now take a bite. You need your strength." She slapped the red folder down on the table. "While you've been off having fun with the Macho Twins, *I* have been busy."

"And you think I haven't?" I said through a mouthful of toast. It was whole grain—Sofia's idea, of course. I took another sip of black coffee to wash it down before I made my announcement. "Last night Tim told me something of great importance, missy. Angie—excuse me, Anjelica—suspected her hubby of having an affair."

Sofia's lower jaw dropped in slow motion. "GET. OUT."

"No, thanks. I live here." I pushed the plate of toast away and concentrated on the coffee. I was going to need it.

"We have to find out who she is," Sofia said, scribbling furiously on her pad. "Then we have to find out if she was anywhere near Oceanside when Parisi started feeling sick. Ooh, can I have this one?"

I waved a hand at her. "Knock yourself out. Now what have *you* got, SIL?"

"I've got Mikey and Fifi—that's who."

"Who?" Mikey and Fifi sounded like names for a pair of Scottish terriers.

"Mike Gemelli, aka Mikey G, and Francesca Cavatoppi, affectionately called Fifi," Sofia said, wrinkling her nose. She tapped her nail on the folder. "Both stars of *The Jersey Side* were with him that day. They both had access. And I wouldn't put it past that little *puttana* to kill him just to get her raise."

"You've lost me."

"You don't read at all, do you?" She shook her head in disgust. "Both those kids are in contract talks. They were asking for ridiculous amounts of money."

"But then killing their producer doesn't make sense."

Sofia looked at me, her impatience tinged with pity. "Parisi wasn't the only producer on the show. His partner, Harvey Rosen, was willing to meet the kids' terms. Our victim wasn't, and now he's out of the way. Convenient, no?"

My blurry thoughts were starting to clear. "They were the two kids up on the boards with him, right?" I looked at Sofia. "If he had anything to eat or drink up there, it's possible one of them could have given him something."

"You bet, SIL." She leaned across the table, her eyes shining. "And you're the one who's gonna find that out."

"Me?" I sat back in my chair. "Why me?"

"You're a writer," she said, as if that explained it all.

"And?"

"Geez, you're slow today." My sister-in-law shook her head. "You're going to approach them about your book."

I narrowed my eyes. "What do they have to do with Isabella?"

"Not that book. Your *other* book. The one you're writing about reality show stars and their path to fame."

I put my head in my hands. "How did I get into this?"

Sofia gathered her notes in the red folder. "That would be me. And your crazy nonna." She stood up and pushed in her chair. "I'm headed up to the boardwalk to see which stands were open that day and if anyone noticed Parisi eating or drinking. Then I'm gonna find out who Parisi's girlfriend was." She paused. "I should probably talk to Anne McCrae, too. She comes in for yoga."

"Oh, right! I forgot our redoubtable mayor was there that day."

But McCrae was a big supporter of the show coming to town, much to the dismay of many of her constituents, my family included. Though she tolerated me because I was a writer, she was no fan of the Rienzi clan, as Nonna and my dad had a habit of showing up at town meetings to express their very decided opinions on town politics. Dealing with the mayor might be a bit tricky. "She wouldn't have a motive, though, would she?"

Sofia shrugged. "Who knows? But she was stuck to him like glue that day, and maybe she knows something." She pointed at me. "And you also have more than one job. You need to find out about those herbs."

"Oh my God. I almost forgot." Luckily, or grossly, I was still wearing last night's jeans. I pulled the crumpled packets from my pockets, along with the Tiffany receipt.

"Give me that." Sofia grabbed the receipt and tucked it into her red folder. "You cannot be trusted with important evidence. And get crackin' on contacting those kids. They're still down here; they're staying at that fancy historic place in Bay Head."

"They're at the Villa Fortuna? C'mon. I need to put a dress on just to walk into that place, and all my good clothes are back in the city. You think I can just waltz in and ask to see them? They probably have handlers and security and entourages and—" But she was already out the door. And I had a choice: I could try to approach the *Jersey Side* kids to pump them for information, or I could go back to the restaurant and face Nonna. There was really no contest.

After showering and finding a passable skirt and blouse, I made the drive to Bay Head, with Bruce in the CD player for courage. I pulled up to the Villa Fortuna, my shabby Honda a standout among the BMWs and Land Rovers lining the sidewalk. Smoothing out my wrinkled skirt, I gazed up at the massive Italianate Victorian structure. It was a bit hard to imagine Mikey G and Fifi taking up residence in here. By some miracle, I had managed to get both kids on the phone; Fifi was amenable to a meeting, and as it turned out, Mikey's father was a Bernardo Vitali fan, so I was in with him, too.

I started with Fifi, who occupied one of the more modest rooms on the second floor. As the cost of even a modest room at the Villa Fortuna was still about equal to a month's rent on my cottage, her digs were impressive. The minute she greeted me at the door, I knew why Fifi had gotten her name; her curly mane and poufy bangs suggested a large-eyed, well-groomed poodle, but a miniature one. Fifi barely made five feet; when I reached down to shake her tiny hand, I felt downright willowy.

She took a seat on a velvet settee and blinked her thickly coated lashes at me. She was actually a pretty girl, under all the foundation, blush, bronzer, eyeliner, mascara, and lash extensions. Despite her plump proportions, her legs were shapely. She wore a thick silver ankle bracelet graced by a heart-shaped charm, which clanked every time she moved. On her slender ankle, it suggested a manacle. *A slave to fame?* I wondered. I sat down across from her to get a better look—was it from Tiffany? Or Canal Street? Sofia would have known in seconds. It wasn't a necklace, but if Fifi were Parisi's mysterious girlfriend, he may have bought more than one gift there.

I pointed to her ankle. "That's a great piece."

"Thanks." She lifted her foot, revealing a pedicure that included tiny rhinestones. "I also have the bracelet, necklace, and ring that match it." She wrinkled her pug nose. "But I think it's tacky to wear them all at the same time."

This from a girl with diamonds on her toenails. She grinned suddenly, and I got a look at the child she really was. *Please,* I thought, *if he was cheating, don't let her be Parisi's girlfriend.* He was old enough to be her father.

"So I hear you wanna write a book about me," she said, studying her fingernails, which also sported gems. "There's already a whaddayacallit—an *unauthorized* one—some bitch wrote and made a bundle off of."

"Uh, well, this isn't actually a biography."

"It isn't?" She sounded as though I had said no to buying her ice cream.

"Not really, Francesca. I'm looking at young reality stars to see how they're handling fame."

She waved a glittery hand. "Geez, I could talk for hours on that one. And call me Fifi, 'kay? Everybody else does." She frowned a little, and I wondered if she was sick of the nickname.

"But Francesca's such a pretty name."

She shrugged. "At home I was Frannie, which I hate."

She sat up to her full fifty-nine inches. "Do we start today?"

I was prepared for resistance, not enthusiasm. I scrabbled in my bag for a pen and notebook. Then I took the plunge. "So, Fifi, first I want to apologize for the timing."

"Timing?" Her face was a bronzed blank.

"Well, after what happened to your producer," I said, lowering my voice to convey some respect.

"Oh, right. I feel kinda bad about that. He had, like, a heart attack, right?" She picked at one of the rhinestones on her thumb. "God. Ya can't get a decent mani around here."

"I think so," I said, as I wrote, *Not too shaken up*, on my pad. "Did you work very closely with him?"

"Not really. Harvey was on set more than he was." At the mention of Rosen's name, her face softened. "Harvey's really cool. He's young. And he's nice to us."

"And he's supporting you in your contract talks?" *Is she involved with Harvey?* got added to my notes, along with *Check out Rosen*. When I looked up at her, she was no longer smiling. "Are you from the newspaper?" she asked, her voice shrill.

"Absolutely not, Fifi!" I was relieved to be telling the truth for once. "I just wanted to convey my condolences about Mr. Parisi."

She sat up primly. "Well, I feel sad for his wife."

My head jerked up from my pad. "Do you know her?"

"I only met her once." Her large eyes grew wider. "She's soooo pretty. I wish I looked like that."

The subject of Angie/Anjelica's looks grated on me like sand in the bedsheets. "Right, well—"

"And I know Harvey thought so, too," Fifi continued. A sly note had crept into her voice. "I don't think Gio liked that him and his wife were BFFs."

While I would have loved nothing better than adding another motive to Anjelica's growing list, kids Fifi's age used "BFF" to describe a wide range of relationships. Still, I scribbled *How close were A and Rosen?????* as quickly as I could.

"Hey." Fifi was now standing, her arms crossed over her unnaturally high bosom. "I thought we were talking about me."

"Just getting some background notes." I smiled up at her in what I hoped was a winning manner. "So you must do lots of promotional appearances. How did things go in Oceanside Park last week?"

Fifi plopped back down on the couch and made a face. "Ugh. That place is a dump. I can't believe they want us to film there."

"So, is that happening?" I asked, trying to keep my tone neutral.

"I dunno. They don't tell me shit."

"Oh." *Bring it back to the boardwalk, Vic.* "So did you have fun on the boardwalk?"

"Please." She rolled her eyes. "It's not like it's Seaside."

"No, it certainly isn't," I said heartily. "But we . . . uh, *they* have great homemade lemonade and amazing pizza. So I hear."

"I guess. Mikey mostly ate. Me, I graze 'cause that's healthier. So I just had the cheese fries."

"So did you *all* get a chance to sample the food?" I wondered how much longer Fifi would stand for these questions. I sounded lame even to my own ears.

She shook her head. "Nah. Gio is on some natural diet. He just brings his special water." Clearly, Fifi's patience was at an end. "Are we gonna, like, talk about the book, or what?"

"Of course. If you'll give me a few more minutes, I

can outline the project for you and you can run it by your agent."

I spent another fifteen minutes talking about my nonexistent nonfiction project, wondering how many purgatory hours I'd be logging for all the lies. But in talking to Fifi, I could sense a sadness and confusion under the bravado and the makeup. She was barely twenty and had quit college to be filmed drinking, screaming, and making a fool of herself on a weekly basis. As I closed the door behind me, I realized that Parisi—along with his buddy Rosen—had exploited this girl and made her a joke for posterity. For some of us, that would be a motive for murder. I left Fifi's hotel room with a head full of questions about Anjelica, Rosen, and Parisi, but pretty sure of one thing: Fifi Cavatoppi was no killer.

Next up was Mikey G. I was unaccountably nervous as I made my way up the marble staircase to the penthouse suite that housed the Gemellis. The door was opened by a fiftyish man in a razor-sharp Italian suit. It was all I could do not to stroke his lapels.

"Ms. Reed?"

"Yes." I held out my hand, praying he wouldn't connect Vick Reed with Victoria Rienzi. "Mr. Gemelli?"

He covered my hand with his. "Call me Michael, please. It's our pleasure to have you here."

I fumbled in my bag for my ticket inside the penthouse—an advance copy of the latest Bernardo Vitali mystery, *Murder Della Casa*. "A small token of thanks," I said, handing him the book.

"Wow," he said. "It hasn't even come out yet. Am I the first kid on the block to get one of these?"

"You bet," I said. *If you don't count* Kirkus, Publishers Weekly, *and about a hundred book bloggers.*

"Where are my manners? Please, come in." Michael Gemelli ushered me into a sumptuously furnished

apartment that looked like something out of an Edith
Wharton novel—all velvet drapes and plaster cherubs.
In one corner of the room, lounging on a carved wood
sofa, was Mikey G himself, texting madly and grinning
to himself with each response. Michael Gemelli swept
his arm across the room and held it out toward his pride
and joy. "Ms. Reed, may I present the man of the hour,
Michael Junior?"

The man of the hour didn't look up from his phone.
"Hey," he said.

"Hey, yourself," I responded. I held out my hand.
"I'm Vick Reed."

As Mikey halfway shook my hand, I noticed that there
was a lacquered shine on his fingernails that matched the
one on his hair. His face was already tanned, and when he
smiled, I squinted at its brightness. "Nice to meetch ya. I
hear you wanna write a book about me."

"Well, about you and other young people who find
sudden fame on reality shows." Oy. I didn't even believe
myself. "I was hoping to do a nonfiction project, you
know, to take a break from the mysteries."

"Uh-huh." Mikey looked back down at his phone.

His father frowned. "Michael Junior, please put that
phone away and listen to Ms. Reed. She wants to write
about you," he said through his teeth. He shot me an
apologetic smile. "You'll have to excuse him. He hasn't
been the same since our producer passed away." He
rolled his eyes heavenward. "God rest his soul."

Mikey raised one dark eyebrow—waxed, I noted—
and tried to look sad. "Yeah, I'm all broken up about it."

I'll just bet you are, I thought. *You* and *Daddy. Parisi
was the only thing standing between you and a big pile of
cash.* Gemelli Senior had used "our" when he spoke
about the show; that career, not to mention that giant
paycheck, belonged to both of them. But at least they'd

given me an opening. I cleared my throat. "Yes, I heard about that on the news. It was fairly sudden, right?"

Michael Gemelli nodded. "A terrible thing."

"It is," I agreed. "Mikey, weren't you with him at that appearance in Oceanside Park?"

Mikey's lazy gaze moved from his phone to my face. When I caught the shrewd expression in his eyes, I knew this was no Fifi I was dealing with. "Yeah, me and Feef were there." He lifted one broad shoulder, and as he moved, the muscles in his neck rippled; his pecs and arms were well-defined. This dude spent a lot of time at the gym. If he were going to kill somebody, it's a safe bet he'd do it with his fists, or possibly a bullet. Slipping something into Parisi's "special water," just didn't seem his style. I looked over at his father. While it was hard to imagine Gemelli Senior getting his hands dirty, he might just hire somebody else to do it. A ripple of anxiety echoed my fear from the previous night. What had I gotten myself into?

"So he seemed okay when you were with him?" I asked.

Mikey shrugged again, and his father frowned. "Miss Reed, aren't you here to talk to Michael Junior about a book project? Why are you so interested in Gio Parisi?"

Uh-oh. "Well, I . . ."

Before I could finish, Mikey struck. "C'mon, Dad, don't you know who she is?" He swept one manicured finger across the screen of his smartphone and then held it up for us to see. Captured in the window was a screen shot of my interview with Nina LaGuardia, just at my "no comment" moment. "She says she heard about it on the news." Mikey sneered. "She *was* the news."

Michael Gemelli slowly turned his head from the phone to my face. "Wait a minute. You're connected to that restaurant where Gio died."

"You could say that. My parents own it." I tried to smile, which was hard to do with trembling lips. "Small world, huh?"

Gemelli Senior's voice was as rough and gravelly as our unpaved parking lot. "What are you *really* here for, Ms. Reed?"

My mind racing to come up with some kind of explanation, I was (in a change for me) struck dumb. There was no good reason to be here. There was no book. There was just me playing amateur sleuth, and doing a bang-up job of it, apparently.

"Wait a minute—I know what this is about!" He shook his finger at me, and I winced, waiting for the inevitable. Did he think I suspected his precious son of murder? What might he do, or more likely, *have done* to me in response? My mouth went dry.

"You're doing research. And not for a book about Mikey, but for one of your mysteries." There was menace in his voice, enough to make me break a sweat in that air-conditioned room and to wonder where *he* was on the day Parisi died. "My son's life is not fodder for one of your books. And now I'd like you to leave."

He held the door open, and I couldn't escape fast enough. Better to have him think I was researching a mystery than searching for a murderer.

As Mikey G followed me to the hallway, he flashed me a wolfish grin and leaned close enough for me to smell his wintergreen Tic Tacs. "Whatever you might think, Miss Rienzi, I'm not some dumb guido," he said. "I just play one on TV."

As I drove home from Bay Head, I tried to process all I had learned, but it was all what my mother calls a *giambotta*, which is informal Italian for "great big mess." Thinking I would do better to talk it through with Sofie,

I turned my attention to my second job: identifying those herbs I'd taken from the pantry. And as I turned down Ocean Avenue and hit my hometown, I knew exactly who could help me.

"Victoria!" Iris Harrington greeted me at the door of her shop, the Seaside Apothecary, which contained all manner of things herbal and organic. It had been an old pharmacy and still had racks of wooden shelves that Cal would appreciate. The store smelled medicine-y and flowery at the same time, and Iris—with her peasant blouse, long skirt, and leather sandals—fit perfectly in her surroundings. She still wore her hair long, as she had in high school, only now it was streaked with gray. Fresh-faced and devoid of makeup, she was an attractive woman, though Sofie was itching to get her hands on her for a makeover. Iris gave me a quick hug, and I caught a whiff of her patchouli scent.

Her blue eyes were bright as she looked me over. "It's so good to see you back. You look wonderful. So you're here to work on a book?"

I grinned. "Gotta love the Oceanside grapevine. Yeah, I'm here to work on a book, do some research. You know."

"So, is there something you need? Still getting those tension headaches of yours?"

"Yes, and yes, but this is actually part of my research." I pulled the herbs from my bag and laid them out on the counter. "Do you think you can identify these for me?"

Iris took a small leaf from one of the packets and rubbed it between her fingers. "This one's easy. It's dried sage. A nice savory herb." She grinned at me. "I'm surprised you didn't figure that out for yourself," she said.

I probably would have recognized the sage if I'd been willing to put it close to my nose. "My grandmother would be ashamed of me," I said. "She makes a butter-and-sage sauce for her ravioli."

She opened another packet and sniffed. "This one's raspberry leaf. Some people make infusions from it or even mouth rinse. It has astringent properties."

"Could somebody get sick from it?" I asked. "Or even die?"

Iris laughed. "No. Pregnant women drink it. I think it's pretty safe." She pointed to the third packet. "And that last one is lovely lemon verbena. It dries nicely and has a wonderful scent. In Europe they make tisanes with it to treat colds. Oh, and it's a natural insect repellent."

"Would somebody use these in something like, say, salad dressing?"

She frowned. "The sage, possibly. But it's a pungent herb; it's often used with meats or in stuffings."

I wrapped the packets back up and slipped them into my bag. "So none of this stuff would kill anybody?"

"Goodness, no. I suppose in large amounts they might make someone a little sick, but I don't think any of these are toxic unless someone had an allergy." She patted me on the shoulder. "Sorry to disappoint."

"No, actually, that's what I thought." Relief coursed through me; I could be fairly sure that nothing in that pantry killed Parisi. And while I never seriously considered her a suspect, it let my grandmother off the hook, too.

She cocked her head and grinned. "If you're trying to kill somebody off with a plant, there are better ways to go."

"Such as?"

"Such as *Phytolacca*, also known as pokeweed; the roots are toxic. And foxglove, of course, also known as *Digitalis purpurea*. Enough of that will stop your heart. Oh, and oleander; there's a nasty one. In some places you're not even allowed to plant it. Now, some people think holly berries can kill you, but they mostly just make you sick . . ."

I only half listened as Iris talked. While I was relieved the herbs were harmless, I was now left with more questions. If some toxic substance caused Parisi's fatal heart attack, how was it delivered? Until those test results came in, we had only conjecture and supposition.

I left Iris's shop feeling a bit better until my phone rang. I recognized the number, even though I'd deleted it from my contacts ages ago.

"Vic," Tim said. "Can you stop by the restaurant for a minute?"

"I'd rather not; I'm trying to avoid my grandmother."

"It's important. It's about last night." At this moment, last night felt like an experience glimpsed through the mirrors at Tillie's Funhouse: distant, distorted, and a little nightmarish. I didn't particularly want to relive it. "What about last night?"

"I'd rather talk in person. Just get over here, okay? Come in through the back."

It was good advice. I parked as far from the door as I could, hoping I wouldn't see my grandmother—or anyone else in my family, for that matter. Tim was waiting outside for me.

He strode over and took my elbow. "C'mere. I want to show you something," he said, and led me to the Dumpster at the corner of the lot.

"You want to show me the garbage?" I wrinkled my nose. Few odors were as pungent as restaurant refuse.

Tim lifted the top and pointed. "Look."

I stood on tiptoe and leaned forward. "I don't see anything."

"That's just it," Tim said. "It's empty. And we don't have pickup until Monday."

"I don't understand."

"The garbage is gone. That means whoever was here last night took it."

I shook my head. "That's impossible. The police would have taken it on Tuesday."

Tim looked around and lowered his voice. "They only took the kitchen trash."

"How do you know that?"

"I talked to Danny, who probably shouldn't have talked to me. The OPPD screwed up, plain and simple. I saw the bags myself; there's been trash in there all week—until today."

"Trash that might have held evidence," I said.

"Maybe evidence that could have proved me innocent if this guy was murdered." Tim sighed. "Too bad I didn't think of it till now. Now that it's gone."

And probably destroyed, if that's why the intruder was rummaging around the restaurant last night. I shivered at the memory. Looking at Tim's worried face, I was fairly sure he wasn't a murderer. But how would we ever prove it?

Chapter Eleven

Isabella stared at the young man's open collar, the white fabric a stark contrast against the tanned skin of his neck and chest. Shyly, she lifted her eyes to his face—

I groaned. At what point had my book become a romance novel? The vibration of my cell phone was a welcome interruption. Until I saw who it was.

"Vic! How's the sleuthing going down there? Guess you haven't had much time to work on the new novel, huh?"

"Don't sound so cheerful, Josh. I *was* working on it. Until you interrupted me, that is."

"Oh, I'll let you get back to it. But I thought you should know that I talked to Sylvie."

I took a quick swig of cold coffee to fortify myself. Much as I adored my editor, I stood a little in awe of her. "And?"

"Well, she's happy that you're doing this book-of-the-heart project." He paused. "But she's also happy about Bernardo's sales. She thinks the series still has traction, and she's worried you won't have time to promote the new release."

"Josh, I haven't forgotten my obligation to Agatha Press or to Sylvie. Or to you, for that matter. I'll do as much promo as you need me to do on the new book."

Sure I will. In between solving a murder and getting my family's business back on its feet, as well as dodging my old boyfriend and *a guy who might be interested in becoming my new one.*

"You don't have to convince me, Vic," Josh said a shade too heartily. "I figure it's only a matter of time before you'll be back in New York. How're things going with that grandmother of yours, by the way?"

"Peachy. Now, if you don't mind, I'd like to get back to work."

"Sure, absolutely. So did ya figure out who killed Parisi yet?"

"No, Josh. I'm gonna let the police work on that one."

"Ha! You won't be able to help yourself. Listen, you know he wouldn't budge on the contract talks, right? Think one of the kids from the show knocked him off?"

He had hit upon one of our theories, and it occurred to me that Josh might be a valuable source of information. "Hey, Josh? Do you still have that connection at ARC Entertainment?"

"You mean Chaz? The guy who handles TV talent?"

"Yes. Could you find out what he knows about Harvey Rosen?"

"Parisi's partner?" Josh's voice took on an excited tone. "You think he killed him, don't you?"

"Hold your horses there, dude. I don't think anything. I'm just looking for some information."

"Sure you are. And if that information happens to give you the plot of the next Bernardo mystery—"

"Don't get any ideas, okay? Yes, I'm looking into this Parisi thing. The restaurant is losing business, more every day. I've got to find out what happened to this guy. Could you please talk to Chaz? Find out whatever you can about Rosen's relationship with Parisi and especially his relationship with Parisi's wife."

"You got it, Vic. I'll call you as soon as I know something. Now I'll let you get back to your writing."

But as I ended the call, I realized there would be no more work on the book today. I had to get over to the restaurant. My mom and dad had called the staff in for a meeting this morning, and Nonna would certainly be there. It was time to face the Italian music. And if I knew my grandmother, I'd be hearing the entire opera.

When I got there, Massimo, Tim, and Nando were already seated at the family table, espresso cups in front of each of them. A platter of pastries occupied the center of the table; I could smell the almond paste from fifty paces. On the plate were macaroon cookies studded with pignoli nuts, several kinds of biscotti, and shell-shaped *sfogliatelle* filled with sweetened ricotta and dusted with sugar.

Mouth watering, I sat down across from the men; Massimo poured me a coffee and handed me a plate. I took a *sfogliatelle* and bit into it with a satisfying crunch and a puff of powdered sugar.

"Umm. My first taste of pastry from Roberto's. Now I know I'm home."

Massimo lifted his cup. "And welcome you are, *cara*. Especially now."

I nodded my head toward the kitchen. "They here yet?"

Tim grinned. "What's the matter, Vic? Can't face Nonna?"

"Very funny. Like you aren't afraid of her, too." I took a sip of the hot, strong espresso, savoring the bitter aftertaste.

"Don't matter to me." He shrugged. "I've been on her S-list for months." His mouth lifted in a sneer. "Right now her boy is *Cal-vino*."

"Jealous, Tim?" I slid my eyes toward his, but he just scowled.

Nando, on the other hand, was enjoying himself immensely. He shot me a toothy smile. "Tim and Cal, Miss Victor—they are *aceite* and *agua*."

"Yeah, and I know who the oily one is." Tim leaned across the table and spoke in a low tone. "I don't trust the guy, Vic. We don't know a thing about him. And he was here that day."

Massimo and Nando exchanged a look; I shook my head at Tim, but he refused to get the message. "He's as phony as that bayou accent he lays on so thick, and for all we know, he had a connection to Parisi—"

"*Who* had connections to Parisi?"

I jumped at the sound of my grandmother's voice. She sure had a way of sneaking up on people. "Another producer on the show, Nonna," I said, avoiding her eyes and marveling at what an adept liar I'd become.

She snorted in my general direction, which was probably the best I would get until she got over finding me and Tim in the pantry. And it was better than calling me a *puttana*. She came into the dining room followed by Danny and my parents—and one other person. "I've asked Calvino to join us," Nonna announced. "He is on staff here now, and what we decide affects him as well."

From Cal's impassive expression, it was difficult to tell how much he had overheard. But he did make a point of sitting next to me at the table. He looked across at Tim and nodded. "Where ya at, brother?"

Tim's face tightened. "I'm not your brother, dude."

Cal held up his palms and grinned. "Just tryin' to be polite . . . *dude*."

While he and Tim threw each other dark looks, I got to enjoy an entirely new sensation—two men fighting for my attention. My mom kissed Tim on the cheek and made a point of ignoring Cal, probably because Cal was now in my grandmother's favor. Danny lifted an eyebrow and shook his head, and my dad seemed blissfully unaware of the family undercurrents flowing around him. I wondered if he knew about the broken wine bottle left in the pantry.

My grandmother folded her hands on the table and looked around at the rest of us, her eyes hard behind her glasses. I took another gulp of coffee, wishing it was Frank's Chianti instead. "I have called you here, today," she began, "because the Casa Lido is in trouble. Our receipts are pitiful. Even our regulars have stopped coming." She waited to let the words sink in. "And this will continue"—she slowly turned her gaze upon me—"until we know who killed that *cafone*."

"But, Nonna, I—" I began.

"You what?" My mother frowned. "You're not getting mixed up in this, are you?"

"She is merely gathering information, Nicolina," Nonna said.

"You will do no such thing, young lady." My mother's curls shook in indignation as she spoke.

"For one thing, Mom, I'm thirty-three years old, and I'm not—"

"I don't care how old you are." How often had my mother spoken these words? I stifled a sigh as she went on, her volume increasing with every word. "There was an intruder here the other night. You could have been injured. Or worse."

"Ma, calm down," Danny broke in. I winced, because I knew exactly what was coming. Did men never learn?

"Don't you dare tell me to calm down, Daniel. I am still your mother." She pointed a bright pink fingernail in his face for emphasis. "You are not to drag your sister into this investigation. Do you understand me?" As she went on lecturing him, I caught a sly glance from Cal and fought the urge to smile. Instead, I stuffed a chocolate biscotti in my mouth.

When my mother finally finished, Danny sighed. "Ma, you know I wouldn't compromise the investigation, and I'd never put Vic in danger."

"I wouldn't have let anything happen to her, Mrs. R," Tim said.

My mother rewarded him with a bright smile. "I know that, Tim. But the fact remains that someone was in this restaurant. Someone rifled through the kitchen."

And someone stole the garbage. I didn't feel the need to share that with the family, though I had told Danny.

My dad patted my mother's hand. "Baby, you worry too much." He picked up a pastry and waved it around. "You *all* worry too much." He turned to Danny. "Those results will be in soon, right? They'll prove that nothing he ate killed him, and we can all go back to normal."

"In a perfect world, Dad," I said. "Look, this has hurt us; there's no denying it."

Massimo crossed his arms and lifted his chin. "I cannot have my reputation sullied."

Tim groaned. "You weren't even here, Massi. Anyway, it's *my* reputation on the line, isn't it? I'm the one who served him. I'm—"

"Basta!" my grandmother shouted, startling all of us except Cal, who had the same bemused look on his face. "Quiet, all of you!" She held up one knobby finger. "Our season begins in a week. *One week*." She looked around the table at each of us. "I don't care what those test results are—the Casa Lido will be keeping its doors open." She shifted a beady glance in my direction. "Now, if someone was to find out what really happened to Mr. Big Shot Television Producer in the meantime—"

"Mama," my mom interrupted, "I will not have Victoria mixed up in this."

"Was I speaking to you, Nicolina? No. I was speaking with my granddaughter; was I not?"

"But she's *my* daughter!"

As the two women went back and forth, I watched Cal's eyes slide from one to the other and then back to me. Was he checking out my gene pool? If so, he was probably finding some pretty murky water that would douse any spark of interest he might have for me. While I tried to figure out whether I cared or not, the front door swung open.

"Vic," Sofia called, "you have to see what I found! Oh my God. It's—"

Danny got to his feet and looked his wife straight in the eye. "It's what, Sofia?"

She skidded to a halt about halfway across the dining room, and her eyes locked with his. "Oh . . . hey, Danny."

Though my brother's expression was stern, I knew he was fighting the impulse to head straight across the room to his wife. Instead, he jammed his hands into his pockets and spoke softly. "Was there something you needed to talk to Vic about?"

Sofia never even looked my way. I watched in admiration as she lifted one eyebrow in my brother's direction, her mouth curling into a slight smile. She dropped her voice to a caressing tone. "Just girl talk, baby. You know."

The air between them was charged. Sofia stepped toward him, and Danny took a quick breath. Any moment now, he would take her into his arms and they'd get back together, just as we all wanted. I caught a look at my mother's frowning face. Well, maybe not all of us.

But instead of pulling her into a clinch, he held his hand to stop the oncoming Sofia traffic. "Don't even try it, sweetheart," he said. "You wouldn't be playing detective, by any chance, would you?"

Sofia lifted her chin and gave a little sniff. "What I do is no longer your business."

My grandmother stood up. "Sofia, *mia*, would you like to join us?"

"No, thank you, Nonna." She came over to the table and raised her hand in a little wave. "Hi, everyone." I saw her steal a look at my mother, whose grim expression said it all. Then her eyes landed on Cal. As his amused glance met hers, I found myself making a silent wish: *Please don't find my sister-in-law attractive.* "You must be Cal," Sofia said.

He got to his feet and held out his hand. "Pleasure, ma'am."

Ma'am? Now, that was encouraging.

Sofia grinned and nodded her head in my direction. "I've heard about you."

"Have ya now?" He sat back down and shot me a sly look.

Good going, SIL. Remind me to kill you later.

Danny took the long way back to his seat, pointedly avoiding Sofia. My mother smiled in approval and then sent Sofia a silent message—*Time to go.*

I caught Cal's eye across the table and he winked. "You have quite an interesting family, Victoria."

"You have no idea," I whispered back.

By the time I could extricate myself from the family meeting, Sofia was already finishing her second class of the day. After bidding her young charges good-bye, she threw a towel around her neck and motioned me to her office.

"So what happened there, Mata Hari?" I said. "I thought you'd have my brother eating out of your hand."

"I will—just give me time. Anyway, it's your mother I'm worried about."

"She'll come around. She's protective of Danny, and she doesn't like that Nonna's taking your side. They're doing the same thing with Tim and Cal at the moment."

"Let me guess—your mom's on Team Cal and Nonna's backing Tim."

I shook my head and circled my finger in the air. "Other way around. Don't forget, Tim besmirched my honor in the pantry."

"Oh my God," she said. "You need a freakin' score-card with that crazy family of yours."

"You married in."

"I know." She sighed. "And I'd like it to stay that way."

I patted her arm. "Be patient. You guys will work it out."

"I hope so." She raised an eyebrow at me. "By the way, your Cal is kinda hot, in a 'Down on the Bayou' sorta way." She wrinkled her nose. "Too old, though."

Why was I relieved? "He's not 'my Cal.' And he's not that old."

"Pushin' forty." She waved her hand. "Anyway, never mind that stuff now. There's something you have to see." Sofia called me over to her desk. "Pull up that chair." The RealTV Web site was open on her screen, and I watched her type "Jersey Side, cow" into the search bar.

"'Cow'?" I asked.

She turned serious eyes on me. "Just wait till it loads."

As the pumping theme music rolled, we watched a montage of three girls and two guys that included Fifi and Mikey G in various activities that were dominated by dancing, drinking, and brawling. "I've never really watched this," I said, "but even the opening credits offend me."

"Oh, it gets better," Sofia said.

The episode began with the group rolling out of bed at two in the afternoon and feasting on a breakfast of cold pizza. This riveting scene was followed by one at the beach, during which the kids compared the merits of tanning oil versus tanning lotion in an eye-glazing discussion that went on forever. By the time Mikey G was making his pecs dance, I'd had enough. "Please, Sofe, make it stop. Can't you just fast-forward?"

"There's not much more of it." She put the volume up. "Okay, listen to this part. They're talking about their plans for that night."

"I can hardly wait." She shushed me again, and I concentrated on listening to Mikey and his sidekick, the quaintly named Jimmy Juice, aka JJ, as they debated about which night spot offered the most "cows."

"So that's how they talk about women?" I asked, but already knew the answer.

Sofia's expression was tight and angry. "Yup. But this is only part of that episode. The network doesn't air the rest of it anymore."

"Why not?"

"Because it's too awful, even by reality TV standards." She pointed to the computer screen. "But I can give you the gist of it: Good ol' Mikey and his buddy pick up a not very pretty overweight girl at the bar who recognizes them from the show and is thrilled with their attention. Cut to commercial break, after which the guys and about half the bar are screaming names at her and pouring drinks over her head."

"Oh my God. That's awful."

"It sure is," Sofia said. "And here's what's worse: Before the network pulled it, clips from that episode had gone viral, so that girl's humiliation had nearly a million views."

I gasped. "That poor girl."

"'That poor girl' is right," Sofia said. She closed the page and opened a new tab, then logged into Facebook. "And here she is." She turned her screen so I could see it clearly: There was a picture of a young woman with a cheerful, round face holding a small dog. She had a long list of friends and a number of recent messages on her page. It appeared she had survived her public humiliation. But when I saw her name, I inhaled sharply: Tina Biaggio, of Oceanside Park, New Jersey.

My eyes met Sofia's, and she nodded. I pointed to the screen. "That's not . . ."

"It sure is," she said. "That's Mr. Biaggio's daughter. Your grocery guy. The one who was part of the protest that day." She paused. "And the one who delivered the produce for Gio Parisi's salad."

Chapter Twelve

"**S**o we've got opportunity *and* motive," I said.

Sofia nodded. "I'd wanna kill somebody who did that to my daughter. Wouldn't you?"

"But Parisi didn't actually do it. Those disgusting kids did."

She shrugged. "He aired it. And don't forget that Mr. Biaggio was opposed to the show filming here; in a way, that gives him two motives." She drummed her fingers on the desk. "I'd like to know if he tried to take any action against the network." She clicked open a blank document. "Let's get some notes down on this."

"But even if he complained to the network, he wouldn't have gotten anywhere." I said. "Tina probably signed a release."

"Wouldn't that be all the more reason to take revenge on him?" Sofia tapped quickly on her keyboard.

"Maybe." As I watched Sofie's notes appear on the screen, I tried to picture Mr. B as a viable suspect. I'd known him for years, but only as our produce man. What did we really know about him? Was he violent? Did he have a temper? I had a sudden image of his reddened, furious face when he realized who was sitting in the dining room that day. And with Tim so busy and me in and out, he could have had time to put something in Parisi's food.

"There's something else, SIL." Sofia stopped typing and looked over at me. "Your intruder was somebody who knows the restaurant and who would know where to find the breaker box and the pantry key."

I shivered at the memory of that dark hallway and the pantry door closing behind us, but another thought swiftly overtook that one. "If he's the intruder, he also took the trash." I shook my head. "I'm having trouble buying it. I mean, is Mr. B smart enough to work that all out? To trap us that way and then take away the trash in case of food evidence?"

"That's what we've got to find out. We need to talk to him." Sofia saved her notes and turned toward me in her chair. "And by 'we,' I mean you."

"Why me?"

"You know him. He's comfortable with you. He might let something slip."

"Great. First, I have to deal with Mikey G's scary father and have his damn kid sneer at me. Now you want me to face down a possible murderer."

"All in a day's work, Bernardo. Look, we have to do this. For one thing, you have exactly five days before Nina LaGuardia pounces for an interview."

"I was trying not to think about that."

"You don't have a choice. You've got to clear the restaurant and everybody connected with it." She cast me an innocent look. "Think of Isabella."

"What about her?"

"Well, a murder at the Casa Lido might sell some mysteries, but I don't see it doing much for your literary work-in-progress."

Now there was a troubling thought. I had dreamed of publishing this book under my own name, but if that name were tainted, how many editors would be willing to take a chance on me? Now I had one more reason to clear up Parisi's death. "You don't play fair, SIL."

"That's why I usually win." She handed me a sheet of paper. "Here. While you've been whining, I made a list of questions for Mr. B."

I looked down at the paper and back at Sofie. " 'Where were you on the afternoon of the murder?' Really, Sofe?"

"So edit them. But the important thing is to talk to him."

"I'll talk to him, but only in the restaurant, preferably with somebody else on the premises. And it has to be a *conversation.* If he thinks I'm interrogating him, he'll clam up." I paused. "And if he did it, he could be dangerous."

"Focus on his daughter, then. Start by asking about her; people love talking about their kids. Then you can lead up to the television show."

I rested my head in my hands, trying to gather thoughts that were too slippery to hold.

"What's the matter?" Sofia asked.

I looked up at her. "It's just that none of this fits together."

"That's 'cause you're used to writing the plot." She grinned. "This one's writing you."

"C'mon, Sofe. Look at what we've got. A jewelry receipt, some dried-up herbs, and an Internet video. Aside from the fact that it's all circumstantial, there's nothing cohesive here. Certainly not enough to build a case on."

But Sofia talked right over me, ticking off her points on her fingers. "We've also got a mysterious break-in and some missing garbage. Right there, that's suspicious. Now throw in a protective father, a sketchy wife, a chef who has a history with said sketchy wife and who faints when he sees the body—"

"Hey, I told you Tim is—"

She held up her hand. "Let me finish. And I'm not ruling out Mr. Down on the Bayou, either."

"We don't know if he even knew Parisi."

"So we'll find out." She looked at me, her expression serious. "And you're positive we can rule out Lori? I know she's your friend, but—"

"Absolutely. I was with her the whole time. She went over to Parisi's table exactly once, and that was to clear up his stuff. When I went back to give him the check, he was already sick and sweating." I shook my head. "The timing just isn't right. And anyway, what possible reason would Lori have to kill Parisi? It's ludicrous."

My sister-in-law's glossy lips were set in a stubborn line. "We can't ignore the fact that she was there."

"So was I, for that matter."

Sofie dismissed me with a flutter of her slender hand. "Don't be ridiculous. The only way you can kill people is in print."

"Thanks. I think."

She went on. "Listen. Our list aside, I'm beginning to think we need to look at other people who weren't on the scene. Rosen, Mikey G and his father, and anybody else who might have had a grudge against him."

"But depending on what the tox results are, that person needed access to Parisi within a specific window of time. We have to find out how he spent his day up to the minute he walked into the restaurant at three thirty." I shook my head. "I don't know. I think his 'special water' had a little something extra in it."

"Could be. When I made the rounds of the food stands on the boardwalk, no one remembered Parisi eating anything. I think one of us should ask Danny if the police found the water bottle on the body."

I narrowed my eyes at her. "'One of us'?"

"Okay, you. I don't want to push it."

As she talked, I had a sudden image of a different sort of bottle. "Holy crap. I can't believe I forgot the water."

"That's what we're talking about, right? His water bottle."

"No, he ordered a bottle of San Pellegrino with his lunch. He finished it, and I threw the bottle into the recycling bin. I'm not even sure I remembered to tell the police that when they questioned me."

"Did you open it for him?"

I shook my head. "No. I brought it out to him sealed. I know that for sure. He opened it and poured the water into his glass."

"Which means that anybody in the dining room could have slipped something into either the bottle or his glass."

"Or into his tea or his salad, or even the salad dressing."

Sofie tapped away on her keyboard. "I need to get all this down." She stopped and looked up at me. "Did the police take the recycled containers?"

I shut my eyes, thinking back to that night. "Yes. I remember a uniformed officer carrying the bin." I breathed a small sigh. "They're probably testing everything in it, but—"

"But what?"

"I'm betting that San Pellegrino bottle is clean. It's much easier to drop something into a water glass than into a narrow bottle. And anyway, that glass was sterilized in a dishwasher, along with his plate, teacup, silverware, and the gravy boat that held the dressing." I rubbed my temples. "This is making my brain hurt."

"What about his hot water?" Sofia asked.

"You mean for the tea? I boiled it and poured it into

his cup myself. Then I brought the carafe back to the kitchen."

"Too many liquids," Sofia grumbled. "Okay, let's walk through this. If his salad, tea, dressing, or water was poisoned, the murderer is most likely somebody who was in the restaurant."

"Or," I said, finishing the thought, "if the poison was in his own water bottle, it's anybody who might have had access to it." I groaned. "Without those autopsy results, there's so much we don't know."

"Okay, Vic. Maybe we don't know how or what, but something killed that guy. Those broken blood vessels in his eyes prove it."

"And if you dare tell Danny I told you that, you are dead, sister."

Sofia rolled her eyes. "As if I couldn't take you with one hand." She pushed her chair back from her desk. "Okay, let's regroup and get our assignments lined up. You're talking to Biaggio."

"Reluctantly, but, yes, I'll talk to him. Hey, I forgot to ask you if you got in to see Anne McCrae."

"No." Sofia shook her head. "I thought I could catch her after her regular exercise class, but she skipped out on me."

"Okay, I'll also talk to Her Honor the mayor; she's been trying to get me to come to her book group, so I'll have an excuse. And at least she tolerates me." I pulled out my pad to make some notes while Sofia scribbled a few of her own.

"Meanwhile, I'm gonna do some research," she said. "Starting with Cal, Mikey G, and his possibly connected father."

"Oh, speaking of connections, my agent has a contact who might be able to tell us about Harvey Rosen—what kind of terms he and Parisi were on and how close

Rosen and Angie really were." I pointed with my pen. "And let's not forget that Tim said Angie claims Parisi was cheating on her. I'd sure like to know who that mystery woman is, because that's another name to add to our list."

Sofia sighed. "Now *my* brain hurts. How many people wanted this guy dead?"

"Only one, SIL. It's just a matter of finding out who."

Chapter Thirteen

On Monday morning I headed over to the mayor's office. Our little town hall shared space with the police department, and I had a vague sense of guilt as I entered the building. My brother might be willing to turn a blind eye to my detecting, but what about his superiors? I slipped down the corridor toward her office, relieved not to see anyone in a blue uniform.

"Victoria. It's lovely to see you again." Mayor Anne McCrae stretched out a hand devoid of rings and nail polish and gripped mine firmly. Her browned callused hands represented days spent in the sun, whether on the beach or in her award-winning garden. A shore person born and bred, Anne was in her midforties and single, but with her salt-and-pepper hair and pale gray eyes, she seemed a decade older. She cared for little beyond her town, its beaches, and her regular tennis game. She would have found a husband an encumbrance, and there were times that I (and probably much of the town) wondered whether she even liked men.

"You too, Anne," I said. "How have you been?"

"Oh, you know what it's like a week before the season begins. I've been as busy as those bees in my *Buddleia* bushes. Sit down, please." She leaned forward on her desk and clasped her hands together. "So, have I finally talked you into speaking with my book group?"

"Yes, if you don't mind waiting until the fall." *And may September never come.* "I'm back to do some research about our family business, and I've been helping out at the restaurant. You know how busy we are during the season."

"I do, yes," she said slowly, and then paused. "However, I hear the Casa Lido has not been very busy these days."

Way to turn the tables, Anne. I cleared my throat. "Yes, that's true. Things have been quiet at the restaurant lately."

"It's a shame what happened."

I pondered what she meant. Was it a shame that the restaurant was losing business or a shame that Parisi died there? "Yes . . . yes, it was."

"Such a vital man." She sighed. "With such vision and so full of ideas."

He was full of ideas, all right, and none of them good. Yet here was our brisk, no-nonsense town leader sighing over a guy who might have brought ruin to our little beach community. I glanced at her wistful face, and a thought struck me: Was Anne McCrae Parisi's mystery mistress? It might explain why she was so willing to hand us over to RealTV. Admittedly, it was hard to imagine this weather-beaten woman a match for the polished producer. Without realizing it, I shook my head.

"Don't you agree?" Anne asked.

"Oh. Well, no, Anne, I don't. I'm sorry he's dead, of course, but I wouldn't have wanted *The Jersey Side* to film here."

She pressed her palms against the top of her desk and leaned forward in her chair. "I know your family was against it, too. They made that clear enough with that silly protest."

I would never learn anything if this meeting became adversarial, so I pasted a smile on my face. "Yes, it's true. My family was against the show filming in Oceanside, as were a number of other merchants." I crossed my fingers in my lap as I was about to engage in another round of lies. "But if it turns out the show ends up filming here, we'll make the best of it."

"That's not likely to happen now, is it? Something that would have been such a boon to our economy, too. Well, we'll find some other way to survive. We always do, don't we?" She cocked her head, and her eyes narrowed. "I do hope we can say the same for the Casa Lido, though."

"Me too, Anne." I couldn't quite make out the mayor's tone, but I would swear she was relishing the Casa Lido's troubles. We were a small gold mine for the town, and it wouldn't make sense for her to take delight in our downfall. Since she had steered me to the subject, I figured it was time to throw caution to the winds and come clean. I was sick of telling lies anyway. "In fact, that's part of the reason I'm here. If it turns out that Gio Parisi died from more than a simple heart attack, it's going to look very bad for the restaurant. It's no secret that people are already staying away."

"But how can I help you?" There was so much caution in her tone, there should have been an amber light blinking over her head. So much for sincerity.

"I'm hoping you can answer a few questions for me. You spent some time with him on the day he died. Did he seem ill in any way?"

She shook her head firmly. "Absolutely not. He was the picture of health. As I said, he was a vital man. And an attractive one. But what he saw in that wife of his, I'll never know."

Don't stop now, Anne. "You know, she grew up near here," I said.

"Hmmph," she said with a little sniff. "All I know is that she must have called him three or four times during his appearance on the boardwalk."

"Is that so?" I tried hard to keep my tone neutral. "Lots of husbands and wives call each other during the day to stay in touch."

"Checking up on him is more like it. Where was he? What was he doing next? When would he be home?" She clucked her tongue like a disapproving hen.

It took all my control not to grab my notebook from my purse and start writing. Why would Angie be checking on Parisi's every move? Was she afraid he was with his mistress? I glanced at Anne's frowning and, frankly, rather plain face and had trouble believing she was the producer's mystery girlfriend. But who was? In any case, it was time to turn the questions back to the heart of the matter.

"Did you notice whether he had anything to eat or drink up at the boardwalk?" I couldn't take Fifi's word for gospel on this one, and I knew Sofie couldn't have gotten to every stand and restaurant.

But our mayor shook her head again. "No. He mentioned that he was trying to eat more healthily, and he was sipping a water bottle. But that was it." She looked me full in the face. "Perhaps he was allergic to something he ate in the restaurant."

"That's possible, of course."

"Or perhaps it was food poisoning."

I felt my insides tighten with anger, but I couldn't afford to unleash my inner Nonna. Not now, anyway. "There's no possibility of that, Anne." And no possibility of finding out, now that the trash was gone.

"Well, we'll know after the autopsy results are in."

She gestured to the door of her office. "I should really step out and ask the chief if we have any more information about that."

It was a clear signal, and I didn't think I'd get much more from her today anyway. I stood up and reached out my hand. "Thank you for seeing me today, Anne."

I winced as she gripped my hand. "You're very welcome. And let's plan to have you come speak to the group after Labor Day, all righty?"

"Absolutely. I'll put it on my calendar." I turned to go, and it was then that Mayor McCrae dropped her little bomb.

"And, Victoria, do keep me posted on how the restaurant is doing, won't you?" She smiled in a practiced politician sort of way and paused. "Because if your grandmother and parents decide to sell, I have a very interested buyer. He's hoping to turn the space into a Starbucks—and won't that be a lucrative little business!"

I blinked, unable to utter a word. She swept around from behind her desk and held open her office door. "Now, do stay in touch, hon. And have a nice day!"

Still reeling from the fallout of my encounter with Mayor McCrae, I stopped at the laundry to pick up all the linens Tim and I had dirtied in the pantry, hoping to drop them back at the restaurant before my grandmother noticed. When I got back to the Casa Lido, there was a visitor waiting for me outside. From a distance, her small stature and short denim skirt gave her a youthful look, but once I got close, I could see that she was over fifty. Her blond hair was cut in a chin-length bob, her bangs reaching almost to her bright blue eyes. Her makeup was expertly but heavily applied. The whole effect was one of a woman trying too hard.

"May I help you?" I asked. "We're closed for business on Mondays."

"I'm looking for Victoria Rienzi," she said.

"I'm Victoria."

She held out her hand. "I'm Emily Haverford. A friend of Gio Parisi."

I had barely taken in this information when my eyes were riveted by a flash of silver at her neck. If only Sofia were here. Knowing I couldn't whip out my cell phone to take a picture, I made a point of memorizing the piece, but my gut told me it came from Tiffany. And I'd lay my father's odds it was the same one purchased at the Red Bank store the day Parisi died. I was imagining Parisi with a younger girlfriend, not one his own age. I unlocked the door and held it open for her. "Please come in."

"Thank you. Is there somewhere we can talk?"

"Pretty much anywhere." I dropped the laundry boxes in a corner and gestured to our family table at the back of the dining room. "Over there is fine. Would you like something to drink? Water or coffee?"

"No, thanks." She sat down and shrugged off her sweater, and my eyes were again drawn to the silver chain around her neck.

"Beautiful necklace," I said.

She smiled slightly. "Thank you. You must be wondering why I'm here."

Not just that. Where'd you get that dang jewelry? "Yes. I mean, I'm not sure how I can help you."

She leaned across the table, her voice urgent. "You found him, didn't you? Do you think someone killed him?"

"Wow, you get straight to the point, don't you?" But I refrained from answering her question.

She tapped the table nervously. "I have to know. It's eating me up inside."

"I'm sorry, but I'm not sure if I can help you. It's not like I knew him. I hadn't ever met him until the day he . . . walked in here."

"I have to know about his last hours. It had been a while since I'd seen him." She twisted a ring on her right hand, but her left was bare. Not married, I thought. Maybe divorced? "You see, I'd known him before. He left me for . . . her." She shook her head.

Angie strikes again. Join the club, lady. I looked at Emily Haverford with sympathy but resisted the urge to share what we had in common.

"I'm sorry. Mrs. Parisi was here asking me the same things, but there isn't a lot I can tell you." Certainly not what Danny had told me about the broken blood vessels in his eyes. I took a breath. "He came in and had a salad, water, and a cup of tea. By the end of the meal, he was sweaty and sick. He asked for the men's room, and that was the last I saw of him until I found him outside."

I met her intense blue stare. "Would you mind describing what he looked like when you found him?" she asked.

"I'm not even sure I should."

She gripped my arm. "Please. I cared for him deeply."

I wondered if "cared for him deeply" was subtext for "we were still sleeping together." I sighed. "It wasn't pretty. He was facedown in his own vomit."

She dropped her head in her hands, and I felt a rush of pity for her. "Look, Emily, until the results of his death are released, no one knows for sure how he died. Right now it looks like a heart attack."

"But you're a mystery writer. You've done research about these things. Do you think he was murdered or not?"

I uttered four words that were completely truthful. "I can't really say."

She hesitated, clearly struggling. "Listen, there's something . . ." She stopped and shook her head. "No, it wouldn't be fair, and much as I hate her—"

Her could be only one person. I put my hand on her arm. "If you have information that's relevant to his death, you need to tell the police." *And me. Tell me.*

Her startling eyes locked onto my own. "Gio told me that Anjelica had only married him for his money."

Yeah, that's a shocker. Then again, a man might say anything when he's cheating on his wife. I had to keep an open mind, but my curiosity was threatening to burn a hole in the tablecloth. "Is that so?" I asked.

She nodded. "In fact, he had a stringent prenup drawn up. She wouldn't have gotten much in a divorce." A pained expression crossed her face. "Not that he would have left her."

"So Anjelica stands to gain by his death?"

"Enormously. He has no other next of kin. He never had children, and both his parents are dead."

Much as I wanted to believe Angie a murderer, I had to ask the next question. "What about you?"

She looked at me steadily. "As far as I know, he left me a small provision. We did spend a number of years together, after all. But I loved him." Her voice broke. "I was *not* interested in his money."

"I'm sorry," I said. And I really was. This detective stuff was weighing heavily on my conscience. Lying, nosing into people's business, hurting them unnecessarily—what else would I be reduced to before this was over?

Emily sighed and slid a business card across the table. "If you're able to tell me more at some point, would you please call me?" She stood and put her sweater back on.

I tucked the card in my pocket and stood up. I reached out my hand. "Sorry I couldn't be more help."

"That's okay." She ducked her head to search for

something in her purse, but I could see that it was an excuse to compose herself. She gripped her keys and looked at me again; in that moment, her age showed clearly in her face. Without another word, she turned and left the restaurant.

I pulled my phone from my pocket and hit speed dial. "Sofie, you're not gonna believe this one. Parisi's girlfriend showed up at the restaurant. And she just handed me Angie's motive on a silver platter."

Chapter Fourteen

When I got back to the cottage, Sofia was already waiting for me, her laptop and red folder in tow. We had barely sat down before she started.

"Tell me everything," she said.

"There's a lot to tell, because I saw Anne McCrae, too."

Sofie leaned across the table. "You can tell me about her later. It's Parisi's girlfriend I want to know about."

"Trust me, she's no girl. She's fifty if she's a day."

"He was cheating on his wife with an *older* woman?"

"Not older. His age. And she knew him before."

Sofia narrowed her eyes. "So?"

"*So* they were together a long time, and he left her for Angie."

"Don't make it right," Sofia said, shaking her head. "He was a married man." She looked at me. "You want to excuse her because you have something in common with her: Angie took your man, too."

"Thanks for the reminder, Sofe. I'm now officially in cringe mode."

She grinned. "Sorry. But we can't let our personal feelings get in the way of the investigation."

"Right, except this isn't a real investigation. And while I'd love to get into the morality of the situation, there's more. Emily told me that Angie signed a prenup that would have left her with a pittance." I pointed to the red folder. "So add Lady Anjelica to the list." I indulged in a brief fantasy in which I detailed Angie's capture to Nina LaGuardia on national TV and couldn't help smiling. "After all," I said, "who else would have access to his 'special water' besides his wife?"

Sofia's expression was grim. "His mistress."

"Maybe. I will say that Emily claimed she hadn't seen him in a while, but she *was* wearing a lovely silver necklace. In fact, is your computer on? Pull up the Tiffany site, okay?"

In two clicks, the page opened. "Got it," she said.

"Geez, that was quick."

She shrugged. "It's in my favorites."

"Of course it is. Will you click on the necklaces for me?"

"I'm already on the page." Sofia turned to look at me. "That wench was wearing a piece of Tiffany, wasn't she?" She pointed to the screen. "Dollars to doughnuts it's the same one Parisi bought last Monday. Hang on." She clicked through several pages and stopped. "I bet it's on this page."

"How the heck did you know it was one of these?" Clearly, Watson was out-Sherlocking Sherlock.

"It's pretty simple, really. Tiffany's been skewing to a younger audience. I knew a woman her age wouldn't be wearing a heart or an ice-cream cone."

"You're right." I pointed to a simple chain-link necklace. "That's the one."

Sofia pulled the receipt from the folder and held it next to the computer screen. "Same item number. Same description. Unless it's a huge coincidence, she saw him the day before he died. And we just caught her in a big fat lie."

"That doesn't make her a murderer," I said.

"But it's suspicious, SIL, and you know it. And I'd like to know if she's getting anything in that will."

"Actually, she told me he left her a small bequest. So that lets her out of a motive."

The pity on my sister-in-law's face was evident. "And I thought you were a fricken mystery writer. You never heard of a crime of passion?"

"But you didn't see her, Sofe. She was really broken up about his death. I would swear her grief was real."

"Her grief might be real. But she *lied*, Vic. She told you she hadn't seen him in a while. Yet she's wearing a shiny new necklace that he bought the day before he died. If she lied about that, she might be lying about other things. For all we know, she might be making a bundle from his death."

I pulled out my notebook and jotted some questions. "I wish we could find out the provisions of that will."

"Whether we do or don't, Haverford goes on the list."

"I guess so," I said reluctantly. "But she wasn't in the restaurant."

"That wouldn't matter if she put something in his water."

"A minute ago you said it was a crime of passion; now you're saying it's premeditated. Make up your mind."

"Either way you look at it, Vic, she was a scorned woman. Her longtime lover leaves her for a younger woman. He takes up with her again, but doesn't leave his wife." She shook her head. "It amazes me how stupid some women can be."

"Are you talking about me or Emily?"

Sofia merely raised one brow in response, an answer I interpreted as "both."

I scribbled more notes on my pad.

"In any case, we need to find out more about Emily Haverford, right?"

I dug into my jeans pocket and slid her card across the table. "Here's one place to start."

Sofia studied the card. "All this says is 'human resources.' That could mean anything. And there's no firm listed."

"Maybe she's a consultant of some kind."

"Wouldn't it say that?" She rubbed the card between her fingers. "This card's not real good paper stock."

"So?"

"So I don't know yet." She slipped the card into the red folder. "But I'm gonna do some digging; something's not right about this." She looked up at me expectantly. "What else we got?"

"Well, our esteemed mayor confirmed that Parisi had nothing to eat or drink up at the boardwalk, but he did sip from his water bottle. He also told her he was trying to eat healthy, which was borne out by his choice of a salad with dressing on the side."

"Didn't you tell me he didn't want the bread, either?"

"That's right—he made me take it back."

Sofia shook her head. "Bread from the best Italian bakery in Brooklyn, and he doesn't want it."

"No accounting for taste. And here's another tidbit: Anne said that Angie called Parisi three or four times that day."

"Huh." Sofie snorted. "She's probably checking up on him to make sure he is where he says he is."

"Maybe. But I can't help feeling there's more to it than that." I grinned at my sister-in-law. "You know, for a while there I was actually wondering if Anne might be Parisi's girlfriend."

"Ha!" She slammed her palm down on the table.

"That's a good one. Her skin's like leather. And that awful gray hair. She needs a good colorist."

"Okay, point taken. But it's not like Emily Haverford is any prize, either. I did learn something else about Anne, though: Her Honor the Avaricious will apparently stop at nothing to bring the bucks to Oceanside Park."

"What do you mean?"

"Well, she made a point of asking me about the restaurant; she said she'd heard we'd lost customers."

"So?"

"So this—as I'm on my way out the door, she informs me that if the Casa Lido goes under, she's got a buyer for the restaurant. A buyer who wants to turn a seventy-year-old family business into a Starbucks."

Sofia let out a slow breath. "Your grandmother will have a cow. Make that two cows."

"Which is why I won't be sharing that news with her. But I feel like it's important, for some reason." I drummed my fingers on the tabletop while I thought it through. "Hey, Sofe," I said slowly, "if you wanted to drive somebody out of business, what better way to do it than drop a dead body on the premises?"

Her mouth dropped open so far, I could count her pretty white teeth. "You can't really believe that she killed Parisi just to make the Casa Lido close down? That doesn't make any sense. She *wanted* the show to film here."

"So she says. But I'm not taking anything at face value. Don't forget, she also has a problem with my family. She'd probably love to see us go down."

"But, Vic, if she's the murderer, wouldn't it follow that she's the intruder, too? You said yourself that it had to be somebody who knew their way around."

"She's been in the restaurant a number of times. But more important, our blueprints are on file in town hall, where she'd have ready access to them."

"And she just happened to find the key to the pantry?" Sofie shook her head. "It's a reach, SIL, and you know it."

"But she was with him up on the boardwalk. Close enough to put something in his water. She had opportunity and possibly motive."

Sofia held up a fist and released her fingers one by one, starting with her thumb. "So did Tim. So did Angie. So did Mr. B, and so did Emily Haverford."

I held up my pinkie finger. "And Annie makes five."

Sofia sighed. "We're supposed to be *eliminating* names from the list, not adding them."

"We're stuck," I said. "Without the autopsy and toxicology results, we're flying blind. Assuming he was poisoned, unless we know how it was delivered, the field of suspects is wide-open."

Sofia nodded. "If you know how, you know who."

"Exactly. We've got to figure out what killed him. And how it got into his system." *And please let it be that water bottle,* I thought, *because anything else spells doom for the Casa Lido.*

Chapter Fifteen

Since Tuesday was Mr. Biaggio's regular delivery day, I got to the restaurant early in hopes of catching him. Much to my grandmother's chagrin ("Only desperate people give out coupons!"), we'd begun running some two-for-one luncheon specials, so the afternoons gave us some work to do. But things got quiet in the evenings; it was almost as if people were afraid to be in the restaurant after dark, and we couldn't survive on lunch trade alone. I stood in the doorway taking in the familiar sights—the dark-paneled woodwork and wide-planked floors, the old-fashioned tables and chairs, and the cheerful red-checked curtains, which now looked forlorn. It wasn't so long ago I'd wanted to run from this place, and now I couldn't bear the thought of losing it.

"You okay?"

Tim's voice came from behind me, almost as though I'd been expecting it. "Yeah, I guess. Just a little worried."

He rested his hand on my shoulder. "Me too. But I think we'll get through it, Vic." He motioned me in ahead of him.

"From your lips to God's ears. So, Chef Tim, what's cookin' for lunch?"

Tim cocked his head, and an errant curl brushed his

forehead. My fingers itched to stroke it back into place; instead I jammed my hands in my jeans pockets. "Ah, you're gonna love today's menu," he said. "My hand-cut *tagliatelle* with your grandmother's walnut pesto, roasted asparagus with prosciutto, and pork medallions in a balsamic glaze."

"Sounds amazing." It also sounded like an opportunity, if I could sweet-talk my ex into letting me help him. "Hey, Tim? Is Nando coming in today?"

"Nah. I can pretty much handle lunch alone. I can always call him in if it looks like we'll get busy." He glanced outside at the empty sidewalks. "Which I don't think is gonna happen."

"Listen, can I give you a hand prepping? I can trim the asparagus, grab some basil from the garden—whatever you need."

A wicked grin spread across Tim's face. "Babe, what I need is not out in that garden." He caught my hand, but I pulled it back.

"You're terrible with rules. You know that, don't you?" But I couldn't help smiling, because despite everything, he was still my Tim. *More fool you*, said a voice in my head. "You haven't answered my question. Can I help you today?"

"Yes," he said, "If you're a good girl and listen to everything I tell you to do."

"Ha. Fat chance, dude."

"It was worth a shot," he said with a grin. "Come, then, lass, and join me in the kitchen. And tie up that hair, or I'll make you wear a net."

As I washed up, Tim brought the large wooden pasta board over to the island countertop. I grabbed the eggs and then measured out the flour and salt. I watched as Tim created a "flour mountain" and then hollowed out the top so that it looked like a mini volcano. Pasta-making in the restaurant is a time-honored process; Nonna must have taught Tim when he was still on her good side. He looked up at me, his eyes a pale gray in the bright sun of the kitchen. "Eggs, please. One at a time and no shells."

I dropped the eggs into the flour volcano, pausing to admire their shiny golden yolks. "Is that a pretty sight, or what?"

Tim reached over and tapped the end of my nose. "It's a beautiful sight," he said.

I tried to approximate a stern expression. "Don't you have some kneading to do?"

He laughed and started working the eggs into the flour, using only his index finger. It was a pleasure to watch his skilled hands gently scoop flour from the inner edges of the circle and work his way outward until he had a beautiful ball of dough. I reached out to pinch a small piece and got my hand slapped.

"C'mon. I just want a taste!"

"Get your hands outta my dough." He wrapped the first ball and set it aside, then measured out another pile of flour and salt. Just as we were finishing the fourth batch, the back door banged open, and Mr. Biaggio appeared, carrying a wooden crate of vegetables.

"Is that my asparagus, Mr. B?" Tim called.

"*Sì*, Timoteo. Nice and fresh, like always." He set the crate down on the counter and swiped the back of his hand across his red face. "Hello, Victoria. *Come stai?*"

"*Bene*, Mr. B. Thank you." I stared at the pudgy grocer, trying to imagine him slipping something into Gio Parisi's salad. He pulled a bandanna from his back pocket and wiped his face again.

"Is it getting hot out there?" I glanced at Tim, who was carefully flouring the pasta board. Rolling and cutting the pasta would take forever, and at this rate I'd lose the chance to talk to Mr. Biaggio alone.

"Yes, like summer already." He shrugged. "Well, the season starts soon. And then we will all be busy, right?"

"We hope." I peered into the vegetable crate. "Is this the whole delivery?"

"That's all Tim ask for," Mr. B said. "But I got the basil on the truck if you need it."

Tim paused just as he was about to unwrap one of the balls of dough. "I'm not sure. I haven't decided how many batches of pesto I should make." He furrowed his brow, counting in his head, looking so adorable that I was distracted from my purpose. As I struggled to get my head back in the game, I was struck with an idea.

"Nonna's already got basil going in the garden, Tim." I smiled at our produce man. "No offense, Mr. B."

I knew Tim's preference would be stuff that came directly from our garden, and I watched him hesitate. "They're young plants, though," I said carefully, "so I'm not sure how much is there. One of us should probably go check."

"I will." Tim grabbed a plastic bag from the closet and looked at Mr. Biaggio. "Can you hang out for a minute?"

I sent a little prayer up to whatever saint was in charge of gardens in the hopes that Tim would be picking basil for a while. But once he was out the door, I got nervous, wondering how to begin. Mr. B began emptying the crate; I brought the asparagus over to the sink for washing. "These look good," I said. "I could almost eat them raw."

The produce man grinned. "Very sweet. They make a nice dish."

Okay, I complimented his vegetables. What next? I couldn't plunge right in to the subject of his daughter, but my time with him was limited. How long would it take Tim to pick basil?

"So, business is good?" I ventured.

"Can't complain," he said. "I'm trying to get some new accounts, though, because I got the tuition in September."

Thank you for that opening, Mr. B. "Where is your daughter going to school?"

"She finish at the community college this week, but in the fall, she go to Rutgers."

"Oh, that's my alma mater."

"Cosa?" he asked.

"I mean, that's where I went to college."

"Such a good school, no?" He smiled broadly, his pride all over his face. "I already buy the sweatshirt, the sticker for my car." He pointed outside, still smiling. "And I put the magnet on the truck."

My determination weakened in the face of Mr. B's paternal pride, but I had to press on. Tim might be back any moment. I smiled. "That's great. I know that she had, well, a difficult year."

In slow motion, his smile faded and his face hardened. His hands were bunched into fists at his sides. I swallowed, my mouth dry as I prepared myself for the blast.

But instead of shouting, he dropped his voice to harsh rasp. "What those kids do to her is unforgivable. And that man—no, that *animale*—who show it for everybody to see: He get what he deserve," he said, his last word no more than a whisper. Then he crossed himself. "May God forgive me."

"I understand why you would feel that way. I mean, none of us were fans of the guy. Not that we would have wished him dead, of course," I added. *Good going there, Vic. Way to win him over with your moral superiority.* I took a breath in preparation for my next question. "You were here that day, right?"

The look of contempt in his dark eyes was replaced by wariness. "*Sì.* You know I was here for the protest. I already tell that to the police." He lifted the empty crate and held it against his barrel chest.

But he was also here much later delivering vegetables. Did the police know about that? Or about the Internet video and the *Jersey Side* connection? I made a mental note to ask Danny.

"Right," I said, "but you came back later with a delivery, remember?" An awfully late delivery, I thought, and one timed exactly when Parisi was eating his lunch. Could Mr. B have followed him here that day?

"Victoria, why you asking me these questions?" Sweat broke out on his forehead, his large hands tightened on the wooden box, and I suddenly wondered whether Tim was within screaming distance. But I wasn't the only one fearful. Mr. Biaggio blinked nervously, swallowed once, and hugged the crate to himself as though he needed protection.

"Oh, no reason, Mr. B." I forced a smile. "It's the mystery writer in me, I guess. Just wondering what happened to the guy."

"It was a heart attack, no?" He nodded, his eyes still afraid.

"Probably," I said. From the corner of my eye I could see Tim approaching with the plastic bag. While I was glad I had a means to get rid of him, I'd be in hot pasta water with my grandmother if he'd stripped too many of those plants. "Oh, look, here's Tim." I pushed open the back door, glad to get out into the air.

Mr. B followed. While he and Tim talked over the next delivery, I mentally replayed my conversation. Mr. B had a clear motive, two if you counted the fact he was one of the protesters. He was protective of his daughter and obviously hated the dead producer. He was here that day and got spooked when I reminded him of it. He was afraid of something; of that, I had no doubt.

Tim went back to the kitchen and I turned to follow, but Mr. Biaggio laid a sweaty palm on my arm. "Victoria," he whispered. "What happened to that Parisi, it was the hand of God, I think."

Not God's hand, Mr. B, but quite possibly yours.

Chapter Sixteen

*B*ack in the kitchen, I prepped the asparagus and basil while Tim rolled out the thin sheets of pasta dough. Once they were the right consistency, they would still have to rest before cutting.

"Tim, should we get that pesto started while the dough dries?" I shook the basil leaves over the sink and twisted off the stems.

"We?" Tim cleared a spot on the island for the last batch of dough, and I found myself admiring his arms as he worked my grandmother's giant rolling pin.

"Yes, 'we.' Have you looked at the time?" I started tearing the basil leaves into a colander.

"Just keep that basil comin', okay?"

He came up behind me and peered over my shoulder, his face close enough to mine that his morning stubble brushed my cheek. I turned to face him. "Are you checking out my basil leaves?"

"Among other things." His voice had a lazy quality that had always had a hypnotic effect on me. He rested his hands against the sink on either side of me, his arms brushing mine. I put my wet hands against his T-shirt, and he curled his own around them.

"Oh, Tim." I sighed. "This is such a bad idea."

He rested his forehead against mine. "Why?" he

whispered, and letting go of my hands, he slid his arms around my waist.

The sensations were sweetly familiar—how he smelled, how his palms felt pressed against my back, and how his eyes looked when they darkened with emotion. I wanted to give in to them because, more than anything, being with Tim felt like home. A home I'd missed keenly during my years in New York. I lifted my face and closed my eyes, but the moment I did I flashed upon a pale face with creamy skin and raspberry lips. And just as I dropped my arms to my sides, the kitchen door swung open.

"What's cookin' in here, y'all?" Cal stood grinning, hands shoved in his jeans pockets, a mischievous look in his green eyes.

Tim stepped back, and I turned to the sink, my heart thumping. "Not much, Cal," I said, wondering if one of the conditions of being back in Jersey was lying my butt off all the time.

"That so, Victoria? You couldn't prove that by me. Not judging by what I see."

My face burning, I dropped my head over the sink, tearing basil leaves with frightening force.

"What are you talking about, Lockhart?" Tim growled.

Cal swept his hand across the kitchen. "Looks to me like you fixin' to make some *pasta fresca*."

I turned quickly from the sink. "How do you know what it's called?"

"Well, *cher*, you'd have no way of knowing this, but my mama's half Italian."

"You're kidding me!" For some reason, I found this heartening news and flashed Cal an answering smile.

He nodded. "We got Italians down Louisiana way; I'm one of 'em." He grinned. "Well, a quarter anyway."

At this, Tim gave a snort of skepticism. I motioned to him with my thumb. "He's half."

"That settles it then. You win, brother." He walked over to the refrigerator and took out a bottle of San Pellegrino.

"Hey, easy on the stock," Tim said. "Who said you could just come in here and take what you want?"

If Tim's question was laden with meaning, Cal either didn't get it or chose to ignore it. "My boss, Giulietta, that's who." He pointed to the pasta dough on the counter. "And I'm looking forward to a nice plate of pasta for my lunch."

"Get out of my kitchen, Lockhart. I won't say it again."

"I'm on my way." He paused with his hand on the door to look back at me. "Catch ya later, Victoria," he said, lifting the San Pellegrino bottle with a wink, and pushed back through the door.

"What is it with that guy?" Tim exploded. "He thinks he can just come and go whenever and wherever he wants. This is our restaurant, damn it."

I frowned in Tim's direction, but he didn't pick up on it. "Oh, it's 'ours,' is it?" I said. "Since when?" The edge in my voice finally got his attention.

"What do you mean?"

"You know what I mean. This restaurant belongs to the Rienzi family." I paused for effect. "It's not like you *married into it* or anything."

"C'mon, Vic. You know what I mean; I love this place. I grew up here."

"There's growing up and there's growing up, Tim." I sighed. "And I'm not sure you're grown-up enough for me. I must have been crazy to forget the rules, even for a minute."

"The hell with the rules!" He grabbed my hand. "Look at me. We still love each other, and you know it."

I gently pulled my hand from his and rested it against his cheek. "And I used to think that was enough. But now I know better."

With only a few twinges of guilt, I left Tim to finish the lunch prep on his own. I couldn't trust myself around him, plain and simple. According to my deal with Nina the TV reporter, I had less than two days to get to the bottom of Parisi's death. I couldn't afford any distractions. I stepped outside to call Sofia and fill her in on my conversation with Mr. B when I noticed a text from Josh:

> *Chaz says Rosen and Parisi on good terms despite difs. Rosen close to P's wife, but see pic he sent colleagues via e-mail.*

The photo was taken the day of the murder. It showed two handsome men, one dark and one fair, with the ocean in the background. The caption read: "On our honeymoon in Miami."

"Sofie," I said into the phone, "looks like we can eliminate a suspect. Rosen was getting married around the time that Parisi was killed."

"Are we sure that rules him out? Just because he's married doesn't mean he wasn't involved with Angie," she said.

I laughed. "Not an issue, Sofe. The bride's name is Michael."

"Go, Harvey. Now I get to take my red pen and put a great big line through his name. Did you talk to Biaggio?"

When I was finished summarizing the key points of that conversation, Sofia asked a question. "So you think he was being evasive about coming back to the restaurant that day?"

"Sort of. I'm not sure he told the police he came back a second time."

"But they'd know based on your interview and Tim's."

"True. But Mr. B clearly didn't want to talk about the fact that he was here just before Parisi was digging into that salad. And he was afraid, Sofe. That's for damn sure."

"Does afraid equal guilty?" she asked.

"Maybe. But here's the real question: What is he afraid *of*?"

After finishing my call, I thought about where we were. Gio Parisi had been dead exactly one week. The autopsy results had yet to be made public. And while we had a list of names and lots of supposition, we still had no idea who had killed him. If Danny was correct, the county prosecutor's office would be taking over the case, if they hadn't already. And I was likely to be questioned again; I had found the body, after all. My stomach turned over at the thought, particularly as there were little matters of interest—such as the Tiffany receipt and a bag of stolen garbage—that I had neglected to share with the Oceanside PD.

And my involvement in this case could well be compromising my brother's career; even if Danny's cop friends in town would protect him, I was pretty sure that blue wall of silence wouldn't extend to the prosecutor's office.

I turned to look over at the boardwalk and beyond that to a blue-green strip of sea that glittered in the sunlight. The Ferris wheel was making its slow revolution, and the smells of pizza and cotton candy were wafting across the street. The season was starting, and it would pick up momentum as fast as those rides out on the pier. Would the Casa Lido be part of it, as we had every summer? Or would we have to close our doors for good?

*   *   *

Our two-for-one special helped us fill a few tables during lunch, though I noticed they all seemed to be visitors, rather than regulars—visitors who likely hadn't heard that a man had dropped dead after eating at Table Five. Once Lori came in, I stopped to have a plate of *tagliatelle* with pesto; after one bite, I knew I could fault Tim for a number of things, but his cooking wasn't one of them. The pasta was light and eggy, but it held up to the swirl of flavors coating it—sweet basil, rich walnuts, and the sharply nutty imported parmesan. After going back for seconds, I made a mental note to do some extra bicycling this week to work off all these luscious carbs.

I stepped over to the bar to offer Cal a plate, but he'd already eaten.

"I'll say one thing for the Iron Chef in there," he said, pointing to the kitchen. "Pleasant he ain't, but the man can cook."

"Oh, he's pleasant enough when he wants to be." I narrowed my eyes at him but couldn't help a smile. "You just like goading him."

"Ya got me there." He cut a small piece of sandpaper, than wrapped it tightly around a pencil.

"What are you doing with that?"

He held it up. "This here's for sanding those tiny places in the wood." He pointed to a floral carving in the mantel over the bar. "See where I filled in with the new wood on that rosette? That's gotta be smoothed fine before I can stain it."

I went behind the bar and squinted at the spot where he was pointing. There was only a fine line where Cal had replaced the cracked piece. "Did you hand carve that?"

"Yup." He took the dowel and lightly sanded the raw wood, blowing the dust away after each pass.

"And do you think you can match that stain?"

"Pretty near," he said over his shoulder. "Might have to do some mixing to get it right."

"I had no idea this was such precise work." I walked back to the front of the bar and perched on a stool. "God knows what we're paying you."

He gave me a sideways grin, and my face grew warm.

"No Saints cap today?" I asked.

"Nope. Don't need it at the moment." He ran a hand through his hair, and it struck me that he was less shaggy than usual.

"Calvin Lockhart, you're sporting a new haircut."

"Guilty as charged, ma'am." He turned to face me and cocked his head. "No reason a man has to go 'round looking like he just rolled out of bed, now, is there?"

As he stood there in a snug black T-shirt with his arms crossed over a tightly muscled chest, it occurred to me that the sight of Cal rolling out of bed might not be such a bad thing. And despite the innocent tone in his voice, the look in his eyes suggested he was following the train of my impure thoughts. Come to think of it, he was more like the engineer.

"Well," I said primly, "you look very nice."

He nodded, but seemed to be enjoying a private joke.

I jumped down from the stool in an attempt to derail the conversation. "I should be getting back."

"Hang on there, Victoria. Before you go runnin' off—I got a question."

"Um, okay."

He set his hands down on the bar and leaned toward me. "I been hearing so much about this boardwalk of yours. I don't suppose you'd like to take a turn with me up there later on?"

"You mean like a date?" I blurted out.

He grinned and shook his head. "You Northern girls

aren't exactly subtle, are ya? Yes, *cher*. I mean like a date. You've heard of 'em, I take it?"

"Yes, I've heard of them." So the enigmatic Cal Lockhart was asking me out. An unforeseen development, surely, but one I could live with. He was fun, he was good-looking, and he had been here the day of the murder, possibly a suspect, and an evening together would afford me the opportunity to ask him some questions. At the very least, he might have seen something the rest of us had missed. And I would be safe; there were few places more public than the Oceanside boardwalk.

I met his amused green stare. "But I won't be taking a turn with you—you'll be taking one with *me*. It's my boardwalk, after all. And I know all the best spots."

He inclined his head and smiled. "I look forward to you showing them to me. How's six?"

"Six would be fine. We can meet outside the restaurant."

"Sounds good. I'm looking forward to learning all about your 'best spots.'" He turned back to his work, leaving me zero words and two pink cheeks.

As I walked back to the kitchen, I told myself that a date with Cal might help move the case forward. That a chance to talk to him alone might provide more information about his own background and explore the possibility that he knew Parisi. That it was all about the case.

So why was I so worried about what to wear?

Chapter Seventeen

I arrived at a few minutes after six to find Cal waiting for me. *Good start, dude. You don't keep a girl waiting.* But the Cal who stood outside the Casa Lido this evening was a far cry from the guy who worked on the bar during the day. His hair was combed back off his face and tucked behind his ears. He wore a crisp tailored shirt in a faded blue that set off his tanned skin, a pair of dark jeans, and black canvas shoes. As I got closer, I noticed he wasn't wearing the earring, but instead sported a vintage wristwatch. His rolled-up sleeves were the only vestige of Cal-the-woodworker, and I couldn't help noticing he had forearms to rival Tim's.

"'Evening, Victoria." He held out his hand, and it seemed the most natural thing in the world to take it. His broad palm was warm, and my fingers slipped easily through his. When he leaned in for a quick kiss on the cheek, he smelled so good, it disoriented me.

"Good evening," I said, struggling to get my equilibrium back.

"You're lookin' lovely."

"Thanks. I figured it was warm enough for a dress." Of course it was. And the fact that it showed off my legs was entirely coincidental. He was still holding my hand when Tim emerged from the restaurant sweaty, disheveled, and still wearing a bandanna on his head. The contrast between him and the neatly turned-out Cal was not lost on either man, as they eyed each other up and down. And was it my imagination that Cal's grip on my hand tightened just the tiniest bit?

Tim planted himself in front of me. "Where the hell are you two going?"

"Not that it's any of your business, brother, but Victoria and I were just headed up to the boardwalk there for a bite to eat, maybe even go on a couple of them rides." His accent got thicker by the word, and I knew he was trying to get Tim's goat.

I turned to Tim, expecting to bask in his disapproval, but to my shock (and a bit of dismay), he just smiled. "Oh," he said, "that sounds like fun. But you might want to go easy on the rides." He pointed to me. "The last time I took Vic on the Tilt-A-Whirl, she threw up all over my pants." His smile grew wider. "You two have fun now."

"We will," I called out, trying to sound cheerful through gritted teeth.

We crossed the street and walked up the ramp to the boardwalk. "Listen," I said, "about the throwing-up thing—"

"Hey, no worries about that, okay?" He pointed at his jeans. "They're washable. For future reference though, there are easier ways of separatin' a man from his pants."

I glanced sideways at him and raised an eyebrow. "Pleasanter ones, too."

He raised an eyebrow back. "Ms. Rienzi, I do b'lieve you've just said something naughty."

"Mr. Lockhart, it's that mind of yours that's naughty."

"I won't deny it. But right now it's my stomach that concerns me. What do you recommend?"

We stood at the top of the ramp, and I pointed to the

right. "That way lies the best pizza outside of north Jersey. To the left resides a sausage sandwich that rivals my nonna's. They also make a nice fried calamari."

"Squid and sausage it is, *cher*. Lead the way." As we walked, I pointed out my favorite spots for saltwater taffy and frozen custard.

"I haven't been up here in a long time," I said, "but I would know this place with my eyes closed."

He grinned. "All you gotta do is follow the smell."

"True enough. And if you inhale deeply right now, you should be picking up the fine scents of peppers, onion, and pork spiced with fennel, as we have reached our destination: Louie's Famous Subs."

We ordered at the counter and brought our food to a table that faced the ocean. I dunked a piece of calamari in Louie's fresh marinara and popped it in my mouth, savoring the competing textures of tender and crispy. "Ummm—oh, that was worth coming home for."

Cal took a bite of his sausage sandwich and nodded vigorously. "And that was worth comin' north for."

"Told you. Hey, what are you doing? Don't you like onions?"

I watched Cal carefully remove all the onions from his sandwich and push them to the side of his plate. "I like them fine, Victoria." He smiled, and I admired the crinkles at the corners of his eyes. "But not when I'm on a date with a lady."

"Ahh, I see. You don't want to offend, should we find ourselves in close quarters. Is that it? I think that's a bit presumptuous. Don't you?" I took a hearty, onion-laced bite of my own sandwich for emphasis.

"Girl, I admire your spirit." Cal held up his beer bottle in a toast and then forked the onions back into his roll.

As we finished our sandwiches and the rest of the

calamari, Cal asked me questions about my writing. They were thoughtful and respectful, and he didn't ask me to name a character after him—a request I got frequently from friends and acquaintances.

"So tell me about the new book," he said.

"Oh, yes, the new book. Well, it's a departure for me. I mean, I've branded myself as a mystery writer, and the series has been good to me—"

"But?"

I laughed. "You knew there was a 'but,' right?"

"There usually is." He took a long swig of his beer.

"It's just that I realized I wanted to write a different kind of book." I looked out over the ocean. "It's what writers call 'the book of your heart.' It's the one you're aching to write, even if nobody will publish it."

"It's a tough business, ain't it?"

"My God, yes. Don't get me wrong. I'm grateful for my success. Me and Bernardo—that's my detective— we're a pretty formidable team."

He grinned. "But." He held out his beer to me, and I took a sip. "It sounds to me you got what your boy Bruce calls a 'hungry heart.'"

"Yes, exactly!" I held my hand out for his beer again and drank more deeply this time. "But don't we all?"

He nodded. "Most of my work's in restoration, but I make furniture of my own. One-of-a-kind pieces. That's where the real love is for me." He shook his head. "I appreciate a fine antique, and I love bringing a piece back to life. But for me it's the creation of something new."

"I'd like to see some of that work. Do you have any of it up here with you?" It occurred to me that I had no idea where Cal lived. Was he renting a place in town? There was so much about this guy I didn't know. Beyond that, he'd charmed me into talking a whole lot about myself (not difficult) and revealed little about himself.

Somehow I had to work the conversation back to the afternoon of the murder.

"No," he said. "It's all in storage."

"Do you sell them?"

"I sold one piece a couple of weeks ago. A garden bench. But for the hours I put into 'em, I normally have to charge too much to make a profit." He shrugged. "In the end, it's not worth it."

"Hmm. You need to take your stuff to Manhattan." I put the last piece of calamari in my mouth. "You would be amazed at what the market can bear in the city."

"Maybe." He grinned and pointed out toward the pier. "So, we gonna take a turn on that Ferris wheel, or what?"

I looked over at the giant ride and my stomach fluttered. "I don't know. As Tim made clear earlier in the evening, I'm not a fan of rides."

He caught my hand and lifted me to my feet. "Tell you what. You get up there and feel afraid, I'll jump down and stop the ride myself."

"Oh, right."

"C'mon, *cher*. It goes nice and slow. We'll get a great view of the water and plenty of time to talk. I promise I'll distract you."

Time to talk. Maybe time to talk about the murder and to find out if Cal had seen anything I'd missed.

To my chagrin, there wasn't much of a line for the Ferris wheel, and before I knew it, I was stepping shakily into an open seat. Cal slid in next to me, and the operator locked the bar into place. I gripped it with both hands.

Cal flashed me a sideways grin. "You okay there?"

I tightened my hands on the bar. "Uh, I'm good. Thanks." I looked over at him with a frozen smile. "It's not—"

I'd been about to say *as bad as I thought it would be,*

but then it was. We were lifted up and backward, and I had that familiar dropping sensation that I got on airplanes. The one that made me feel that I'd left my stomach somewhere on the ground and that I was flying away without it. My eyes darted for an escape, but Cal put an arm around my shoulders.

"It's okay. They're just raisin' the car to bring the next one up on the platform." He assumed the slow, gentle tone one might use with a skittish horse, and I frowned at him.

"I said I'm fine, okay? So if you're worried about your p-pants—" The car jerked upward, and I squeezed my eyes shut. "Oh my God, what the hell are they doing?"

"Victoria, open your eyes. They're just filling up the cars, is all. Once they do that, we'll make a couple of nice, slow circles and be back down on the ground before you know it."

I opened one eye and glared at him with it. "This ride is interminable." My grip on the bar was so tight, I was losing feeling in my hands. I shifted in the seat, which set the car rocking and me wondering whether sausage and peppers had been such a good idea. At that moment we began our slow ascent, and my whole body stiffened. Cal tightened his arm around me, but I was too terrified to tell whether or not I enjoyed the feeling. "Uhh, you said you'd distract me. So let's t-talk."

"You got it. But would you mind opening your other eye?" I could hear the amusement in his voice.

"Right. Both eyes open." *Ha, that could be the theme of my investigation.* But *was* I keeping both eyes open? I glanced at Cal's hand on my upper arm. "You don't have to keep holding on to me, you know."

He lifted his arm away from my shoulder and then patted my hands. "I can see you're doing fine. So what do you want to talk about?"

"Well . . . whoa, we're getting a little high here." I swallowed, wishing I had Cal's cold beer in my hand. For all the good it would do me; to drink it, I'd have to let go of the bar. "So, uh, I told you about me, but you didn't tell me much about you. When did my parents hire you?" *Now, there's a friendly opening, Vic. That's sure to disarm him.*

He frowned slightly and rubbed his chin. "Last month."

"And before that where were you working?"

"The country club over to Belmont. They gave your daddy a reference." He slid his eyes toward me. "And there's no outstandin' warrants for my arrest, in case you're wondering."

"Sorry. I didn't mean to sound like I was grilling you. It's just that—"

"You don't know anything about me."

"Right. I mean, we only met about a week ago." I looked down at my still-clenched hands; I'd have to pry them from this bar finger by finger. "And then we have this death at the restaurant." *And you were there the day it happened.*

"Victoria, just what is it you are trying to ask me?" Cal crossed his arms over his chest. A defensive gesture? Or an angry one? We were about to crest the top of the ride, and I hazarded a look down. The sun was setting in swaths of orange and deep blue; the lights of the boardwalk twinkled below. It was so beautiful that for a few seconds, I wasn't afraid. Until the ride stopped with us at the very top of the wheel.

"Oh God," I whispered, as afterimages of the boardwalk lights danced behind my eyelids.

Cal tapped my forehead. "Will you please open your eyes?"

"Uh, okay." I looked at Cal's stern expression and fought the urge to close them again.

He leaned closer to me, his face inches from mine. "What's going on?"

"Nothing." I sighed. "It's just that business has been falling off since Parisi's death, and Nonna's been bugging me to try to find out what happened before the season starts. Then my sister-in-law, Sofia, got involved, and well—"

"Oh, so you and Miss Firecracker been playin' detective. Is that it? Then let's get a couple of things straight right now. One: I'd never seen that Parisi guy before he came into the restaurant, and didn't know him from Adam. Two: I didn't notice a dang thing. You waited on him and your old boyfriend made his plate. *He's* the one you oughta be talking to."

"C'mon, I didn't accuse you of anything!"

"Didn't you?" He reached out a finger and turned my face toward his. "Now, if I *were* a murderer, it'd be mighty stupid of you to be up here on this ride with me, wouldn't it?" His eyes were hard to read, as clouded as a piece of dark green sea glass. *Oh God, have I stepped out of my life right into the middle of a Hitchcock film?*

"Oh, for goodness' sake," I sputtered. "Don't be silly. I'm just wondering if there's something I missed."

Before he could answer, the wheel creaked into motion and the car began to descend. My body stiffened as we dropped, and I gulped in a big breath of sea air. "Listen, Cal," I said. "Are you absolutely sure that nobody else came into the restaurant while Tim and I were in the kitchen?"

"You mean the widduh, don't you?" He pointed. "You'd just love it if I said, 'Oh, silly me. I just remembered that Anjelica came in and sprinkled poison all over her husband's salad.'"

"Cut it out."

"I'm right, lady, and you know it."

"Okay." I admitted. "Maybe I wouldn't mind seeing Angie arrested for murder."

"Because of her and the Iron Chef, right?"

My eyes widened. "How do you know about that?"

"The Casa Lido's a small place, *cher*. Things get around."

"And by 'get around,' you mean Lori told you."

Just then we came to a stop, our chair swinging slightly over the platform. I let out a long breath, my heart still pounding, whether from the ride or my little interrogation, I didn't know. I released my hands from the bar and flexed my fingers, then wiped my damp palms on the sides of my skirt. Cal unfastened the bar and reached for my hand, saw me hesitate and frowned.

"You don't wanna take my hand?"

"It's not that." I held up my hands. "Sweaty palms."

He laughed and caught my hand. "A little sweat don't bother me. Long as you don't think you're holding hands with a murderer."

"Hilarious." I stepped down from the ride with rubbery legs, glad to be on terra firma. I looked back up at the huge wheel and shivered. "I can't believe I let you talk me into that."

"And thus far my pants are still clean and upon my person." He shot me a wicked grin, and I narrowed my eyes at him.

"And likely to remain that way." I tugged his hand. "C'mon, you're not leaving here without a classic frozen custard."

As we walked and ate our ice creams, I thought about our conversation up on the Ferris wheel. Had Cal really not seen anything at all on the day of the murder? He struck me as someone who missed very little. Maybe he would remember something later, even a small detail that might be important.

"By the way," I said as we headed back to the restaurant, "my sister-in-law will be interested to hear that you call her 'Miss Firecracker.' It's kind of fitting, though. Coincidentally, she has a nickname for you: 'Mr. Down on the Bayou.'"

"Hell, girl, what does she think? That I'm out there mixin' moonshine and wrasslin' gat-uhs?"

"Keep layin' on the accent like sugar syrup and I'll think the same thing."

"Whatsamatta?" Cal's voice shifted quickly from the bayou to the Meadowlands. "Don't I tawk like what yuh used to?"

"Wow," I said, turning to look at him. "It's like all the South just dropped out of your voice there for a minute." Impressive, but for some reason, also disconcerting.

"Well, Victoria, I got you here safe and sound." We stood in front of the Casa Lido, Cal still holding my hand. "Thank you for a lovely evening. Hope we can do it again sometime." After the briefest brush of his lips against my cheek, he said good night. As I watched his slim-hipped figure recede into the darkness, I was left with a faint sense of unease. He'd been in Jersey for almost eight years, yet acted as though this was his first trip to the boardwalk. He also was a guy with the ability to sound like somebody else. Finally, he had specifically mentioned Parisi's salad in the course of our conversation on the Ferris wheel.

Was it merely a joke? A coincidence? Or an unconscious slip of the tongue?

Chapter Eighteen

Isabella gripped the side of the deck, taking in lungfuls [lungs full?] *of the salt air, trying to focus her eyes on the distant horizon.* The illness can't last long, *she thought as she—*

I jumped at the buzzing sound coming from the vicinity of my elbow. "Why didn't I leave this thing off?" Still bleary-eyed the morning after my date with Cal, I turned my phone to read the name I knew I would see there: Sofia.

"You rang, SIL? This is early even for you." I stared at the computer screen, willing more words to magically appear in the paragraph.

"Geez, good morning to you, too."

"I was writing. 'Was' being the operative word."

But my snark had little effect on my sister-in-law. "Good," she said. "That means you're at your computer. Minimize your document, please."

I waited a beat, but left my page up. "Okay, what?"

"I'm not saying another word till you close that document."

Letting out a loud sigh, I clicked the minus sign across the top of the doc. "What are you, on video phone or something?"

"I just know my Victoria. Listen, get on the Entertainment Channel Web site. There's a video on the home page you should probably see. Call me back when you're finished."

The Entertainment Channel Web site, with its black-and-gold EC! logo, was an amalgam of gossip and "info-tainment." Its Web page was a pastiche of lurid colors and sound effects, and the show's theme song blared through my computer's speakers as the page opened. Wincing, I turned the volume down; it was way too early for this. I scanned the tabs across the top and clicked on the featured video, a screen shot of Angelina Jolie. But once I hit the play button, I blinked and peered closer at the screen. The tall woman in the dark hair was not Angelina, but none other than her doppelgänger, Anjelica, aka Angie Martini. What the hell?

It looked like a news conference, with Angie at a podium flanked by two men. She was saying something into the mike I couldn't quite catch, and I raised the volume.

". . . and was the recipient of several threatening letters before his death." Threatening letters? Angie continued, clearly reading from a statement. "More than a week has passed, yet I know nothing more today than I did one week ago." She stopped to dab at her eyes, and I groaned aloud. "And the local police in Oceanside Park have provided me with absolutely no information."

A muffled question came from the audience, and Angie shook her glossy hair. "They have not released any autopsy results. At this point, I know nothing about what caused my husband's death."

Another inaudible question and another shake of Angie's head. "No, he had no food allergies." She frowned, glanced at one of the men, who shook his head. "I'm sorry. We really can't comment further on that."

At that, one of the men stepped in front of the mike.

"Mrs. Parisi has made her statement. There will be no more questions, but I will make one more comment for the record: If Mrs. Parisi is not provided a satisfactory answer from local law enforcement regarding her husband's death, we will be launching our own investigation and possible lawsuit. Thank you."

And the screen went blacker than my thoughts.

Thus far I had tried to keep my brother out of my "investigation," but now the situation was desperate. The Black Widow had gone public with some new information and just stopped short of naming the restaurant in a suit. Tomorrow my time was up on the deal with Nina; if I didn't have something for her, the Channel Ten van might well end up outside the Casa Lido doors. We would never survive another media onslaught, let alone a wrongful-death suit. Danny was my only hope in getting some answers before the worst happened.

I found him in the one place I knew he'd be on his off-hours: on his boat in the marina.

"Hey, bro." I stepped gingerly onto the boat's deck; despite being born and bred near the water, I was not a fan of boating, mostly because I tended to seasickness and dark fantasies involving sharks. Danny reached out a hand and led me to a seat. "I figured this would be the best place for us to talk," I said.

Danny glanced over to the slip at his left. "For now," he said. "Nobody's here yet."

He looked at me over the top of his black wraparound sunglasses. "You wanna know about the autopsy, right?"

"Yes. And you've been out here, so you probably haven't seen the latest news. The Widow Angie just announced publicly that her husband was receiving threatening letters in the weeks before he died. Her lawyer or some PI with her implied there'd be a lawsuit." I shook my head. "It's looking worse and worse for us, Danny."

"We know about the letters," he said, "but I can't say any more about that." He looked around once more and lowered his voice. "The cause of death was heart failure, but the medical examiner has sent all the fluids out for testing. Those results could take weeks."

"We don't have weeks." And I had only twenty-four hours before Nina descended. "Memorial Day is right around the corner," I told him. "And I knew all this already. Isn't there anything else you can tell me?"

Danny looked out over the water, then back at me. "I'm not on the investigation, Vic, and even if I were, you know I shouldn't be telling you anything."

"That's not an answer. I know your brothers in blue are keeping you posted on this case." I gripped his arm. "Please, Danny. I have to figure out what happened to this guy."

"And what are you gonna do with that information? Besides put yourself in harm's way?"

I bit my lip. "I don't exactly know. Maybe force a confession? Get somebody to incriminate himself? Or herself?"

Danny blew out a loud breath. "That only happens in your books, sis. You've gotta be careful here."

"I won't do anything stupid. I promise."

He cracked a smile for the first time. "Because getting yourself locked in the pantry wasn't stupid."

"Gimme a break here, will ya? Okay. What if I ask you a couple of questions and you just answer them?"

He sighed. "Hell, I know I won't get any fishing in otherwise."

I pulled out my notebook and a pen. "Was he on any meds? Maybe something he accidentally overdosed on?" The hope in my voice was pathetic.

"He was on beta blockers for his heart. But it wasn't an overdose."

"He's on heart meds, yet he dies of heart failure." I scribbled the medication on my pad. "So Parisi must have been given something that caused his fatal heart attack, correct?"

My brother nodded, tight-lipped.

"Okay, the question is, how was it delivered?"

He raised one thick brow over his sunglasses, but remained silent.

"You are maddening—you know that? All right, we know everything he ate *from* went through the dishwasher. What about the San Pellegrino bottle? It tested negative, right?"

"What do you think?"

"I figured as much. Listen, I found out he was drinking from a water bottle up on the boardwalk, one he brought from home. Was that bottle tested, too?"

"Yes," he said quietly, "and it was clean."

My heart sank like a penny dropped into the bay. "That means he most likely ingested whatever killed him at lunch. In the restaurant."

"Yeah," he said, and that one syllable was laden with meaning.

"But the kitchen trash turned up nothing?"

"Right."

"But we don't know what might have been in the garbage that was already outside."

A muscle in his jaw tightened. "Don't remind me. The CP wants my chief's ass on a platter for that one."

I thought of the portly Chief O'Brien and grimaced. "Now there's an image I won't be able to shake." I jotted a few more notes and then looked up at my brother. "Wait. Does 'CP' stand for county prosecutor?"

"Uh-huh."

"Crap. There must be *something* else you can tell me about that autopsy." I waited, hearing only the slap of the water against the side of the boat. "C'mon, Danny!" I wailed.

He suddenly grinned. "You sound just like you did when you were ten. Next thing I know, you'll be threatening to tell Mom."

"Funny." I nodded toward the water. "Bet those fish are starting to bite. Too bad you're not out there."

"Okay," he said, holding up his palms. He shot a quick glance across the marina and lowered his voice again. "Listen, they won't know for sure for weeks, but the ME's hunch is that a natural substance was used to kill him."

"A natural substance? Like . . . from a plant?" My stomach thumped with a terrible foreboding. He nodded again, and a kaleidoscope of impressions swirled around my brain. The herbs in the pantry. Iris's words about poisonous plants. Cal's joke about the salad. And fresh bunches of greens laid out in the kitchen delivered by Mr. B. Was Parisi's lunch a crazy salad of arugula laced with poisonous leaves?

"This is not good," I whispered.

"No," Danny said. "It isn't."

"But there's more. If we go under, do you know that the mayor already has a buyer lined up for the restaurant? A buyer who wants to turn it into a Starbucks."

Danny swore under his breath. "That's just great. That would kill Mom and Pop." He shook his head. "Nonna would just kill the buyer."

"Please don't joke like that, okay?" I tucked my pad and pen back into my purse and grabbed my keys. "Danny, thanks for talking to me. I know it's a risk, and this will be the last time. I promise."

But as I turned to go, Danny put his hand on my

shoulder. "Hey, Vic. Is Sofia involved in this little investigation of yours?"

"What do you think? She's like a cute little dog with a bone."

One side of his mouth lifted, and I had to smile back. "She's smart, Dan. And she's a tough cookie."

"Don't I know it," he said grimly.

"Why are you so against her applying for the police academy? Are you worried about her safety?"

"Of course, but it's not just that. I'm just not sure about both of us on the job. I've seen what it can do to marriages."

I put my hand on his arm. "Would you say that you have a marriage right now?"

"No, I wouldn't. I want her back home with me, damn it." There was sadness in his tone.

"I know that's what she wants, too. Look, I know how you feel about this, but why don't you consider counseling?"

He grinned. "No shrink would last an hour with us. Two hotheaded Italians in therapy?"

"You forgot 'hardheaded.' Still, I wish you'd consider it. It's better than this limbo you're in right now."

"And what about you, sis? How's it been, having to work with Tim?"

"In some ways, really difficult." I thought back to our near kiss in the kitchen. "In some ways, just like old times. Having Angie Martini in the picture sure threw me for a loop, though." I searched my brother's face. "Danny, you don't think Tim . . ."

He shook his head and spoke firmly. "Absolutely not. I've known the guy twenty years. He's not capable of it."

But you could be wrong about him, Dan. We both could. "Mr. Biaggio was also there. Do the cops know about that Internet video clip from *The Jersey Side*?"

"Yeah." He crossed his arms, and his face hardened. "I'd like to bang those kids' heads together."

"Me too. Imagine how Mr. B feels. He's got at least one motive, maybe two. And in his line of work, he would have to know plants, right?"

"I don't know, Vic." Danny pulled a cooler from a hatch along the side of the boat, and any minute I'd lose him to today's catch. "I just don't like him for this; I'm not sure why."

"Okay. Then who, Dan? Who *do* you like for this?"

He shrugged. "Well, we usually look at the spouse. In this case, there's also the mistress."

"Oh, you know about her." But for some reason, I hesitated about telling my brother I'd spoken to Emily Haverford.

"Trouble is," Danny continued, "they weren't on the scene."

"How do we know that for sure? It's not outside the realm that one of them could have slipped into the kitchen or the dining room at some point. And my money's on Angie."

"No." He shook his head. "They both have an alibi."

"You're kidding me. Where *were* they that afternoon?"

"I don't know specifics," Danny said. "But I do know this: Neither of those women was anywhere within a mile of the Casa Lido when Gio Parisi was killed."

Chapter Nineteen

I had just pulled my car door shut and was about to leave the marina when my phone rang. "You never called me back."

"Sorry, Sofe." I clipped my seat belt and cradled the phone against my chin. "That video freaked me out, and I thought it was time to break out the big guns."

"You went to see Danny."

"Are you stalking me?" I glanced out my car window, half expecting to see a trench-coated Sofia lounging in a nearby alley with a pair of binoculars.

"Nope. I just got off the phone with him." She dropped her voice in an approximation of Danny's gruff baritone. "*Interfering in police investigation* blah blah, *risking your safety* et cetera, et cetera, *sticking your nose in places you shouldn't*, blah blah blah. God, he pisses me off."

"I'd say you have that effect on each other. But cool down long enough for me to tell you what he said, okay?" After I was finished, there was only silence on Sofia's end of the phone. "Are you there?"

"Yeah, I'm here. I'm busy crossing off names. You know who we're down to, don't you, Vic? I mean, leaving out you and Lori—"

"It's Tim, Cal, and Mr. B who had access to Parisi's lunch," I said with a sigh. "I know."

"Unless—" Sofia paused.

"Unless what?"

"Unless we're missing something."

"We must be," I said.

"Remember I said we needed to look at other people who might have wanted Parisi dead? I'm gonna follow up on Mikey G's dad."

"Gemelli?"

"He and that little turd of a son were holding out for more money. And it's rumored that Daddy has some unsavory connections."

"People always say that about Italians with money."

"And sometimes it's true, SIL. You said yourself he struck you as the type who might hire somebody to do the dirty work."

"Maybe. But could somebody have gotten into the restaurant that day without us noticing?"

"That's what we have to find out, isn't it? I'm gonna do some digging. Speaking of digging, I can't seem to find a thing on Mr. Down on the Bayou."

That would have been the moment to tell Sofia about my date with Cal, but I wasn't in the mood for a lecture on getting involved with suspects. "Um, I'm working on that one. I'll let you know what I find out." I shifted the phone to the other side of my chin. "By the way, he has a nickname for you, too: Miss Firecracker."

"Ha. It's fitting. I'll say that."

"Why?" I asked. "Because you're hot, colorful, and dangerous in close proximity?"

"That works," she said.

"Listen, Sofe. It's getting warm in this car, and I need to get out of here. So you're gonna work on Gemelli Senior?"

"Yeah. I'll let you know what I find out. What about you?"

"Me?" An idea was forming as Sofie asked me the question. "I'm planning to have a one-Martini lunch."

"Thank you for meeting me," I said as I sat down across from Anjelica Parisi in a quiet corner of the Cupping Room. The café was in nearby Belmont Beach; I didn't think Angie wanted to be seen in Oceanside, and I didn't want to be seen with *her*.

She looked up from the menu, her face a bored blank. "I don't have much time, and honestly, I have no idea why you want to talk to me."

I leaned across the table and looked steadily into the widow's blue-violet eyes. "You know what I've noticed? That when people say 'honestly,' they're usually anything but."

She frowned, and I noticed a telltale lack of lines between her brows; her forehead was smooth as well. Then she wrinkled her nose as though an offensive odor had just wafted past her. "Just tell me what this is about, please. Do I need to remind you that I lost my husband a week ago?"

"Oh, no, indeed, Angie. I don't need any reminding on that score. I saw your little video on the EC! Web site."

She shook out her napkin and placed it across her lap. "I'd like to know what happened to my husband," she said without looking up.

"So let the police force do its job."

She arched her fine brows until they disappeared under her side-swept bangs. "I could say the same to you, couldn't I? I hear someone's been going around asking questions." She shook her finger at me. "Naughty, naughty."

"That restaurant is my family's livelihood," I said through my teeth. "I have a right to know what happened there."

A waitress appeared at Angie's elbow. She closed the menu and trained a bright smile on the girl. "I'll have a nonfat decaf iced latte, hon. And some herbal sweetener, please."

"Any biscotti or pastries?" the girl asked.

"Not for me, sweetie." She nodded in my direction. "It's my friend there with the sweet tooth," she whispered, sending our waitress into a fit of giggles.

"Just a double espresso, thanks." I waited until the girl walked away and turned my attention back on Angie. "As I was saying—"

"You were saying you want to find out what happened to my husband. So do I. And if the police can't help me, I'll go to somebody who can."

And then bring a lawsuit against us. "Look, Angie—"

"My name is Anjelica," she said, lifting her chin.

"Got it. As I was saying, *Angie*, the Casa Lido is very important to my family."

"So that's why you're playing detective. Because you've written a few books, you think you can jump in and save the day." Her voice dropped, and she suddenly sounded like the Jersey girl she was. "Life doesn't work that way, sweetheart," she snarled.

At that auspicious moment, our waitress returned with our drinks, and I took a deep sniff of my coffee. The rush gave me all the courage I needed, and I looked at Angie over my cup. "So where *were* you the day he died?"

"Ha!" Her throaty laugh rang out across the coffee shop. "Barely five minutes," she said, tapping the gold watch on her wrist. "I didn't think you could hold out that long." She pressed her fingertips against her lips and yawned. "God, this is getting *so* predictable."

"You didn't answer my question."

"I don't have to, do I? I've already told the police

where I was. But I'll play along, Nancy Drew." She leaned across the table, her voice conspiratorial. "At the time in question, I was in Ocean Grove, New Jersey. I attended a yoga class, followed by a stop for one of these. They're yummy." She held up her latte and sucked deeply on the straw. With her pale face and dark red lips, she looked positively vampiric.

Her story would be easy enough to check. Ocean Grove was a small community; how many yoga classes could they offer? And there were only a couple of coffee shops in town.

"So that leaves me out, doesn't it?" she was saying.

"Possibly."

"Sorry, Victoria. I know you'd like it to be me, but no can do." She patted my hand, and I recoiled from her icy touch. "After all," she continued, "I loved my husband."

To the tune of millions. "Of course," I said, smiling. "So you would have no motive, correct?"

She took another sip of her drink and nodded. "Correct." She motioned to me with her cup. "You should be looking for someone *with* a motive. Say, someone who didn't want *The Jersey Side* filming in town. Or someone who had a grudge against my husband."

"Can you think of anyone?"

Her lips formed a menacing red curve. "You mean besides people in *your* family? The person who was sending him letters, obviously. But I have no idea who that might be."

"Right," I said.

In the silence that followed, she played with the straw in her coffee and then looked up at me. "Poor Tim," she said with a sigh.

My shoulders tensed, and I leaned forward in my chair. "What does Tim have to do with this?" I desperately wanted to believe that "nothing"—not "everything"—was the answer to that question.

"He's just so gal-LANT," she said with a French pronunciation, and I resisted the urge to groan. She tilted her head and blinked her thick lashes in a practiced way. "There isn't anything he wouldn't do for me."

I froze with the coffee cup halfway to my mouth. "Leave Tim out of this."

"I'm not sure I can, sweetie." She shook her head in an approximation of regret. "You see, he's very protective of me. And he knew Gio and I were, well, having some troubles. As all marriages do," she added.

It was time to play my trump card. "You mean Emily Haverford."

At the mention of Emily's name, Angie's pale face went even whiter. Her eyes narrowed and her nostrils flared, and in that moment, I thought, *This is a dangerous woman*. "How dare you even mention her name to me?"

I lifted one shoulder and took a sip of my coffee. "She came to see me."

Angie gripped the edge of the table, giving me a full view of her new manicure—a deep red the color of blood. "Why would she do that?"

"She has questions, too. She also wants to know how your husband died."

"She has no right to know anything about Gio."

I shrugged. "Well, to hear her tell it, she does. Apparently, they were together for a number of years." I stared into her cold eyes. "Until you came along."

She curled her lip into a sneer. "He married *me*. I have no use for women who poach on another woman's territory."

I nearly spit out my coffee. "That's hilarious, coming from you." I downed the rest of the espresso and held my cup to her in a toast. "And the hunting metaphor is fitting, by the way. Well done."

She raised her thin black brows. "Isn't it funny," she began, "how some people just can't let go?"

"If you're talking about me, don't flatter yourself, Angie. I got over what you did a long time ago." *Sure I did, which is why I'd like to reach across this table and strangle you where you sit.*

She laughed. "I wasn't talking about you, sweetie." She scrounged in her purse and brought out a mirror and lip gloss. After carefully applying another coat of Bride of Dracula Red, she snapped the mirror closed and shot me a feral smile. "I meant Tim."

"What's that supposed to mean?" The words tumbled from my mouth. "He hadn't even seen you until the week before your husband died."

She pressed her lips together and then blotted them on a napkin. I raised my eyes from that bright red imprint up to her face, which held an expression that was a toxic combination of sympathetic and sly.

"Oh, hon," she said. She shook her head slowly from side to side. "Is that what he told you?"

Less than an hour later, I arrived at Sofia's studio, tapping my foot in her office until she finished her last class. The espresso with a Martini chaser had left me jittery, and the implication that Tim had lied about when he'd last seen Angie left me pissed. I needed to take action.

"What's up?" Sofia came in a little breathless, mopping her face with a towel. "Aren't you supposed to be at the restaurant?"

"I took the day off. Listen, you up for a road trip, SIL?" I pulled a sheet from the office printer, a black-and-white image of the EC! screen shot of Anjelica, and tucked it into my purse.

"Where? Can I shower first?"

"Ocean Grove, and yes. But hurry up. And bring the red folder!" I called after her.

We took her car, as her air-conditioning was less temperamental than that in my Honda. Summer was still a month away, but the Jersey heat was already upon us as we headed north on the Garden State Parkway.

"So I did some research on Gemelli Senior," Sofia said as she zipped into the left lane, heedless of the Range Rover barreling up behind us.

"Hey, take it easy." I automatically pressed my right foot down on the floor. "I'd like to get there in one piece."

"Anyway," she continued, "he definitely has some sketchy connections."

"What does he do?"

"Mostly he manages Mikey's career, such as it is. But he owned a construction firm for a long time; that's how he made his money."

"And that's where the sketchy stuff comes in?"

Sofia nodded. "I dug up some old newspaper articles online about possible kickbacks on bids, but nothing was ever proven. I don't think he was even investigated."

"Is that it?"

"Not quite." She made a sudden lane change, and I gripped the armrest. "He's built houses up in north Jersey for the Rossini family."

"The Rossini family or the Rossini *family*?"

"Both."

"Okay, just because he has some connected clients doesn't mean—"

Sofia held up her hand. "Is this where I get a lecture about Italian-American stereotypes?"

"Keep both hands on the wheel, please. I just meant that building houses for an alleged mobster isn't a crime."

"You're right," Sofia said. "It's not. But it puts him in close contact with people who kill for money."

"And people who could slip in and out of places without being seen and who wouldn't think twice about coming back to retrieve evidence." I shuddered at the thought of a Rossini henchman sneaking around the restaurant at night and locking us in the pantry.

"And Gemelli had a motive, don't forget. With Parisi out of the picture, those kids on *Jersey Side* will probably get the money they're asking for."

I nodded. *"Cui bono."*

"What does that mean?"

"It's Latin for 'to whose benefit?' It's a question you ask when greed's a motive."

"So Gemelli Junior and Senior both benefit when Mikey G gets his raise," Sofia said.

"And Angie benefits big-time," I added. "And speaking of the Black Widow, let me tell you about my very interesting lunch with her."

My sister-in-law was uncharacteristically silent as I recounted the salient points of my conversation with Angie/Anjelica, but the minute I paused for breath, she jumped in.

"You think she's telling the truth about those letters?"

"Danny told me the cops knew about them, so I assume they exist."

"If the murderer sent them, wouldn't that give the cops a strong lead? I wish we could get a look at them."

"Not that I'm not curious, SIL, but they wouldn't tell us much." From my own research I knew that people who sent anonymous letters usually knew enough to wear gloves, avoid licking the envelope, and post the letters far from where they lived.

I was about to explain that to her when she sailed through the EZPass toll at top speed, then changed the subject as quickly as she changed lanes. "So she claims she was in Ocean Grove taking a yoga class last Tuesday." She tapped restlessly on the steering wheel. "I don't get it."

"What do you mean?"

"I mean, what's in Ocean Grove to interest Angie?" she asked. "Antiques and little shops? She sure wasn't there for a prayer meeting." She shook her head. "It's a weird choice. Now, if she'd said she was in Atlantic City or Wildwood—that I could believe."

"Well, we'll find out, won't we? Exit's coming up."

As we entered the quaint confines of the little town, I couldn't help but agree with Sofia's assessment. Ocean Grove had been established as a Methodist community and still held prayer meetings every summer. Any night-life was next door in Asbury Park. It was a dry town and home to an eclectic mix of people that didn't normally include the glamorous wives of television producers.

Our first stop was the art center at the top of the main street in town. "I haven't been here in a long time," I told Sofia, "but I know there used to be a community bulletin board with events and stuff. Let's see if there's a yoga class."

As we scanned the board, we saw flyers for a local theater production of *Much Ado About Nothing* and an upcoming appearance by the New Jersey Ballet. There was also a tour of historic houses planned for June. But no yoga.

"May I help you?" A middle-aged woman got up from behind a desk.

"Yes," I said. "We were looking for a yoga class in town that a friend told us about."

"Oh, that's on Tuesdays in the studio upstairs," she said. "You missed it by a day."

Sofia dug her elbow into my side. "But are we sure this is the class Angie meant?" she asked, her brown eyes the picture of innocence. I gave her a quick elbow jab in return.

"We're pretty sure our friend took last Tuesday's class," I said, "but maybe you remember her? People say she looks like Angelina Jolie."

"Oh my goodness, yes," the woman said. "Such a striking woman. She was here for the two o'clock class last week. I remember her clearly." She smiled and handed us a brochure. "Just fill this out, and we can get you both in starting next week."

Sofia tugged at my arm. "Oh, we'll just take it with us. Thanks!"

As we walked toward the town center, we started to put a time frame together. "If she was here for a two o'clock class," Sofia said, "that means the latest she could have left our area was one thirty."

"And at one thirty Parisi was still up at the board-walk; he didn't come into the restaurant until two hours later."

Sofia opened the brochure. "This says the class is forty-five minutes. If she didn't stop for coffee like she said, she could have made it back to the restaurant."

"On to the coffee shops, then."

We walked the length of the main street in a matter of minutes and counted the cafés.

"Should we split up?" Sofie asked. "We'll get done quicker, and then we can have lunch."

"There's only a few places," I said. "And I think it's better if we have two pairs of eyes and ears. And we can eat somewhere along the way."

The first two shops yielded nothing more than blank looks and head shakes from the staff. We walked into the third one, Café au Lait, and were greeted by a bearded bear of a guy behind the counter.

"What can I get you ladies?" As the offerings included lunch, we decided to refuel first and ask questions later. Big Bear motioned us to a table and then brought our sandwiches out to us.

Sofia batted her eyes at him while I rolled my own. "Can we ask you a question?"

He rested his hands across his generous belly. "Sure."

"A friend of ours was in town last week and raved about an iced latte she had. Do you make those here?" Sofia asked.

"We do, indeed," he said. "Can I get you one?"

"Not right now," she said. "Thanks, but—"

"Actually," I interrupted, "may we presume on your time just one more minute?" I dug into my bag and produced the picture. "This is our friend. Can you tell us if she came in last Tuesday?"

Big Bear chuckled and raised his thick eyebrows. "Oh yeah, she was here all right. Came in around three. Her and that other lady."

That other lady? I glanced at Sofia, who looked up sharply. "Somebody was with her?" I asked, straining to keep the curiosity out of my voice.

"Yup. I'm not likely to forget either one of those two." He glanced over at a customer at a nearby table and lowered his voice. "They had a screaming match, the two of 'em, right there at that table. I hadda ask them to leave."

Sofia's eyes were wide. "You're kidding."

He shook his head. "It was pretty bad. I mean, in this economy, who kicks out paying customers?"

"This other lady," I said slowly. "Do you remember what she looked like?"

"Hell, yeah. She was a tiny woman, especially next to the other one. I thought she was on the younger side until I got up close. She had blond hair." He paused. "And a lotta makeup."

Thank you, Big Bear, for being so observant. "Did she have long bangs?" I asked. "Blue eyes? They're an unusual color—almost turquoise."

"Yeah. Sounds like you know her."

"Slightly," I said.

"I don't remember Angie telling us about a fight. Do you, Vic?" Sofia said with exaggerated emphasis. *Real smooth, Sofe.* "Could that have been her friend Susie?"

I opened my mouth, but Big Bear got there first. "Nah," he said, "that wasn't her name. Just before I threw them out, when they were getting really loud, the short one said something that really pissed the big one off. Then I hear the big one say—clear as day, mind you—'You bitch, Emily. I'll kill you for this.'"

Emily. There was only one Emily in this scenario. And my brother had been right: If they were in the Café au Lait at three o'clock, neither one of these women was anywhere near the restaurant the day Gio Parisi was killed.

Chapter Twenty

*T*hat evening I took a walk on the boardwalk to clear my head (and to grab some saltwater taffy). I passed the arcades and the rides pier, already lit up for the start of the season. I eventually made my way to the old movie theater, where I'd spent many a rainy Saturday afternoon. The Paramount didn't show first-run films anymore, but it had a new life as an art house. I wandered over to look at the posters on each side of its massive doors. Next month was a French film retrospective, featuring *Diabolique* and *Jules and Jim*. That didn't interest me much, but I looked with longing at tonight's offering, an Astaire-Rogers double feature. But the sad truth was that I didn't have time for Fred and Ginger or walks down memory lane. I sighed as I turned to go. I had work to do, and it was time to get started.

Back at the cottage, I settled down at my computer to break down this case, much in the same way I planned Bernardo's mysteries—with a chart.

I stared at the screen, my heart sinking. Laid out like this, there were only two clear front-runners: Mr. B and Tim. Which brought us right back to where we had started a week ago. *Unless you're missing something, Vic. Think!* I glanced at the chart again. Cal was also on the

	Motive?	Means?	Opportunity?	Alibi?	Other Info?
Mr. B	Parisi humiliated daughter on TV/ did not want show filming in town [PASSION]	Access to plants of all kinds	Was in kitchen at the time; could have added plant material to salad	No	No regret for Parisi's death; acting afraid; unlikely intruder
Gemelli Senior	Parisi standing in way of raises for cast [GAIN]	Connections with Rossini family; could have hired killer; (would plant poison be the means for hit man?)	Not personally	*Check on this!*	Sketchy connections; protective of son; ruthless in business; threatening manner
Cal	None known/no known connection to Parisi	None known	Was on the scene; known to be in the kitchen at least once	No	Mentioned poisoning the salad; able to mimic voices/ accents; little known about his background
Tim	Protective of ex- girlfriend/still in love with her? [PASSION]	As chef, might know toxic plants	Prepared Parisi's lunch; leaves could be hidden in salad	No	Anger at Parisi; washed plates; may have lied about contact with Angie
Angie	Stands to inherit large estate; jealousy over Emily [GAIN/ PASSION]	None known	Unlikely	Yes—in Ocean Grove from 2 to 4 p.m.	Likely married for money; has a temper; hates Emily
Emily	Spurned by Parisi [PASSION]	None known	Unlikely	Yes—in Ocean Grove from before 3 to 4 p.m.	Parisi left her for Angie; lied about when she saw P last

scene, but he had no motive—that we knew of, anyway. But I couldn't rule him out.

"If you know how, you know who," I said to myself. And it was time to find out more about how Parisi may have been murdered. Danny had said the medical examiner suspected a plant poison, but I didn't know the first thing about them. (In my Bernardo series, I had yet to kill anybody with poison. They're unpredictable, messy, and not always easy to get ahold of. Give me a nice clean shove off a cliff any day.)

There had to be dozens of poisonous plants that grew in Jersey, so where to begin? It seemed logical to talk to Iris Harrington first, but the shop was closed, and Iris, who was not a believer in cell phones, had only a landline. Since she didn't believe in answering machines, either, I was left with only my spotty memory of our conversation.

What had she said? I remembered something about holly berries—or was it juniper berries? But either way, there was nothing on Parisi's salad that looked remotely like a berry. I struggled to remember the salad plate and the greens that were on it. Arugula, certainly, but nothing else—at least that I could remember—that looked leafy. *But leaves could be chopped up*, said a voice in my head. And the bitterness of the arugula might have disguised the taste of those leaves.

What other plants had Iris talked about? I closed my eyes to concentrate. There was a name I recognized because it had been in the title of a book I'd read whose cover had a white flower. White lily? White narcissus? No. *Oleander*. That was it.

I clicked open my browser to get started. A quick look on garden Web sites indicated that the flowers were definitely grown in Jersey. I also learned that the plant contained a substance that could cause heart failure. Ingesting it caused nausea, vomiting, and diarrhea, all signs consistent with Parisi's symptoms. But the articles I read pointed out another fact: Oleander causes burning in the mouth. I watched Parisi shovel that salad down his throat in a matter of minutes; if his mouth burned, wouldn't he have stopped eating it? I made a few more notes about the plant, but I doubted this was our candidate.

As I mentally replayed my conversation with Iris, I remembered the word "weed." A poisonous weed? And for some reason I kept imagining a cowboy—maybe it grew out West? I scrolled down the poisonous plants page until I hit *Phytolacca*, commonly known as pokeweed. My eyes widened when I read what pokeweed leaves are used for—salad. "But leaves must be cooked twice in separate water," the article read. "Roots and berries are poisonous. Improper cooking of leaves may result in serious poisoning." I stared at the image of the plant; the long green leaves did indeed look like salad greens. And if those greens were uncooked, they might well have been responsible for killing Parisi.

I added pokeweed to my notes and strained to recall what else Iris had mentioned. The last thing I remembered from that conversation was a plant I thought she called "purple digit," but a Google search brought up only a bunch of medical articles about circulatory diseases. I rubbed my tired eyes; I'd spent too much time in front of a screen and too many hours playing detective. I opened my e-mail, ignored the full in-box, and sent Sofia a copy of the chart I'd made and links to the articles about poisonous plants.

It was a relief to shut down the computer and put the day behind me. I took a hot bath, threw on my favorite sleep attire—an oversized T-shirt from the Boss's last Meadowlands appearance—and slipped under the covers of my narrow bed. The cool night air, carrying the smell of the sea, washed over me from the open window. I had come here for a peaceful place to write my book, to learn about my family's business and its roots in America. And here I was researching poisons and making lists of suspects. Beyond that, I had been pulled back into Tim's orbit, yet found myself attracted to another man. Both of whom, I reminded myself, were on the premises when Parisi was killed.

I sighed and straightened the covers under my chin. Closing my eyes, I tried to let the sound of the sea lull me to sleep, but my mind fought back. I saw Parisi sitting at Table Five. Tina Biaggio's horrified face on film. Tim's dawning fear as Angie asked, *What have you done?* Emily Haverford's grief. Cal's stony expression of denial. Angie's red-lipped, predatory smile. The images made a slow circle in my head, a mental Ferris wheel that wouldn't stop turning. I lay awake another hour, until exhaustion finally won out. But when I did sleep, it was only to have uneasy dreams about white oleanders, purple fingers, and salads made of noxious weeds.

Too groggy to write, the next morning I made a mental promise to Isabella that I would spend more time with her once I figured out how to keep the restaurant open. Tomorrow was the kickoff of Memorial Day weekend; in fact, by dinner hour today, Oceanside would be getting the first wave of summer weekenders who had tomorrow off. As I biked down to the restaurant, I thought again about the list of suspects I'd made last evening and couldn't shake the niggling worry that I'd forgotten something—or somebody. I wondered again about our mayor, Anne McCrae. But Parisi's water bottle was clean. And even if we couldn't take Anne's word that he hadn't eaten anything, Fifi had said the same thing. When would Anne have had the opportunity to poison him? And if the toxic substance came from plant matter, the most likely way Parisi would have ingested it was through his lunchtime salad. But Anne was a gardener, and she would have known plants.

I swerved quickly on the old Schwinn and doubled back a block to the Seaside Apothecary, where I hoped that Iris would translate her "purple digit" reference for me. But I got there to find a hand-scrawled note on the shop's front door: *Away until Monday. See you then!*

"That's great, Iris," I muttered. "Let's hope Monday's not too late."

I was surprised to find my parents and grandmother at the Casa Lido ahead of me. "What are you guys doing here?" I asked, after dutifully making the rounds to kiss them.

My dad rubbed his hands together. "Tim says we're busy at lunch again, sweetheart. The Casa Lido's coming back, just like I said."

I looked from my mother to my grandmother, whose skeptical faces reflected my own, but not one of us opened our mouths. I patted my dad's shoulder. "That's the spirit, Daddy. We've got to be ready for tomorrow, right?"

"Never mind tomorrow, honey. By tonight all those vans will be driving into town, filled with people hungry for a plate of real Italian food."

But will they be pulling into our parking lot, Dad? Not likely.

My grandmother snorted, either in disgust or assent. Maybe both. "I have given Tim the day off," she announced.

"Oh?" I said. "Is he coming in for dinner?"

She shook her head. "Massimo and Nando will be handling things today and tonight. Perhaps tomorrow, too."

My mother turned to face her mother-in-law. "Is that necessary, Mama?" she asked quietly.

Nonna gave a classic Italian shrug, lifting one shoulder slowly, followed by a lift of her palm. "The boy needs a break."

Sure, Nonna, and now maybe you'd like to sell me the Driscoll Bridge. "I know why you told Tim not to come in," I said. "You think he's bad for business."

"Victoria!" My mother and father gasped in unison. Whether they were shocked at my intimation or my challenge to my grandmother was not clear.

"It's true, isn't it?" I said.

My grandmother blinked once behind her glasses, the only sign I'd ruffled her. "Why do you defend him, after what he did to you?"

My face burned. What happened with Tim was a topic my grandmother had studiously avoided. But it was gratifying (and kinda shocking) to know that she cared. "Nonna, that's old history."

"Whether it is or isn't," she said, "it's better he's not here." She turned to go into the kitchen, the doors swinging behind her

"Mom—Daddy, c'mon. Are you gonna let her do that?" I was surprised by how upset I sounded.

My mom put her arm around me and rested her head against mine. "People are talking, honey. It's just how it is in small towns."

I pulled away from her quickly. "You know Tim didn't kill him. You both know that!" My words echoed across the empty dining room, and in the silence that followed, a thought struck me: Did my parents know that Anjelica was actually Angie Martini? If they did, they'd have even more reason to suspect Tim. But if my mom had made that connection, she would have mentioned it to me—that was for darn sure. In the meantime, I had to hope they wouldn't find out just yet. I turned to my dad. "He's not a murderer, Daddy."

"Baby, nobody suggested such a thing," my dad said. "But we're struggling to stay alive here. Tim's been working hard anyway. He could use a day or two off, right?" He reached over and grabbed my chin. "Now let me see my girl smile."

"Okay, okay." I grimaced just long enough for him to let go of my face. "But really, since when does the Rienzi family care what people think?"

"Since their business has fallen off," my mom responded with a sigh. "It's just temporary, honey. This will all blow over and Tim will be back, and the customers will be back—you'll see."

But it sounded as if my mother was trying to convince herself of her own words. "I hope so, Mom." I looked around the dining room. "Where's Cal this morning, by the way?"

"He's been and gone already," my mother said shortly, turning to me with her hands on her hips. "And why are you interested in where Mr. Lockhart is?"

"'Mr. Lockhart,' is it? My, aren't we formal. I was just wondering."

She waved a manicured hand in my direction. "Well, you can just stop wondering. He's not for you."

"Who said anything about him as a romantic prospect, Mother?" I tied on a black apron in the hopes of conveying the impression that I wanted to get to work.

"I know you were up at the boardwalk together the other evening."

I'd started to get the coffee urns ready and paused with the filter basket still in my hand. "Do you have spies out following me?"

"Of course not, Victoria. Mrs. Foglia, who works at the fudge shop, was told by Jenny at the Surf Shack, who heard it from Louie Ianuzzi, who saw you at his stand. How was the calamari, by the way?"

"The calamari was delicious. Thank you." I dumped coffee into the basket without measuring, telling myself that it was surely too soon to give up and go back to the city. "What else did you learn?"

"Well, you must like him, darling, or how else could he have gotten you up on that Ferris wheel? I mean, the last time you went on a ride with Tim, well—"

"Yes, Mom. I remember. Thank you. Aren't you going to ask whether he kissed me or not?" *If I hurry, I can be packed and heading north on the Parkway this afternoon.*

My mother tossed a few hair extensions over her shoulder. "I am well aware that he did not."

"Why? Because it was our first date?"

"No, darling, because Daniel happened to be driving by in his squad car as Mr. Lockhart was taking his leave of you."

"'Taking his leave of me'?" I couldn't help smiling. "How many Regency romances are loaded on that Kindle of yours, anyway?"

"Don't be smart, missy. And don't try to change the subject. I think you should stay away from Calvin Lockhart."

"No worries on that score, Mom, okay? And now I need to face the dragon in the kitchen."

"Don't be disrespectful, Victoria!" she called after me, and I groaned. Being back here made me feel like I was sixteen again, and not in a good way. And if I was hoping my grandmother would let me do some cooking this morning, I sure had another thing coming.

"Have you set up the coffee station?" she asked without looking up from her pad. I peeked over her shoulder to see a list forming for Nando and Massimo.

"Yes, Nonna," I said dutifully, and she cast me a suspicious glance.

"And what progress have you made about the other thing?"

The other thing. *Oh, you mean that thing where a man dropped dead outside the restaurant, Nonna?* "Some," I admitted.

She turned from her list and narrowed her eyes at me. "'Some' is not enough. Tomorrow is Friday!"

"I know what day it is, Nonna. What would you have me do? Torture a confession out of somebody?" I held up my hand. "Never mind. Don't answer that."

My grandmother slammed down her pencil and hit me with her best shot. "Don't you care about your family?"

I groaned. "Of course I do. And I care about the Casa Lido. But I'm not a cop. I'm not a real detective. I've been doing research and talking to people."

But my brother's question echoed in my head: to what end? Did I really believe the murderer would come forward because I was digging around? Would I round up all the suspects in the dining room and have a showdown á la Poirot? Bullied by my grandmother and egged on by Sofia, I may have already tipped off a murderer. And it certainly could be argued that I was hindering a police investigation. All because I was treating this as an intellectual exercise instead of the crime that it was. Maybe it was time to pack it in.

"I've done all I can, Nonna. We have to leave this to the police now." I steeled myself, expecting an Italian blast. But there was only silence. Instead of anger on my grandmother's face, all I saw was her age.

Then she shrugged and shook her head. "All right, Victoria. Now please go out to the garden and pick some mint for the *tea freddo*."

I stopped at the back door. "Nonna, you'll let Tim come back, won't you? You know he didn't do this."

She straightened up and lifted her chin, her face once again hard. "I know no such thing," she said, turning back to her work.

As I headed toward the garden, I had to remind myself only plants were out here now. *No dead bodies, Vic. It's okay.* Skirting around the shed, I found the patch of herbs and sniffed out the spearmint plants. I rubbed a leaf between my fingers, and the rich scent brought back summertime and childhood—a childhood that was inextricably bound up with the Casa Lido. What would happen to it now?

I sighed, picked a handful of leaves, and looked over the garden. The herbs had taken nicely, and the tomato plants were all in, thanks to a couple of Nando's cousins. I bent to look at the plants Nonna had ready to go. Her usual flats of impatiens and begonias threw bright color against the green grass. Larger pots of perennials flanked both sides of the bed. Few had flowered, so I stooped to read their tags. There were balloon flowers and daisies and sunflowers that would grow as tall as the fence. At the back of the row was a pretty purple flower on a long stalk. When I bent closer to read the white plastic tag that poked up from the soil, I felt exactly as I had when I looked down at Parisi's corpse. My knees buckled; I dropped the tag as though it were toxic, because it was. The Latin name swam before my eyes. The plant I couldn't remember wasn't "purple digit," but *Digitalis purpurea*, commonly known as foxglove.

And that's when Iris's words finally came back to me: *Enough of that will stop your heart.*

Chapter Twenty-one

Dropping the handfuls of mint at my feet, I slapped at my front pocket. *Phone, yes.* I dug it from my jeans pocket and held it in my shaking left hand, tapping wildly at the screen to pull up Google. My fingers felt thick and clumsy as I spelled out "f-o-x-g-l-o-v-e" in the search bar. Sweeping my finger across the screen, I scrolled down to read about the plant's toxicity, and there it was: The substances in the foxglove plant were known to cause "deadly disturbances of the heart." I would have to do more research later, but for now I had seen enough. I backed away from the plant and shoved my phone into my pocket. I scooped up the mint leaves with trembling hands, and for the second time in ten days, ran from that garden as though the hounds of hell were nipping at my heels.

I went straight to the sink, keeping my back to my grandmother. Because if she looked at my face, I was certain these words would be scrolling across my forehead: *There is a poisonous plant in the garden ... a poisonous plant in the garden ... a poisonous plant ... a poisonous plant ... Holy Mother of God, what am I going to do?*

"Victoria?" My grandmother's sharp tones took the tiniest edge off my rising hysteria.

"What?" I said, only a few decibels shy of a shriek.

"What are you doing at the sink? That water is running too long."

"I'm, uh, rinsing the mint leaves." Scrubbing them raw was more accurate. I turned off the water and grabbed a paper towel, patting the leaves dry while a new phrase took hold in my tortured brain: *deadly disturbances of the heart. Ha,* I thought. *Sounds like one of Mom's books.* But this story was real and playing itself out right in front of me.

"Here." My grandmother dumped a large bag of greens on the counter. "Now you can wash the escarole."

I peeked inside the bag. The leafy green heads certainly *looked* like escarole. I pulled off a leaf and stared at its curly edges and the creamy whiteness of the stem. When I snapped it, I recognized the fibrous strings and figured it was safe.

"What, you never seen 'scarole before?" Nonna spoke right into my ear and I jumped, slapping my hand on my chest.

"Don't do that, Nonna! You scared me to death." And then I realized what a poor choice of words that was.

"Victoria, what is wrong with you? You say you want to help in the kitchen, but all you do is daydream." She pointed to the bag of greens. "Get moving. I am going out to the dining room."

"Daydream" was not the word I would have chosen; "surreal nightmare" was a much better description for the state I found myself in. I forced myself to take a breath and used the job at hand to focus. While I automatically rinsed and tore the greens, I collected my thoughts in a rational manner.

Okay, there was no proof that a foxglove plant was used to kill Parisi. Those leaves didn't look like salad

greens, for one thing. But I would have a better idea
about that as soon as I could get to a computer and do
more research. And just because there was a foxglove
plant behind the Casa Lido kitchen did not mean that
someone here used it to kill him. *But*, cara, said the
voice of my detective, Bernardo Vitali, *what have I
taught you about coincidence?*

"Shut up, Bernardo," I muttered, furiously tearing escarole leaves. At least I was calmer now, but I needed a
plan. Once I was done with prep, I would sneak back to
the garden and do what I had been too panicked to
think of earlier: use my phone to take a couple of pictures of the plant. The minute I could get away from the
restaurant today, I'd learn everything I could about *Digitalis purpurea.*

But after the escarole came the carrots for Chef Massimo's famous puree, and after the carrots came a bin full
of flatware to be wiped clean, and after the flatware
came water pitchers to be filled. When Lori showed up
at ten thirty, my grandmother still had not released me
from my bondage.

"Hey, you wanted to come back," Lori said as she
tied on her apron. "You know the drill."

"That I do, girlfriend." I sighed as I folded linens
around the forks and knives.

She took a seat next to me. "I'll help with the setups.
You'd better get sharper points on those napkins. Your
nonna will check 'em all."

I groaned. "Of course she will."

"Where is everybody, by the way?"

"Nonna's back in the kitchen, Mom's in the office,
and last I saw my dad, he was prepping the bar."

"Ha," Lori said. "You mean avoiding the womenfolk.
Is Dreamboat working this morning?"

"No. Massimo and Nando are in the kitchen." I made a face. "They kicked me out."

"Massi doesn't like anybody in there. He barely tolerates Nando." She slipped a knife and fork into a napkin and folded it with expert ease. "I guess they gave Tim the day off, huh?" she said carefully.

"Yup." I studied the napkin in front of me, not wanting to pick up this particular conversational thread.

Lori patted my arm. "We know Tim would never do such a thing. I don't care if he was involved with that Angie again."

At her words, I had the sudden sensation of the Ferris wheel, with the ground under my feet falling away. My stomach churning, I smoothed out another napkin and flattened it with my fingers. It seemed minutes before I could find my voice. "What do you mean 'involved' with her?"

"Maybe 'involved' isn't the right word. But she was in here a couple of times before her husband died. I just never connected her with Parisi until after he—"

"Dropped dead in the restaurant?" I said harshly.

"Hey, you might want to lower your voice on that one."

"Right." But in that moment, I didn't care if the whole town heard me, because all *I* could hear were Lori's words: *She was in here a couple of times.* A couple of times. Not once, as Tim had implied that night in the pantry. I flashed on Angie's look of false pity as she taunted me: *Is that what he told you?* And if he lied about that . . . "No," I said aloud.

Lori frowned at me. "You okay? Listen, I'll finish these up. You go take a break."

"Thanks, LJ, but it's almost time for lunch to start, and we have to get these out on the tables. And listen, do me a favor, would you? Don't mention to my parents that Anjelica is actually Angie, okay?"

She winked at me. "You got it."

Just as we finished setting the last table, our first customer came through the doors. She was a large woman, broad-shouldered and curvy. Her bright orange suit set off the deep caramel color of her skin; she wore her hair in a cropped afro, the ends tipped in blond highlights.

"May I help you?" I smiled, and though her face was serious, I was mesmerized by her brownish gold eyes. *Tiger eyes,* I thought, and some instinct told me it was an apt description for her.

"Table for one, please." After I seated her and left her with a menu, I stepped back to the coffee station to pick up a water pitcher. But I couldn't take my eyes off our customer. As she shifted in her chair, her jacket opened, and I clutched Lori's arm.

"Oh my God." I gasped. "Is that a gun in her pocket?"

"Or is she just glad to see us?" Lori said with a grin.

"It's not funny," I hissed. "She's got a *gun!*"

"She's allowed to have a gun, Vic." Lori's patient, explanatory tone was similar to one I heard her use on her son. "She's the county prosecutor, Regina Sutton."

Chapter Twenty-two

I wanted to panic. In fact, I wanted to run out the door as fast as my little waitress clogs could carry me. Instead, I just said, "Oh," and had the following thoughts:

1) There's a county prosecutor in the dining room.
2) There's a poisonous plant in the garden.

Considering the lady tiger that was burning bright over there at Table Four, the fearful symmetry of those two truths circled me like a chain. And there was no escape.

Regina Sutton looked up at me and beckoned in a manner worthy of her name. Lori nudged me in the side. "She's ready for you to take her order."

"Ohhhh-kay, then." I groped for a pad and pen inside my apron pocket; unluckily, they were both there, so I couldn't stall any longer. I stepped stiffly toward the table, feeling as though I were walking through a bowl of my grandmother's *zabaglione*. Standing at Sutton's elbow, I flinched when she trained those scary golden eyes on my face.

"I'd like a half order of the pasta special. And the house salad, please." Her voice was low, melodious, and commanding, but I was barely able to hear it over the one screaming in my head. *She ordered the salad!*

I gripped my pen, scribbled something on the pad, and nodded. She tilted her head and looked at me. "Would you mind telling me what's in it?"

"Wh-what's in what?" I stammered.

"The salad," she said, pronouncing each syllable separately.

"Uh, it's got spring greens, arugula, olives, tomatoes—" *And no foxglove or pokeweed. I promise. Calm down, Vic,* I told myself. *You're getting hysterical.*

"Thank you," she interrupted. "That will be fine. Dressing on the side, please."

My head snapped up and my mouth went slack. Was she re-creating the crime? I blinked, and Sutton frowned. "Are you quite all right?" she asked.

"Fine, yes. Sorry. I'll just go put in that order." I spun around, quick to escape, but froze at the sound of the rich contralto behind me.

"And, Ms. Rienzi, when you come back with my lunch, do sit and join me for a moment." It wasn't a request.

How did she know my name? Worse yet, what did she want with me? My mind offered several terrible possibilities: She was arresting me for murder; she was arresting me for withholding evidence; she was arresting me for obstructing a police investigation. Or perhaps all three.

I lurked behind the kitchen door while Nando prepared her order, watching with equal parts admiration and dismay as he swiftly arranged her salad on a platter. And because Tim's *pasta fresca* cooked up quickly, her whole lunch was ready in less than ten minutes. I loaded a tray with the two plates and a container of dressing, took a deep breath, and stepped into the dining room to meet my fate.

Sutton put an e-reader aside and watched in silence

as I set her plates down in front of her. I looked down at her and attempted to smile brightly. "I'll just go get you more water."

I looked down to find a restraining hand on my arm, a hand with five gorgeously decorated fingernails, and I wondered how she fired a gun with that manicure.

"No need for that," she said. "The other waitress already filled my glass, as you can see." She tilted her head and bared two rows of very white teeth. "Please sit down, Ms. Rienzi."

I dropped into the chair across from hers. "You know who I am."

"Yes, I do." She waited a beat and smiled again. *"Ms. Reed."* She patted the cover of her device. "I was just reading your latest. It's nicely written. Good solid prose."

"Oh. Thank you." My smile, no longer forced, now spread across my face. Like all writers, I crave praise. I waited happily for her to go on.

"For the most part, you do your homework," she announced. She settled her napkin on her lap. "But while you're careful with the crime scene details, you cut corners in other places. You skim over some things that might get in the way of your plot. Now and then your detective behaves in ways that would never fly in real life. But I imagine that's all in service of the story, correct?"

Always up for a discussion of my work, I sat up expectantly in my chair. "Yes. I guess you'd say it's author license."

"Exactly: author license. In your books, you have built a world. And in that world, you have license." She folded her hands and rested her chin on them, capturing my cowardly eyes with her own. "But in this world—in *my* world—you do not. Is that understood?"

Brazen it out, Vic. I also folded my own hands in front

of me—okay, it was to keep them from shaking—and forced myself to meet her eyes. "I'm not sure what you mean, Ms. Sutton."

One thin brow arched. "Given that you know who I am, I'm fairly certain that you do know what I mean." She motioned to me with her fork. "But I will be happy to elucidate. Interviews with the cast of *The Jersey Side*. That little trip to Ocean Grove. And meetings with at least two other people whose actions have bearing on this case." She tapped the tabletop with her fingernail for emphasis. "These actions could all be construed as obstruction."

"Or . . . research." I gulped and eyed her glass of ice water. "Um, for a book," I continued.

"Perhaps." But a small quirk of her lips conveyed skepticism. She speared some pasta, put it in her mouth, and her eyes widened. She chewed it slowly and then nodded. "This is delicious. It would certainly be a shame if this restaurant had to close."

In that moment, I felt as though my grandmother had suddenly taken possession of my body, and my fear dissipated. "That sounds like a threat," I said quietly.

"Not a threat, Ms. Rienzi. Just a possibility. You realize, don't you, that this place could have been closed down days ago? And that it was only through the good auspices of local law enforcement—of which your brother is a part—that it has remained open this long."

What was Sutton suggesting? That Danny had used influence to keep the restaurant from closing? "As I'm sure you are aware," I said, "my brother has no part in this investigation. It would be a clear conflict of interest."

"It would be indeed, Ms. Rienzi. Just as it would be a conflict of interest—and highly unethical—for your brother to share any information about this case with you. And such actions could cost him his position on the force." She forked a few more pieces of fresh pasta into her mouth and briefly shut her eyes. "Truly wonderful food," she murmured. "What kind of sauce is this?"

I couldn't keep up with this woman. One minute she's threatening Danny's job, and the next she's waxing poetic over the sauce. "That's our marinara sauce, made with fresh basil and tomatoes we harvest each August." I leaned toward her, flattened my palms on the table, and uttered a statement that was mostly true. "Look, my brother hasn't done anything wrong."

She smiled again, but her eyes were questioning. "Exactly what I would expect a loyal sister to say. And you Rienzis are a loyal bunch. I wonder if that loyalty extends to your employees as well." Without waiting for an answer, she took a bite of greens and nodded again. "The salad is lovely."

Was it coincidence that she mentioned the salad, with unnecessary emphasis on the word, in the same breath as she referred to our "employees"? She had to be talking about Tim. In the space of three minutes, she had implied that my brother was corrupt and that my family was harboring a murderer. I had the distinct impression that Tiger Lady was batting me back and forth between her predatory paws. I stood up from my chair and met that golden gaze with my own. "Ms. Sutton, I'm not sure why you wanted to speak to me, but I don't appreciate games and—"

"Games?" she asked, her voice low and harsh. "I don't play games, Ms. Rienzi. And certainly not where a man's death is concerned." She sipped her water, her eyes never leaving my face.

Predictably, I blinked first. "Please," I said. "I know you can't talk about it, but if you're planning to make an arrest, wouldn't it be the kind thing to let us know?"

And then Regina Sutton did a strange thing. She

chuckled. And then the chuckle grew into a deep laugh that shook her shoulders. "Oh, Ms. Rienzi," she said, still smiling. "Perhaps you should turn to humor writing." She blotted her mouth with her napkin and shook her head. "In case you have missed my point here today, this is *not* one of your books."

Oh, how tired I was of that particular phrase. "I understand that." I glanced around me and lowered my voice. "Look, my parents and grandmother are on the premises. They're naturally upset by what happened here and its effect on our business. Our season is about to start."

"So you're hoping we can wrap things up nicely for you in time for Memorial Day. Is that it? So long as we arrest someone with no ties to the Casa Lido?"

I smiled weakly. "In a perfect world, yes."

"Or in a perfect story, perhaps?" She ate her last bite of salad, dabbed at her mouth, and reached into her jacket pocket.

I gripped the side of the table, ready for her to train her gun on me. Instead, she handed me her business card. "In the event you come across any information that should be shared with my office." As I stared at the raised gold letters and law enforcement seal, the reality hit me like a cold ocean wave: What I'd gotten myself into was no longer merely an intellectual exercise.

"And in the interest of open communication," she continued, "I will say this: The persons of interest in the case all seem to be tied to this restaurant, and we will be questioning them." She pointed to me with her fork again. "Including you, Ms. Rienzi." Her mouth curved in satisfaction. "After all, you were the one who discovered the body, were you not?"

*   *   *

After she left, I hightailed it back to the kitchen with the excuse that I wanted to watch Nando start the dinner prep. To my great relief, my parents and grandmother had missed the customer at Table Four. Luckily, Regina Sutton had paid in cash, so there would be no telltale receipt in the bottom of the register. (Strangely, however, she'd left me a generous tip.) And may my luck hold, I wished silently, glancing out the open back door toward the garden.

Because Massimo had left for the afternoon, I could remain in the kitchen with impunity. I even talked Nando into showing me how to butterfly chicken breasts. As I pounded them flat between sheets of butcher paper, I obsessed about getting outside to look at that plant again. I jerked my head up as a hopeful thought occurred to me. Had the foxglove even *been* there the day I found Parisi? I remembered seeing a bunch of potted plants, but was that purple flower among them?

"Hey, Nando," I said, my head bent over the chicken, "when did your cousins come and plant the tomatoes?"

"Monday, I think. I know, because we were closed."

"I must have left already, because I didn't see them. Boy, was I glad to get out of that job."

Nando grinned. "Your *abuela* will come up with a new one."

"Probably. In fact, there're still some plants out there in pots." I looked up from the meat I was pounding into submission. "Do you know why your cousins didn't plant those, too?"

"Oh, *sí*, I do. Luis say one of the plants can make you sick."

A chill crept over me. "Is that so?"

He nodded vigorously, his braid bouncing. "He say he and Miguel no mess with that flower." He handed me a plate of neatly sliced cutlets. "And anyway, Miss Guilietta tell them only to do the tomatoes, and she will do the flowers."

They were innocuous words, but the creeping chill grew colder, and I looked down to see goose bumps forming on my arms.

"Luis say they should go in the ground, though," Nando continued. "They been sitting in the pots too long."

I tried to keep my tone casual, a little difficult with my heart pounding harder than my meat mallet. "Really? How long, Nando?"

He paused, his chef's knife poised over the cutting board. "Oh, I dunno, maybe coupla weeks."

A couple of weeks? Had the murder weapon been sitting out in that garden all along? Who would have known it was there? My grandmother, who wasn't on the scene when Parisi was killed. And thank you, Lord, for that small mercy. That left two people—the same two people whose names were in bold on my handy chart: Tim and Mr. Biaggio. Tim, because he knew the Casa Lido as though it were his own home, and Mr. B, because he knew plants. I consoled myself with the thought that of the two, Mr. B was more likely to have known the flower was poisonous. But either way, both men had clear opportunity. But wasn't there a third person? Would Cal have known about the plant? And if he knew, would he have used it to kill Parisi? For what possible reason? I stopped my work, holding the mallet like a judge's gavel, feeling as though I were about to pass sentence upon the Casa Lido and my family's whole future. If *Digitalis purpurea* was indeed the natural substance that killed Parisi, there was a lovely specimen of it not thirty yards from the kitchen door.

Crash! Down came the mallet, loud enough and hard enough to bring Nando to my side. He peeled back the top sheet of paper to look over at my work and shook his head. "Miss Victor, you pound them too thin." He pointed to a spot where the meat was in shreds. "See what happened there."

I saw what happened, all right. Only too clearly—and the thought was making me sick. I dropped the mallet with a clatter. "You're right, Nando. I'm sorry." I had to get out there and get a closer look at that plant. "Listen, I have to make a quick phone call. Do you mind if I take a little break?"

"Go 'head. I'll finish these."

I strode out to the garden blindly. My hands shook as I shot a couple of pictures of the foxglove, then made sure they were saved to the phone. As I stared at the pretty bell-shaped blooms, comprehension dawned: This plant might be the one thing standing between the Casa Lido and complete ruin.

Without giving myself time to think, I slipped the white tag into my jeans pocket, grasped the heavy pot, and looked around wildly for somewhere to put it. A voice in my head—one that sounded strangely like Nonna's—was saying, *Get rid of it. Get rid of it. No one will know.* But a second voice, the one imagined as I created him, came to me in heavily accented Italian. *No, cara. That is not the way,* Bernardo whispered. *You know this will come to no good . . .*

And then another voice broke into my thoughts. One I'd heard quite recently in the dining room.

"Going somewhere with that plant, Ms. Rienzi?"

Chapter Twenty-three

I dropped the plant, straightened up, and smiled into the face of Prosecutor Sutton. "Just moving it to a sunnier spot." Maybe I had been possessed by the spirit of my grandmother; lying was coming much easier to me these days.

"Is that so?" Sutton reached out to finger one of the leaves. "You have any idea what kind of flower this is?"

I shrugged. "I'm not sure. I leave the gardening to my grandmother." It took all of my control not to slide my hand into my jeans pocket to make sure the tag was safely stowed away. I turned to look at her. "Is there anything I can help you with?" Because I couldn't ask, *Why are you snooping around the garden?* Though the answer was obvious.

"Not at the moment." She tilted her head and looked from me back to the foxglove. "But I'll certainly be calling upon you one of these days." She turned to leave, stopped, and smiled slightly. "Just so you are aware, my team has been over this area. And we've taken a careful inventory." Her smile widened. "Lunch was delicious, by the way. You have a nice day now," she called out as she strode away.

I was left staring at the foxglove. *They already know it's here. And if that's what killed him . . .*

"No," I said. "I can't think this way. Not until I know more." Unfortunately, the one person who could tell me more was Nonna.

I found her back in the kitchen, inspecting Nando's work. And my own as well, judging by the scowl on her face. She pointed to my handiwork on the counter. "Victoria, you made a mess of this chicken."

"Sorry, Nonna. I'll do better next time." I glanced over at Nando and then whispered to Nonna, "Could I show you something in the garden?"

Her scowl deepened. "What do you need to show me in the garden? Those basil plants you stripped?"

"Uh, no. Something else."

"Aren't you supposed to be serving?"

"Lori's up front, and this won't take long." I strained for a smile. "If I want to learn about the restaurant, I need to learn about the garden, too."

She made a *humph*ing sound, but followed me out the door to the spot where the foxglove stood in all its deadly innocence.

"This plant," I said. "Isn't it dangerous? Nando said his cousin wouldn't even touch it."

"Victoria," she snapped, "this is what you drag me out here for?" She crossed her arms over her chest. "I have been planting foxglove for years. They're safe if you know how to handle them. I even harvest the seeds."

All parts of the plant are poisonous, I had read, *including the flowers, leaves, and seeds.* Seeds could be well hidden in a salad dressing filled with dried herbs. I swallowed. "Did you say you harvest the seeds?"

"Some years, yes. I put them with the herbs in the pantry."

I closed my eyes. *Oh dear Lord, did I have to do a sweep of the pantry, too? Get a grip, Vic. As if you'd tamper with evidence, even to protect your family or Tim.*

That's what I told myself, anyway. But out here earlier, I had acted on instinct, an instinct that fairly screamed at me to dump that plant.

"Victoria, I don't have all day to stand around here talking about the garden."

My grandmother's sharp tones brought me out of my anxious reverie. "Sorry, Nonna." Would that I had a buck for every time I uttered those words. "I was just a little worried about that plant."

The sun glinted off the lenses of my grandmother's eyeglasses, making it impossible to see the light dawning in her eyes. "You think somebody used this to kill that *cafone*, don't you?" she asked.

Before I could answer, she had already heaved the pot into her arms, and her intention was clear. *Hmm*, I thought, *the tomato doesn't fall too far from the vine*. I put my hand on her scrawny but surprisingly strong arm. "Don't even think about it."

She held the plant against her as though it were a precious commodity. "I don't know what you're talking about, Victoria."

"Yes, you do," I hissed. "You need to put that plant back right now."

"No, I do not. And anyway, it's dying. I think I'll go put it out in the compost." She turned to walk away.

"Nonna," I called. "You can't. The police know it's here."

She shrugged and kept walking. "If you do that," I called out, "Danny will lose his job."

She paused, but didn't turn around. "You don't want Danny to be kicked off the force, do you?"

I watched her shoulders droop and felt a pang of pity for her. She was only following the same impulse I'd had earlier—to protect her family and the livelihood that meant so much to her. She turned back to me, and I took the heavy pot from her arms and set it back down.

"Look," I said, "there's no proof this is what killed him. That's the trouble; we don't know what killed him."

She narrowed her eyes and pointed straight at my nose. "You promised me you'd find out!"

I hadn't exactly promised; in fact, I'd been strong-armed and guilted into this little investigation. But now that I *was* in it, there was no turning back. "I'll try, okay?" I said with a sigh. "In the meantime, you leave that plant right where it is." And then I did something I'd been afraid to do for months: I kissed my grandmother on her paper-thin cheek. She looked at me with an expression of suspicion and something that might have been pleasure. Or a touch of *agita*. Without saying another word, she walked back into the kitchen, leaving me in the garden to review.

A poisonous plant discovered in the garden. A visit from the county prosecutor. And a small spot of evidence tampering.

Just another day around the Casa Lido.

I pulled out my phone and texted Sofia. *Can you meet me at the cottage around 3? New developments!*

If I knew my partner-in-solving-crime, she'd be at my door at 2:58. In the meantime, though, I had to finish out the lunch shift. And pray there would be no more visits from Regina Sutton.

Sofia made the wise decision to stop for coffees before showing up at my door. We sat out on the deck, facing the ocean, sipping the reviving caffeine and scribbling notes as we talked.

"I can't believe Sutton actually showed up at the restaurant," Sofia said. "What do you think that was about?"

"Well, to warn me off, of course. And maybe to check things out for herself. She said her 'team' had already been over the garden. And probably noted everything in it."

"Including this." Sofia held up the white plant tag, then slipped it into the red folder.

"Don't remind me."

"Vic, there's no proof this plant killed him. And wouldn't his stomach contents show that anyway?"

"Yes, they would—in another couple of weeks, when the testing is done."

"But all Danny said was that the medical examiner had a 'hunch about a natural substance,' right?"

"Right. But if there's one thing I've learned from writing mysteries, it's not to trust coincidence. And symptoms of *Digitalis* poisoning plus a foxglove plant on the scene is a bit too coincidental for me." I looked across at Sofia. "And for Nonna, apparently." Then I shared the conversation with my grandmother, right up to the moment Nonna was ready to dump the evidence out on the compost heap.

Sofia shook her head and grinned. "I could just see her carting that plant off the premises."

"She almost did. You don't think a little thing like a felony arrest would stop her, do you? No, it was the thought of her precious Danny getting kicked off the force."

"Speaking of my beloved husband, SIL, let's go over again what he told you that day out on the marina." She pulled out a page from the folder. "Okay. So the police know about the threatening letters Angie talked about."

"Right. But that's as much as he would say."

"Do you think the person who sent the letters is the same person who killed him?"

"Of course it's possible. But in a sense, he was a public figure. He produced a reality show that's a sensation, but was also crude and offensive." I shrugged. "To tell you the truth, I'm surprised he didn't get *more* threatening letters."

"Okay," Sofia said. "What else is here? Both water bottles were clean, right? The one you served him and the one he brought with him."

"Yup. And the biggest bombshell of all was, of course, that both Angie and Emily have an alibi."

Sofia held up her pen. "Which checked out."

"Unfortunately." I stared out at the water, my mind returning to the same thought: It's Tim or Mr. B. But something else buzzed around my brain, something as annoying and elusive as the sand flies that tormented us each summer. But just as quickly, it flew away.

"Hey, Vic," Sofia said, her voice rising. "Hang on a minute. Danny also told you Parisi was on medication. Who's to say one of those two crazy women didn't slip something into his medicine bottle? Maybe it just *looks* like something he ate killed him."

I sat straight up in the deck chair. "Holy crap. I hadn't thought of that. Gosh, Sofe. I wonder if he took a pill during lunch? Angie would have had access to his medicine."

"So would Emily," Sofie said firmly, "and you know it. She saw him the day before. It would have been easy enough to switch a medicine bottle or add something to his." She grabbed my arm with a samurai grip. "Wait— they use *Digitalis* for heart medication, don't they? It must come in a pill form."

"Of course! And he was already on beta blockers. Who knows what that combination might do to somebody with a bad heart?" I grabbed my sister-in-law's face and gave her a big smacking kiss on the cheek. "You're a genius, Sofia Delmonico."

She grinned at me. "You mean I'm a fricken genius." She already had her laptop open for a search. She tried "beta blockers and *Digitalis*" and got a bunch of articles from medical journals that weren't for the lay reader. She groaned. "I might be a genius, but I'm no doctor. I'm lost here."

"Let me try." As I read over her shoulder, I learned a few important facts. The substance in *Digitalis* used in heart medication was digoxin. Sometimes digoxin was prescribed with beta blockers, but there were a number of warnings listed about using the drugs together. And then I read the sentence that changed everything. "Here it is, Sofe!" I pointed at the screen. "I don't get the chemistry either, but listen to this: 'Digoxin concentrations are increased with beta blockers, causing serious decrease in heart rate.'"

She turned to look at me, her eyes wide. "One of those women fixed him a nasty pharmaceutical cocktail."

"And whichever of them did it also engineered that meeting in Ocean Grove to give herself an alibi." I nodded slowly. "It makes sense, SIL. Finally, something makes sense. And my money's still on Angie for the culprit."

She shook her head. "I vote Emily. That business card is a fake, and there's something suspicious about her showing up at the restaurant to see you." She shut down her computer and stood up. "In fact, it's high time we did some digging into her life, and I'm gonna start right now. I'll check in with you later."

After she left, I watched the waves break on the shore and my heart lifted. For the first time in days, I had some hope. Hope that Tim wouldn't end up on trial for murder. Hope that the restaurant wouldn't close down. And hope that I'd finally get back to my book and put all of this behind me. And then my phone rang.

"Hello, Victoria!" I winced as Nina LaGuardia's trilling TV voice assaulted my ear. "Do you know what day this is?"

"Uh . . . Thursday," I said weakly.

"Now, really, do you think that playing dumb will work with me? You know very well your time is up. We need to schedule that interview, and pronto!"

"Listen, Nina. I'm close. I really am. And if I'm right, this story will be huge." I needed to throw her something, and quickly. "I happen to know the county prosecutor will be bringing in persons of interest any day."

"I know that," she said impatiently. "What I don't know is who killed Gio Parisi, which is what you promised to find out. Are you telling me you don't have that information for me?"

I swallowed, and the sound seemed to echo across the entire beach. "I need more time. Just a couple of days."

"Uh-uh. Sorry, darling. We had a deal. So you'd better be ready to have your skinny behind in hair and makeup at five tomorrow morning."

"Wait, Nina." I had to hold her off. What could I possibly give her that would buy me a couple more days? And then inspiration struck. "Would you hear me out for a second?"

"I'm very busy, Victoria, so make this quick."

"You give me two more days, and I'll do another exclusive interview with you when my next mystery comes out."

She yawned loudly into the phone. "Not interested."

"That's too bad because the next book in the series is the HBO tie-in." I crossed myself and sent up a quick Act of Contrition, neither of which would be enough to keep me from burning in hell for this one.

Her voice quickened with interest. "HBO picked up your books?"

"I really shouldn't even be talking about it, so this is all on the down low at the moment, okay?" I lowered my voice for effect. "I mean, De Niro's people still have to get back to us."

"Robert De Niro!" she squealed. "Oh my God, is he playing Bernardo?"

"That's the plan." *In my dreams, anyway.* "So can I have a couple more days?"

She sighed. "Victoria, you'd better come through on this. On *all* of it. Or that little 'no comment' snippet is going to look like an award-winning production compared to what I'll do to you next time."

I had no doubt of that. So now I had about forty-eight hours to find Gio Parisi's murderer. Or to get Robert De Niro on the phone.

Chapter Twenty-four

*T*he next morning officially kicked off Memorial Day weekend, and a reprieve for the Casa Lido hovered tantalizingly near. But only if we could prove that Parisi took something that caused his fatal heart attack, most likely in tandem with the beta blockers he was already prescribed. Did the dead man habitually carry his medicine? Or did he take it at home and leave it in a medicine chest where anyone (and by "anyone," I meant Angie) could have substituted something else for it? But how easily could that be done? How could the Black Widow have obtained the drug, for example? There were still so many missing pieces, the most important being what the police knew about Parisi's meds. I was about to risk a phone call to my brother when Sofia's number appeared on my phone.

"Listen, Vic," she said. "I've done every people search imaginable online, and I can't find Emily Haverford. At least not one fitting the description of *our* Emily Haverford. There're only two in New Jersey. One's a baby and the other died last year."

"Did you try some other states?"

"New York and Connecticut. It didn't make sense to look anywhere else. She told you she'd known Parisi for years, and he's got two addresses, one in New York and one in north Jersey. If she saw him on a regular basis, she'd have to live somewhere nearby, right?"

"True. But I think we should do a countrywide search just to make sure."

"Well, I also did a reverse lookup on the phone number on her business card. It's a cell phone in Ocean County, which argues that she's living in Jersey. I'll do a US search, but I doubt I'll get anything. Let's face it, SIL. There's only one logical explanation: The woman who came to the restaurant is using a fake name. Which means she has something to hide."

"It could be that she's married. Maybe she was living a double life, carrying on an affair with Parisi using another name."

Sofie's tone was doubtful. "What makes you think that?"

"Don't forget, Angie knows her as 'Emily.' The guy in Ocean Grove heard her use that name. If that's not her real name, she's been using that alias for a while."

"It all sounds sketchy to me. I think you should try that phone number on her card."

"That's a good idea. I could call her on the pretext that I've got more information about Parisi's death."

"And then get more information about *her*. Keep me posted."

As soon as I ended Sofia's call, I tried the number Emily Haverford gave me, only to get her voice mail, in which she identified herself as "Emily." I was beginning to agree with my sister-in-law—there *was* something sketchy about the woman calling herself Emily Haverford.

Would Danny tell me anything at all? In my desperate state, it was worth a try.

"What is it, Vic?" His voice held suspicion, impatience, and a small note of warning.

"Can you talk?" I whispered.

"Yes. Why are *you* whispering?"

"Good question, since I'm alone in the cottage." I hesitated, knowing I could be compromising him with this call. "Look, Dan, I know I said I wouldn't—"

"You can stop right there, sis. I heard all about Sutton showing up at the restaurant."

I winced. "You did?"

"We all did—my fellow officers, my chief, the mayor—you name 'em, they heard it."

"Oh, shi . . . shoot. I'm sorry, Danny."

"Can't be helped," he said shortly.

For some reason, I was whispering again. "So I guess this means that if, for example, I had a question about Parisi's medication, you couldn't answer it."

"Got it in one, kid."

"Or," I continued, "if I wanted to know about Parisi's stomach contents. Or Emily Haverford's real name."

I heard him sigh loudly. "Listen, Vic, I know that Nonna's on your back about this. But you have to stop this little investigation you've got going—and that includes my wife."

"But, Danny, you don't understand. I—"

And what was I to say? *I have a theory that hinges on information you can't give me. Oh, and I just found a foxglove plant in the garden, and it's poisonous, in case you didn't know.* Of course, the police might already have this information. But if they didn't, and I told Danny, he'd have no choice *but* to tell them. And he was already in some hot water.

"*What* don't I understand?" His question came out as a snarl.

"Nothing, okay? Don't go all 'bad cop' on me." I looked out my window at the peaceful blue sky and calm gray ocean. "There's just one thing I have to ask,

Dan. Is there even a chance that Tim could be arrested for this?"

The silence that stretched out between us said it all.

When I got on my bike that morning, I didn't head in the direction of the restaurant, but toward the other end of town to a place I hadn't visited in more than eight years. As I pedaled down the familiar street, the years melted away and I was once again a gangly girl with a desperate crush on an older boy, riding past his house in hopes of a glimpse of him.

I stopped the bike in front of a white seaside colonial with black shutters and a wide porch with tall columns—the house where Tim had grown up. I stood there thinking how different this classic home was in comparison to our two-family house across town. But when I fell in love with Tim, I'd also fallen in love with this house and his elegant, educated parents.

I wheeled the bike down the stone driveway to where I'd find Tim, in the carriage house at the back of the property. Tim had occupied this house on and off since he'd turned eighteen, a fact that scandalized my parents, who firmly believed their children should be under their roof at all times, even after they married. I had a rush of memories as I stood in front of the arched doorway of the cottage; I raised my hand to knock when Tim opened the door.

He was unshaven, wearing pajama pants and a ripped T-shirt bearing the faded letters of the Stone Pony. "Hey," he said. "I heard your bike on the driveway stones."

"You used to listen for that sound, once upon a time."

He rubbed his stubbly chin and smiled slightly. "I remember."

I followed him into the cottage, unprepared for the mess that met my eyes. Dirty dishes lined the tiny kitchen counter; there were clothes draped over every available surface, and the pullout couch seemed to be serving as both eating *and* sleeping area. I wrinkled my nose. "It smells like boy in here."

"Thanks, Vic. If I'd known you were coming, I would have tidied up." He heaved open the small kitchen window, letting in the sweet sea air.

"Much better." I shifted a pair of jeans and a nachos bag to one side of the bed and sat. "What's up?"

He slumped into the only other seat in the small living room, stretching his long legs out in front of him. "You tell me. Am I fired?"

"Don't be ridiculous."

"Why? It wouldn't be the first time."

"You know why they fired you the first time."

He lifted his head and looked at me steadily. "Because I hurt their daughter so bad they couldn't stand to look at me."

I blinked, surprised to feel the tears. "They forgave you a long time ago, Tim. And right now, I think they just want you to lie low for a while. Until it all blows over."

" 'Lie low' suggests I did something." He sat forward in the chair and planted his hands on his knees. "And you know I didn't, Vic."

I looked at this man I'd known for more than half my life. He was bleary-eyed and stubbly, his hair a mess of unruly curls, yet I still felt a surge of affection (and other things) when I looked at him. I saw a man who'd been my friend and my lover, a man who'd brought me both grief and joy. I saw an indulged only son who had found his calling late in life and had trouble committing either to a woman or a job. He was temperamental and passionate, flirtatious and funny. Tim Trouvare was many things. But he wasn't a murderer.

"You're right. I do."

He got up from his chair and sat down next to me. "You believe me?" he asked, taking my hand.

I nodded, but slipped my hand from his. "About that I do." I pushed the curls back from his forehead. "I don't think you're capable of killing anybody. Unless perhaps they got in your way in the kitchen."

He grinned, making my heart do a little somersault. But then his face grew serious. "This doesn't look good for me, Vic." He stood abruptly and started pacing the length of the small room. "*I* served the guy his last meal. *I* washed his plates afterward."

"And you had a history with his wife," I added, a bit more acerbically than I intended.

Tim plopped back into the chair, both arms hanging at his sides. "Right. You don't need to remind me."

"I think maybe I do, Tim."

He frowned. "What's that supposed to mean?"

"It means that when I asked you about Angie, you implied you'd seen her only one time before Parisi came into the restaurant. But you'd had more contact with her than that. I saw you on the phone with her."

"Well, yeah, there were some phone calls." He hesitated.

"And despite what you told me, she'd been to the restaurant more than once, right?"

Tim blinked and squirmed as though there were a white light shining in his face. "Yeah, maybe a couple of times."

Funny how those words—*a couple of times*—could propel me back eight years in time to this very room. To the night Tim confessed he'd fallen in love with somebody else. Back then the pain had had a knife-edge so sharp, it took my breath away; now it was simply a dull ache. But it hadn't gone away. "That night in the pantry," I said, "I asked you if you'd been involved—"

"You meant was I sleeping with her," he interrupted. "And the answer is no." He came over to where I was sitting and knelt at my feet, his hands resting on my knees. "She and I were done a long time ago, Vic. If she cheated on her husband, it wasn't with me."

I let out a breath I'd been holding, and he sat down next to me at the edge of the bed. But I slid over a couple of inches so I wouldn't get distracted by his leg touching mine. "All right, Tim," I said. "Help me here. Why do you think she contacted you in the first place?"

"I'm not sure. A sympathetic ear, maybe? Male attention?" He smiled grimly. "She likes male attention."

"Tell me something I don't know. Did she confide in you?"

He nodded. "A little. She would talk about Parisi. They fought a lot. She said he was verbally abusive."

"That doesn't surprise me," I said. "But forgive me if my heart doesn't exactly break for her. She knew what she was getting into."

"She also suspected he was seeing the old girlfriend again."

"Emily Haverford."

Tim frowned. "Is that her name? How do you know it? She never mentioned it to me."

I struggled with how much to tell Tim. I wasn't sure if he knew how deeply I was insinuating myself into this case; he might try to talk me into dropping it or, worse, allowing him to help me. Some instinct told me not to share my conversation with Emily. I looked at him and shrugged. "You hear things. So basically, Angie was crying on your big, strong shoulder. Is that it?"

"I guess. But she was interested in what I was doing, too."

I'll bet. "What do you mean?" I asked.

"Well, she heard I was at the restaurant. She wanted to come down and see where I worked."

More likely to case the joint, I thought. *And to set you up, Tim.* I wanted to lay my father's odds that Angie had found some way to poison Parisi *before* he got to the restaurant, but I couldn't indulge in too much wishful thinking. Not as long as that foxglove plant occupied the Casa Lido garden.

I heard Tim say something; then he waved a hand in front of my face. "Hey? You in there, Vic?"

"Sorry. My mind's in a million places. Did you ask me something?"

"Yeah. Do they know how Parisi died? I haven't read anything about an autopsy."

"I'm pretty sure the investigators are keeping that quiet. They know it was his heart, but something caused the fatal attack. Toxicology screens take a long time."

"Danny must know something."

I shook my head. "That well is dry, my friend." I hesitated and then made a decision. "Tim, what do you know about the garden behind the restaurant?"

"Um, I get my herbs there. And we harvest the tomatoes in August. That's about it."

"What about the other plants? Do you know the different flowers Nonna's got out there?"

He wrinkled his brow in a manner I found adorable. "Should I?" he asked.

"No, actually. In fact, it's better if you don't. But there's a plant out there that's poisonous. And there's a substance in it that can cause heart attacks."

Tim held up both hands. "I did not put a *thing* in that guy's food."

"I know that, Tim. But the prosecutor's office doesn't have my faith in you."

"What?" The word came out in a whisper.

"I had a visit from the county prosecutor, Regina Sutton. She said that the 'persons of interest' in the case all seem to be connected to the Casa Lido. It's likely we're all gonna get pulled in for questioning. It's also likely they know that plant is out there and that we had access to it."

Tim dropped his head and raked his hands through his hair. "God, my life is over," he said.

I grabbed his arm. "Look. There's nothing definite about any of this. Okay, right now everyone's assuming there was something in his food. But there might have been another way he died. Something I'm looking into."

His face took on a guarded expression. "Does this have to do with Angie?"

"Maybe, but I can't really talk about it."

"Don't you trust me, Vic?"

How to answer that question? The truth was, I trusted Tim with my life. I just didn't trust him where Angie was concerned. But I wasn't going to go there at this moment. "Tim, the less I tell you, the better. Don't you see?"

He crossed his arms. "Not really."

"Men." I sighed. "Listen, if Sutton pulls you in for questioning, you have to answer her honestly. I think I've already said too much, so I won't be sharing any theories I might have with you, either. Without the tox screen, they're only educated guesses anyway." I stood up and kissed him on the cheek. "I have to get over to the restaurant. You hang in there. Go do something useful." I grinned at him. "You might want to start with a shower."

"That's the plan."

I turned to leave when I heard his voice behind me.

"Hey, Vic? Are you seeing Lockhart?"

Didn't see that one coming. I turned to look at him. "I wouldn't say 'seeing.' We just went out that one night."

"Yeah?" He slid me a sideways glance. "You likely to do it again?"

What I said next surprised me. "I honestly don't know. But it's not like I have to explain anything to you."

He patted my shoulder. "You're right; you don't. But in the end, Vic, it's always gonna be me and you—you know that, don't you?"

I looked at him steadily. "I used to know that. But I'm afraid of being vulnerable again."

He took both my hands. "Angie was a mistake; it didn't take me that long to figure it out. But by then it was too late. You were gone." He let go of one hand and tapped the piece of sea glass I wore around my neck. "You're still wearing this. I must still mean something to you." He cupped my face with his free hand. "Do I, Victoria?"

Just for a second, I rested my cheek against his hand. "You'll always mean something to me," I said. "But we have much bigger problems at the moment—like keeping you out of jail."

Chapter Twenty-five

I never got back to the restaurant that day, hoping Nonna would forgive me if she knew I'd spent the day laboring over my notes and creating more suspect charts. I was mulling over how I'd put off Nina again when my phone vibrated. I jumped. Thankfully, it was only my agent.

"Hey, Josh. What's up? I'm not coming back to New York, if that's what you called to bug me about."

"C'mon, Vic. I know you're committed to your new project. For now, anyway. Actually, I had some information I thought you might be interested in—about the Gemellis."

My senses were on high alert; I shifted the phone closer to my ear. "I'm interested."

"Well, it turns out the issue with Mikey G wasn't a contract dispute. That's just what Gemelli Senior was putting out there. Word was, Parisi wanted Mikey G dropped from the show. Apparently, the kid and his father were more trouble than they're worth."

I scrabbled in my purse for my notebook and a pen. "Not surprising. Thanks, Josh. Did this come from your friend Chaz?"

"Yup."

"Let me know if he tells you anything else, okay?"

"Will do, Vic. Hey, how's Isabella these days?"

"She's barely out of the port of Naples."

He gave a short bark of laughter. "Let me know when she reaches our welcoming shores, okay?"

"Funny, Josh. And thanks again."

Sofia and I had been focused on Mr. B and the two women—perhaps too much so. It was time to find out a bit more about Gemelli and son.

"Here're all my notes on them," Sofia said as we sat at her office computer. "There's some business articles, the old piece about the connection to the Rossini family, and a couple about Mr. G acting as his son's manager."

"What about his personal life?"

Sofia frowned. "Do you think there might be a personal connection with Parisi?"

"Or Angie, maybe?" I added.

"Wishful thinking, SIL." Sofia tapped quickly on the keyboard. "Well, let's start with Facebook."

"The kid's or the dad's?"

"Both."

But Mikey's page was a predictable amalgam of photos featuring Mikey and his friends in various states of inebriation. His father's, on the other hand, yielded more interesting results. His profile picture showed him with his arm around a woman who was much too young to be Mikey's mother.

"Second marriage?" I asked.

"Obvi," Sofia said. "Now, what else is here?" She scrolled down the page.

As the images came into view, I held my breath and leaned closer to the screen. "Are those pictures of his yard?"

"That's what the tags say." Sofia turned from the screen to look at me. "This guy's hobby is gardening."

She pointed to the images. "And just *look* at all those pretty flowers."

"But he wasn't in the restaurant; we just keep getting back to the same thing."

But judging from the sparkle in Sofia's brown eyes, she wasn't bothering with such petty details. Instead, she opened the Web pages we'd found on poisonous plants and starting printing.

"You're gonna owe me a cartridge after this," she said. "In fact, make that two cartridges." She grabbed the pages as they emerged and slipped them into the infamous red folder.

"Listen, Sofe. This is just a waste of time. It's obvious that either Angie or Emily messed with Parisi's medication."

Sofia shook her head. "Maybe. But we got so excited about the pill scenario that we forgot about the stomach contents."

I made a face. "How could I forget? I had a clear view of them all around his body."

"What I mean is, the pill theory works only if there were no plant leaves in his stomach." She wrinkled her nose. "Or in what came *out* of his stomach."

"Exactly. But we don't know that yet. And if we go with the most logical way, it's the pills."

"Even if you're right, we need to rule out Gemelli completely. For all we know, he's got a garden full of poisonous flowers." She shut down her computer and stood up.

I frowned. "You wanna tell me what you're doing?"

"You mean what 'we're' doing, don't you?" She took her purse from the doorknob and fished out her keys. "*We* are taking a little ride to Shelter Point."

I finally caught up with her train of thought but had no intention of boarding. "Oh no, we're not. If you think

I'm gonna go snoop around Michael Gemelli's garden in the middle of the night and compare those pictures," I said, snatching the red folder from her hand, "you are crazier than I thought."

"Fine. Don't find out who killed Parisi." She studied her fingernails in a maddening show of indifference and then looked up at me. "How do you think Tim will look in an orange jumpsuit?"

I sighed as she held out her hand for the folder. "How did I get roped into this?"

So once again I found myself riding shotgun as my sister-in-law sped down the Garden State Parkway.

"I'm sure he's got a giant alarm system," I said. "And probably booby traps out in the yard. Along with a Rossini henchman standing guard." My empty stomach gurgled audibly.

"Stop being such a nervous Nellie. Here." She handed me a protein bar.

I wrinkled my nose at the list of healthy ingredients. "I don't suppose you have any Kit Kats in there?"

Instead of answering such an obvious question, she handed me her GPS. "His address is in the folder. You wanna type it in, please?"

As we entered Shelter Point, I let out a sigh. "I love this town. Too bad you need millions to live here."

"Which Gemelli apparently has." She motioned out the window. "Here's our turn. He's on an ocean block, of course."

"Just drive by once, okay? So we can kind of get the lay of the land." I squirmed in my seat, wishing I hadn't gone along with my sister-in-law's harebrained scheme.

"Will you chill out, already? If it looks like anybody's around, we'll keep going. We can always play it off like we stopped to take a walk on the beach."

"Is that it?" I pointed at a monstrosity of a house;

newly built in a Victorian style, it was crammed with towers, gables, and crenellations. It even had a widow's walk.

"Holy cats." Sofia let out a soft whistle. "Imagine what that thing cost to build. On a beach block in Shelter Point, yet."

"It's reason enough to keep his little cash cow on that show," I said. "But is it reason enough to kill somebody?"

"Maybe," Sofia said, looking past me out my window. "I don't see a car."

"And there aren't any lights on, either."

"We might just be in luck, Vic." Sofia cruised slowly past the house toward the ocean and made a K-turn at the end of the block. "I don't want to park too close, though. We'll stay across the street, nose out for a quick getaway."

"What are we, Bonnie and Clyde?"

She giggled. "More like Thelma and Louise."

"Please, Sofe. I don't plan to drive off any cliffs with you." We sat in the car quietly, staring over at the Gemelli villa. Since she didn't make a move, I dared to hope that she might be changing her mind about this little escapade. But her hand was already on the door handle.

She opened it slowly and looked over at me. "What are you waiting for?"

Oh, I don't know. A bolt of lightning. A minor earthquake. Anything that will get you back in the driver's seat and me back on the Parkway. But my sister-in-law's grim look told me everything I needed to know; then she handed me a flashlight. There was no turning back.

Considering it was Memorial Day weekend, I would have expected more activity around us. At the beach end of the block, there seemed to be a party going on, but near the Gemelli abode, a number of the houses were dark. How long would our luck hold?

"Hey," Sofia whispered. "Do you remember our cover story?"

"Give me a little credit, Sofe, okay? We're friends of the Gemellis from north Jersey. There was no answer at the front door, and we came around the back to see if anyone was out here. But why would we be arriving in the middle of the night?"

She flashed me a grin in the darkness. "Weekend traffic's a bitch."

Once we reached the front of the house, we halted at the sidewalk. "It's a big piece of property," Sofie whispered. "Which is good, because it puts a lotta distance between us and the houses on either side."

"It doesn't mean we won't be caught," I hissed.

"Remind me not to take you on the next stakeout," Sofia said. She motioned with her flashlight. "C'mon. But avoid the garage side; there's probably a sensor light."

I was much more worried about an alarm system that might be connected to the local police station. We crept to the back of the yard and split up, each of us with a flashlight. We had tried to memorize the pictures on the way down, and as I swept my light across the garden beds, I didn't see any oleander or foxglove. Though the beds were well kept and nicely designed, they contained only the usual suspects—day lilies, some hostas, roses, and lots of annuals.

Sofia hurried to my side, a little breathless. "I don't see anything."

"Me neither. Let's just get the hell out of here, okay?"

"I'm with you."

"For once," I muttered. I switched off my light and blinked in the darkness, my attention caught by a dark rectangle in the corner of the garden. I reached out to touch Sofia's arm. "Hang on a second."

"Wait," she said behind me. "Not toward the garage."

But it was too late. I stepped into a circle of bright light that illuminated the whole yard, including the square shape—a garden bench. Without thinking, I hurried over for a closer look. It was a beautiful piece, simple and clean, stained in a deep mahogany that had already started to weather. This piece did not look like it had come from a catalog. It looked handcrafted by a professional, and I had a sinking feeling I knew who.

But before I could look for a marking or signature, a light went on in the house next door. I turned to meet Sofia's frozen gaze. She jerked her head, motioned to me to follow, and we sprinted out of the yard and into the car.

Sofia pulled away swiftly, her tires spraying gravel. I held my breath until we turned on to the main road, my heart and mind racing. *Gemelli could have gotten that damn bench anywhere. Really, what are the odds that Cal made it?* But if he had? If he *had*, there was a clear link between him and Gemelli. Tim's words came back to me with frightening intensity: *Tell Lockhart to stay out of my kitchen.*

I jumped at the sound of Sofia's voice in my ear. "Vic, what the hell were you doing over by the garage?"

"I saw something. A wooden bench in the back of the garden." Still breathless, I made a promise to myself to do more biking. The minute this mess was over.

"A bench? We were supposed to be looking for poisonous plants."

"And look how well that turned out." I rubbed my eyes, suddenly aware of how tired I was. "Okay, this probably means nothing, but Cal told me he makes furniture and that he sold a garden bench recently."

"Oh my God." Sofia breathed. "Did he say who he made it for?"

"No, and don't get carried away. The bench in the Gemellis' yard looked expensive and handmade, but I didn't get close enough to look at it for a maker's mark or signature." I let out a sigh of exhaustion laced with frustration. "This was just a wild-goose chase tonight. A risky one."

"What do you mean?"

"We didn't think this through. Either Parisi's murder was premeditated—which argues for one of the women to have switched his pills—or it was committed on impulse, because somebody had the opportunity."

"And that brings us back to Tim or Mr. B." She turned to look at me. "But why not Cal? If Cal made that bench for Gemelli, that's a connection."

"A tenuous one. And we don't even know that he *did* make it."

"You could ask him," she said hopefully.

"Sure," I said. "I could ask him if he made a garden bench for a guy with sketchy connections who just happens to have a motive for murdering Parisi. And I could follow up with a nice 'By the way, Cal, did he hand you a fistful of foxglove leaves to sprinkle over Parisi's salad?' "

Sofia let out a little sniff. "You don't have to be so snarky."

Why *was* I on the defensive where Cal was concerned? Was my attraction to him getting in the way of logic? "Sorry, Sofe. I don't mean to be. I'm just so tired of this whole thing. We keep running into one dead end after another, and nothing makes any sense."

"It will," she said. "We just have to keep digging."

"Right," I said. "We'll dig ourselves right into a charge of hindering a police investigation. Or maybe obstruction of justice?" I drummed my fingers on the armrest as I went through the possibilities. "At the very least, trespassing."

Sofie rolled her eyes. "You're such a worrywart."

I nodded. "Damn right I am. Do you have any idea how lucky we were not to get caught tonight?"

That's when we heard the sirens.

Chapter Twenty-six

*A*s the sound blared around us, my stomach clenched in fear. "You need to slow down, Sofe. We're getting pulled over."

"I see that," she said calmly. Putting on her signal, she braked gradually and eased the car over to the shoulder. The squad car pulled behind us, its siren off but the lights still flashing.

As we sat on the side of the road, our faces reflected in the squad car's blue and red lights, I turned to my sister-in-law. "Did you say we're Thelma and Louise? Because I'm thinking Lucy and Ethel."

She patted my arm. "Don't get hysterical, and please open the glove box. There's a plastic folder with my registration and insurance card in it."

I had to press the button a number of times, but finally got it open, only to have a bottle of nail polish fall out. "You have nail polish in your glove box?"

"It's for emergencies. Can you find my papers, please?"

My hands were still shaking as I held the folder out to Sofia, but she shook her head.

"Just put it on the seat next to me. I need to keep my hands on the wheel, Vic. And you shouldn't make any sudden moves."

"Sudden moves? I couldn't move if I wanted to." I stared into the rearview mirror. "Why doesn't he get out of the car? He wants to torture us, right?"

"The officer probably has to check into headquarters, maybe run my license through his computer system to make sure the car's not stolen or to see if I have any priors."

"'Priors'? Like in arrests? I don't know how you can be so calm about this." I took my eyes away from the mirror and tried to stare straight ahead. "You watch for him; I can't stand it. Think if we mention Danny's name, he'll go easier on us?"

"Probably not." She flicked her eyes to the mirror and suddenly did a strange thing. She smiled. I could hear the cop's boots crunch on the gravel as he got closer to the car. I gulped and risked a look. And then I finally exhaled.

"Good evening, Officer." Sofia rested her chin on her hand and batted her eyes at the handsome cop who leaned in her window. "You know, I never could resist a man in uniform."

"Just what the hell do you two think you're doing?" my brother barked.

"Oh my God, Danny! We were scared to death," I said. "Did you follow us?"

"I did not follow you. I *had* you followed."

"Nice, Dan." Sofia's voice was petulant. "You have your own wife and sister tailed like criminals."

"Trespassing, my darling, is a crime," he said through his teeth. "And you're damned lucky you weren't arrested tonight."

"That's what I tried to tell her!"

My brother shot me a look. "You're not making this any better, sis."

Sofia gazed at Danny and ran a finger down his forearm. "What *would* make it better, honey? Would you like me to lean over the car so you can pat me down?"

My brother closed his eyes, probably to rid himself of the mental picture of his wife's perky little butt perched over the back of his police car. He slowly lifted her hand from his arm. "There will be no need for a body search, Sofia."

She winked at him. "Maybe another time, then?"

I elbowed her in the ribs. "You wanna take it easy there, Miss Firecracker? He's already pissed off."

"You bet I am. Now, here's what's gonna happen: You two are going to get back out on Route 71 and drive the hell home. You are going to stop playing detective—"

Sofia thrust her finger in Danny's face. "You started it. *You're* the one who told her about the broken blood vessels in his eyes."

Danny slowly shifted his glare to me, and I smiled weakly. "She wormed it out of me."

"That was my mistake. But it's enough now; I mean it. You head back to Oceanside and quit nosing around." He eyed his wife. "And make sure you drive the limit, Sofia."

"Wait, Dan," I said. "I think Sutton's eyeing Tim for this. She implied the restaurant could be shut down, and—"

He hunched down at the window, and when he spoke he sounded like my brother and not a policeman. "I know that, Vic. It doesn't look good for us. Now will you two please go home?"

I reached across Sofia and gripped Danny's arm. "We'll go. I promise. Just listen for a minute. For one thing, Gemelli had a reason for wanting Parisi out of the way; so did his wife."

"And the girlfriend," Sofia added.

"And we've been so focused on the food," I contin-

ued. "But maybe he was poisoned another way. Like
through his medicine. Either of the women, or Gemelli,
or even somebody we don't know about yet could have
had access to his medicine bottle and..." My voice
trailed away as my brother shook his head.

"Listen, you're not coming up with anything that law
enforcement isn't already investigating." He gently loosened my hand from his arm. "And just having this conversation could cost me my career. You know that, don't
you?"

"We're sorry, baby," Sofia said, closing her hand over
his.

"I'm sure," Danny muttered, pulling his hand away.

"We are, Dan," I said. "We never wanted to put you
in this position."

"Then the best thing you can do is go home and forget about all this," he said.

Right. With Nonna and Nina LaGuardia breathing
down my neck? With the future of the Casa Lido hanging in the balance? And I couldn't help voicing my biggest worry. "But what about Tim?" I asked.

"Tim?" My brother straightened up and adjusted his
cap, the picture of law and order. "Tim needs a good
lawyer."

I sat out on my deck the next morning, holding coffee I
wasn't drinking and a newspaper I wasn't reading. And
there was no use trying to write, as my thoughts were
consumed by the case. It was time to take stock. There
were no test results as yet for Parisi's death. And even if
there were, Danny was in no position to share that information. Based upon what Sofia and I had found out
about *Digitalis*, it was high on the list of possible toxins
used to kill Parisi. If either Angie or Emily had tampered with his heart medication and he had taken *Digi-*

talis instead of his beta blocker, that might well have caused his death. However, there was also a pretty fox-glove plant sitting right in the Casa Lido garden, giving anyone in the restaurant that day access to it. And while I had ruled out Tim as a suspect, Regina Sutton certainly hadn't.

That left Cal and Mr. Biaggio and narrowed our field of suspects to four: the two women, Cal, and Mr. B, with the outcome contingent on how that toxin got into Parisi's system. Mr. B and both women had clear motives, but what about Cal? If that garden bench was Cal's work, that would signify a connection to the Gemellis, but would it necessarily follow that Gemelli Senior had hired him to kill Parisi? How would Gemelli have known the producer would show up at our restaurant? Unless Cal called him . . . ? The timing would be tight, but just possible. Still, I kept coming back to Mr. Biaggio or one of the women.

Thus far Emily Haverford hadn't returned my phone call, and I suspected I wouldn't be hearing from her at all. Then why come see me in the first place? To satisfy her curiosity about where her lover had died? To find out how much I knew? Or to throw suspicion on Angie?

I took a sip of my cold coffee and leafed idly through the paper. I hadn't seen the *Asbury Park Press* in a while, and I wondered if there were any stories about the dead producer. There were articles about the governor's upcoming visit, an annual fishing tournament, the county college graduation, and a piece about tourism at the shore. Thankfully, there was nothing about Gio Parisi's death. I set my coffee down on the deck, and a coupon insert slid from my lap.

It was a circular for Drug World, a statewide chain with several stores in the shore area. I was about to tuck it back into the paper when my eye was caught by a photo of a woman in a lab coat. The caption read, "Our pharmacists are part of your family." I tilted the paper out of the sun's glare and squinted at the image. The woman was middle-aged, with shoulder-length brown hair and long bangs. Even in the tiny mug shot, the startling blue of her eyes jumped from the page. The hairs on my forearms stood up, and I let out a small gasp. Cut the hair and dye it blond, and she'd be a dead ringer for Emily Haverford.

Chapter Twenty-seven

My fingers burned to call Sofia immediately, but she had classes on Saturday mornings; I had no choice but to work on my own. I brought the circular inside, flattened it out on my kitchen table, and stared at the woman's image. While the hair was different, she couldn't hide those bright blue eyes. If my hunch was right, the woman calling herself Emily Haverford did not work in human resources but was, in fact, a pharmacist. How easy for her to tamper with Parisi's medication! And with such an intimate connection between them, she likely knew about his heart condition and the medication he took for it. Assuming, of course, that he was poisoned through his meds and not his food.

"It had to be the pills," I said aloud. "It's the most logical scenario." *And the foxglove would be what—a coincidence?* "Shut up," I told the voice in my head, and I got down to work.

Since the circular helpfully listed all the Drug World stores in Monmouth and Ocean Counties, I didn't need to drag out my computer. But I got my story ready: I was a faithful Drug World customer who was wondering where her favorite pharmacist had been transferred. I couldn't remember her name, but she was a petite woman with brown hair and pretty blue eyes. Could anyone there give me her name or the store where she could be reached? I grabbed my notebook and pen and got started on my first call.

I worked my way through the four Monmouth stores with no luck, slowly realizing that I might have to call every Drug World in the state before I tracked Emily down. The fact that her cell phone carried an Ocean number didn't necessarily mean she lived in this area or had worked here. This was going to take longer than I thought. I trudged upstairs, settled in at my desk, and turned on my computer. The Drug World Web site included a store locator, but where to begin? Sofia had said that Parisi had a house in north Jersey; there was a lot of money in Bergen County, so that seemed the place to start. I was on the last Bergen store, waiting for the voice menu I now knew by heart, when a cheerful young woman finally answered.

"Hi, this is Kristen at the pharmacy desk. May I help you?"

"I hope so," I said, launching into my story.

"Oh, you're looking for Sarah Crawford."

Yes! I had a name at last. "Of course, Sarah. Now I remember. Does she still work there?"

"Not for a couple of years. Last we heard, she was engaged. Her fiancé used to come into the store. That's how she met him."

"Oh," I said, trying to sound disappointed despite my excitement. "I bet she's married by now. I wonder if I've lost my pharmacist."

The young woman giggled. "Are you kidding? If I snagged a rich guy like that, I wouldn't work either."

A chatty one. Thank you, Lord. "Well, good for her," I said. "So did you ever meet him?"

"Nah, but I saw him a few times. He reminded me of

somebody from *The Sopranos*. Not Tony, but the other one."

The other one could have been any number of thugs in Italian designer suits, but the description sure fit Parisi. "Well, thanks a lot, Kristen," I said. "Listen, I don't suppose you'd have her number?"

"No, sorry."

"That's okay. Thanks for your time; I really appreciate it."

I certainly did. Even if Kristen couldn't supply me with a phone number, I had a name and crucial information. Emily/Sarah had not only known about Parisi's medication, but she had likely *dispensed* it. And according to Kristen, Parisi had been more than Crawford's customer—he'd been her fiancé as well.

A computer search for Sarah Crawford yielded two addresses for her, one in north Jersey and a more recent one in Ocean County. Not so coincidentally, she was listed as Sarah *Emily* Crawford. Had she followed Parisi to the shore when the show started filming here? *The Jersey Side* had already run for a season, and she'd left the Drug World pharmacy about two years ago. The timing seemed right. But Parisi and Angie had been married about two years. Had Parisi been living a double life himself—engaged to one woman but actively courting another? Maybe Emily/Sarah had simply bided her time until she could take revenge on the man who dumped her for a younger woman. And she had obscured her identity to do it. As Sofia pointed out, she had something to hide. And I was beginning to believe that *something* was murder.

I hopped on my bike to ride into town, but not to the restaurant just yet. With only a day to go before Nina LaGuardia would be pounding on my door for an interview, I needed every minute. How would we close in on

Sarah Crawford? If I had to, I'd show up at Sutton's office and present my theory, consequences be damned. And while I didn't relish facing the tiger in her den, I'd still rather deal with her than an angry Nonna. I locked the bike on a rack along Ocean Avenue and hurried to the Shell Café, where I was due to meet Sofia for lunch.

She was already waiting, shifting impatiently in her chair. "I ordered us salads, Vic, if that's okay. I only have a half hour before I need to get back."

"Sorry, but wait till you hear what I've got." I slid into a chair, took a sip of water, and recounted the Sarah Crawford story from start to finish, while Sofia interjected with various "oh my Gods" and "get outs."

She sat back in her chair and crossed her arms. "So I was right about that wench."

"Maybe. The girl at Drug World told me she'd left almost two years ago. But that doesn't mean she's not at a different pharmacy somewhere and still dispensing Parisi's medication. Here's what I'm thinking: Either on the evening before or on the morning of his death, Emily/Sarah switched his meds. Then she gave herself an alibi by calling a meeting with Angie and picking a public fight."

"Assuming she was still Parisi's pharmacist." Sofia frowned slightly. "But that would mean she was also the intruder. That she was the one who locked you and Tim in the pantry and stole the garbage."

"The garbage!" Suddenly my beautiful theory was showing its ugly seams. "I didn't even think about that. If she used pills, what could possibly be in the garbage that was incriminating?" I groaned. "Please don't tell me this is another dead end."

"Hang on," Sofia said. "Let's think this through."

At that moment the waitress set our salads in front of us, but I didn't have much of an appetite. I stared at the pile of leafy greens, which seemed to be saying, *C'mon Vic. You know how he died.* "What is there to think through, Sofe? If Emily/Sarah killed him via his pills what could she have wanted from the trash?" I speared a few salad leaves but couldn't quite get them to my mouth.

Sofia, who had no such trouble digging in to her lunch, took a big bite of her salad and then pointed her fork at me. "Well, how about an empty pill bottle? There'd be a label with her name on it."

"True. And if she'd been planning this for a while wouldn't it make sense for her to wait to switch it until he had only one pill left?" Cheered by that thought, I started to feel the tiniest bit hungry.

"It's not a bad theory," Sofia said. "But it's based on two assumptions: He was down to his last pill and he threw the empty bottle away in the restaurant." She paused and set her fork down. "Or that she *thought* he did." Her voice grew excited. "Don't you get it, Vic? It doesn't really matter if there was something incriminating in the garbage, but only that the murderer *thought* there was. She might have been trying to cover her tracks. Then she came to see you to see how much you knew."

"Maybe," I admitted. "But if she locked Tim and me in the pantry, how would she know the layout of the restaurant?"

"She could have been there before. It's possible, right?"

"I don't know. Is it possible? Sure. Is it likely? Not so much." I pushed my salad around on the plate. "Remember when you're a kid and working on a jigsaw puzzle? And there's that piece that doesn't quite fit, so you force it in? I think that's what we're doing right now."

"Still," she said, "we're close, SIL. I know we are."

I shook my head. "Not close enough. I have to have something for my pal Nina by tomorrow." As I thought about our Emily/Sarah theory, I once again had the sensation of a fly buzzing around the edge of my consciousness. What was it? I looked down at my half-eaten salad. Did it have to do with Parisi's lunch? Was it in what Sofia said about the pill bottle and Sarah covering her tracks? The buzzing grew louder as the image of the boardwalk rose in my consciousness—was there something from my date with Cal I should be remembering? But the buzzing stopped, and the thought flew away.

We paid our bill and walked out together, still talking about Sarah Crawford. Just as we got to the bike rack, we heard a voice behind us.

"Victoria! How are you?"

We turned to look into the weather-beaten face of Anne McCrae. "Oh, and your sister-in-law is with you. How nice." She was smiling, but her eyes were not. "You Rienzis do stick together, don't you?"

I put a hand on Sofia's arm before Miss Firecracker went off in the middle of Ocean Avenue. "We do, Anne," I said. *Which is why there won't be a Starbucks opening anytime soon, Your Honor.* But I stuck to a safe subject and one close to the mayor's heart—tourism. "Isn't it good to see the town come alive again?"

"Yes, indeed. The stores are busy, the parking spots are all taken, and the boardwalk is already buzzing with people. We're off to a fine start to the season." She tilted her head. "Can the Casa Lido say the same?"

"Listen, lady," Sofia exploded. "Stop circling like a vulture, okay? Because the restaurant is doing just fine—"

"Now, Sofia," Anne said. "There's no reason to lose your temper." She stepped back, as though Sofia might haul off and hit her. Which was not unimaginable. Then Anne smiled innocently into my sister-in-law's face. "Your business is booming. In fact, weren't you looking to expand your studio space, dear? You've got all your paperwork lined up and ready, I take it?"

Once again, I grabbed Sofia's arm on the chance she'd been too angry to miss the mayor's not so veiled threat. "Well, Anne," I said hastily, "we've got to get going. It was nice seeing you." I unlocked the bike and shifted it from its spot on the rack.

"Nice seeing you, too, Victoria," she said, but made no move to leave. "By the way, how's your little investigation going?"

I stood holding the bike awkwardly. "Uh, I wouldn't say it's an investigation, actually . . ."

"No, of course not. That would be left to Reggie Sutton."

Reggie? It was hard to imagine the regal Regina with such a casual nickname. "Right," I said.

"In fact," Anne continued, "she just issued a statement to the press this morning." She lowered her voice. "As a public servant, one hears these things, you know."

"What was in it?" Sofia asked.

"Nothing too surprising," Anne said. "That they have probable cause to treat Gio Parisi's death as a homicide. And that her office will begin interviewing persons of interest right after the holiday." She looked at me and smiled. "So I would expect a phone call bright and early on Tuesday morning, Victoria. You did find the body, after all." She snapped her fingers. "Oh, there is one other thing that may interest you."

And you just remembered that. Right. "Okay, Anne, I'll bite. What else did you find out?"

"Well, Chief O'Brien let something slip in the office yesterday." She looked around quickly. "I probably shouldn't be telling you, but it's only fair that you should know." She paused and then dropped her voice to a stage whisper. "It's looking more and more that Mr. Parisi died as the result of something he ate."

Sofia and I exchanged a look, but neither of us responded to Anne, who smiled again and lifted her hand in a wave. "Bye-bye, girls!"

Still holding the handlebars of the bike, I watched her walk down the street, greeting townspeople and tourists cheerfully. "She probably offed him herself," Sofia hissed, "just so she can open a stupid Starbucks."

"Doesn't seem to so far-fetched now, does it?"

"Maybe not," Sofia said, glancing at her phone. "Listen, I'm late. I've gotta get back. We can talk more later, okay?"

As I got on the bike, I wondered what there would be to talk about. If the police and the county prosecutor were pursuing poisoning of Parisi's food, his stomach contents must have revealed something crucial. *And please don't let it be a bunch of partially digested foxglove leaves.* In any case, my pill theory was receding like the tide, as was my prime suspect, Sarah Crawford. The fact that she was a pharmacist—*Parisi's* pharmacist—had to be important. But I couldn't make it fit.

I pedaled quickly along the bike lane, heedless of the weekend traffic around me. By tomorrow I'd be hearing from Nina LaGuardia. By Tuesday I'd be hearing from Regina Sutton. My time was running out. On impulse, I turned down Ocean Avenue. I'd go to the restaurant. I'd walk myself through the events of that day and re-create every action I took to help me remember something I'd missed. *C'mon, Vic. You've written this stuff. Every piece of it is in front of you. You just have to put it together.*

My heart racing from exertion and a surge of hope, I zipped into the driveway and dropped the bike in the lot out back only to find the kitchen door locked. I came around to the front, but that door was locked, too. And taped to the inside of the glass was a neatly printed sign: CLOSED UNTIL FURTHER NOTICE.

Chapter Twenty-eight

"**N**o." I leaned close to the glass and cupped my hands around my eyes to peer inside, but there was nothing to see except empty tables. When had this happened? And more important, why? Well, it was time to do something I'd avoided in the two weeks since I'd been back in Oceanside—go home.

It was no more than a couple of blocks to Seventh Street and the house where I'd grown up. The once stately Victorian had been chopped up into two large apartments, with Nonna upstairs on the third floor and my mom and dad occupying the first and second. As I stood on the wide porch, I briefly indulged my fantasy of restoring the house to its original splendor. *Maybe someday*, I thought. *After I sell about a billion books*.

I knocked at the front door, then realized where they'd be on such a gorgeous, almost summer day. I walked to the back, with its deep green yard and gardens along both sides, one for flowers and one for vegetables. My mom was at her potting bench and my dad sat out on the deck, reading the paper and sipping coffee.

"Hey," my dad said. "This is a nice surprise."

"Unlike the one I got at the restaurant." I kissed his cheek and waved to my mom. She frowned, shaded her eyes, and then dropped her trowel. "Hi, Mom," I called.

"Hi, honey!" She bounded up to me, but stopped short, holding out her gloved hands. "I can't hug you. I'm a dirty mess."

I took in my mother's neatly twisted hair, designer T-shirt, and pressed khaki shorts. "Hardly," I said. "You even do your gardening fashionably."

"Please sit, honey." She peeled off her gloves. "There's still coffee in the pot. Or maybe some nice iced tea?"

"I'm good, Mom, really. Just wondering about that sign in the restaurant window."

My parents exchanged a glance; then my dad closed the paper, reached over and patted my hand. "Listen, honey, it's just temporary. Until all this blows over."

"It might not 'blow over' for a while, Daddy. In a couple of days, the county prosecutor is going to start dragging us all in for questioning. And you know it looks bad for Tim. If there's an arrest—"

"Don't even say it, honey!" My mom shook her head so vigorously, two long curls escaped from their barrette. "No one at the Casa Lido had anything to do with that man's death."

"We know that, Mom, but I don't think Regina Sutton does. As I started to say, if there's an arrest, there will also be a trial, with lots of publicity." I didn't feel the need to mention my deal with Nina LaGuardia; they'd find out soon enough. "This is likely to drag on for a while. Are we just going to give up?"

"No, baby, of course not," my dad said. "But it's expensive to keep the Casa Lido open, and we've lost so much business as it is . . ." He raised both shoulders in a shrug, as if that said it all.

"Nonna's gotta be crazy. How'd you talk her into this?"

My mom and dad looked at each other and then back at me. "It was her idea," my mom said.

"No way. She was one who was insisting on staying open. She wanted business as usual."

My mom nodded. "She did. But now she's discouraged. She's eighty, Victoria. It's all too much for her."

"Since when?" I got to my feet and pointed. "Is she up there?"

"I think so, hon," my mom said. "But we've barely had a visit."

"I'll be back. I promise." I gave her a hasty kiss on the cheek. "Right now I need to find out what's up with my grandmother."

I walked up the outside stairway that led to her kitchen, and before she even opened the door, the smell told me I was home. She opened the door and frowned. "What are you doing here?"

"Hello to you, too. Why are you making Sunday Sauce on a Saturday?"

She shrugged and gestured for me to come inside. "What else do I have to do?" She took a plate from the cabinet, put two meatballs on it, and set it down in front of me.

"You could be at the restaurant, bossing everybody around," I said. "Dictating the sauce recipes to Massi and yelling at him when he doesn't follow them. You could be fighting with Mom and talking to Nando in Span-Italian. And you haven't made me a list in a while."

Her eyes were sad behind her glasses. "You know what I wanted you to do."

"And I'm doing it, Nonna. I promise. I'll have an answer soon."

"It's too late. The season already started and we're losing money every day. And if there's a big trial and all that publicity, well . . ." She shook her head.

I put my hand over hers. "Don't talk like that. It's not like you to give up."

Instead of answering, she gestured to my plate. "Eat."

"Nonna, I'm not hungry. I just had lunch."

"What did you have?"

"I had a salad, just a little while ago."

She was silent, but here is what her face said: that I considered a mere salad "lunch" was an affront to my grandmother, her meatballs, and all of Italian culture. "You're skin and bones," she said, taking a roll from a brown bag on her counter. She threw it down in front of me, a clear challenge. Unless I started eating, she'd cook up a pound of pasta, too.

I cut a meatball into quarters and brought the first piece to my mouth. I closed my eyes for the flavor implosion of tomato, meat, basil, garlic, eggs, and cheese; it was almost enough to make me forget the reason for my visit. "Umm. Nonna, they're amazing. Just like I remember."

When I opened my eyes, she was smiling in her charming, tight-lipped way. Now was the time to strike. "Can I have the key to the restaurant?"

She crossed her arms and scowled. "What for?"

"I won't do any cooking. I promise. I just want to go over everything again. All the events of that day. There might be something we missed."

She left the kitchen and came back with a ring of keys. "You know which one?"

"Of course." I stuck the keys in my pocket, knowing I was now compelled to finish the meatballs and bread. All in service of the case, of course.

I left my grandmother's house, having made her two promises. One, I wouldn't touch a thing in the Casa Lido kitchen. Two, I'd come up with Parisi's murderer before the weekend was out. So now I had to answer to not one formidable woman, but three—Nina LaGuardia, Regina Sutton, and my grandmother, the scariest of them all.

*   *   *

I let myself into the empty restaurant, struck by the contrast of its quiet interior with the bustle of the street outside. Oceanside was coming alive for the season, but the Casa Lido was eerily still. That would change, starting right now. Determined to re-create the day of Parisi's death, I started by putting on an apron. Instead of an order pad, I tucked a notebook and pen in its pocket and stationed myself in the spot where I'd stood that afternoon. I closed my eyes, let out a breath, and tried to see it all in my head:

Parisi shows up at the door, and I tell him we're closed for regular business. He walks past me, sits at Table Five, says he wants a house salad with grilled chicken. Cal notices him arguing with me but doesn't move from the bar area. Parisi asks for a San Pellegrino and a cup of tea. He says he wants the chicken well-done and the dressing on the side.

At this point, I stopped the scenario and walked into the kitchen, as I had that day. I took out my phone and noted the time and started walking and talking myself through the events:

Tim is in the kitchen, and I ask him to grill some chicken. I tell him Parisi is out there. I offer to make the salad. Tim gets angry and says he won't make Parisi's lunch. Mr. B comes in the back door, asks who we're talking about and gets angry. Calls Parisi a cafone *and offers to "throw him out like garbage." I tell him we don't want any trouble and put the kettle on to boil Parisi's hot water. I take out some bread and the bottled water and ask Tim again to make the lunch. He starts prepping the chicken and says, "Tell Lockhart to stay the hell out of my kitchen."*

I looked at my phone; about three minutes had passed. Allowing for all our movements in the kitchen, I added another three to four minutes. So once he sat down, Parisi was alone in the dining room for approximately five to seven minutes. Except for Cal, who at some point had been in the kitchen, according to Tim. And five minutes was plenty of time to slip Parisi something, but how? There was no food or drink on his table yet. However, Parisi *could* have swallowed a pill dry or used his own water bottle to take one. Despite what Anne McCrae said about the food, I wasn't ready to give up on my switched-medication theory just yet. I went back to the kitchen and noted the time again. I took a bread basket and a water bottle, as I had that day, and backed out through the kitchen doors.

I stop at the coffee station for a cup, a saucer, and a tea bag. I take everything to Table Five and set them down in front of him. I tell him the hot water is coming. He says no to bread and starts to bait me about the protest. I pick up the bread basket and start to leave, and he reminds me that he wants the hot water.

My second exchange with Parisi can't be more than a minute or so. If he'd taken a pill, it would probably be too soon for his symptoms to start. So far so good.

I go back to the kitchen, where the water is now boiling. I fill a carafe and bring it to Parisi. He takes a packet of sweetener from the dish on the table and empties it into his teacup. Then he asks me to pour the hot water.

I froze in place, holding the empty carafe over the imaginary teacup. The sweetener. There was something about the sweetener . . .

"I'm looking for Victoria Rienzi."

The deep rumble came from somewhere behind me; I swung around, heart pounding, realizing too late that I hadn't locked the door behind me. The man in the middle of the dining room was thickset, with broad shoulders and the face of a prizefighter, a look that was at odds with his peach-colored golf shirt, green madras shorts, and boat shoes. I pointed to the door with a shaking hand. "Um, we're closed, sir."

"I noticed." He stood with his arms clasped in front of him. "I'm not here to eat." His words were ominous, as was his hooded expression. "Michael Gemelli is a business associate of mine." He smiled, flashing me a row of nicotine-stained teeth. "Michael Senior, that is."

I gripped the carafe, wondering how true my aim would be if I had to hurl it at his head. He took a step closer and I took a step back. "Who are you?" I asked.

"Oh, I apologize. I should have introduced myself. My name is Rossini. Fredo Rossini."

Fredo? They sent Fredo to threaten me? I don't know why this reassured me, as I was still alone in the restaurant with a thug. A preppie thug, but a thug all the same. Now holding the carafe in front me, I asked what he wanted.

He held up two thick fingers. "Well, miss, I'm here to talk about two things: trespassing and serendipity."

I got the trespassing part, all right. Somehow Gemelli had gotten wind of our little trip to his house. I opened my mouth to speak, but Fredo kept going.

"Now, about the first matter, Mr. Gemelli has no wish to pursue any action. With the understanding, of course, that you desist from pursuing any action of your own. And that is where serendipity comes in."

"Uh, Mr. Rossini, I'm not sure what you're talking about."

"Ah, but you're a writer. You must understand serendipity. It's something that is fortuitous."

Or as he pronounced it, *faw-TOOH-it-tiss.* "I know what it means," I said, "but I don't understand its application here."

"Well, sometimes in life we have to make things happen. And sometimes"—he opened his palms and tilted his head—"we don't. Mr. Gemelli would like me to inform you that a recent happening—one that transpired on these very premises—was, in fact, serendipitous. And was not in any way planned or calculated."

In other words, Gio Parisi's death was just a lucky break for Gemelli and son. I was no fan of Gio Parisi, but this was a pretty cold-blooded attitude to take toward a man who'd made Mikey G and his daddy very rich men. I gripped the metal carafe. Much as I'd like to give in to righteous anger, I couldn't afford the luxury. Gemelli was offering me a veiled deal—he wouldn't have me arrested for trespassing if I crossed him off our list of suspects. But he still had a powerful motive. And there was also the question of that garden bench. "I understand, Mr. Rossini."

"*Brava*, Miss Rienzi. You're a smart girl. But you'd have to be, right?" He reached into his back pocket, and my insides turned to water. But he wasn't holding a Glock, just a beat-up copy of *Molto Murder*. "While I'm here, could I bother you to sign this for me?"

This scene was growing more surreal by the minute. "Uh, okay." I dug into my apron pocket for my pen and scrawled a shaky "Vick Reed" on the flyleaf, while Rossini hovered over my shoulder.

"Could you make it out to 'Fredo'?" he asked.

Did I have a choice? I complied and handed the book back to him, looking nervously toward the door. Surely he'd leave now.

Fredo Rossini inclined his head and smiled. "Thank you, Miss Rienzi. I'll tell Mr. Gemelli our talk was a productive one."

In a way, he was right. My gut was saying that Gemelli was telling the truth. If he had wanted Parisi out of the way, he had better and more efficient means at his disposal than poison.

A bit shaky from the encounter, I locked the door behind my visitor and, still carrying the carafe, walked back to Table Five. I'd left off at pouring the hot water and noticed the sweetener. Something about it was important, but what? Poison in the saccharine was too far-fetched. Should I start over? But the more I tried to retrace my steps, the less I knew. So I would treat this just as I would a case of writer's block—with a distraction. And I knew exactly what that distraction would be.

Completely disregarding my grandmother's orders, I headed back to the kitchen. If she wouldn't teach me to cook, I'd have to teach myself. I would start with our fresh marinara sauce. At the salad prep station, I laid out garlic, basil, and parsley. I found a saucepan and drizzled in some olive oil. It was then I performed the most dangerous task of my mission—pilfering a jar of my grandmother's tomatoes. I found an open one in the refrigerator, but didn't dare risk grabbing another from the pantry. So it would have to be a small batch.

I peeled two garlic cloves and starting chopping, hoping their pungency might unlock that secret in my brain. As I rinsed the herbs, I thought again about Parisi's meal. *Salad, chicken, water, tea. Which delivered the poison? Or was it the pills?*

I chopped the basil and parsley fine, started the flame under the pot, and got ready for my favorite part. It was time to stop and smell the garlic. While I was no culinary expert, I had learned at least one thing at my mother's knee: Don't burn the garlic. I threw in the chopped pieces, stirred them quickly in the pan, and turned off the heat. Then I inhaled the scent and concentrated. *Who had access? Tim, Cal, Mr. B., if the food was poisoned. Sarah or Angie, if pills were used. Who would be likely to know that a foxglove plant was outside in the garden? Mr. B.*

I stirred the tomatoes into the oil, breaking them up with the back of my spoon, knowing I should have seeded them first. (Nonna would never serve a customer tomato seeds, but I didn't mind.) Next came the fresh herbs, then a couple of twists of pepper and some salt; while I crushed the tomatoes, I thought some more. *Who had motive? Tim, Mr. B, Sarah, Angie, Gemelli.*

I brought up the heat and waited for the tomatoes, and possibly my ideas, to come to a boil. *Who knew the layout of the restaurant? Tim, Cal, Mr. B, Angie. Who would have reason to steal the trash? Tim, Cal, Mr. B, possibly Sarah.* The tomato mixture bubbled to a foam, and I turned the heat to low.

I pulled a stool over to the counter and sat down. As I listened to the soothing sound of the sauce, I mulled it over.

Tim had motive and opportunity, but would he lock himself in the pantry? And if he'd stolen the trash, why tell me?

Angie had motive and opportunity only if she switched his pills. If that were the case, why steal the trash?

Sarah had motive and opportunity, and she might steal the trash if she thought the empty pill bottle was in it. But pills were the least likely means of poisoning.

Mr. B had motive and opportunity; he would recognize a foxglove. But the footsteps in the pantry were too stealthy to be his.

Cal had opportunity but no motive.

Gemelli had motive but no opportunity.

No single person fit the bill, and I was still left with the biggest question of all—how did that *Digitalis* get into Parisi's system? Because if I only knew how, without a doubt I'd know *who*.

*   *   *

Once I had the sauce made, it was natural for me to cook up some pasta to give it a try. And while it wasn't my grandmother's, my marinara was at least edible. As I ate, I put all thoughts of the case from my mind, concentrating only on my food. By the time I'd finished the dishes and removed all evidence of my culinary crime, it was growing dark outside. I was putting the pots away when I heard a tentative rap on the back door and jumped. Had my pal Fredo returned?

I crept to the door, my heart fluttery. "Who is it?"

"Is that you, Victoria? It is Rocco Biaggio."

Rocco? All these years and I'd never known Mr. B's first name. More important, what was he doing here? "Yes, Mr. B, but we're closed. I'm just here . . . working."

"Please. I must speak to you." His voice broke on the last word, and I heard a choking sound. Was he crying? Or was he faking? I pressed my ear against the door.

"Please," he said again, banging harder on the door. "It is time. I must confess."

Chapter Twenty-nine

*C*onfess? I let out a long breath. Was Rocco Biaggio about to spill his guts and clear Tim's name? Would this nightmare for the restaurant finally end tonight? I needed to hear what he had to say.

But I'd had one run-in with a thug today, and it would be the height of foolishness to be alone with a possible murderer. But tomorrow was Sunday. If I could end this right now, the Casa Lido might recover in time, and I'd have some exclusive to offer Nina LaGuardia. I had to risk it, but not without calculation.

I slipped a knife from the rack and laid it on the counter next to me. I also took out a heavy skillet, tested its heft, and put that on the counter, too. The banging on the door grew louder, and I faltered. Then an idea struck. *Please be home, Sofe*, I thought as I dug my phone from my pocket and crept to a far corner of the kitchen.

"Sofie," I whispered. "You have to do me a favor."

"Vic, are you okay? You sound funny."

"Biaggio's at the door. He says he's gonna confess. But I'm here alone."

"Victoria, please!" came the shout from the other side of the door, followed by more banging.

"Holy crap," Sofie said. "Don't you dare let him in until I get there."

"No! Danny will kill us both."

"Unless Mr. B does it first."

"I don't think he's dangerous. But just in case, I'm leaving the phone open, on speaker. I'll put it somewhere he won't see it."

"I don't like this, Vic. I'm calling Danny."

"Not yet. I don't want to involve him unless we have to. Just listen carefully, okay? You hear anything at all that sounds off, you call the police." The banging resumed. "Just a minute, Mr. B," I called.

"God, Vic. Be careful, will ya?"

I set the phone down in a corner of the counter and hoped the speaker would pick up our conversation. Then I sent up a small prayer, took a deep breath, and opened the back door. At which point, Rocco Biaggio fell inside. I jumped out of the way to escape being crushed by a sweaty—and clearly drunken—250-pound man. He staggered to his feet, and I was treated to the sight of his bloodshot eyes and a blast of wine-soaked breath. I sneaked the knife from the counter and held it to my side, staying in range of my phone. I shoved a stool toward him with my foot.

"Sit, please, Mr. B." My voice was calm, though the hand holding the knife was trembling. If I were reading this scene in a book, I'd never be able to suspend my disbelief at a character doing something this stupid. I held the knife out where he could see it. "And don't move from that stool. Say what you came to say."

He blinked in confusion at the sight of the blade. "Victoria, I didn't come to hurt you. I told you; I came to confess my sins." The last word was a wail of anguish. Sofie would hear that much, at least.

"Why come to me?" I asked, still gripping the knife.

He licked his lips and swallowed, clearly dried out from all the alcohol. I didn't offer him water because I didn't dare move, nor did I want *him* to. "I know you were asking questions," he said. "I know you know about that show and what those animals do to my poor Tina." He dropped his head in his hands and sobbed.

Good grief. I'd never get anything out of him at his rate. "Mr. B, do you think you can calm down and tell me what you want to confess?"

He swiped a large paw across his eyes and nodded. "You remember, Victoria, that my wife, she die about ten years ago."

I tightened my hold on the knife. What the hell? Had he killed his wife, too? "I remember, yes. I'm sorry."

"So I have to be mama *and* papa to Tina." He spread his broad palms. "At first it was okay. But then she grows up, and what do I know about teenagers? And what do I know about the things they watch and the things they put on the computers for people to see?" He shook his head sorrowfully. "So she come to me and say, *I'm gonna be on TV. I sign a paper and I'm gonna be on this show*."

"I'm not sure what—" I began.

He held up his hand. "Wait. I tell you. So they make a fool of her on the television, and I call and complain. And I get a lawyer to make them take it off the air so no one will ever see her shame again. But—"

"But she signed the release," I said quietly. "And there was nothing you could do."

He lifted his head, his eyes clearer now and his voice sober. "Oh, there was some-ting I could do. And I did it," he said through his teeth. I glanced over at my phone. *Are you there, Sofie? It's me, Vic, and I'm getting a little scared here.* I had to keep him talking.

"But then Parisi wanted to film the show in our town," I said.

"*Sì!*" he shouted. "To add insult to the injury. So I take matters into my own hands."

Had he just admitted to murder? "Mr. B, why don't you go to police with this?" *And leave me alone*, I did not add.

"Because I am *il vigliacco*. A coward." He put his hand to his barrel chest. "But this presses on me. Like a weight it press on me, and I must tell what I have done. I tell you, and if you want to tell your brother, I give you permission. And then he can take me to jail." His voice cracked, but he kept speaking. "The first time I do it was maybe a couple of months ago. And after, I feel such power, such relief that I have avenged my little girl."

The first time? Was there a trail of bodies behind our produce man? Just whom had I let into this kitchen? My heart thumped wildly in my chest as I slowly lifted the knife.

"And then I can't stop," he continued. "Three, four, five." He held up stubby fingers. "I keep going until I no can stop."

I lifted the knife and held it right under his bulbous Italian nose. "Well, you're stopping now," I said loudly. "Do not move. You are not going to hurt anyone else. The police are on their way over." *Please God and Sofia.*

His red eyes grew wide. "Victoria, you think I am speaking of bodies—*people*?" His mouth opened in surprise. "You think I killed that *cafone*?"

"Well, what the hell are you confessing to?" I waved the knife, and he jumped from the stool, holding up both his hands in surrender.

"The letters," he said. "The letters I write with—what do you call it?—the poison pen."

"Do you think you should have let him go, Danny?" Still shaky, I sat at the Casa Lido bar swirling the Scotch in the bottom of my glass. Sofia sat at my right, drinking a seltzer.

"I don't think he's a flight risk. Come Tuesday, Sutton's office will be dragging him in, anyway." He turned to me, his mouth tight. "But what you did was stupid, sis."

"He's not a murderer." After a fortifying sip, I closed my eyes, giving in to the warming effects of the drink.

"You don't know that," Sofia said.

My brother glanced over at his wife, his expression softening. "She's right. And she was right to call me."

"C'mon, guys," I said. "If he was so guilty about those letters, don't you think he would have spilled his guts about murdering Parisi?"

"Damn it, Vic. We can't take anything for granted," Dan said.

Sofia put her hand on my arm. "At least this will take some of the focus off Tim, right?"

"Maybe," I said. "But we still don't have an answer. Danny, Anne McCrae told me the police believe Parisi was poisoned through his food, but isn't it possible Angie or the girlfriend switched his pills?"

Dan's eyes met mine, and he slowly shook his head. "That's a horse that won't run, kid."

"So it *is* the food. Oh God." I dropped my head in my hands, exhaustion settling deep into my bones. "I just want this to be over."

"We all do," Sofia said. "And it will be, one way or another."

Dan got up from his stool. "Well, it's over for tonight, anyway. I want you both to get out of here. I'll wait in the car until you go."

I stood up, my legs leaden. "I'm not sure I can ride my bike after downing that Scotch."

"I'll take you," Sofia said. She turned to Dan. "Thank you for coming to the rescue."

My brother flashed her a smile. "Anytime, sweetheart."

Sofia watched him go and sighed. "I really need to get him back."

"Could we worry about your love life another time, please? I've got to clean these bar glasses and close up."

As we locked the doors behind us, Sofia asked, "What were you doing here anyway, Vic?"

"Trying to retrace my actions from the day Parisi died. I thought I might remember something that was important."

"Well, did you?"

"I think so, but I was interrupted." I told her about my visit from Fredo Rossini and his lesson in serendipity.

Sofia shook her head. "You do attract them, don't you?"

"Hey, we're lucky we didn't get arrested. And we can probably rule out Gemelli now." We wheeled the bike over to her car and hoisted it into the trunk.

"And if it wasn't the pills, we lose Emily Slash Sarah *and* the widow." Sofia paused. "You said you started to remember something, though."

"I did." I slid into the passenger seat. "When I poured Parisi's hot water, there was already a packet of sweetener in the bottom of the cup."

She glanced over at me. "Before he put the tea bag in?"

I nodded. "Definitely. I remember the moment because he was deliberately nasty, calling me by my pen name and talking about the HBO deal."

"Okay, so then what?"

"I went back to the kitchen. The salad was made, but I had to wait for the chicken, so I got the dressing ready." I paused, remembering the smell from the grill and the salad out on the counter. "Then Tim brought in the meat and threw it on the salad."

"And you brought the salad to Parisi."

"Right. Then he started eating, and his table manners were disgusting."

"Don't get off track," she warned. "You were talking about the tea. Try to remember."

We were turning onto my block now. "Okay." I closed my eyes and struggled to see Parisi at the table. *He's saying how the show could bring us business. Or hurt our business. He takes a sip of tea. He grimaces.* And in unconscious imitation of Parisi, I did the same. And then my face froze that way, just as my mother once warned me it would.

Sofia pulled into my driveway and cut the engine. "What is it, Vic? You have a really weird look on your face."

I let out a slow breath, my heart pounding from the sudden rush of clarity. "Oh my God, Sofe. I assumed the tea was too sweet. But what if it was too *bitter*?"

"Vic," she said slowly, "how long were you waiting for the chicken?"

"I was in the kitchen at least five minutes, maybe more."

"While he was alone in the dining room, somebody spiked that tea with *Digitalis*. Between that and the beta blockers he was on—wham!" She slammed the steering wheel with her palm.

"It does make the most sense. But we're back to opportunity."

"And now we ruled out Mr. B after his 'confession,' " Sofia said.

"If the tea *is* the culprit, he would have been ruled out anyway. He wasn't in the dining room. And neither was Tim."

Sofia's eyes met mine. "And Lori came later, so—"

"So that leaves Cal," I said softly.

Chapter Thirty

The opening strains of "Thunder Road" sounded tinnily in my ear as I struggled awake. What was Bruce doing in my bedroom? Another second's consciousness told me my phone was ringing. By the time I found it, the call had gone to voice mail.

"I haven't heard from you, Victoria!" Nina LaGuardia sang out in the message. "I believe you owe me an interview. I'll be waiting for your call. And soon!"

I sat up in bed, rubbed my eyes, and it all came flooding back. The closed sign on the restaurant. My reenactment and my encounter with Fredo, the preppie mobster. Mr. B's confession. The realization that something was wrong with Parisi's tea. I shook my head to clear it.

Today was Sunday, tomorrow Memorial Day. On Tuesday, Sutton would launch her formal investigation of Parisi's murder. I could probably put off Nina LaGuardia, but the Tiger Lady was another story. I had work to do and only a matter of hours to do it in. And I would start with the one person with access to Parisi's cup of tea: Calvin Lockhart.

I hadn't seen Cal since the night we'd gone up to the boardwalk. Since then, he had texted me once to say that he'd enjoyed himself and hoped we could do it again. But some instinct had told me not to respond, and I didn't hear from him after that. But it was time for another conversation with the mysterious Mr. Lockhart. Was that garden bench in Gemelli's yard a clue or just a stinky red herring? Had Cal been lying when he said he didn't know Parisi? And why had our digging into his past turned up so little? I would get him to meet me in a public place, the more crowded the better. I found his last message in my phone and texted a reply:

You up for a walk on the beach this morning? Meet me at the corner of Ocean and Seaside at 11.

Cal arrived at the appointed spot a few minutes before eleven. He wasn't exactly dressed for a date, but he wasn't wearing work clothes, either. I'd never seen him in shorts, and his tan, well-shaped legs were a pleasant surprise. But I couldn't afford to be distracted by Cal's physical charms.

He greeted me with a grin. "You didn't say anything about swimmin', Victoria, so I left my Speedo at home."

"Probably a good move." I found myself smiling back. "I'm glad you came."

"You think I wouldn't?"

"I wasn't sure. C'mon, you're my guest today." At the gate I flashed the seasonal badge Sofia had left me and paid for Cal. Though the beach was relatively quiet, it was filling up. If Cal were a threat to me, he'd have a hard time pulling anything with so many witnesses around. I stole a glance at him from the corner of my eye. What did I know about this guy?

He was probably in his late thirties; he'd lived in New Orleans until Katrina hit. He'd had a furniture business, which he'd lost in the storm. He claimed to be divorced and hadn't mentioned kids. Sofie's Internet search had turned up one old address in New Orleans, but nothing local. I didn't even know where the guy lived. *And yet here you are on a second date with him, Vic. And like it or not, he's a murder suspect.*

"Victoria? Which way would you like to go?"

I jumped at the sound of his voice. "Oh. We can head down toward the rock jetty if you like. It's the fishermen's area."

"I'm more of a lake fisherman, myself, but why not?" He slid a glance my way. "I was kinda surprised to hear from you this morning."

"Really?"

He nodded. "I mean, I thought you'd had a pretty nice time up here at the boardwalk. But I didn't get the impression you wanted to repeat the experience."

"You make it sound like a visit to the dentist." I looked at his guarded expression and went with the truth. "I did have a nice time. But I don't know anything about you."

He grinned and caught my hand. "Then let's remedy that right now."

"Not so fast there, pardner," I said, pulling my hand away. "How about we start with some conversation?"

"Fine by me." He looked out over the horizon. "You know, I'm always surprised by how pretty your Jersey beaches are."

"It's not the Gulf, but it's got its charms. C'mon. Let's walk along the shoreline." I rolled up my jeans, took off my flip-flops, and tentatively reached out with my toes, but jerked them back again. "Oooh, definitely not for swimming yet. What are the beaches like in Louisiana?"

Cal splashed his hand in the surf and shook it dry. "Water's a lot warmer—that's for damn sure."

"Do you miss the South?" My shoes in hand, I continued barefoot, relishing the feel of wet sand under my feet.

"Sometimes. I go back once or twice a year. Usually avoid hurricane season, though."

"So have you established yourself up here?"

"I have. Been doin' fairly well, mostly through word of mouth. I guess my work's pretty specialized. Besides some of the historic work, I do some private jobs now and then."

Like a garden bench, maybe? "What about your furniture?"

"Like I told you, I did a piece for a guy a little bit ago."

"Is his house nearby? I'd love to see it."

Cal shrugged. "I dunno. I didn't deliver it. He hired somebody to come pick it up."

It wasn't hard to imagine Gemelli hiring someone to pick up the furniture. But any number of wealthy guys would do the same thing. And I couldn't come out and ask him his customer's name, much as I wanted to. It would look too suspicious. And Cal was already looking a little skeptical. "So is your workshop around here?" I asked.

"My workshop's my garage. I got a place in Seaside."

"Oh, so you're pretty close by." I pointed to a mound of shiny black rock. "There's the jetty. The rocks can be a little slippery, so be careful." I put my flops back on to start the climb, and Cal followed me. I turned to look back at him. "Have you done work for anybody else in the area?"

He frowned, his face puzzled. "Maybe one or two last year. Did you need references or something?"

Yes, but I can't very well ask for them. "Oh, no. I was just curious about your work."

"About my work, huh?"

Definitely time to switch tacks. "So I haven't seen you around the restaurant much lately."

"I haven't seen you, either. But I gotta work around the lunch and dinner hours."

"You know that we're closed, right? But I'm hoping it's temporary."

"I'm sorry to hear that. But I guess I'm not surprised after what happened."

"No." I watched the waves rise and break against the rocks, uncomfortably aware that Cal stood close behind me. Was my discomfort due to attraction? Fear? A little of both? It was time to get down off this jetty. I slid down from the rocks and Cal followed; I headed in the direction of my cottage.

We walked a bit in silence, and then I turned to face him. "Cal, there were only a couple of us there that day."

"I guess I know which day you're talking about." His voice was as cold as the seawater. "You're still playin' detective, aren't you?"

"I'm not playing anything," I said.

"I don't know what this is about, Victoria, but it sure ain't about us getting acquainted." He stopped abruptly and stood with his arms crossed, his green eyes hard. All his warmth and humor receded with the tides, and standing in front of me was an angry stranger.

"Look, I—"

"Look, nothing," he interrupted. "I know what you're doing." Gripping my wrist, he leaned in close to me. "You need to leave this alone, Victoria. Do *not* be messin' with this. I'd hate as hell to see you get hurt."

I jerked my arm away, and he turned without another word. I watched him stalk down the beach, my insides churning like the waves. I thrust my hands into the cold water and pressed them against my face to stop the rise of panic. But I couldn't stop the question that had risen in my mind. Had Calvin Lockhart just threatened me?

There was only one thing to do. I hiked the last half mile down the beach to the cottage, stopping long enough only to jam a ball cap on my head and grab a pair of sunglasses. Gripping the car keys in my sweaty hand, I jumped in the Honda. There was no time to call Sofia, but I had to make one last road trip, this time alone.

As I sat in holiday traffic, I thought about Cal's parting words. Why had he been so suspicious? Why the flash of temper? Had he warned me off out of concern for me—or out of fear for himself? The traffic was at a crawl as I left town, and my anxiety intensified with each slow mile I put behind me. I was putting myself in harm's way yet again. Only this time wearing a lame disguise in broad daylight. To quote my brother, I was taking a helluva chance.

When I finally reached Shelter Point, I pulled the hat down low and crouched in my seat. Michael Gemelli's block was quiet, with most of its residents probably down on the beach. I cruised slowly past the house and parked at the end of the street. Once I was sure the street was empty, I walked rapidly down the sidewalk and cut through the yard next to his, once again avoiding the garage, edging ever closer to his grass. I wiped my wet palms on my jeans, conscious of the blood pounding in my ears and the breakfast threatening to come up any minute.

Stop thinking, Vic. Just go! I sprinted across the yard and dove behind the bench. Breathless, I searched the back and arms of the bench, but there were no markings. I would have to crawl under it for a better look. I slid beneath it, blinking against the sun that was pouring through the slats of the bench. As my eyes adjusted, I could make out black printing in one corner of the seat. I shimmied closer, took a breath, and read exactly one word: "Sears."

*   *   *

I spent the rest of the day holed up in the house with my outline for Isabella's book. I sat at my desk upstairs, alternating between scribbling ideas on index cards and looking absently out at the ocean. *You could write this book in New York, Vic. You don't have to stay here.* I sighed loudly. What *was* keeping me here? I was about to get dragged into Sutton's investigation, along with the rest of my family. The Casa Lido would probably not weather the media storm, and the best we could hope for was a fat check from the guy who wanted to open a Starbucks. I should get out now, before things grew ugly and before I got any closer to Tim.

Feeling foolish after that impulsive trip to Shelter Point, I had a sudden longing for the anonymity of the city. Where nobody knew my real name or my checkered history with Tim. Where nobody cared how often I visited and where cooking was beside the point. I stood up and paced my little bedroom. If I left now, it would be like quitting on a book before the last chapter was written. But the Mystery of the Poisoned Patron wasn't any closer to a solution, and I was no Bernardo. My detective was methodical and wise and experienced. He had blinding insights at crucial moments that always led to the solution. (Because I put them there, of course.) *So think, Vic. What would he do right now?* Go back over his notes to see if there was anything or anyone he'd missed? Maybe do more interviews of suspects? Make one of his pithy pronouncements about fate or human nature?

I grabbed my pocket notebook and wandered down to the kitchen, and over a dinner of cold pizza, I reviewed my notes. On the first page was the original list Sofia and I had made of those in the restaurant on the day of the murder. Tim, Cal, and Lori. And I'd added Mr. B. As I stared at the names, it struck me like one of

Bernardo's mental lightning bolts. I'd interviewed everybody on the list except the one person who'd seen what was left of Parisi's lunch that day.

After a quick phone call, I changed into shorts and a T-shirt for the bike ride across town; there was no way I was getting back in a car. Lines of cars filled Ocean Avenue, narrowing the bike lane. A green sedan came up close behind me, and I swerved and hugged the curb. Though I tried to pay attention as I rode, my thoughts drifted to Cal again. The bench was just another blind alley, and I couldn't prove a connection between him and Gemelli or Parisi, but he *was* there.

But I'd reached my destination—Lori's street on the bay side of town, and I parked the bike in the driveway of her neat little Cape Cod.

"Hey, girl." Lori met me at the door and motioned me inside. "We're in luck. Billy and Will are fishing, so it's just us." She led me to the kitchen, where there were two glasses of iced tea waiting. "Took ya long enough to get here."

"I know, LJ, and I wish this were a social call. You know the restaurant's closed, right?"

She nodded. "Your mom called me. I think it's just temporary, Vic."

"Maybe. But Sutton will be calling us in after the holiday. It doesn't look good for Tim, and it doesn't look good for the Casa Lido either." As if on cue, a few musical notes sounded on my phone—a text from Nina LaGuardia. *Where are u?!?!?!?* Turning off the phone, I dropped it into the bottom of my crowded purse. "Lori, would you mind going over the day he was murdered? Start from when you noticed his car outside."

"Sure." As she spoke, her account bore out my own memory of events. "Then you asked me to clear his table," she continued. "And I brought his plate to the kitchen."

"How did Parisi look when you took his plate? Was he sweating or anything?"

She shook her head. "Maybe a little pale, but that's all."

"So in the time I got his bill ready, he was starting to feel sick." But still drinking the tea, I remembered. "Let's go back to his plate for a minute. How did it look before you cleared it up?"

"Hang on." She shut her eyes. "Okay. There's a lunch plate that's empty. On top of that is his dirty napkin and silver." She frowned in thought. "Next to that is the gravy boat with the dressing in it. And on the other side of the plate—I think—is his teacup and saucer." She opened her eyes. "That's it."

"Okay," I said. "Now focus on that teacup. Where's the tea bag? In the cup or on the saucer?"

Lori's freckled face was thoughtful. "Which tea bag?"

Tiny prickles of apprehension traveled up the back of my neck, and when I spoke, it was only a whisper. "Are you saying there was more than one tea bag on that table?"

She nodded. "Yup. But only one of them was used."

Chapter Thirty-one

*I*n that moment, I heard Parisi's voice in my head. He hadn't asked for "a cup of tea." He'd asked for "hot water *for* tea." *He didn't need a teabag because he had his own.* A bag that was probably full of *Digitalis* prepared by Angie or Emily, one that let both Tim and Cal off the hook.

"Do you remember anything about the tea bags, Lori?" It was hard to keep the excitement out of my voice; I wanted to do a dance of joy right there in her kitchen.

"Well, one was the brand we use. That was dry. I don't remember much about the other one, except that it was wet. I'm pretty sure he left it on the saucer."

"You are the best." I threw my arms around her in a tight hug. "I gotta run, but I owe you big. And expect to be back at work tomorrow!"

Before getting back on my bike, I fished out my phone. Ignoring two more messages from Nina, I texted Tim instead: *Don't worry. This will all be over soon.* Then I left a message for my grandmother to let her know I had an answer. By tomorrow the Casa Lido would be ready to open its doors for the season, just as it had every other Memorial Day. Because first thing tomorrow morning, I would be calling Prosecutor Sutton myself, holiday or no. And I would give her exactly what she needed to make an arrest.

I pedaled furiously across town, my mind spinning in rhythm with the wheels of the bike. I thought of Parisi drinking his special water. Turning away the bread and asking for dressing on the side. These were all signs of a man on a diet, and I was betting that a diet tea was part of his regimen—something both Angie and Emily/Sarah would have known. I had to get to Sofia, because I needed her help for the last vital piece. As I neared the restaurant, the curb was lined with cars, including the green sedan that had nearly clipped me earlier. *Tourists. Too bad we need their money to survive.* I skidded to a halt in the driveway at the back of the restaurant, dropped the bike, and scrabbled in my purse for my phone. When she didn't pick up, I left a frantic message:

Sofe, we just got a huge break. Meet me at the Casa Lido as soon as you can. Bring the red folder. And a shovel.

My sister-in-law pulled into the parking lot of the Casa Lido with her brakes screeching. Slamming the door behind her, she strode toward me carrying the folder and a small shovel. "What's going on? And why the hell do we need a shovel?"

"Here. Put these on while I explain." I handed her a pair of latex gloves from the kitchen. "Okay, so we've already figured out the poison had to be in Parisi's tea, but the only one with access was Cal."

"Who doesn't have a motive. As far as we know."

"Right. But I went to talk to Lori. She cleared up his plates—I don't know why I didn't think of it before. And she gave me the answer." I held up my fingers in a V. "There were two tea bags, Sofe. Two."

Sofia's gasp echoed in the empty parking lot. "He

brought it with him. Oh my God, Vic. *He brought it with him.*" She frantically pulled papers from the red folder. "It's in one of these articles," she muttered. "I just didn't put it together." She shoved a paper at me. "Look. It's all the way at the bottom."

I held the flashlight over the sheet. "'Accidentally brewing foxglove leaves into tea has led to poisonings and death,'" I read aloud. "But this was no accident."

Our eyes met and Sofie nodded. "One of those crazy bitches gave him a doctored tea bag."

"Angie had access," I said, unable to keep the triumph out of my words. "She must be the one who locked us in the pantry and stole the trash."

"Emily/Sarah knows drugs," Sofie said. "But whichever of them did it has the evidence from the garbage. We'll never be able to prove it now."

"Don't bet on it," I said. "Grab that shovel."

I was surprised by the flicker of fear that crossed Sofia's face. "Please don't tell me there's another body back here," she said.

"Not that I know of. Nope, we're digging up evidence, not a body. Care to follow me to the back of the garden?"

"What for, Vic? They *took* the trash."

"It wasn't in the trash." I couldn't keep the grin from my face. "Because here at the Casa Lido we don't throw away our tea bags. We *compost* them."

"Yes!" Sofia pumped one arm and lifted the shovel with the other. "One of those wenches is goin' down!" She paused with the shovel in midair. "But we've got two weeks of crap to dig through."

"It's just some vegetable peelings and eggshells. It'll go fast. C'mon."

We hurried to the back corner of the garden, where the composter was overflowing with all manner of food refuse. "When I found the body, Tim came from here with the empty compost bucket." I pointed with the flashlight. "That tea bag was in there—I know it."

Sofia eyed the dark mound and made a face. "It's a little stinky. And there's a lot of it."

"All the more reason to get started. Now give me that shovel."

Fifteen minutes later, we were up to our elbows in potato skins, coffee grounds, and carrot curls. Our gloves were black, and we both had smears across our faces. We also had a pile of wet tea bags, none of them the one we needed.

"Ugh, this is gross," Sofia said. "And we're not getting anywhere, Vic. We've got one flashlight we have to share, and we're looking for a tiny little tag." She wiped the back of her hand across her forehead, adding another dark streak to her dirty face. "Wouldn't we do better in daylight?"

"Probably, Sofe." I looked around the dark garden, the blue shed rising ominously in the distance. "But I have this sense of urgency. I can't really explain it, but we have to do this now."

She shivered. "Okay, but it's a little creepy out here."

We worked in silence, each of us pawing away, strewing compost everywhere. Just as I was wondering how I would explain the mess to my grandmother, Sofia let out a shriek. She held the bag gingerly by its tag, her eyes glittering in the darkness. I trained the flashlight on it. The tag was a faded yellow, with some Asian characters. I could just make out the letters "Chinese diet tea." I fumbled to get the plastic bag open, and Sofia dropped it in.

"SIL," I said, "I would kiss you if you weren't so disgusting."

"Right back at ya." She groaned and got up stiffly, and I did the same.

I stuck the bag in my jeans pocket and patted it. "We have evidence now."

"I wouldn't be too sure of that if I were you." And then she stepped out from the shadows and swiftly circled Sofia's neck with one arm. In her other hand, she held a hypodermic needle—aimed straight at my sister-in-law's heart.

Chapter Thirty-two

"Drop that tea bag on the ground, please." Sarah Crawford, aka Emily Haverford, pointed with the toe of her sneaker. "Right here at my feet."

The blood pounded in my ears as I looked at Sofia's calm face and stared into her eyes. I read two messages there: *Don't give it to her* and *I told you so*. I swallowed hard and shifted my gaze to Crawford. Even in the darkness, her blue eyes were crazed. "Listen, Em...er, Sarah," I said softly. "I can't give it to you unless I know my sister-in-law is safe. You let her go, and I'll drop the bag."

She swung her head from side to side, tightening her grip on Sofie's neck. "You don't tell me what to do. I tell you." She made a stabbing motion with the needle. "Or maybe your cute little sister-in-law would like a nice shot of adrenaline."

Sofia's eyes fluttered briefly, but she remained still. A tiny incline of her head told me to keep trying. I went in a new direction. "I'm sorry for your loss."

She peered at me through her long bangs. "I'm not," she said simply. "I gave him years of my life—for what? So he could leave me for a younger woman?" She gave a bitter laugh. "It's a tired old plot, isn't it, Miss Mystery Writer?" She jerked her chin at me. "What do you know?

You *or* her?" She slid her eyes toward Sofia. "You're both young and pretty. Wait. Wait till you're middle-aged and no one wants you."

As she talked, her hold on Sofia loosened. All at once my sister-in-law let out a fighting shriek, stamped down on Sarah's foot, and elbowed her once hard, knocking the hypodermic from her hand. As the needle rolled toward me, I kicked it a safe distance away. When I looked up, Sarah Crawford was on the ground with Sofia's foot planted firmly on her neck. "You move, bitch," Sofia growled, "and I'll crush your scrawny neck."

"Wow," I gasped. "Those karate lessons really paid off."

"Thanks," she said breathlessly. "Now grab that needle."

I stuffed the tea bag into my shorts first, then glanced over at the hypodermic, afraid to turn my back on Sofia and the crazy woman she had pinned on the ground. Grateful I was still wearing my gloves, I picked it up between two fingers and held it out in front of me. "Now what?"

But Sofia's eyes grew wide; she opened her mouth to speak, but the voice I heard wasn't hers.

"You stupid bitch." I turned to see Angie Martini behind me, holding a small but menacing little pistol. It wasn't aimed at me, but at her rival for her husband's affections. And it was then that I finally remembered.

My walk down the boardwalk. The French movie posters. The convenient alibi that put both women in the same place at the crucial time, having a very public argument.

"Oh my God," I whispered. "It *is* diabolical."

"Angie, I didn't say anything. I swear," Sarah whimpered. "I was trying to help."

Get her talking, Sarah. Get her talking, please. I gripped the barrel of the needle. But would I have the nerve to use it if I had to? One corner of Sofia's mouth lifted; she got the message and slid her foot down to Sarah's chest.

"Help?" Angie sneered. "Oh, you're a great help."

"But I did what you said. I watched her so I could figure out what she knew. I followed her here."

The green car. Some detective you are, Vic. Sarah flailed an arm in my direction. "And they found the tea bag. They led us right to it."

"And now we're stuck with two hostages. You're pathetic—you know that?" Angie's eyes glittered in the darkness, her voice a guttural rasp. "We used to laugh at you, Gio and me. He used you, and so did I."

"No," Sarah whispered. "He loved me." She turned her head to the side, weeping softly. I had to remind myself that she had helped plan a man's death. And that I was about to become a hostage to two psycho women.

"And now for you two." Angie swung her arm around and trained the gun at my chest, her red nails looking like drops of shiny blood. I held the needle so tightly, my hand trembled. "First, you're gonna drop that needle on the ground," she said. "Then the tea bag."

"Angie," I said. "You don't want to do this."

"Don't tell me what I want to do!" She jerked her head toward Sofia. "Let Sarah the Spy get up."

But Sofia didn't move a muscle. "Looks like we're at an impasse, Angie," she said coolly, her foot still resting on Sarah's chest.

"I've got the gun," Angie said.

Sofia nodded. "True. But we've got the evidence." She glanced at me. "I say we give them a head start, Vic. This way no one gets hurt."

"Please, Angie," Sarah said. "Just listen to what they say so we can get out of here."

"Why should I listen to them?" she asked harshly. "We had a perfect plan, and they ruined it."

"Listen, Angie," I said. "If you drop the gun, I'll give you the tea bag. And you can both go." My voice shook and my fingertips were numb from clutching the hypodermic. "But I'm hanging on to the needle, okay?"

"How many times do I have to say this, Victoria? You don't tell me what to do." She waved the gun wildly, and I flinched, wishing I had a chance to see Tim one last time. To finish my book. To say good-bye to my mom and dad. I slid my eyes toward Sofia; she saw my fear and shook her head.

I was about to close my eyes and wait for the inevitable when a third crazy woman stepped out of the shadows, a frying pan raised high. "Oh no," I whispered. "Not the head. Please not the head."

My grandmother let out a primal cry as she brought the pan down, connecting hard with Angie's right shoulder. I cringed as Angie, howling, crumpled in a heap. The second she let go of the gun, Sofia was on it. I watched in surprise as she emptied the chamber.

While Angie wailed on the ground, Nonna stood over her with the frying pan inches from her face. "You touch either of my granddaughters, *puttana*, and the next place this lands is your skull."

The moments that followed were a blur of sights and sounds. Sirens. Lights. Sarah sobbing. Angie clutching her shoulder and moaning in pain. Men in blue uniforms, one of whom stepped from the group, his face white.

"Wanna tell me what the hell is going on here?" he growled.

Sofia threw herself against his chest. "Am I glad to see you, Detective."

Dan glared at me over the top of his wife's head.

"You should have seen her, Danny," I babbled. "She was awesome. She disarmed that crazy Emily. I mean, Sarah."

Sofia gripped Dan's arm. "Oh, but Vic was great. She was afraid, but she kept Psycho Angie talking. And then—" Her eyes grew wide. "Bam! Nonna comes out of nowhere and whacks her with that pan."

"She dropped like a rock!" I said. "You should have seen it. Then Sofie got the gun and—"

"What you did was dangerous!" he shouted. "I warned you both, damn it!" He jerked a thumb toward Nonna, who was still holding the frying pan and calmly giving a statement to an Oceanside officer. "And she's worse than the two of ya put together."

"But we're okay," I said.

He reached out an arm for me and let out a loud sigh. He squeezed the two of us tightly, lifted his eyes to the heavens, and muttered a prayer. "Please, God, preserve me from crazy broads."

Sofia lifted her head and smiled. "But they're in custody, Danny."

My brother frowned, and just for a second switched to Stern Cop mode. "I wasn't talking about *them*," he said.

Chapter Thirty-three

*T*he Casa Lido opened its doors the next morning, just as it had every other Memorial Day for seventy years. We sat at the family table, fortifying ourselves with espresso for the busy morning ahead.

"That phone is ringing off the hook," my dad said, snapping open the *Asbury Park Press*, which featured "Wife and Mistress Conspire to Murder RealTV Producer" as its top story.

"Curiosity seekers." My mom leaned over to read the headline and pursed her lips. "I still can't believe you and Sofia put yourselves into that kind of danger."

"I tried to tell them that, Ma." Danny's arm tightened around Sofia's shoulder, while she glanced at him adoringly. Judging from their high-watt glow, it appeared a reconciliation was in the works. I smiled at Sofia, who didn't notice it. Or the frown my mother was casting in her direction. Ah, love.

"We're fine, Mom." I patted her arm. "And now that little black book of yours will be filled right up. Aren't you relieved that the Casa Lido isn't under a cloud of suspicion anymore?"

"*Certo*," Massimo said. "I could not work under such conditions." He tossed his head, then held out his coffee cup in a toast. "To Signora Giulietta, who save the day."

"To my ma," my dad said proudly. "Who took down a murderer."

Nando nodded. "To our *abuelita*."

I lifted my cup. "To Nonna, who saved my . . . behind."

"Hmmph," my grandmother grumbled. "That *puttana* is lucky it was my stainless-steel pan and not the cast-iron.

I grinned at her. "Don't sound so disappointed."

My mother shook her head. "Those two women took an awful chance. How did they know it would work?"

Danny shrugged. "They didn't. But every murderer takes a risk. Theirs almost paid off."

"But, Victoria," my mom asked, "how did you know they were in it together?"

I downed the rest of my espresso and shook my head. "I didn't. Not till it was too late. But one night I took a walk down to the Paramount, and there was this poster for a French film festival and—"

"Oh my goodness," my mom interrupted, her eyes growing wide. "I know which film you mean. Daddy and I saw it years ago. It's the one with Simone Signoret where the wife and the girlfriend plan the husband's murder—*Diabolique*."

"You got it, Mom. Too bad I didn't. But it was in the back of my mind all the time, bugging the heck out of me. That alibi was just too convenient." I turned to my brother. "Danny, are they talking at all? I'm wondering how they got together in the first place."

"Right now," he said, "it's just a lotta 'she said, she said' as far as who came up with the plan. But apparently Parisi was threatening Angie with divorce. And Sarah was still furious over being burned by the guy." He finished his coffee and set the cup down. "At some point they decided they'd team up and get their revenge. And a whole lotta dough at the same time."

"Well," I said, "you have to hand it to them."

"Hand it to them? Victoria, they are evil!" Nonna's eyes narrowed. "Especially that Angie, who finally got what she deserved."

I had a feeling Nonna was talking about more than murder, and apparently so did my mother. She raised her brow and smiled. "You know what they say about karma, don't you, honey?"

I shot my mom a quick wink. "Yes, I do, Mother. And it's especially apt in this case."

"Well, they should both burn in hell." My grand-mother crossed herself and looked at the ceiling. "May God forgive me."

"Evil or not, Nonna, it was brilliantly simple. They knew he was drinking that diet tea every day. So they doctor it with a substance they know will kill him and wait."

"They did more than that, Vic," Sofia said. "Remember Angie called him a bunch of times to see where he was. I bet she egged him on to come here and eat."

"Absolutely," I said. "She checked the place out. Think about it: She knows Tim works at a restaurant near the boardwalk where Parisi was appearing. So she employs her dubious charms on him and cases the Casa Lido. She sees the plant in the garden, and the plan takes shape. And then her ex ends up making the 'fatal' lunch. It was the perfect setup."

"Almost perfect," Sofia said. "They didn't think about the police searching the trash."

"Until it was too late," I added. "So they locked Tim and me in the pantry."

My mother sighed and shook her head. "Poor Tim, to have been involved with that woman. To have her use him in that way—"

"What about 'poor Tim'?"

The conversation stopped abruptly as its subject came through the front door. He looked pale, with dark smudges under his eyes.

"We're, uh, talking about last night," I said.

"Right." He strode past us and pushed through the kitchen doors.

I pushed away from the table. "Excuse me a minute, guys."

In the kitchen, Tim was pulling packages from the refrigerator and slamming them on the counter. "What are you here for, Vic?" he asked over his shoulder. "To gloat about Angie? Or for my undying gratitude for saving my ass?"

"Tim, will you look at me, please?" He turned, crossed his arms, and waited. "I'm sorry about Angie. God knows, I have no love for her, but it can't be easy knowing you were involved with a murderer."

He flinched, and when he spoke, his voice was hard. "She could have killed you. Probably would have if your crazy nonna hadn't shown up."

"But I'm okay. And now you are, too. It's over, finally."

His lips were drawn into a thin line. "Did you want a thank-you, Vic? Is that it?"

"Well, a little gratitude would be nice, but that's not what I came to talk to you about."

He lifted a shoulder, his arms still crossed. "So talk."

I stepped closer, about to lay a hand on his arm, but thought better of it. "Look, Tim." I sighed. "I finally figured out something important. In a way, Angie Martini did me a favor all those years ago. If we hadn't broken up, I'd never have gone to New York or had a writing career. Don't you see? Things happened for a reason—"

"And this is your great epiphany," he said, his voice

harsh. "That losing me was the best thing that ever happened to you."

"I didn't say that!" I gasped. My anger rising, I jabbed a finger at his chest. "Losing you nearly killed me. But I survived. And I'm the better for it."

He tilted his head, his eyes two dark stones. "Glad to be of service, Vic," he said bitterly, turning back to the sink without a word.

I stalked past him out the back door of the restaurant and stood facing the garden, breathing in its smells for comfort. So this was what I'd come home to. I shook my head.

"Hey, SIL." Sofia put her hand on my shoulder. "What's up with Top Chef?"

"Apparently he's mad at me for keeping him out of jail."

She grinned. "Makes perfect sense."

"Never mind me. What's going on with you and my brother?"

She tilted her head, her eyes innocent. "Nothing."

"Yeah, I could tell that when you were draped all over him at the table."

Before she could answer, the sound of tires on gravel pulled our attention to the parking lot. Cal jumped from his truck and grabbed his toolbox from the back. He turned, smiled briefly at Sofia, and nodded.

"Hey, Cal," I said. "Listen, can we talk for a minute?"

"Sorry, Victoria," he said. "Runnin' late." He hurried past us into the restaurant and I sighed. I seemed to be doing a lot of that today.

"Well, that message was loud and clear."

"Did you expect him to ask you on a date?" Sofia asked. "You practically called him a murderer."

"Not in so many words." I shook my head. "Men. What can you do with them?"

"Can't accuse them of murder," Sofia said.

"Can't save their sorry asses."

"Can't live with 'em—" she began.

"And ya can't kill 'em," I said.

"Oh wait," Sofia said, her dark eyes full of mischief. "Sometimes you can." She stopped, her face suddenly serious. "Vic, were you scared last night?"

I looked around to make sure no family members were in earshot. "Shitless," I told her. "What about you?"

She nodded, but her eyes shone. "Well, yeah, but . . ."

"But what?"

"It was kind of a rush, don't you think?" Her words gathered speed, and I knew just where they were headed. "I mean, it was exciting. All of it. Figuring it out, digging for evidence—"

I grinned. "Literally."

"Literally, exactly! And taking them out just felt so good, Vic. It felt right to me." She lowered her voice and put her face close to mine. "I mean, wouldn't you like the chance to do that again?"

"Oh, no, you don't. Don't even say it." I backed away from her, holding up my hand to stop my sister-in-law's crazy train before it flattened me. "I will never get mixed up in anything like this again. No way. Do you understand me?"

But Sofia just smiled.

I peeled the garlic clove slowly and sliced it neatly down the middle. As I pushed it to the side of the cutting board, a hand closed around my arm like a steel claw.

"Did you take out the green sprout?"

"Yes, Nonna."

"And you're not cutting them too small?"

"No, Nonna."

"Don't roll your eyes at me, Victoria. Do you want to learn how to cook, or not?"

I looked at my grandmother's upraised chin, her square shoulders, and the still-strong arms that had protected me from a crazed killer. I wouldn't risk a kiss, but maybe I could hazard a smile.

"Yes, Nonna," I told her. "I do."

Author's Note

I turned in the manuscript for this book less than a day before Hurricane Sandy struck. As the storm progressed, it devastated many areas along the Jersey Shore, including locales mentioned in my story; it also caused the deaths of at least five people in Monmouth and Ocean Counties. Since October 2012, many have come to associate the Jersey Shore with that terrible storm. But I made a conscious decision not to include mention of it in this book.

I wanted my fictional world to be a Jersey Shore that was untouched by the ravages of Sandy, a place where readers could find escape in descriptions of the beach and boardwalk. I wanted to present a picture of the Jersey Shore that I, and so many of us, remember and hold precious.

I also worried it might be insensitive to fictionalize an event that had such a drastic impact on so many lives. As of this writing, many people in shore towns remain homeless, businesses are still shut down, and thousands of residents are struggling to put their lives back on track. Perhaps I will include a hurricane in a later book in the series, but only at a respectful distance from an event that shook us all to the core.

To support rebuilding efforts along the Jersey Shore, please consider a donation to www.restoretheshore.com.

Recipes from the
Italian Kitchen

Vic's nonna makes her marinara with peeled and seeded tomatoes she puts up herself each August, as does my brother, who's an awesome cook. My version takes a couple of shortcuts and can be served either chunky or smooth. (I don't bother with peeling and seeding. Don't tell Nonna. Or my brother.)

My sauce takes only about an hour from prep to table and requires just a knife and a cutting board. In the summer, I make it with any kind of tomatoes my gardener friends are kind enough to share—plum, beefsteak, even cherry. Out of season, plum tomatoes will give you the closest approximation of that garden taste. Make this once, and you'll never open another jar!

Rosie's Quick Marinara Sauce

10–12 fresh basil leaves, snipped into small ribbons
2 large cloves of garlic
2–3 lbs. fresh plum tomatoes (about a dozen)
¼ cup of chopped fresh parsley
2 tbs. extra-virgin olive oil
Salt and pepper, to taste

1. Prep fresh herbs and set aside.

2. Using the side of your knife, bruise the garlic cloves so that the peel slides off easily. Slice off the stem ends and cut cloves long ways; remove the "sprout." Chop garlic roughly and set aside.

3. In a 4-qt. heavy-bottomed pot, heat the olive oil over medium heat. Add garlic and stir so that pieces are coated in oil. Watch them carefully—once they start to

sizzle, turn off the heat. The garlic will continue to cook in the hot oil without burning.

4. Slice off stem ends of tomatoes and cut into large dice. Turn heat back on to medium high and add chopped tomatoes to garlic and oil. As tomatoes start to soften, stir to coat them in oil and their own juices. Press on tomato chunks with the back of your spoon. Add herbs and stir until well blended.

5. Allow tomatoes to cook, uncovered, at medium high until mixture comes to a moderate boil (about ten minutes or so). Smoosh tomatoes again, turn heat down to low and cover the pot. Simmer the mixture for 30–35 minutes.

6. Turn off the heat and season with salt and pepper. (I use about two teaspoons of salt and about 10 twists of the pepper mill, but I have a heavy hand with both. Go light and taste first!) Continue pressing tomatoes with spoon until preferred consistency.

7. If you like a chunky sauce, you're good to go. But if you like a smoother sauce and have the time, allow the mixture to cool, uncovered, for at least 20 minutes. Pour into food processor and pulse until the tomatoes lighten and consistency is smooth. Put back into pot and heat gently for about 10 minutes.

I generally don't follow a recipe when I make pesto, so the measurements below are only guidelines. Depending upon whether you prefer your pesto herby, cheesy, or nutty, feel free to play around with the proportions. Use more oil for a thinner paste and less for a thicker one. For a milder pesto, substitute pignoli nuts for the walnuts and parmesan for the Pecorino Romano.

Tim's Basil Walnut Pesto

½ cup of walnuts, lightly toasted
½ cup of extra-virgin olive oil
2 cloves of garlic
2 cups of fresh basil leaves
½ cup freshly grated Pecorino Romano cheese
Freshly grated pepper and salt, to taste

1. In a shallow skillet, toast the walnuts quickly over medium heat. Turn off the heat as they become golden brown and fragrant—don't scorch them.

2. Set nuts aside to cool. Use about ¼ cup of the olive oil and pour into the same pan; heat the oil over a medium flame. Peel garlic cloves, slice long ways and remove the green sprout. Drop garlic pieces into the hot oil. Once small bubbles form, turn off the heat and tip the pan so that cloves are completely coated in oil. They will continue cooking in hot oil without burning; set them aside.

3. In a food processor, pulse the basil leaves, the nuts, the garlic, and the oil from the pan until mixture is smooth. With processor running, slowly add the rest of the oil until the desired consistency. Add the grated cheese. Season with salt and pepper, to taste.

Think of a frittata as an Italian quiche without the buttery crust (and the extra calories). This supersized omelet can accommodate any number of vegetable/ meat/cheese combinations and works for breakfast, lunch, or dinner. In my family, no frittata is complete without the addition of flavored bread crumbs for a crispy topping. This version is similar to the one served in the Casa Lido.

Chef Massimo's Frittata with Arugula

1–2 tablespoons of extra-virgin olive oil
1 quarter of a Vidalia onion, thinly sliced
5 ounces of baby arugula
8 large eggs
¼ lb. of Fontina cheese, cut into ½ inch cubes
½ teaspoon of salt
¼ teaspoon of black pepper
Italian-flavored bread crumbs for topping

1. Preheat oven to 350°

2. Heat oil in a well-seasoned 10-inch cast-iron pan or other heavy ovenproof skillet. Cook the onion over medium heat, separating it into ribbons, until nicely browned. Add arugula and cook, stirring frequently until wilted, for about 1–2 minutes.

3. Whisk together the eggs, cheese, salt, and pepper until frothy. Pour over arugula and onions in skillet and cook over medium heat without stirring until almost set, for about 5–6 minutes.

4. Remove from heat and sprinkle flavored bread crumbs over the top. Bake for 15–20 minutes until edges are golden brown and center is set.

Read on for a sneak peek
at the next Italian Kitchen Mystery,

The Wedding
Soup Murder

Coming in summer 2014 from Obsidian.

"**W**hat are you doing in here, Vic?" The deep, familiar tones of my ex's voice still had the power to set my heart pounding. But I didn't look up.

"What does it look like I'm doing, Tim?" I released the scoop, gently dropping the thirteenth meatball onto the sheet pan. That left a mere 987 to go. At the rate I was going, I'd be spending my thirty-fourth birthday in the Casa Lido kitchen, still scooping ground meat from this bottomless aluminum bowl.

He stood with his hands on his hips, frowning. "Who said you could make the meatballs?"

"I'm not *making* them." I tried to keep the impatience out of my tone. "I'm forming them." I held up the scoop, covered in flecks of raw meat. "Nando mixed them up."

"Good." Tim strode over to the stockpots, lifted the lid of the nearest one, and sniffed. Then he stuck a spoon into it, blew on it, slurped its contents noisily, and nodded. He pointed the spoon at me. "You didn't make this stock."

I slammed the scoop down on the worktable. "No, I didn't make the stock. My grandmother started it and Nando finished it." I gestured to the slow simmering pots. "But it will probably be my job to pick every piece of edible chicken from those bones, right after I finish making—sorry, *forming*—a thousand tiny meatballs for the Wedding Soup." I imagined tray after tray of meatballs, lined up until the crack of doom, and shook my head. "It's like some mythological punishment Nonna dreamed up."

"You wanted to learn the business." His voice was terse. "That's why you came back, wasn't it? I mean, it sure wasn't for me."

I tried to concentrate on the task in front of me. I had to make these quickly, while the meat was still cold. Aside from health reasons, if the ground beef, pork, and veal mixture sat out too long, I'd get misshapen *polpetti*. And then there would be hell to pay, extracted by my eightyish, but still formidable, grandmother.

But even fear of my nonna wasn't enough to take my mind from Tim's powerful presence a few feet from my elbow. I'd come back to Oceanside Park to learn the family business and research a new book, a departure from my mystery series. Instead, I'd stumbled into a murder and briefly back into Tim's arms. But my role in its outcome had left him furious with me. I glanced up and met his cold gray stare.

"Yes," I said, "that's why I came back." It was only a partial truth, and we both knew it. I've been in love with Tim Trouvare for more than half my life, and trying to push away those feelings was about as easy as fighting a riptide. "Look, Tim, I'm sorry about the way things turned out in May. But it could have been much worse."

"Right," he said. "I could have been arrested for murder."

"Can't we just get past this?"

"Oh, I'm past it, sweetheart." He patted me on the

shoulder, and I jumped. "I'm past it all." And with that, he swept through the kitchen's swinging door.

"Ohhhh-kay." I stuck the scoop back into the meat and tried to concentrate on the task at hand. I could only work in two-hour intervals, as Nonna was strict about how long the meat could stay unrefrigerated. I looked down at the raw mixture, catching whiffs of fresh parsley and garlic. Once the stock was skimmed and strained, it would be brought to a simmer, and the *polpetti* would be quickly dropped in to cook. But that was only the last step of the process. There was still the escarole to be cleaned and blanched, another job that would likely fall to me. And the whole thing had to be done in stages. I dropped another meatball onto the sheet pan and counted. Again.

As a favor to an old friend of my dad's, we'd agreed to make our special Wedding Soup for his daughter's reception. With two hundred guests, we needed God knows how many gallons of soup. My grandmother had specified five meatballs per bowl—hence the thousand count. But while we could make the stock ahead of time, we needed to complete the last steps at the reception just before serving. That meant making up all the meatballs and freezing them. Prepping the stock and greens. And transporting all of it to the Belmont Beach Country Club a couple of hours before the service. And Nonna had put me in charge.

"You wanted more responsibility," she'd said with a shrug. "So now you're responsible."

"But, Nonna," I told her, "Belmont probably has its own staff. But you know Chef Massimo—he'll want to oversee the prep and service. And we'll never keep Tim out of there. How will we do this with two kitchen staffs butting heads?" The panic rose in me as I imagined all those culinary egos clashing in one small space. "Can't we just make it here and drop it off?"

"No." She crossed her arms, frowning over the top of her glasses. "The *polpetti* and greens must be cooked just before service." She shook a knobby finger at me. "Not one moment sooner."

I could still hear her voice in my ears as I shook out the last tiny meatball. At fifty per tray, I'd need twenty sheet pans. Each would have to be double-wrapped in plastic and set carefully into the freezer. How would we get it all there? How many trips in my little Honda would it take? Not to mention the soup itself—how would we transport all those gallons of chicken stock down Ocean Avenue?

"Good Lord," I said, staring down at the tray of tiny pink spheres. "How did I get myself into this? If I never see another meatball again, it will be too soon."

But as it turned out, meatballs were the least of my troubles.

"Now, darling," my mom said, fluttering around me in the Casa Lido kitchen like a stiletto-wearing butterfly. "When you go over there, make sure you clear everything with Elizabeth Merriman. She's very particular about how things are done." Mom smoothed the collar of my cotton blouse. "Would you like me to give this a quick press before you go? It is the Belmont Beach Country Club, after all."

I looked into my mother's freshly bronzed face. Her long curls, now a purple-tinted auburn, brushed her shoulders, bared slightly by her lime green boat-neck top. The combination of colors was blinding. "Mom, I'm fine. I'll be spending most of my time in a hot kitchen. Once that soup is made and served, I'll be hightailing it out of there."

"No, you won't." Like an avenging ghost, my grandmother materialized out of nowhere, pronouncing her words with a finality that sealed my fate. And whatever it was, it wouldn't be pleasant. But it was a price I was willing to pay. I'd even left my apartment in Manhattan to come back to the Jersey Shore so I could spend a year learning about our restaurant business. But thus far, things hadn't quite turned out as I'd planned.

"You will stay until the end of the reception," Nonna said, setting a tray of cookies down on the butcher-block worktable. I stared at the pale, plump pillows with golden brown edges, each perfectly formed. The licorice scent of anise wafted upward, pulling my hand toward the tray like a magnet. And then the sound of my grandmother's slap resounded across the kitchen.

"Hey!" I rubbed the back of my hand. "Why can't I have one? You know your ricotta cookies are my favorites."

"They are for the reception. You'll put these out on the dessert table." She crossed her arms, pressing her lips together in a tight red line of warning. It was a line I knew better than to cross.

Waiting for the dessert service meant I'd be stuck at that wedding all night. I'd hoped to be back at my cottage and at my computer by seven to put in a couple of hours of work on my novel.

"But why?" I wailed, sounding like the ten-year-old who'd helped my grandmother set tables in the restaurant more than two decades ago. "Aren't they having some overloaded Venetian table filled with cannoli and eclairs and napoleons? Do they really *need* more cookies?" The second the words dropped from my mouth, I realized how foolish they were. This was an Italian wedding, after all. We always need more cookies. Then a sense of dread overcame me like fog over the ocean. "Nonna," I said slowly, "these aren't iced."

"Of course they aren't. You'll ice and decorate them two hours before service, not a minute before or after." She produced a plastic container of what looked like silver BBs. "One teaspoon of icing per cookie and three nonpareils on top. No more, no less."

My mouth gaped open like one of my brother Danny's fresh-caught tuna. "I . . . but . . ."

" 'But' nothing, Victoria." Nonna glared at me from behind her bifocals. I turned an imploring look upon my mother.

"Now, Mama," my mom said. "We can prep these ahead, don't you think?"

Nonna turned her stony gaze on my mom, who despite forty years' acquaintance with her mother-in-law, still flinched. "Nic-o-lina." My grandmother pronounced each syllable separately and crisply, a sure sign of danger. "The Casa Lido has a reputation to uphold," she said. "I will not be sending out dry cookies that are imperfectly iced." Nonna trained her laser beam stare back on me. "Especially after what happened in May."

St. Francis, give me patience, I prayed. "Nonna," I said gently, "what happened in May was no one's fault." But I knew that on some level, she held me responsible. "And we've recovered."

"Thank God," my mom said. "In any case, Mama, can you really expect Victoria to make all that icing as well as oversee the soup service at the club? It seems like an awful lot to ask."

"No. Tim will make the icing." My grandmother's tight lips curved into either a smile or a sneer. With her it was hard to tell. But Tim had been in her bad graces ever since that little mishap in the pantry, and this was her version of revenge. Tim saw himself as an up-and-coming chef de cuisine, not an assistant baker. It was bad enough we'd have to work together all night, but now he'd be in a fouler mood than usual.

I exchanged a look with my mom, who gave a small shake of her auburn extensions that spelled it out for me: Give it up.

"Okay," I said. "So fill me in on how all this is going to work."

My grandmother rested her palms on the worktable in a war room pose. Any minute now she'd get out a wall map and pushpins. "All right," she said. "The *polpetti* will remain in the freezer until the moment we are ready to load the van. The stockpots are sealed. The escarole is prepped. Both are in the walk-in. Nando will load the van and drive; Chef Massimo will follow. You will take Tim in your car."

Just what I needed. Forty minutes alone in the car with my ex-boyfriend.

"And when we get there?"

"By all the saints, have we not gone over this?" My grandmother shook her head at my obtuseness. "You set the stock to simmer, adding the greens in bunches. At the very last, you add the *polpetti*, and you cook them only until they are no longer pink inside. Understand?" She spread her fingers wide. "And when you plate, only five meatballs per bowl. As for the cookies—"

"I know: Ice before service and only three silver balls per cookie. I get it."

She narrowed her eyes at me. "Remember that you are representing the Casa Lido, Victoria."

"I will, Nonna. Speaking of which, what about our service here tonight?"

"Nando will drive back for prep, and Massimo will return after the soup is served at the reception. You and Tim will stay for the dessert service and bring back our stockpots."

"I probably have to wash them, too," I muttered.

"What was that, Victoria?" my grandmother asked sharply.

"Nothing, Nonna," I said with a loud sigh. It was the first of many to come.

WEDDING CAKE KILLER
A Fresh Baked Mystery

LIVIA J. WASHBURN

After all the planning, decorating, and cake tasting, the big day has finally arrived. Phyllis Newsom has opened up her house to host the wedding of her best friend Eve to Roy Porter.

But all the to-do lists in the world won't prepare them for what happens after the honeymoon. When the groom is found dead at a local bed-and-breakfast, Eve is the top suspect. Now Phyllis must find out who iced Roy before her friend finds herself eating breakfast behind bars...

<u>And don't miss</u>
A Peach of a Murder
Murder by the Slice
The Christmas Cookie Killer
Killer Crab Cakes
The Pumpkin Muffin Murder
The Gingerbread Bump-Off

**Available wherever books are sold or
at penguin.com**

OM0080

3 2953 01171745 3

M884G101